An History of Birmingham (1783)

by William Hutton

Copyright © 10/2/2015
Jefferson Publication

ISBN-13: 978-1517636470

Printed in the United States of America

All rights reserved. No part of this book may be reprinted or reproduced or utilized in any form or by any electronic, mechanical, or other means, now known or hereafter invented, including photocopying and recording, or in any form of storage or retrieval system, without prior permission in writing from the publisher.'

Table of Contents

PREFACE. 7
AN HISTORY &c. 8
SITUATION. 9
SOIL. 10
WATER. 10
BATHS. 11
AIR. 11
LONGEVITY. 12
ANCIENT STATE OF BIRMINGHAM. 13
BATTLE OF CAMP-HILL. 19
   1643. .... *19*
MODERN STATE 20
   OF. *20*
BIRMINGHAM. 20
OF THE STREETS, ... 24
   AND *24*
THEIR NAMES. 24
TRADE. 26
THE BUTTON. 30
THE BUCKLE. 31
GUNS. 31
LEATHER. 32
STEEL. 32
NAILS. 33
BELLOWS. 33
THREAD. 34
PRINTING, ... 35
   By JOHN BASKERVILLE. *35*
BRASS FOUNDRY. 36
HACKNEY COACH. 36
BANK. 37
GOVERNMENT. 37
CONSTABLES. 39
A LIST OF THE 40
HIGH BAILIFFS, LOW BAILIFFS, AND CONSTABLES, ... 40
OF THE TOWN OF BIRMINGHAM, FROM 1732, TO 1782. 40

COURT OF REQUESTS.	42
LAMP ACT.	44
RELIGION AND POLITICS.	45
PLACES OF WORSHIP.	47
SAINT JOHN'S CHAPEL,	48
DERITEND.	48
SAINT BARTHOLOMEW'S.	49
SAINT MARY's.	51
SAINT PAUL's.	52
OLD MEETING.	52
NEW MEETING.	54
CARR's LANE MEETING.	54
BAPTIST MEETING.	55
QUAKER's MEETING	55
METHODIST's MEETING.	55
ROMISH CHAPEL.	56
JEWISH SYNAGOGUE.	57
THEATRES.	58
AMUSEMENTS.	59
HOTEL.	60
WAKES.	62
CLUBS.	62
IKENIELD STREET.	64
LORDS OF THE MANOR.	68
ULUUINE, (SINCE ALWYNE, NOW ALLEN,)	69
RICHARD,	69
1066,	69
WILLIAM,	70
1130,	70
PETER DE BIRMINGHAM,	70
1154.	70
WILLIAM DE BIRMINGHAM,	71
1216.	71
WILLIAM DE BIRMINGHAM,	71
1246.	71
WILLIAM DE BIRMINGHAM,	71
1265.	71
WILLIAM DE BIRMINGHAM,	72
1306.	72
WILLIAM DE BIRMINGHAM,	72
LORD BIRMINGHAM.	72
1316.	72
SIR FOUK DE BIRMINGHAM,	72
1340.	72
SIR JOHN DE BIRMINGHAM,	73
1376.	73
WILLIAM DE BIRMINGHAM,	73

1430.	73
SIR WILLIAM BIRMINGHAM,	73
1479,	73
EDWARD BIRMINGHAM,	74
1500,	74
1537,	74
JOHN, DUKE OF NORTHUMBERLAND,	76
1537,	76
THOMAS MARROW,	76
1555,	76
THOMAS ARCHER, ESQ.	77
for 1,700l. in 1746,	77
ANDREW, LORD ARCHER,	77
SARAH, LADY ARCHER,	77
1781,	77
MANOR HOUSE.	77
(The Moat.)	77
PUDDING BROOK.	78
THE PRIORY.	78
JOHN A DEAN'S HOLE.	81
LENCH'S TRUST.	81
FENTHAM'S TRUST.	82
CROWLEY'S TRUST.	82
SCOTT'S TRUST.	83
FREE SCHOOL.	85
CHIEF MASTERS.	87
CHARITY SCHOOL:	88
COMMONLY,	88
The BLUE SCHOOL.	88
DISSENTING CHARITY-SCHOOL.	89
WORKHOUSE.	90
OLD CROSS,	93
WELCH CROSS.	94
SAINT MARTIN's.	95
UPON ONE OF THE CENTRE PILLARS.	99
NORTH GALLERY.	99
SAME GALLERY.	99
RECTORS.	101
A TERRIER OF THE RECTORY, WRITTEN BY THE RECTOR, ABOUT 1680.	102
SURPLICE FEES.	103
SAINT PHILLIP's.	105
IN THE FRONT GALLERY.	107
BIRTHS AND BURIALS.	108
GENERAL HOSPITAL.	109
PUBLIC ROADS.	110
CANAL.	112
DERITEND BRIDGE.	114

ADJACENT REMARKS.	114
SOHO.	*114*
DANES CAMP;	114
DANES BANK, OR BURY FIELDS.	*114*
GENTLEMEN'S SEATS.	115
THE MOATS.	115
BLACK GREVES.	116
ULVERLEY, OR CULVERLEY.	116
HOGG'S-MOAT.	116
YARDLEY.	117
KENT'S-MOAT.	117
SHELDON.	118
KING'S-HURST.	118
COLESHILL.	119
DUDDESTON.	119
SALTLEY.	120
WARD-END.	120
CASTLE BROMWICH.	121
PARK-HALL.	122
BERWOOD.	122
ERDINGTON.	122
PIPE.	123
ASTON.	124
WITTON.	125
BLAKELEY.	125
WEOLEY	126
SUTTON COLDFIELD.	127
PETITION FOR A CORPORATION.	128
BRASS WORKS.	130
PRISON.	130
CLODSHALES CHANTRY.	131
OCCURRENCES.	132
EARTHQUAKE, &c.	*132*
PITMORE AND HAMMOND.	133
RIOTS.	133
THE CONJURERS.	134
MILITARY ASSOCIATION.	135
BILSTON CANAL ACT.	136
WORKHOUSE BILL.	137
THE CAMP.	139
MORTIMER's BANK.	139
F I N I S.	140

PREFACE.

A preface rather induces a man to speak of himself, which is deemed the worst subject upon which he *can* speak. In history we become acquainted with things, but in a preface with the author; and, for a man to treat of himself, may be the most *difficult* talk of the two: for in history, facts are produced ready to the hand of the historian, which give birth to thought, and it is easy to cloath that thought in words. But in a preface, an author is obliged to forge from the brain, where he is sometimes known to forge without fire. In one, he only reduces a substance into form; but in the other, he must create that substance.

As I am not an author by profession, it is no wonder if I am unacquainted with the modes of authorship; but I apprehend, the usual method of conducting the pen, is to polish up a founding title-page, dignified with scraps of Latin, and then, to hammer up a work to fit it, as nearly as genius, or want of genius, will allow.

We next *turn over a new leaf*, and open upon a pompous dedication, which answers many laudable purposes: if a coat of arms, correctly engraven, should step first into view, we consider it a singular advantage gained over a reader, like the first blow in a combat. The dedication itself becomes a pair of stilts, which advance an author something higher.

As a horse-shoe, nailed upon the threshold of a cottage, prevents the influence of the witch; so a first-rate name, at the head of a dedication, is a total bar against the critic; but this great name, like a great officer, sometimes unfortunately stands at the head of wretched troops.

When an author is too *heavy* to swim of himself, it serves as a pair of bladders, to prevent his sinking.

It is farther productive of a *solid* advantage, that of a present from the patron, more valuable than that from the bookseller, which prevents his sinking under the pressure of famine.

But, being wholly unknown to the great names of literary consequence, I shall not attempt a dedication, therefore must lose the benefit of the stilt, the bladder, and the horse-shoe.

Were I to enter upon a dedication, I should certainly address myself, "*To the Inhabitants of Birmingham*." For to them I not only owe much, but all; and I think, among that congregated mass, there is not one person to whom I wish ill. I have the pleasure of calling many of those inhabitants *Friends*, and some of them share my warm affections equally with myself. Birmingham, like a compassionate nurse, not only draws our persons, but our esteem, from the place of our nativity, and fixes it upon herself: I might add, *I was hungry, and she fed me*; *thirsty, and she gave me drink*; *a stranger, and she took me in*. I approached her with reluctance, because I did not know her; I shall leave her with reluctance, because I do.

Whether it is perfectly confident in an author, to solicit the indulgence of the public, though it may stand first in his wishes, admits a doubt; for, if his productions will not bear the light, it may be said, why does he publish? but, if they will, there is no need to ask a favor; the world receives one from him. Will not a piece everlastingly be tried by its merit? Shall we esteem it the higher, because it was written at the age of thirteen? because it was the effort of a week? delivered extempore? hatched while the author stood upon one leg? or cobbled, while he cobbled a shoe? or will it be a recommendation, that it issues forth in gilt binding? The judicious world will not be deceived by the tinselled purse, but will examine whether the *contents* are sterling.

Will it augment the value of this history, or cover its blunders, to say, that I have never seen *Oxford?* That the thick fogs of penury, prevented the sun of science from beaming upon the mind? That necessity obliged me to lay down the battledore, before I was master of the letters? And that, instead of handling systems of knowledge, my hands, at the early period of seven, became callous with labour?

But, though a whole group of pretences will have no effect with the impartial eye, yet one reason pleads strongly in my favor--no such thing ever appeared as *An History of Birmingham*. It is remarkable, that one of the most singular places in the universe is without an historian: that she never manufactured an history of herself, who has manufactured almost every thing else; that so many ages should elapse, and not one among her numerous sons of industry, snatch the manners of the day from oblivion, group them in design, with the touches of his pen, and exhibit the picture to posterity. If such a production had ever seen the light, mine most certainly would never have been written; a temporary bridge therefore may satisfy the impatient traveller, till a more skilful architect shall accommodate him with a complete production of elegance, of use, and of duration.--Although works of genius ought to come out of the mint doubly refined, yet history admits of a much greater latitude to the author. The best upon the subject, though defective, may meet with regard.

It has long been a complaint, that local history is much wanted. This will appear obvious, if we examine the places we know, with the histories that treat of them. Many an author has become a cripple, by historically travelling through *all*

England, who might have made a tolerable figure, had he staid at home. The subject is too copious for one performance, or even the life of one man. The design of history is knowledge: but, if simply to tell a tale, be all the duty of an historian, he has no irksome task before him; for there is nothing more easy than to relate a fact; but, perhaps, nothing more difficult than to relate it well.

The situation of an author is rather precarious--if the smiles of the world chance to meet his labours, he is apt to forget himself; if otherwise, he is soon forgot. The efforts of the critic may be necessary to clip the wings of a presuming author, lest his rising vanity becomes insupportable: but I pity the man, who writes a book which none will peruse a second time; critical exertions are not necessary to pull him down, he will fall of himself. The sin of writing carries its own punishment, the tumultuous passions of anxiety and expectation, like the jarring elements in October, disturb his repose, and, like them, are followed by stirility: his cold productions, injured by no hand but that of time, are found sleeping on the shelf unmolested. It is easy to describe his fears before publication, but who can tell his feelings after judgment is passed upon his works? His only consolation is accusing the critic of injustice, and thinking the world in the wrong. But if repentence should not follow the culprit, hardened in scribbling, it follows, his bookseller, oppressed with *dead works*. However, if all the evils in Pandora's box are emptied on a blasted author, this one comfort remains behind--The keeper of a circulating library, or the steward of a reading society can tell him, "His book is more *durable* than the others."

Having, many years ago, entertained an idea of this undertaking, I made some trifling preparations; but, in 1775, a circumstance of a private nature occurring, which engaged my attention for several years, I relinquished the design, destroyed the materials, and meant to give up the thought for ever. But the intention revived in 1780, and the work followed.

I may be accused of quitting the regular trammels of history, and sporting in the fields of remark: but, although our habitation justly stands first in our esteem, in return for rest, content, and protection; does it follow that we should never stray from it? If I happen to veer a moment from the polar point of Birmingham, I shall certainly vibrate again to the center. Every author has a manner peculiar to himself, nor can he well forsake it. I should be exceedingly hurt to omit a necessary part of intelligence, but more, to offend a reader.

If GRANDEUR should censure me for sometimes recording the men of mean life, let me ask, *Which is preferable*, he who thunders at the anvil, or in the senate? The man who earnestly wishes the significant letters, ESQ. spliced to the end of his name, will despise the question; but the philosopher will answer, "They are equal."

Lucrative views have no part in this production: I cannot solicit a kind people to grant what they have already granted; but if another finds that pleasure in reading, which I have done in writing, I am paid.

As no history is extant, to inform me of this famous nursery of the arts, perfection in mine must not be expected. Though I have endeavoured to pursue the road to truth; yet, having no light to guide, or hand to direct me, it is no wonder if I mistake it: but we do not *condemn*, so much as *pity* the man for losing his way, who first travels an unbeaten road.

Birmingham, for want of the recording hand, may be said to live but one generation; the transactions of the last age, die in this; memory is the sole historian, which being defective, I embalm the present generation, for the inspection of the future.

It is unnecessary to attempt a general character, for if the attentive reader is himself of Birmingham, he is equally apprized of that character; and, if a stranger, he will find a variety of touches scattered through the piece, which, taken in a collective view, form a picture of that generous people, who *merit his* esteem, and *possess mine*.

AN HISTORY &c.

Some account of the derivation of the name of Birmingham.

The word Birmingham, is too remote for certain explanation. During the last four centuries it has been variously written *Brumwycheham, Bermyngeham, Bromwycham, Burmyngham, Bermyngham, Byrmyngham*, and *Birmingham*; nay, even so late as the seventeenth century it was written *Bromicham*. Dugdale supposes the name to have been given by the planter, or owner, in the time of the Saxons; but, I suppose it much older than any Saxon, date: besides, it is not so common for a man to give a name to, as to take one from, a place. A man seldom gives his name except he is the founder, as Petersburg from Peter the Great.

Towns, as well as every thing in nature, have exceedingly minute beginnings, and generally take a name from situation, or local circumstances. Would the Lord of a manor think it an honour to give his name to two or three miserable huts? But, if in a succession of ages these huts swell into opulence, they confer upon the lord an honour, a residence, and a name. The terminations of *sted*, *ham*, and *hurst*, are evidently Saxon, and mean the same thing, a home.

The word, in later ages reduced to a certainty, hath undergone various mutations; but the original seems to have been *Bromwych*; *Brom* perhaps, from broom a shrub, for the growth of which the soil is extremely favourable; *Wych*, a descent, this exactly corresponds with the declivity from the High Street to Digbeth. Two other places also in the neigbourhood bear the same name, which serves to strengthen the opinion.

This infant colony, for many centuries after the first buddings of existence, perhaps, had no other appellation than that of Bromwych. Its center, for many reasons that might be urged, was the Old Cross, and its increase, in those early ages of time must have been very small.

A series of prosperity attending it, its lord might assume its name, reside in it, and the particle *ham* would naturally follow. This very probably happened under the Saxon Heptarchy, and the name was no other than *Bromwycham*.

SITUATION.

It lies near the centre of the kingdom, in the north-west extremity of the county of Warwick, in a kind of peninsula, the northern part of which is bounded by Handsworth, in the county of Stafford, and the southern by King's-norton, in the county of Worcester; it is also in the diocese of Lichfield and Coventry, and in the deanery of Arden.

Let us perambulate the parish from the bottom of Digbeth, thirty yards north of the bridge. We will proceed south-west up the bed of the river, with Deritend, in the parish of Aston, on our left. Before we come to the Floodgates, near Vaughton's Hole, we pass by the Longmores, a small part of King's-norton. Crossing the river Rea, we enter the vestiges of a small rivulet, yet visible, though the stream hath been turned, perhaps, a thousand years, to supply the moat. We now bear rather west, nearly in a straight line for three miles, to Shirland brook, with Edgbaston on the left. At the top of the first meadow from the river Rea, we meet the little stream above-mentioned, in the pursuit of which, we cross the Bromsgrove road a little east of the first mile stone. Leaving Banner's marlpit to the left, we proceed up a narrow lane crossing the old Bromsgrove road, and up to the turnpike at the five ways in the road to Hales Owen. Leaving this road also to the left we proceed down the lane towards Ladywood, cross the Icknield street, a stone's cast east of the observatory, to the north extremity of Rotton Park. We now meet with Shirland Brook, which leads us east, and across the Dudley road, at the seven mile stone, having Smethwick in the county of Stafford, on the left, down to Pigmill. We now leave Handsworth on the left, following the stream through Hockley great pool; cross the Wolverhampton road, and the Ikenield-street at the same time down to Aston furnace, with that parish on the left. At the bottom of Walmer-lane we leave the water, move over the fields, nearly in a line to the post by the Peacock upon Gosty-green. We now cross the Lichfield road, down Duke-street, then the Coleshill road at the A B house. From thence down the meadows, to Cooper's mill; up the river to the foot of Deritend bridge; and then turn sharp to the right, keeping the course of a drain in the form of a sickle, through John a Dean's hole, into Digbeth, from whence we set out. In marching along Duke-street, we leave about seventy houses to the left, and up the river Rea, about four hundred more in Deritend, reputed part of Birmingham, though not in the parish.

This little journey, nearly of an oval form, is about seven miles. The longest diameter from Shirland brook to Deritend bridge is about three, and the widest, from the bottom of Walmer Lane to the rivulet, near the mile-stone, upon the Bromsgrove road, more than two.

The superficial contents of the parish may be upwards of four miles, about three thousand acres.

Birmingham is by much the smallest parish in the neighbourhood, those of Aston and Sutton are each about five times as large, Yardley four, and King's-Norton eight.

When Alfred, that great master of legislation, parished out his kingdom, or rather, put the finishing hand to that important work; where he met with a town, he allotted a smaller quantity of land, because the inhabitants chiefly depended upon commerce; but where there was only a village, he allotted a larger, because they depended upon agriculture.

This observation goes far in proving the antiquity of the place, for it is nine hundred years since this division took effect.

The buildings occupy the south east part of the parish; perhaps, with their appendages, about six hundred acres.

This south east part, being insufficient for the extraordinary increase of the inhabitants, she has of late extended her buildings along the Bromsgrove road, near the boundaries of Edgbaston; and actually on the other side planted three of her streets in the parish of Aston. Could the sagacious Alfred have seen into futurity, he would have augmented her borders.

As no part of the town lies flat, the showers promote both cleanliness and health, by removing obstructions.

The approach is on every side by ascent, except that from Hales-Owen, north west, which gives a free access of air, even to the most secret recesses of habitation.

Thus eminently situated, the sun can exercise his full powers of exhalation.

The foundation upon which this mistress of the arts is erected, is one solid mass of dry reddish sand.

The vapours that rise from the earth are the great promoters of disease; but here, instead of the moisture ascending to the prejudice of the inhabitant, the contrary is evident; for the water descends through the pores of the sand, so that even our very cellars are habitable.

This accounts for the almost total extinction of the ague among us:--During a residence of thirty years, I have never seen one person afflicted with it, though, by the opportunities of office, I have frequently visited the repositories of the sick.

Thus peculiarly favoured, this happy spot, enjoys four of the greatest benefits that can attend human existence--water, air, the fun, and a situation free from damps.

All the *past* writers upon Birmingham have viewed her as low and watery, and with reason; because Digbeth, then the chief street, bears that description. But all the future writers will view her on an eminence, and with as much reason; because, for one low street, we have now fifty elevated.

Birmingham, like the empire to which she belongs, has been, for many centuries, travelling *up hill*; and, like that, rising in consequence.

SOIL.

The soil is rather light, sandy, and weak; and though metals, of various sorts, are found in great plenty, *above* the surface, we know of nothing below, except sand and gravel, stone and water. All the riches of the place, like those of an empiric, in laced cloaths, appear on the *outside*.

The northern part of the parish, for about four hundred acres, to the disgrace of the age, is yet a shameful waste.

A small part of the land near the town, is parcelled out into little gardens, at ten or twenty shillings each, amounting to about sixteen pounds per acre.

These are not intended so much for profit, as health and amusement.

Others are let in detached pieces for private use, at about four pounds per acre. So that this small parish cannot boast of more than six or eight farms, and these of the smaller size, at about two pounds per acre. Manure from the sty brings about 16s. per waggon load, that from the stable about 12, and that from the fire and the street, five.

WATER.

I think there is not any natural river runs through the parish, but there are three that mark the boundaries of it, for about half its circumference, described above; none of these supply family use. After penetrating into a body of sand, interspersed with a small strata of soft Rock, and sometimes of gravel; at the depth of about twenty yards, we come to plenty of water, rather hard. There are in the lower parts of the town, two excellent springs of soft water, suitable for most purposes; one at the top of Digbeth, the other, Lady-Well. Or rather, one spring, or bed of water, with many out-lets, continuing its course along the bottom of the hill, parallel with Small-brook-street, Edgbaston street, St. Martin's-lane, and Park-street; sufficiently copious to supply the whole city of London. Water is of the first consequence, it often influences disease, always the habit of body: that of Birmingham is in general productive of salutary effects.

That dreadful disorder, the stone, is seldom found among us. I can recollect but very few, in my time, under this severe complaint, which is perhaps owing to that valuable element. I mentioned this remark to an eminent surgeon, who assured me, that, in his long course of practice, he had never been concerned in one operation in that unhappy disorder.

BATHS.

At Lady-Well, are the most complete baths in the whole Island. There are seven in number; erected at the expence of 2000*l*. Accommodation is ever ready for hot or cold bathing; for immersion or amusement; with conveniency for sweating. That, appropriated for swimming, is eighteen Yards by thirty-six, situated in the centre of a garden, in which are twenty four private undressing-houses, the whole surrounded by a wall 10 feet high. Pleasure and health are the guardians of the place. The gloomy horrors of a bath, sometimes deter us from its use, particularly, if aided by complaint; but the appearance of these is rather inviting. We read of painted sepulchres, whose *outsides* are richly ornamented, but *within* are full of corruption and death. The reverse is before us. No elegance appears without, but within are the Springs of life! The expence was great, the utility greater.

I do not know any author, who has reckoned man among the amphibious race of animals, neither do I know any animal who better deserves it. Man is lord of the little ball on which he treads, one half of which, at least, is water. If we do not allow him to be amphibious, we deprive him of half his sovereignty. He justly bears that name, who can *live* in the water. Many of the disorders incident to the human frame are prevented, and others cured, both by fresh and salt bathing; so that we may properly remark, "*He lives in the water*, who can find life, nay, even *health* in that friendly element."

The greatest treasure on earth is health; but, a treasure, of all others, the least valued by the owner. Other property is best rated when in possession, but this, can only be rated when lost. We sometimes observe a man, who, having lost this inestimable jewel, seeks it with an ardour equal to its worth; but when every research by land, is eluded, he fortunately finds it in the water. Like the fish, he pines away upon shore, but like that, recovers again in the deep.

Perhaps Venus is represented as rising from the ocean, which is no other then a bath of the larger size, to denote, that bathing is the refiner of health, consequently, of beauty; and Neptune being figured in advanced life, indicates, that it is a preservative to old age.

The cure of disease among the Romans, by bathing, is supported by many authorities; among others, by the number of baths frequently discovered, in which, pleasure, in that warm climate, bore a part. But this practice seemed to decline with Roman freedom, and never after held the eminence it deserved. Can we suppose, the physician stept between disease and the bath, to hinder their junction; or, that he lawfully holds, by prescription, the tenure of sickness, in *fee*?

The knowledge of this singular *art of healing*, is at present only in infancy. How far it may prevent, or conquer disease; to what measure it may be applied, in particular cases, and the degrees of use, in different constitutions, are enquiries that will be better understood by a future generation.

AIR.

As we have passed through the water, let us now investigate her sister fluid, the air. They are both necessary to life, and the purity of both to the prolongation of it; this small difference lies between them, a man may live a day without water, but not an hour without air: If a man wants better water, it may be removed from a distant place for his benefit; but if he wants air, he must remove himself.--The natural air of Birmingham, perhaps, cannot be excelled in this climate, the moderate elevation and dry soil evinces this truth; but it receives an alloy from the congregated body of fifty thousand people; also from the smoke of an extraordinary number of fires used in business; and perhaps, more from the various effluvia arising from particular trades. It is not uncommon to see a man with green hair or a yellow wig, from his constant employment in brass; if he reads, the green vestiges of his occupation remain on every leaf, never to be expunged. The inside of his body, no doubt, receives the same tincture, but is kept clean by being often washed with ale. Some of the fair sex, likewise are subject to the same inconvenience, but find relief in the same remedy.

LONGEVITY.

Man is a time-piece. He measures out a certain space, then stops for ever. We see him move upon the earth, hear him click, and perceive in his face the uses of intelligence. His external appearance will inform us whether he is old-fashioned, in which case, he is less valuable upon every gambling calculation. His face also will generally inform us whether all is right within. This curious machine is filled with a complication of movements, very unfit to be regulated by the rough hand of ignorance, which sometimes leaves a mark not to be obliterated even by the hand of an artist. If the works are directed by violence, destruction is not far off. If we load it with the oil of luxury, it will give an additional vigor, but in the end, clog and impede the motion. But if the machine is under the influence of prudence, she will guide it with an even, and a delicate hand, and perhaps the piece may move on 'till it is fairly worn out by a long course of fourscore years.

There are a set of people who expect to find that health in medicine, which possibly might be found in regimen, in air, exercise, or serenity of mind.

There is another class amongst us, and that rather numerous, whose employment is laborious, and whose conduct is irregular. Their time is divided between hard working, and hard drinking, and both by a fire. It is no uncommon thing to see one of these, at forty, wear the aspect of sixty, and finish a life of violence at fifty, which the hand of prudence would have directed to eighty.

The strength of a kingdom consists in the multitude of its inhabitants; success in trade depends upon the manufacturer; the support and direction of a family, upon the head of it. When this useful part of mankind, therefore, are cut off in the active part of life, the community sustains a loss, whether we take the matter in a national, a commercial, or a private view.

We have a third class, who shun the rock upon which these last fall, but wreck upon another; they run upon scylla though they have missed charybdis; they escape the liquid destruction, but split upon the solid. These are proficients in good eating; adepts in culling of delicacies, and the modes of dressing them. Matters of the whole art of cookery; each carries a kitchen in his head. Thus an excellent constitution may be stabbed by the spit. Nature never designed us to live well, and continue well; the stomach is too weak a vessel to be richly and deeply laden. Perhaps more injury is done by eating than by drinking; one is a secret, the other an open enemy: the secret is always supposed the most dangerous. Drinking attacks by assault, but eating by sap: luxury is seldom visited by old age. The best antidote yet discovered against this kind of slow poison is exercise; but the advantages of elevation, air, and water, on one hand, and disadvantages of crowd, smoke, and effluvia on the other, are trifles compared to intemperance.

We have a fourth class, and with these I shall shut up the clock. If this valuable machine comes finished from the hand of nature; if the rough blasts of fortune only attack the outward case, without affecting the internal works, and if reason conduces the piece, it may move on, with a calm, steady, and uninterrupted pace to a great extent of years, 'till time only annihilates the motion.

I personally know amongst us a Mrs. Dallaway, aged near 90; George Davis, 85; John Baddally, Esq; and his two brothers, all between 80 and and 90; Mrs. Allen, 92; Mrs. Silk, 84; John Burbury, 84; Thomas Rutter, 88; Elizabeth Bentley, 88; John Harrison and his wife, one 86, the other 88; Mrs. Floyd, 87; Elizabeth Simms, 88; Sarah Aston, 98; Isaac Spooner, Esq; 89; Joseph Scott, Esq; 94; all at this day, January 9, 1780, I believe enjoy health and capacity. This is not designed as a complete list of the aged, but of such only as immediately occur to memory. I also knew a John England who died at the age of 89; Hugh Vincent, 94; John Pitt, 100; George Bridgens, 103; Mrs. More, 104. An old fellow assured me he had kept the market 77 years: he kept it for several years after to my knowledge. At 90 he was attacked by an acute disorder, but, fortunately for himself, being too poor to purchase medical assistance, he was left to the care of nature, who opened that door to health which the physician would have locked for ever. At 106 I heard him swear with all the fervency of a recruit: at 107 he died. It is easy to give instances of people who have breathed the smoak of Birmingham for threescore years, and yet have scarcely left the precincts of of youth. Such are the happy effects of constitution, temper, and conduct!

Ancient State of Birmingham.

We have now to pass through the very remote ages of time, without staff to support us, without light to conduct us, or hand to guide us. The way is long, dark, and slippery. The credit of an historian is built upon truth; he cannot assert, without giving his facts; he cannot surmise, without giving his reasons; he must relate things as they are, not as he would have them. The fabric founded in error will moulder of itself, but that founded in reality will stand the age and the critic.

Except half a dozen pages in Dugdale, I know of no author who hath professedly treated of Birmingham. None of the histories which I have seen bestow upon it more than a few lines, in which we are sure to be treated with the noise of hammers and anvils; as if the historian thought us a race of dealers in thunder, lightning, and wind; or infernals, puffing in blast and smoak.

Suffer me to transcribe a passage from Leland, one of our most celebrated writers, employed by Henry the VIIIth to form an itinerary of Britain, whose works have stood the test of 250 years. We shall observe how much he erred for want of information, and how natural for his successors to copy him.

"I came through a pretty street as ever I entered, into Birmingham town. This street, as I remember, is called Dirtey (Deritend). In it dwells smithes and cutlers, and there is a brook that divides this street from Birmingham, an hamlet, or member, belonging to the parish therebye.

"There is at the end of Dirtey a propper chappel and mansion-house of timber, (the moat) hard on the ripe, as the brook runneth down; and as I went through the ford, by the bridge, the water came down on the right hand, and a few miles below goeth into Tame. This brook, above Dirtey, breaketh in two arms, that a little beneath the bridge close again. This brook riseth, as some say, four or five miles above Birmingham, towards Black-hills.

"The beauty of Birmingham, a good market-town in the extreme parts of Warwickshire, is one street going up alonge, almost from the left ripe of the brook, up a meane hill, by the length of a quarter of a mile, I saw but one parish-church in the town.

"There be many smithes in the town that use to make knives and all manner of cutting tools, and many loriners that make bittes, and a great many naylers; so that a great part of the town is maintained by smithes, who have their iron and sea-coal out of Staffordshire."

Here we find some intelligence, and more mistake, cloathed in the dress of antique diction, which plainly evinces the necessity of modern history.

It is matter of surprise that none of those religious drones, the monks, who hived in the priory for fifteen or twenty generations, ever thought of indulging posterity with an history of Birmingham. They could not want opportunity, for they lived a life of indolence; nor materials, for they were nearer the infancy of time, and were possessed of historical fads now totally lost. Besides, nearly all the little learning in the kingdom was possessed by this class of people; and the place, in their day, must have enjoyed an eminent degree of prosperity.

Though the town has a modern appearance, there is reason to believe it of great antiquity; my Birmingham reader, therefore, must suffer me to carry him back into the remote ages of the Ancient Britons to visit his fable ancestors.

We have no histories of those times but what are left by the Romans, and these we ought to read with caution, because they were parties in the dispute. If two antagonists write each his own history, the discerning reader will sometimes draw the line of justice between them; but where there is only one, partiality is expected. The Romans were obliged to make the Britons war-like, or there would have been no merit in conquering them: they must also sound forth their ignorance, or there would have been none in improving them. If the Britons were that wretched people they are represented by the Romans, they could not be worth conquering: no man subdues a people to improve them, but to profit by them. Though the Romans at that time were in their meridian of splendor, they pursued Britain a whole century before they reduced it; which indicates that they considered it as a valuable prize. Though the Britons were not masters of science, like the Romans; though the fine arts did not flourish here, as in Rome, because never planted; yet by many testimonies it is evident they were masters of plain life; that many of the simple arts were practiced in that day, as well as in this; that assemblages of people composed cities, the same as now, but in an inferior degree; and that the country was populous is plain from the immense army Boadicia brought into the field, except the Romans increased that army that their merit might be greater in defeating it. Nay, I believe we may with propriety carry them beyond plain life, and charge them with a degree of elegance: the Romans themselves allow the Britons were complete masters of the chariot; that when the scythe was fixed at each end of the axle-tree, they drove with great dexterity into the midst of the enemy, broke their ranks, and mowed them down. The chariot, therefore, could not be made altogether for war, but, when the scythes were removed, it still remained an emblem of pride, became useful in peace, was a badge of high-life, and continues so with their descendants to this day.

An History of Birmingham (1783)

We know the instruments of war used by the Britons were a sword, spear, shield and scythe. If they were not the manufacturers, how came they by these instruments? We cannot allow either they or the chariots were imported, because that will give them a much greater consequence: they must also have been well acquainted with the tools used in husbandry, for they were masters of the field in a double sense. Bad also as their houses were, a chest of carpentry tools would be necessary to complete them. We cannot doubt, therefore, from these evidences, and others which might be adduced, that the Britons understood the manufactory of iron. Perhaps history cannot produce an instance of any place in an improving country, like England, where the coarse manufactory of iron has been carried on, that ever that laborious art went to decay, except the materials failed; and as we know of no place where such materials have failed, there is the utmost reason to believe our forefathers, the Britons, were supplied with those necessary implements by the black artists of the Birmingham forge. Iron-stone and coal are the materials for this production, both which are found in the neighbourhood in great plenty. I asked a gentleman of knowledge, if there was a probability of the delphs failing? He answered, "Not in five thousand years."

The two following circumstances strongly evince this ancient British manufactory:--

Upon the borders of the parish stands Aston-furnace, appropriated for melting ironstone, and reducing it into pigs: this has the appearance of great antiquity. From the melted ore, in this subterranean region of infernal aspect, is produced a calx, or cinder, of which there is an enormous mountain. From an attentive survey, the observer would suppose so prodigious a heap could not accumulate in one hundred generations; however, it shows no perceptible addition in the age of man.

There is also a common of vast extent, called Wednesbury-old-field, in which are the vestiges of many hundreds of coal-pits, long in disuse, which the curious antiquarian would deem as long in sinking, as the mountain of cinders in rising.

The minute sprig of Birmingham, no doubt first took root in this black soil, which, in a succession of ages, hath grown to its present opulence. At what time this prosperous plant was set, is very uncertain; perhaps as long before the days of Caesar as it is since. Thus the mines of Wednesbury empty their riches into the lap of Birmingham, and thus she draws nurture from the bowels of the earth.

The chief, if not the only manufactory of Birmingham, from its first existence to the restoration of Charles the Second, was in iron: of this was produced instruments of war and of husbandry, furniture for the kitchen, and tools for the whole system of carpentry.

The places where our athletic ancestors performed these curious productions of art, were in the shops fronting the street: some small remains of this very ancient custom are yet visible, chiefly in Digbeth, where about a dozen shops still exhibit the original music of anvil and hammer.

As there is the highest probability that Birmingham produced her manufactures long before the landing of Caesar, it would give pleasure to the curious enquirer, could he be informed of her size in those very early ages; but this information is for ever hid from the historian, and the reader. Perhaps there never was a period in which she saw a decline, but that her progress has been certain, though slow, during the long space of two or three thousand years before Charles the Second.

The very roads that proceed from Birmingham, are also additional indications of her great antiquity and commercial influence.

Where any of these roads lead up an eminence, they were worn by the long practice of ages into deep holloways, some of them twelve or fourteen yards below the surface of the banks, with which they were once even, and so narrow as to admit only one passenger.

Though modern industry, assisted by various turnpike acts, has widened the upper part and filled up the lower, yet they were all visible in the days of our fathers, and are traceable even in ours. Some of these, no doubt, were formed by the spade, to soften the fatigue of climbing the hill, but many were owing to the pure efforts of time, the horse, and the showers. As inland trade was small, prior to the fifteenth century, the use of the wagon, that great destroyer of the road, was but little known. The horse was the chief conveyor of burthen among the Britons, and for centuries after: if we, therefore, consider the great length of time it would take for the rains to form these deep ravages, we must place the origin of Birmingham, at a very early date.

One of these subterranean passages, in part filled up, will convey its name to posterity in that of a street, called Holloway-head, 'till lately the way to Bromsgrove and to Bewdley, but not now the chief road to either. Dale-end, once a deep road, has the same derivation. Another at Summer-hill, in the Dudley road, altered in 1753. A remarkable one is also between the Salutation and the Turnpike, in the Wolverhampton road. A fifth at the top of Walmer-lane, changed into its present form in 1764. Another between Gosta-green and Aston-brook, reduced in 1752.

All the way from Dale-end to Duddeston, of which Coleshill-street now makes a part, was sunk five or six feet, though nearly upon a flat, 'till filled up in 1756 by act of Parliament: but the most singular is that between Deritend and Camp-hill, in the way to Stratford, which is, even now, many yards below the banks; yet the seniors of the last age took a pleasure in telling us, they could remember when it would have buried a wagon load of hay beneath its present surface.

Thus the traveller of old, who came to purchase the produce of Birmingham, or to sell his own, seemed to approach her by sap.

British traces are, no doubt, discoverable in the old Dudley-road, down Easy-hill, under the canal; at the eight mile-stone, and at Smethwick; also in many of the private roads near Birmingham, which were never thought to merit a repair, particularly at Good-knaves-end, towards Harborne; the Green-lane, leading to the Garrison; and that beyond Long-bridge, in the road to Yardley; all of them deep holloways, which carry evident tokens of antiquity. Let the curious calculator determine what an amazing length of time would elapse in wearing the deep roads along Saltleyfield, Shaw-hill, Allum-rock, and the remainder of the way to Stichford, only a pitiful hamlet of a dozen houses.

The ancient centre of Birmingham seems to have been the Old Cross, from the number of streets pointing towards it. Wherever the narrow end of a street enters a great thorough-fare, it indicates antiquity, this is the case with Philip-street, Bell-street, Spiceal-street, Park-street, and Moor-street, which not only incline to the centre above-mentioned, but all terminate with their narrow ends into the grand passage. These streets are narrow at the entrance, and widen as you proceed: the narrow ends were formed with the main street at first, and were not, at that time, intended for streets themselves. As the town increased, other blunders of the same kind were committed, witness the gateway late at the east end of New-street, the two ends of Worcester-street, Smallbrook-street, Cannon-street, New-meeting-street, and Bull street; it is easy to see which end of a street was formed first; perhaps the south end of Moor street is two thousand years older than the north; the same errors are also committing in our day, as in Hill and Vale streets, the two Hinkleys and Catharine-street. One generation, for want of foresight, forms a narrow entrance, and another widens it by Act of Parliament.

Every word in the English language carries an idea: when a word, therefore, strikes the ear, the mind immediately forms a picture, which represents it as faithfully as the looking-glass the face.--Thus, when the word Birmingham occurs, a superb picture instantly expands in the mind, which is best explained by the other words grand, populous, extensive, active, commercial and humane. This painting is an exact counter-part of the word at this day; but it does not correspond with its appearance, in the days of the ancient Britons--We must, therefore, for a moment, detach the idea from the word.

Let us suppose, then, this centre surrounded with less than one hundred stragling huts, without order, which we will dignify with the name of houses; built of timber, the interfaces wattled with sticks, and plaistered with mud, covered with thatch, boards or sods; none of them higher than the ground story. The meaner sort only one room, which served for three uses, shop, kitchen, and lodging room; the door for two, it admitted the people and the light. The better sort two rooms, and some three, for work, for the kitchen, and for rest; all three in a line, and sometimes fronting the street.

If the curious reader chooses to see a picture of Birmingham, in the time of the Britons, he will find one in the turnpike road, between Hales-owen and Stourbridge, called the Lie Waste, alias Mud City. The houses stand in every direction, composed of one large and ill-formed brick, scoped into a tenement, burnt by the sun, and often destroyed by the frost: the males naked; the females accomplished breeders. The children, at the age of three months, take a singular hue from the sun and the soil, which continues for life. The rags which cover them leave no room for the observer to guess at the sex. Only one person upon the premisses presumes to carry a belly, and he a landlord. We might as well look for the moon in a coal-pit, as for stays or white linen in the City of Mud. The principal tool in business is the hammer, and the beast of burden, the ass.

The extent of our little colony of artists, perhaps reached nearly as high as the east end of New-street, occupied the upper part of Spiceal-street, and penetrated down the hill to the top of Digbeth, chiefly on the east.

Success, which ever waits on Industry, produced a gradual, but very slow increase: perhaps a thousand years elapsed without adding half that number of houses.

Thus our favourite plantation having taken such firm root, that she was able to stand the wintry blasts of fortune, we shall digress for a moment, while she wields her sparkling heat, according to the fashion of the day, in executing the orders of the sturdy Briton; then of the polite and heroic Roman; afterwards of our mild ancestors, the Saxons. Whether she raised her hammer for the plundering Dane is uncertain, his reign being short; and, lastly, for the resolute and surly Norman.

It does not appear that Birmingham, from its first formation, to the present day, was ever the habitation of a gentleman, the lords of the manor excepted. But if there are no originals among us, we can produce many striking likenesses--The smoke of Birmingham has been very propitious to their growth, but not to their maturity.

Gentlemen, as well as buttons, have been stamped here; but, like them, when finished, are moved off.

They both originate from a very uncouth state, *without form or comeliness*; and pass through various stages, uncertain of success. Some of them, at length, receive the last polish, and arrive at perfection; while others, ruined by a flaw, are deemed *wasters*.

I have known the man of opulence direct his gilt chariot *out* of Birmingham, who first approached her an helpless orphan in rags. I have known the chief magistrate of fifty thousand people, fall from his phaeton, and humbly ask bread at a parish vestry.

Frequently the wheel of capricious fortune describes a circle, in the rotation of which, a family experiences alternately, the heighth of prosperity and the depth of distress; but more frequently, like a pendulum, it describes only the arc of a circle, and that always at the bottom.

Many fine estates have been struck out of the anvil, valuable possessions raised by the tongs, and superb houses, in a two-fold sense, erected by the trowel.

The paternal ancestor of the late Sir Charles Holte was a native of this place, and purchaser, in the beginning of Edward the Third, of the several manors, which have been the honour and the support of his house to the present time.

Walter Clodshale was another native of Birmingham, who, in 1332, purchased the manor of Saltley, now enjoyed by his maternal descendant, Charles Bowyer Adderley, Esq.

Charles Colmore, Esq; holds a considerable estate in the parish; his predecessor is said to have occupied, in the reign of Henry the Eighth, that house, now No. 1, in the High-street, as a mercer, and general receiver of the taxes.

A numerous branch of this ancient family flourishes in Birmingham at this day.

The head of it, in the reign of James the First, erected New-hall, and himself into a gentleman. On this desirable eminence, about half a mile from the buildings, they resided till time, fashion, and success, removed them, like their predecessors, the sons of fortune, to a greater distance.

The place was then possessed by a tenant, as a farm; but Birmingham, a speedy traveller, marched over the premises, and covered them with twelve hundred houses, on building leases; the farmer was converted into a steward: his brown hempen frock, which guarded the *outside* of his waistcoat, became white holland, edged with ruffles, and took its station *within*: the pitchfork was metamorphosed into a pen, and his ancient practice of breeding up sheep, was changed into that of *dressing their skins*.

Robert Philips, Esq; acquired a valuable property in the seventeenth century; now possessed by his descendant, William Theodore Inge, Esquire.

A gentleman of the name of Foxall, assured me, that the head of his family resided upon the spot, now No. 101, in Digbeth, about four hundred years ago, in the capacity of a tanner.

Richard Smallbroke, Bishop of Lichfield and Coventry, in the reign of George II. was a native of Birmingham, as his ancestors were for many ages, with reputation: he is said to have been born at number 2 in the High-street, had great property in the town, now enjoyed by his descendants, though they have left the place. The families also of Weaman, Jennings, Whalley, etc. have acquired vast property, and quitted the meridian of Birmingham; and some others are at this day ripe for removal. Let me close this bright scene of prosperity, and open another, which can only be viewed with a melancholy eye. We cannot behold the distresses of man without compassion; but that distress which follows affluence, comes with double effect.

We have amongst us a family of the name of Middlemore, of great antiquity, deducible from the conquest; who held the chief possessions, and the chief offices in the county, and who matched into the first families in the kingdom, but fell with the interest of Charles the First; and are now in that low ebb of fortune, that I have frequently, with a gloomy pleasure, relieved them at the common charity-board of the town. Such is the tottering point of human greatness.

Another of the name of Bracebridge, who for more than six hundred years, figured in the first ranks of life.

A third of the name of Mountfort, who shone with meridian splendor, through a long train of ages. As genealogy was ever a favourite amusement, I have often conversed with these solitary remains of tarnished lustre, but find in all of them, the pride of their family buried with its greatness:--they pay no more attention to the arms of their ancestors, than to a scrap of paper, with which they would light their pipe. Upon consulting one of the name of Elwall, said to be descended from the Britons, I found him so amazingly defective, that he could not stretch his pedigree even so high as his grandfather.

A fifth family amongst us, of the name of Arden, stood upon the pinnacle of fame in the days of Alfred the Great, where perhaps they had stood for ages before: they continued the elevation about seven hundred years after; but having treasonable charges brought against them, in the days of Queen Elizabeth, about two hundred years ago, they were thrown from this exalted eminence, and dashed to pieces in the fall. In various consultations with a member of this honourable house, I found the greatness of his family not only lost, but the memory of it also. I assured him, that his family stood higher in the scale of honour, than any private one within my knowledge: that his paternal ancestors, for about seven generations, were successively Earls of Warwick, before the Norman conquest: that, though he could not boast a descent from the famous Guy, he was related to him: that, though Turchell, Earl of Warwick at the conquest, his direct ancestor, lost the Earldom in favour of Roger Newburgh, a favourite of William's; yet, as the Earl did not appear in arms, against the Conqueror, at the battle of Hastings, nor oppose the new interest, he was allowed to keep forty-six of his manors: that he retired upon his own vast estate, which he held in dependence, where the family resided with great opulence, in one house, for many centuries, 'till their reduction above-mentioned. He received the information with some degree of amazement, and replied with a serious face,--"Perhaps there may have been something great in my predecessors, for my grandfather kept several cows in Birmingham and sold milk."

The families of those ancient heroes, of Saxon and Norman race, are, chiefly by the mutations of time, and of state, either become extinct, or as above, reduced to the lowest verge of fortune. Those few therefore, whose descent is traceable, may be carried higher than that of the present nobility; for I know none of these last, who claim peerage beyond Edward the first, about 1295. Hence it follows, that for antiquity, alliance, and blood, the advantage is evidently in favour of the lowest class.

Could one of those illustrious shades return to the earth and inspect human actions, he might behold one of his descendants, dancing at the lathe; another tippling with his dark brethren of the apron; a third humbly soliciting from other families such favours as were formerly granted by his own; a fourth imitating modern grandeur, by contracting debts he never designs to pay; and a fifth snuff of departed light, poaching, like a thief in the night, upon the very manors, possessed by his ancestors.

Whence is it that title, pedigree, and alliance, in superior life, are esteemed of the highest value; while in the inferior, who have a prior claim, are totally neglected? The grand design of every creature upon earth, is to supply the wants of nature. No amusements of body or mind can be adopted, till hunger is served. When the appetite calls, the whole attention of the animal, with all its powers, is bound to answer. Hence arise those dreadful contests in the brute creation, from the lion in the woods, to the dog, who seizes the bone. Hence the ship, when her provisions are spent, and she becalmed, casts a savage eye, upon human sacrifices; and hence, the attention of the lower ranks of men, are too far engrossed for mental pursuit. They see, like Esau, the honours of their family devoured with a ravenous appetite. A man with an empty cupboard would make but a wretched philosopher. But if fortune should smile upon one of the lower race, raise him a step above his original standing, and give him a prospect of independence, he immediately begins to eye the arms upon carriages, examines old records for his name, and inquires where the Herald's office is kept. Thus, when the urgency of nature is set at liberty, the bird can whistle upon the branch, the fish play upon the surface, the goat skip upon the mountain, and even man himself, can bask in the sunshine of science. I digress no farther.

The situation of St. Martin's church is another reason for fixing the original centre of Birmingham at the Old Cross. Christianity made an early and a swift progress in this kingdom; persecution, as might be expected, followed her footsteps, increased her votaries, and, as was ever the case, in all new religions, her proselytes were very devout.

The religious fervor of the christians displayed itself in building churches. Most of those in England are of Saxon original, and were erected between the fourth and the tenth century; that of St. Martin's is ancient beyond the reach of historical knowledge, and probably rose in the early reigns of the Saxon kings.

It was the custom of those times, to place the church, if there was but one, out of the precincts of the town; this is visible at the present day in those places which have received no increase.

Perhaps it will not be an unreasonable supposition to fix the erection of St. Martin's, in the eighth century; and if the inquisitive reader chooses to traverse the town a second time, he may find its boundaries something like the following. We cannot allow its extension northward beyond the east end of New-street; that it included the narrow parts of Philip street, Bell street, Spiceal street, Moor street, and Park street. That the houses at this period were more compact than heretofore; that Digbeth and Deritend, lying in the road to Stratford, Warwick, and Coventry, all places of antiquity, were now formed. Thus the church stood in the environs of the town, unincumbered with buildings. Possibly this famous nursery of arts might, by this time, produce six hundred houses. A town must increase before its appendages are formed; those appendages also must increase before there is a necessity for an additional chapel, and after that increase, the inhabitants may wait long before that necessity is removed. Deritend is an appendage to Birmingham; the inhabitants of this hamlet having long laboured under the inconveniency of being remote from the parish church of Aston, and too numerous for admission into that of Birmingham, procured a grant in 1381 to erect a chapel of their own. If we, therefore, allow three hundred years for the infancy of Deritend, three hundred more for her maturity, and four hundred since the erection of her chapel, which is a very reasonable allowance. It will bring us to the time I mentioned.

It does not appear that Deritend was attended with any considerable augmentation, from the Norman conquest to the year 1767, when a turnpike-road was opened to Alcester, and when Henry Bradford publicly offered a freehold to the man who should first build upon his estate; since which time Deritend has made a rapid progress: and this dusky offspring of Birmingham is now travelling apace along her new formed road.

I must again recline upon Dugdale.--In 1309, William de Birmingham, Lord of the Manor, took a distress of the inhabitants of Bromsgrove and King's-norton, for refusing to pay the customary tolls of the market. The inhabitants, therefore, brought their action and recovered damage, because it was said, their lands being the ancient demesne of the crown, they had a right to sell their produce in any market in the King's dominions.

It appeared in the course of the trial, that the ancestors of William de Birmingham had a MARKET HERE before the Norman conquest! I shall have occasion, in future, to resume this remarkable expression. I have also met with an old author, who observes, that Birmingham was governed by two Constables in the time of the Saxons; small places have seldom more than one. These evidences prove much in favour of the government, population, and antiquity of the place.

In Domesday-book it is rated at four hides of land. A hide was as much as a team could conveniently plough in a year; perhaps at that time about fifty acres: I think there is not now, more than two hundred ploughed in the parish.

It was also said to contain woods of half a mile in length, and four furlongs in breadth. What difference subsisted between half a mile and four furlongs, in ancient time, is uncertain; we know of none now. The mile was reduced to its present standard in the reign of Queen Elizabeth: neither are there the least traces of those woods, for at this day it is difficult to find a stick that deserves the name of a tree, in the whole manor.--Timber is no part of the manufactory of Birmingham.

Let us survey the town a third time, as we may reasonably suppose it stood in the most remarkable period of English history, that of the conquest.

We cannot yet go farther North of the centre than before, that is, along the High-street, 'till we meet the East end of New street. We shall penetrate rather farther into Moor-street, none into Park-street, take in Digbeth, Deritend, Edgbaston-street, as being the road to Dudley, Bromsgrove, and the whole West of England; Spiceal-street, the Shambles, a larger part of Bell street, and Philip-street.

The ancient increase of the town was towards the South, because of the great road, the conveniency of water, the church, and the manor-house, all which lay in that quarter: but the modern extension was chiefly towards the North, owing to the scions of her trades being transplanted all over the country, in that direction, as far as Wednesbury, Walsall, and Wolverhampton. But particularly her vicinity to the coal delphs, which were ever considered as the soul of her prosperity. Perhaps by this time the number of houses might have been augmented to seven hundred: but whatever was her number, either in this or any other period, we cannot doubt her being populous in every æra of her existence.

The following small extract from the register, will show a gradual increase, even before the restoration:

Year.	Christenings.	Weddings.	Burials
1555,	37,	15,	27.
1558,	48,	10,	47.
1603,	65,	14,	40.
1625,	76,	18,	47.
1660,	76,	from April to Dec. inclusive.	

In 1251, William de Birmingham, Lord of the Manor, procured an additional charter from Henry the Third, reviving some decayed privileges and granting others; among the last was that of the Whitsuntide fair, to begin on the eve of Holy Thursday, and to continue four days. At the alteration of the style, in 1752, it was prudently changed to the Thursday in Whitsun week; that less time might be lost to the injury of work and the workman. He also procured another fair, to begin on the eve of St. Michael, and continue for three days. Both which fairs are at this day in great repute.

By the interest of Audomore de Valance, earl of Pembroke, a licence was obtained from the crown, in 1319 to charge an additional toll upon every article sold in the market for three years, towards paving the town. Every quarter of corn to pay one farthing, and other things in proportion.

We have no reason to believe that either the town or the market were small at that time, however, at the expiration of the term, the toll was found inadequate to the expence, and the work lay dormant for eighteen years, till 1337, when a second licence was obtained, equal to the first, which completed the intention.

Those streets, thus dignified with a pavement, or rather their sides, to accommodate the foot passenger, probably were High-street, the Bull-ring, Corn-cheaping, Digbeth, St. Martin's-lane, Moat-lane, Edgbaston-street, Spiceal-street, and part of Moor-street.

It was the practice, in those early days, to leave the center of a street unpaved, for the easier passage of carriages and horses; the consequence was, in flat streets the road became extremely dirty, almost impassable, and in a descent, the soil was quickly worn away, and left a causeway on each side. Many instances of this ancient practice are within memory.

The streets, no doubt, in which the fairs were held, mark the boundaries of the town in the thirteenth century. Though smaller wares were sold upon the spot used for the market, the rougher articles, such as cattle, were exposed to sale in what were then the *out-streets*. The fair for horses was held in Edgbaston-street, and that for beasts in the High-street, tending towards the Welch Cross.

Inconvenient as these streets seem for the purpose, our dark ancestors, of peaceable memory, found no detriment, during the infant state of population, in keeping them there. But we, their crowded sons, for want of accommodation, have wisely removed both; the horse-fair, in 1777, to Brick-kiln-lane, now the extreme part of the town; and that for beasts, in 1769, into the open part of Dale-end.

Whatever veneration we may entertain for ancient custom, there is sometimes a necessity to break it. Were we now to solicit the crown for a fair, those streets would be the last we should fix on.

If we survey Birmingham in the twelfth century, we shall find her crowded with timber, within and without; her streets dirty and narrow; but considering the distant period, much trodden, yet, compared with her present rising state, but little.

The inhabitant became an early encroacher upon nor narrow streets, and sometimes the lord was the greatest. Her houses were mean and low, but few reaching higher than one story, perhaps none more than two; composed of wood and plaister-- she was a stranger to brick. Her public buildings consisted solely of one, *the church*.

If we behold her in the fourteenth century, we shall observe her private buildings multiplied more than improved; her narrow streets, by trespass, become narrower, for she was ever chargeable with neglect; her public buildings increased to four, two in the town, and two at a distance, the Priory, of stone, founded by contribution, at the head of which stood her lord; the Guild, of timber, now the Free School; and Deritend Chapel, of the same materials, resembling a barn, with something like an awkward dove-coat, at the west end, by way of steeple. All these will be noticed in due course.

If we take a view of the inhabitants, we shall find them industrious, plain, and honest; the more of the former, generally, the less of dishonesty, if their superiors lived in an homelier stile in that period, it is no wonder *they* did. Perhaps our ancestors acquired more money than their neighbours, and not much of that; but what they had was extremely valuable: diligence will accumulate. In curious operations, known only to a few, we may suppose the artist was amply paid.

Nash, in his History of Worcestershire, gives us a curious list of anecdotes, from the church-wardens ledger, of Hales-Owen. I shall transcribe two, nearly three hundred years old. "*Paid for bread and ale, to make my Lord Abbot drink, in Rogation week, 2d.*" What should we now think of an ecclesiastical nobleman, accepting a two-penny treat from a country church-warden?

This displays an instance of moderation in a class of people famous for luxury. It shows also the amazing reduction of money: the same sum which served my Lord Abbot four days, would now be devoured in four minutes.--"1498, *paid for repeyling the organs, to the organmaker at Bromicham, 10s.*" Birmingham then, we find, discovered the powers of genius in the finer arts, as well as in iron. By '*the* organmaker,' we mould suppose there was but one.

It appears that the art of acquiring riches was as well understood by our fathers, as by us; while an artist could receive as much money for tuning an organ, as would purchase an acre of land, or treat near half a gross of Lord Abbots.

BATTLE OF CAMP-HILL.

1643.

Clarendon reproaches with virulence, our spirited ancestors, for disloyalty to Charles the First.--The day after the King left Birmingham, on his march from Shrewsbury, in 1642, they seized his carriages, containing the royal plate and furniture, which they conveyed, for security, to Warwick Castle. They apprehended all messengers and suspected persons; frequently attacked, and reduced small parties of the royalists, whom they sent prisoners to Coventry.--Hence the proverbial expression of a refractory person, *Send him to Coventry*.

In 1643, the King ordered Prince Rupert, with a detachment of two thousand men, to open a communication between Oxford and York. In his march to Birmingham, he found a company of foot, kept for the parliament, lately reinforced by a troop of horse from the garrison at Lichfield: but, supposing they would not resist a power of ten to one, sent his quarter masters to demand lodging, and offer protection.

But the sturdy sons of freedom, having cast up slight works at each end of the town, and barricaded the lesser avenues, rejected the offer and the officers. The military uniting in one small and compact body, assisted by the inhabitants, were determined the King's forces mould not enter. Their little fire opened on the Prince: but bravery itself, though possessed of an excellent spot of ground for defence, was obliged to give way to numbers. The Prince quickly put them to silence; yet, under the success of his own arms, he was not able to enter the town, for the inhabitants had choaked up, with carriages, the deep and narrow road, then between Deritend and Camp-hill, which obliged the Prince to alter his route to the left, and proceed towards Long-bridge.

The spirit of resistance was not yet broken; they sustained a second attack, but to no purpose, except that of laughter. A running fight continued through the town; victory declared loudly for the Prince; the retreat became general: part of the vanquished took the way to Oldbury.

William Fielding, Earl of Denbigh, a volunteer under the Prince, being in close pursuit of an officer in the service of the parliament, and both upon the full gallop, up Shirland-lane, in the manor of Smethwick, the officer instantly turning, discharged a pistol at the Earl, and mortally wounded him with a random shot.

The parliament troops were animated in the engagement by a clergyman, who acted as governor, but being taken in the defeat, and refusing quarter, was killed in the Red Lion-inn.

The Prince, provoked at the resistance, in revenge, set fire to the town. His wrath is said to have kindled in Bull-street, and consumed several houses near the spot, now No. 12.

He obliged the inhabitants to quench the flames with a heavy fine, to prevent farther military execution. Part of the fine is said to have been shoes and stockings for his people.

The parliament forces had formed their camp in that well chosen angle, which divides the Stratford and Warwick roads, upon Camp-hill.

The victorious Prince left no garrison, because their insignificant works were untenable; but left an humbled people, and marched to the reduction of Lichfield.

In 1665, London was not only visited with the plague, but many other parts of England, among which, Birmingham felt this dreadful mark of the divine judgment.

The infection is said to have been caught by a box of clothes, brought by the carrier, and lodged at the White-hart. Depopulation ensued. The church-yard was insufficient for the reception of the dead, who were conveyed to Ladywood-green, one acre of waste land, then denominated the Pelt Ground.

The charter for the market has evidently been repeated by divers kings, both Saxon and Norman, but when first granted is uncertain, perhaps at an early Saxon date; and the day seems never to have been changed from Thursday.

The lords were tenacious of their privileges; or, one would think, there was no need to renew their charter. Prescription, necessity, and increasing numbers, would establish the right.

Perhaps, in a Saxon period, there was room sufficient in our circumscribed market-place, for the people and their weekly supplies; but now, their supplies would fill it, exclusive of the people.

Thus by a steady and a persevering hand, she kept a constant and uniform stroke at the anvil, through a vast succession of ages: rising superior to the frowns of fortune: establishing a variety of productions from iron: ever improving her inventive powers, and perhaps, changing a number of her people, equal to her whole inhabitants, every sixteen years, till she arrived at another important period, the end of the civil wars of Charles the first.

MODERN STATE

OF

BIRMINGHAM.

It is the practice of the historian, to divide ancient history from modern, at the fall of the Roman Empire. For, during a course of about seven hundred years, while the Roman name beamed in meridian splendour, the lustre of her arms and political conduct influenced, more or less, every country in Europe. But at the fall of that mighty empire, which happened in the fifth century, every one of the conquered provinces was left to stand upon its own basis. From this period, therefore, the history of nations takes a material turn. The English historian divides his ancient account from the modern, at the extinction of the house of Plantagenet, in 1485, the fall of Richard the Third. For, by the introduction of letters, an amazing degree of light was thrown upon science, and also, by a new system of politics, adopted by Henry the Seventh, the British constitution, occasioned by one little act of parliament, that of allowing liberty to sell land, took a very different, and an important course.

But the ancient and modern state of Birmingham, must divide at the restoration of Charles the Second. For though she had before, held a considerable degree of eminence; yet at this period, the curious arts began to take root, and were cultivated by the hand of genius. Building leases, also, began to take effect, extension followed, and numbers of people crowded upon each other, as into a Paradise.

As a kind tree, perfectly adapted for growth, and planted in a suitable soil, draws nourishment from the circumjacent ground, to a great extent, and robs the neighbouring plants of their support, that nothing can thrive within its influence; so Birmingham, half whose inhabitants above the age of ten, perhaps, are not natives, draws her annual supply of hands, and is constantly fed by the towns that surround her, where her trades are not practised. Preventing every increase to those neighbours who kindly contribute to her wants. This is the case with Bromsgrove, Dudley, Stourbridge, Sutton, Lichfield, Tamworth, Coleshill, and Solihull.

We have taken a view of Birmingham in several periods of existence, during the long course of perhaps three thousand years. Standing sometimes upon presumptive ground. If the prospect has been a little clouded, it only caused us to be more attentive, that we might not be deceived. But, though we have attended her through so immense a space, we have only seen her in infancy. Comparatively small in her size, homely in her person, and coarse in her dress. Her ornaments, wholly of iron, from her own forge.

But now, her growths will be amazing; her expansion rapid, perhaps not to be paralleled in history. We shall see her rise in all the beauty of youth, of grace, of elegance, and attract the notice of the commercial world. She will also add to her iron ornaments, the lustre of every metal, that the whole earth can produce, with all their illustrious race of compounds, heightened by fancy, and garnished with jewels. She will draw from the fossil, and the vegetable kingdoms; press the ocean for shell, skin and coral. She will also tax the animal, for horn, bone, and ivory, and she will decorate the whole with the touches of her pencil.

I have met with some remarks, published in 1743, wherein the author observes, "That Birmingham, at the restoration, probably consisted only of three streets." But it is more probable it consisted of fifteen, though not all finished, and about nine hundred houses.

I am sensible, when an author strings a parcel of streets together, he furnishes but a dry entertainment for his reader, especially to a stranger. But, as necessity demands intelligence from the historian, I must beg leave to mention the streets and their supposed number of houses.

Digbeth, nearly the same as now, except the twenty-tree houses between the two Mill-lanes, which are of a modern date, about	110
Moat-lane (Court-lane)	12
Corn-market and Shambles	40
Spiceal-street	50
Dudley-street	50
Bell-street	50
Philip-street	30
St. Martin's-lane	15
Edgbaston-street	70
Lee's-lane	10
Park-street, extending from Digbeth nearly to the East end of Freeman-street	80
More-street, to the bottom of Castle-street,	70
Bull-street, not so high as the Minories,	50
High-street,	100
Deritend;	120
Odd houses scattered round the verge of the town	50

	907

The number of inhabitants, 5,472.

An History of Birmingham (1783)

The same author farther observes, "That from the Restoration to the year 1700, the streets of Birmingham were increased to thirty one." But I can make their number only twenty-eight, and many of these far from complete. Also, that the whole number of houses were 2,504, and the inhabitants 15,032. The additional streets therefore seem to have been Castle-street, Carr's-lane, Dale-end, Stafford-street, Bull lane, Pinfold-street, Colmore-street, the Froggery, Old Meeting-street, Worcester-street, Peck-lane, New-street, (a small part,) Lower Mill-lane.

From the year 1700 to 1731, there is said to have been a farther addition of twenty-five streets, I know of only twenty-three: and also of 1,215 houses, and 8,250 inhabitants. Their names we offer as under;--Freeman-street, New Meeting-street, Moor-street, (the North part), Wood-street, the Butts, Lichfield-street; Thomas's-street, John's-street, London-'prentice street, Lower priory, The Square, Upper-priory, Minories, Steel-house-lane, Cherry-street, Cannon-street, Needless-alley, Temple-street, King's street, Queen-street, Old Hinkleys, Smallbrook-street, and the East part of Hill-street.

I first saw Birmingham July 14, 1741, and will therefore perambulate its boundaries at that time with my traveller, beginning at the top of Snow-hill, keeping the town on our left, and the fields that then were, on our right.

Through Bull-lane we proceed to Temple-street; down Peck lane, to the top of Pinfold-street; Dudley-street, the Old Hinkleys to the top of Smallbrook street, back through Edgbaston-street, Digbeth, to the upper end of Deritend. We shall return through Park-street, Mass-house-lane, the North of Dale end, Stafford-street, Steel-house-lane, to the top of Snow-hill, from whence we set out.

If we compare this account with that of 1731, we shall not find any great addition of streets; but those that were formed before, were much better filled up. The new streets erected during these ten years were Temple-row, except about six houses. The North of Park-street, and of Dale-end; also, Slaney-street, and a small part of the East side of Snow hill.

From 1741, to the present year 1780, Birmingham seems to have acquired the amazing augmentation of seventy one streets, 4172 houses, and 25,032 inhabitants.

Thus her internal property is covered with new-erected buildings, tier within tier. Thus she opens annually, a new aspect to the traveller; and thus she penetrates along the roads that surround her, as if to unite with the neighbouring towns, for their improvement in commerce, in arts, and in civilization.

I have often led my curious enquirer round Birmingham, but, like the thread round the swelling clue, never twice in the same tract. We shall therefore, for the last time, examine her present boundaries. Our former journey commenced at the top of Snow-hill, we now set off from the bottom.

The present buildings extend about forty yards beyond the Salutation, on the Wolverhampton road. We now turn up Lionel-street, leaving St. Paul's, and about three new erected houses, on the right[1]; pass close to New-Hall, leaving it on the left, to the top of Great Charles-street, along Easy-hill: we now leave the Wharf to the right, down Suffolk-street, in which are seventy houses, leaving two infant streets also to the right, in which are about twelve houses each: up to Holloway-head, thence to Windmill-hill, Bow-street, Brick-kiln-lane, down to Lady-well, along Pudding-brook, to the Moat, Lloyd's Slitting-mill, Digbeth, over Deritend bridge, thence to the right, for Cheapside; cross the top of Bradford-street, return by the Bridge to Floodgate-street, Park-street, Bartholomew's-chapel, Grosvenor-street, Nova scotia-street, Woodcock-lane, Aston-street, Lancaster-street, Walmer-lane, Price's-street, Bath-street, to the bottom of Snow-hill.

[1] The above was written in May 1780, and the three houses are now, March 14, 1781, multiplied into fifty-five.

The circle I have described is about five miles, in which is much ground to be filled up. There are also beyond this crooked line, five clumps of houses belonging to Birmingham, which may be deemed hamlets.

At the Sand-pits upon the Dudley-road, about three furlongs from the buildings, are fourteen houses.

Four furlongs from the Navigation-office, upon the road to Hales-owen, are twenty-nine.

One furlong from Exeter row, towards the hand, are thirty-four.

Upon Camp-hill, 130 yards from the junction of the Warwick and Coventry roads, which is the extremity of the present buildings, are thirty-one.

And two furlongs from the town, in Walmer-lane, are seventeen more.

I shall comprize, in one view, the state of Birmingham in eight different periods of time. And though some are imaginary, perhaps they are not far from real.

	Streets.	Houses.	Souls.
In the time of the ancient Britons,		80	400
A.D. 750,	8	600	3000
1066,	9	700	3500

1650,	15	900	5472
1700,	28	2504	15032
1731,	51	3717	23286
1741,	54	4114	24660
1780,	125	8382	50295

In 1778, Birmingham, exclusive of the appendages, contained 8042 houses, 48252 inhabitants.

At the same time, Manchester consisted of 3402, houses, and 22440 people.

In 1779, Nottingham contained 3191 houses, and 17711 souls.

It is easy to see, without the spirit of prophecy, that Birmingham hath not yet arrived at her zenith, neither is she likely to reach it for ages to come. Her increase will depend upon her manufactures; her manufactures will depend upon the national commerce; national commerce, will depend upon a superiority at sea; and this superiority may be extended to a long futurity.

The interior parts of the town, are like those of other places, parcelled out into small free-holds, perhaps, originally purchased of the Lords of the Manor; but, since its amazing increase, which began about the restoration, large tracts of land have been huxtered out upon building leases.

Some of the first that were granted, seem to have been about Worcester and Colmore streets, at the trifling annual price of one farthing per yard, or under.

The market ran so much against the lesor, that the lessee had liberty to build in what manner he pleased; and, at the expiration of the term, could remove the buildings unless the other chose to purchase them. But the market, at this day, is so altered, that the lessee gives four-pence per yard; is tied to the mode of building, and obliged to leave the premises in repair.

The itch for building is predominant: we dip our fingers into mortar almost as soon as into business. It is not wonderful that a person should be hurt by the *falling* of a house; but, with us, a man sometimes breaks his back by *raising* one.

This private injury, however, is attended with a public benefit of the first magnitude; for every "*House to be Let,*" holds forth a kind of invitation to the stranger to settle in it, who, being of the laborious class, promotes the manufactures.

If we cannot produce many houses of the highest orders in architecture, we make out the defect in numbers. Perhaps *more* are erected here, in a given time, than in any place in the whole island, London excepted.

It is remarkable, that in a town like Birmingham, where so many houses are built, the art of building is so little understood. The stile of architecture in the inferior sort, is rather showy than lasting.

The proprietor generally contracts for a house of certain dimensions, at a stipulated price: this induces the artist to use some ingredients of the cheaper kind, and sometimes to try whether he can cement the materials with sand, instead of lime.

But a house is not the only thing spoilt by the builder; he frequently spoils himself: out of many successions of house-makers, I cannot recollect one who made a fortune.

Many of these edifices have been brought forth, answered the purposes for which they were created, and been buried in the dust, during my short acquaintance with Birmingham. One would think, if a man can survive a house, he has no great reason to complain of the shortness of life.

From the external genteel appearance of a house, the stranger would be tempted to think the inhabitant possessed at least a thousand pounds; but, if he looks within, he sees only the ensigns of beggary.

We have people who enjoy four or five hundred pounds a year in houses, none of which, perhaps, exceed six pounds per annum. It may excite a smile, to say, I have known two houses erected, one occupied by a man, his wife, and three children; the other pair had four; and twelve guineas covered every expence.

Pardon, my dear reader, the omission of a pompous encomium on their beauty, or duration.

I am inclined to think two thirds of the houses in Birmingham stand upon new foundations, and all the places of worship, except Deritend Chapel.

About the year 1730, Thomas Sherlock, late Bishop of London, purchased the private estate of the ladies of the manor, chiefly land, about four hundred per annum.

In 1758, the steward told me it had increased to twice the original value. The pious old Bishop was frequently solicited to grant building leases, but answered, "His land was valuable, and if built upon, his successor, at the expiration of the term, would have the rubbish to carry off:" he therefore not only refused, but prohibited his successor from granting such leases.

But Sir Thomas Gooch, who succeeded him, seeing the great improvement of the neighbouring estates, and wisely judging fifty pounds per acre preferable to five, procured an act in about 1766, to set aside the prohibiting clause in the Bishop's will.

Since which, a considerable town may be said to have been erected upon his property, now about 1600*l*. per annum.

An acquaintance assured me, that in 1756 he could have purchased the house he then occupied for 400*l.* but refused. In 1770, the same house was sold for 600*l.* and in 1772, I purchased it for eight hundred and thirty-five guineas, without any alteration, but what time had made for the worse: and for this enormous price I had only an old house, which I was obliged to take down. Such is the rapid improvement in value, of landed property, in a commercial country.

Suffer me to add, though foreign to my subject, that these premises were the property of an ancient family of the name of Smith, now in decay; where many centuries ago one of the first inns in Birmingham, and well known by the name of the Garland House, perhaps from the sign; but within memory, Potter's Coffee-house.

Under one part was a room about forty-five feet long, and fifteen wide, used for the town prison.

In sinking a cellar we found a large quantity of tobacco-pipes of a angular construction, with some very antique earthen ware, but no coin; also loads of broken bottles, which refutes the complaint of our pulpits against modern degeneracy, and indicates, the vociferous arts of getting drunk and breaking glass, were well understood by our ancestors.

In penetrating a bed of sand, upon which had stood a work-shop, about two feet below the surface we came to a tumolus six feet long, three wide, and five deep, built very neat, with tiles laid flat, but no cement. The contents were mouldered wood, and pieces of human bone.

I know of no house in Birmingham, the inns excepted, whose annual rent exceeds eighty pounds. By the lamp books, the united rents appear to be about seventy thousand, which if we take at twenty years purchase, will compose a freehold of 1,400,000*l.* value.

If we allow the contents of the manor to be three thousand acres, and deduct six hundred for the town, five hundred more for roads, water, and waste land; and rate the remaining nineteen hundred, at the average rent of 2*l.* 10s. per acre; we shall raise an additional freehold of 4,750*l.* per ann.

If we value this landed property at thirty years purchase, it will produce 142,500*l.* and, united with the value of the buildings, the fee-simple of this happy region of genius, will amount to 1,542,500*l.*

OF THE STREETS,

AND

THEIR NAMES.

We accuse our short-sighted ancestors, and with reason, for leaving us almost without a church-yard and a market-place; for forming some of our streets nearly without width, and without light. One would think they intended a street without a passage, when they erected Moor-street; and that their successors should light their candles at noon.

Something, however, may be pleaded in excuse, by observing the concourse of people was small, therefore a little room would suffice; and the buildings were low, so that light would be less obstructed: besides, we cannot guess at the future but by the present. As the increase of the town was slow, the modern augmentation could not then be discovered through the dark medium of time; but the prospect into futurity is at this day rather brighter, for we plainly see, and perhaps with more reason, succeeding generations will blame us for neglect. We occupy the power to reform, without the will; why else do we suffer enormities to grow, which will have taken deep root in another age? If utility and beauty can *be joined together* in the street, why are they ever *put asunder*? It is easy for Birmingham to be as rapid in her improvement, as in her growth.

The town consists of about 125 streets, some of which acquired their names from a variety of causes, but some from no cause, and others, have not yet acquired a name.

Those of Bull street, Cannon street, London Prentice street, and Bell street, from the signs of their respective names.

Some receive theirs from the proprietors of the land, as Smallbrook street, Freeman street, Colmore street, Slaney street, Weaman street, Bradford street, and Colmore row.

Digbeth, or Ducks Bath, from the Pools for accommodating that animal, was originally Well street, from the many springs in its neighbourhood.

Others derive a name from caprice, as Jamaica row, John, Thomas, and Philip streets.

Some, from a desire of imitating the metropolis, as, Fleet-street, Snow-hill, Ludgate-hill, Cheapside, and Friday-street.

Some again, from local causes, as High-street, from its elevation, St. Martin's-lane, Church-street, Cherry-street, originally an orchard, Chapel-street, Bartholomew-row, Mass-house-lane, Old and New Meeting-streets, Steelhouse-lane, Temple-row and Temple-street, also Pinfold-street, from a pinfold at No. 85, removed in 1752.

Moor-street, anciently Mole-street, from the eminence on one side, or the declivity on the other.

Park-street seems to have acquired its name by being appropriated to the private use of the lord of the manor, and, except at the narrow end next Digbeth, contained only the corner house to the south, entering Shut-lane, No. 82, lately taken down, which was called The Lodge.

Spiceal-street, anciently Mercer-street, from the number of mercers shops; and as the professors of that trade dealt in grocery, it was promiscuously called Spicer-street. The present name is only a corruption of the last.

The spot, now the Old Hinkleys, was a close, till about 1720, in which horses were shown at the fair, then held in Edgbaston-street. It was since a brick-yard, and contained only one hut, in which the brick-maker slept.

The tincture of the smoky shops, with all their *black furniture*, for weilding gun-barrels, which afterwards appeared on the back of Small-brooke-street, might occasion the original name *Inkleys*; ink is well known; leys, is of British derivation, and means grazing ground; so that the etymology perhaps is *Black pasture*.

The Butts; a mark to shoot at, when the bow was the fashionable instrument of war, which the artist of Birmingham knew well how to make, and to use.

Gosta Green (Goose-stead-Green) a name of great antiquity, now in decline; once a track of commons, circumscribed by the Stafford road, now Stafford-street, the roads to Lichfield and Coleshill, now Aston and Coleshill-streets, and extending to Duke-street, the boundary of the manor.

Perhaps, many ages after, it was converted into a farm, and was, within memory, possessed by a person of the name of Tanter, whence, Tanter-street.

Sometimes a street fluctuates between two names, as that of Catharine and Wittal, which at length terminated in favour of the former.

Thus the names of great George and great Charles stood candidates for one of the finest streets in Birmingham, which after a contest of two or three years, was carried in favour of the latter.

Others receive a name from the places to which they direct, as Worcester-street, Edgbaston-street, Dudley-street, Lichfield-street, Aston-street, Stafford-street, Coleshill-street, and Alcester-street.

A John Cooper, the same person who stands in the list of donors in St. Martin's church, and who, I apprehend, lived about two hundred and fifty years ago, at the Talbot, now No. 20, in the High-street, left about four acres of land, between Steelhouse-lane, St. Paul's chapel, and Walmer-lane, to make love-days for the people of Birmingham; hence, *Love-day-croft*.

Various sounds from the trowel upon the premises, in 1758, produced the name of *Love-day-street* (corrupted into Lovely-street.)

This croft is part of an estate under the care of Lench's Trust; and, at the time of the bequest, was probably worth no more than ten shillings per annum.

At the top of Walmer-lane, which is the north east corner of this croft, stood about half a dozen old alms-houses, perhaps erected in the beginning of the seventeenth century, then at a considerable distance from the town. These were taken down in 1764, and the present alms-houses, which are thirty-six, erected near the spot, at the expence of the trust, to accommodate the same number of poor widows, who have each a small annual stipend, for the supply of coals.

This John Cooper, for some services rendered to the lord of the manor, obtained three privileges, That of regulating the goodness and price of beer, consequently he stands in the front of the whole liquid race of high tasters; that he should, whenever he pleased, beat a bull in the Bull-ring, whence arises the name; and, that he should be allowed interment in the south porch of St. Martin's church. His memory ought to be transmitted with honor, to posterity, for promoting the harmony of his neighbourhood, but he ought to have been buried in a dunghill, for punishing an innocent animal.--His wife seems to have survived him, who also became a benefactress, is recorded in the same list, and their monument, in antique sculpture, is yet visible in the porch.

The Alms House.

TRADE.

Perhaps there is not by nature so much difference in the capacities of men, as by education. The efforts of nature will produce a ten-fold crop in the field, but those of art, fifty.

Perhaps too, the seeds of every virtue, vice, inclination, and habit, are sown in the breast of every human being, though not in an equal degree. Some of these lie dormant for ever, no hand inviting their cultivation. Some are called into existence by their own internal strength, and others by the external powers that surround them. Some of these seeds flourish more, some less, according to the aptness of the soil, and the modes of assistance. We are not to suppose infancy the only time in which these scions spring, no part of life is exempt. I knew a man who lived to the age of forty, totally regardless of music. A fidler happening to have apartments near his abode, attracted his ear, by frequent exhibitions, which produced a growing inclination for that favourite science, and he became a proficient himself. Thus in advanced periods a man may fall in love with a science, a woman, or a bottle. Thus avarice is said to shoot up in ancient soil, and thus, I myself bud forth in history at fifty-six.

The cameleon is said to receive a tincture from the colour of the object that is nearest him; but the human mind in reality receives a bias from its connections. Link a man to the pulpit, and he cannot proceed to any great lengths in profligate life. Enter him into the army, and he will endeavour to swear himself into consequence. Make the man of humanity an overseer of the poor, and he will quickly find the tender feelings of commiseration hardened. Make him a physician, and he will be the only person upon the premises, the heir excepted, unconcerned at the prospect of death. Make him a surgeon, and he will amputate a leg with the same indifference with which a cutler saws a piece of bone for a knife handle. You commit a rascal to prison because he merits transportation, but by the time he comes out he merits a halter. By uniting also with industry, we become industrious. It is easy to give instances of people whose distinguishing characteristic was idleness, but when they breathed the air of Birmingham, diligence became the predominant feature. The view of profit, like the view of corn to the hungry horse, excites to action.

Thus the various seeds scattered by nature into the soul at its first formation, either lie neglected, are urged into increase by their own powers, or are drawn towards maturity by the concurring circumstances that attend them.

The late Mr. Grenville observed, in the House of Commons, "That commerce tended to corrupt the morals of a people." If we examine the expression, we shall find it true in a certain degree, beyond which, it tends to improve them.

Perhaps every tradesman can furnish out numberless instances of small deceit. His conduct is marked with a littleness, which though allowed by general consent, is not strictly just. A person with whom I have long been connected in business, asked, if I had dealt with his relation, whom he had brought up, and who had lately entered into commercial life. I answered in the affirmative. He replied, "He is a very honest fellow." I told him I saw all the finesse of a tradesman about him. "Oh, rejoined my friend, a man has a right to say all he can in favour of his own goods." Nor is the seller alone culpable. The buyer takes an equal share in the deception. Though neither of them speak their sentiments, they well understand each other. Whilst the treaty is agitating, the profit of the tradesman vanishes, yet the buyer pronounces against the article; but when finished, the seller whispers his friend, "It is well sold," and the buyer smiles if a bargain.

Thus is the commercial track a line of minute deceits.

But, on the other hand, it does not seem possible for a man in trade to pass this line, without wrecking his reputation; which, if once broken, can never be made whole. The character of a tradesman is valuable, it is his all; therefore, whatever seeds of the vicious kind shoot forth in the mind, are carefully watched and nipped in the bud, that they may never blossom into action.

Thus having slated the accounts between morality and trade, I shall leave the reader to draw the ballance. I shall not pronounce after so great a master, and upon so delicate a subject, but shall only ask, "Whether the people in trade are more corrupt than those out?"

If the curious reader will lend an attentive ear to a pair of farmers in the market, bartering for a cow, he will find as much dissimulation as at St. James's, or at any other saint's, but couched in homelier phrase. The man of well-bred deceit is '*infinitely* your friend--It would give him *immense* pleasure to serve you!' while the man in the frock 'Will be ---- if he tells you a word of a lye!' Deception is an innate principle of the human heart, not peculiar to one man, or one profession.

Having occasion for a horse, in 1759, I mentioned it to an acquaintance, and informed him of the uses: he assured me, he had one that would exactly suit; which he showed in the stable, and held the candle pretty high, *for fear of affecting the straw*. I told him it was needless to examine him, for I should rely upon his word, being conscious he was too much my friend to deceive me; therefore bargained, and caused him to be sent home. But by the light of the sun, which next morning illumined the heavens, I perceived the horse was *greased* on all fours. I therefore, in gentle terms, upbraided my friend with duplicity, when he replied with some warmth, "I would cheat my own brother in a horse." Had this honourable friend stood a chance of selling me a horse once a week, his own interest would have prevented him from deceiving me.

A man enters into business with a view of acquiring a fortune--A laudable motive! That property which rises from honest industry, is an honour to its owner; the repose of his age; the reward of a life of attention: but, great as the advantage seems, yet, being of a private nature, it is one of the least in the mercantile walk. For the intercourse occasioned by traffic, gives a man a view of the world, and of himself; removes the narrow limits that confine his judgment; expands the mind; opens his understanding; removes his prejudices; and polishes his manners. Civility and humanity are ever the companions of trade; the man of business is the man of liberal sentiment; a barbarous and commercial people, is a contradiction; if he is not the philosopher of nature, he is the friend of his country, and well understands her interest. Even the men of inferior life among us, whose occupations, one would think, tend to produce minds as callous as the mettle they work; lay a stronger claim to civilization, than in any other place with which I am acquainted. I am sorry to mutilate the compliment, when I mention the lower race of the other sex: no lady ought to be publicly insulted, let her appear in what dress she pleases. Both sexes, however, agree in exhibiting a mistaken pity, in cases of punishment, particularly by preventing that for misconduct in the military profession.

It is singular, that a predilection for Birmingham, is entertained by every denomination of visitants, from Edward Duke of York, who saw us in 1765, down to the presuming quack, who, griped with necessity, boldly discharges his filth from the stage. A paviour, of the name of Obrien, assured me in 1750, that he only meant to sleep one night in Birmingham, in his way from London to Dublin. But instead of pursuing his journey next morning, as intended, he had continued in the place thirty-five years: and though fortune had never elevated him above the pebbles of the street, yet he had never repented his stay.

It has already been remarked that I first saw Birmingham in 1741, accidentally cast into those regions of civility; equally unknown to every inhabitant, nor having the least idea of becoming one myself. Though the reflections of an untaught youth of seventeen cannot be striking, yet, as they were purely natural, permit me to describe them.

I had been before acquainted with two or three principal towns. The environs of all I had seen were composed of wretched dwellings, replete with dirt and poverty; but the buildings in the exterior of Birmingham rose in a style of elegance. Thatch, so plentiful in other towns, was not to be met with in this. I was surprised at the place, but more so at the people: They were a species I had never seen: They possessed a vivacity I had never beheld: I had been among dreamers, but now I saw men awake: Their very step along the street showed alacrity: Every man seemed to know and prosecute his own affairs: The town was large, and full of inhabitants, and those inhabitants full of industry. I had seen faces elsewhere tinctured with an idle gloom void of meaning, but here, with a pleasing alertness: Their appearance was strongly marked with the modes of civil life: I mixed a variety of company, chiefly of the lower ranks, and rather as a silent spectator: I was treated with an easy freedom by all, and with marks of favour by some: Hospitality seemed to claim this happy people for her own, though I knew not at that time from what cause.

I did not meet with this treatment in 1770, twenty nine years after, at Bosworth, where I accompanied a gentleman, with no other intent, than to view the field celebrated for the fall of Richard the third. The inhabitants enjoyed the cruel satisfaction of setting their dogs at us in the street, merely because we were strangers. Human figures, not their own, are seldom seen in those inhospitable regions: Surrounded with impassable roads, no intercourse with man to humanise the mind, no commerce to smooth their rugged manners, they continue the boors of nature.

Thus it appears, that characters are influenced by profession. That the great advantage of private fortune, and the greater to society, of softening and forming the mind, are the result of trade. But these are not the only benefits that flow from this desirable spring. It opens the hand of charity to the assistance of distress; witness the Hospital and the two Charity Schools, supported by annual donation: It adds to the national security, by supplying the taxes for internal use, and, for the prosecution of war. It adds to that security, by furnishing the inhabitants with riches, which they are ever anxious to preserve, even at the risk of their lives; for the preservation of private wealth, tends to the preservation of the state.

It augments the value of landed property, by multiplying the number of purchasers: It produces money to improve that land into a higher state of cultivation, which ultimately redounds to the general benefit, by affording plenty.

It unites bodies of men in social compact, for their mutual interest: It adds to the credit and pleasure of individuals, by enabling them to purchase entertainment and improvement, both of the corporeal and intellectual kind.

It finds employment for the hand that would otherwise be found in mischief: And it elevates the character of a nation in the scale of government.

Birmingham, by her commercial consequence, has, of late, justly assumed the liberty of nominating one of the representatives for the county; and, to her honor, the elective body never regretted her choice.

In that memorable contest of 1774, we were almost to a man of one mind: if an *odd dozen* among us, of a different *mould*, did not assimilate with the rest, they were treated, as men of free judgment should ever be treated, *with civility*, and the line of harmony was not broken.

If this little treatise happens to travel into some of our corporate places, where the fire of contention, blown by the breath of party, is kept alive during seven years, let them cast a second glance over the above remark.

Some of the first words after the creation, *increase and multiply*, are applicable to Birmingham; but as her own people are insufficient for the manufactures, she demands assistance for two or three miles round her. In our early morning walks, on every road proceeding from the town, we meet the sons of diligence returning to business, and bringing *in* the same dusky smuts, which the evening before they took out. And though they appear of a darkish complexion, we may consider it is the property of every metal to sully the user; money itself has the same effect, and yet he deems it no disgrace who is daubed by fingering it; the disgrace lies with him who has none to finger.

The profits arising from labour, to the lower orders of men, seem to surpass those of other mercantile places. This is not only visible in the manufactures peculiar to Birmingham, but in the more common occupations of the barber, taylor, shoemaker, etc. who bask in the rays of plenty.

It is entertaining to the curious observer, to contemplate the variation of things. We know of nothing, either in the natural or moral world, that continues in the same state: From a number of instances that might be adduced, permit me to name one-- that of money. This, considered in the abstract, is of little or no value; but, by the common consent of mankind, is erected into a general arbitrator, to fix a value upon all others: a medium through which every thing passes: a balance by which they must be weighed: a touchstone to which they must be applied to find their worth: though we can neither eat nor drink it, we can neither eat nor drink without it.--He that has none best knows its use.

It has long been a complaint, that the same quantity of that medium, money, will not produce so much of the necessaries of life, particularly food, as heretofore; or, in other words, that provisions have been gradually rising for many ages, and that the milling, which formerly supported the laborious family a whole week, will not now support it one day.

In times of remarkable scarcity, such as those in 1728, 41, 56, 66, and 74, the press abounded with publications on the subject; but none, which I have seen, reached the question, though short.

It is of no consequence, whether a bushel of corn sells for six *pence*, or six *shillings*, but, what *time* a man must labour before he can earn one?

If, by the moderate labour of thirty-six hours, in the reign of Henry the Third, he could acquire a groat, which would purchase a bushel of wheat; and if, in the reign of George the Third, he works the same number of hours for eight shillings, which will make the same purchase, the balance is exactly even. If, by our commercial concerns with the eastern and the western worlds, the kingdom abounds with bullion, money must be cheaper; therefore a larger quantity is required to perform the same use. If money would go as far now as in the days of Henry the Third, a journeyman in Birmingham might amass a ministerial fortune.

Whether provisions abound more or less? And whether the poor fare better or worse, in this period than in the other? are also questions dependant upon trade, and therefore worth investigating.

If the necessaries of life abound more in this reign, than in that of Henry the Third, we cannot pronounce them dearer.

Perhaps it will not be absurd to suppose, that the same quantity of land, directed by the superior hand of cultivation, in the eighteenth century, will yield twice the produce, as by the ignorant management of the thirteenth. We may suppose also, by the vast number of new inclosures which have annually taken place since the revolution, that twice the quantity of land is brought into cultivation: It follows, that four times the quantity of provisions is raised from the earth, than was raised under Henry the Third; which will leave a large surplus in hand, after we have deducted for additional luxury, a greater number of consumers, and also for exportation.

This extraordinary stock is also a security against famine, which our forefathers severely felt.

It will be granted, that in both periods the worst of the meat was used by the poor. By the improvements in agriculture, the art of feeding cattle is well understood, and much in practice; as the land improves, so will the beast that feeds upon it: if the productions, therefore, of the slaughter house, in this age, surpass those of Henry the Third, then the fare of the poor is at least as much superior now, as the worst of fat meat is superior to the worst of lean.

The poor inhabitants in that day, found it difficult to procure bread; but in this, they sometimes add cream and butter.

Thus it appears, that through the variation of things a balance is preserved: That provisions have not advanced in price, but are more plentiful: And that the lower class of men have found in trade, that intricate, but beneficial clue, which guides them into the confines of luxury.

Provisions and the manufactures, like a pair of scales, will not preponderate together; but as weight is applied to the one, the other will advance.

As labour is irksome to the body, a man will perform no more of it than necessity obliges him; it follows, that in those times when plenty preponderates, the manufactures tend to decay: For if a man can support his family with three days labour, he will not work six.

As the generality of men will perform no more work than produces a maintenance, reduce that maintenance to half the price, and they will perform but half the work: Hence half the commerce of a nation is destroyed at one blow, and what is lost by one kingdom will be recovered by another, in rivalship.

A commercial people, therefore, will endeavour to keep provisions at a superior rate, yet within reach of the poor.

It follows also, that luxury is no way detrimental to trade; for we frequently observe ability and industry exerted to support it.

The practice of the Birmingham manufacturer, for, perhaps, a hundred generations, was to keep within the warmth of his own forge.

The foreign customer, therefore, applied to him for the execution of orders, and regularly made his appearance twice a year; and though this mode of business is not totally extinguished, yet a very different one is adopted.

The merchant stands at the head of the manufacturer, purchases his produce, and travels the whole island to promote the sale: A practice that would have astonished our fore fathers. The commercial spirit of the age, hath also penetrated beyond the confines of Britain, and explored the whole continent of Europe; nor does it stop there, for the West-Indies, and the American world, are intimately acquainted with the Birmingham merchant; and nothing but the exclusive command of the East-India Company, over the Asiatic trade, prevents our riders from treading upon the heels of each other, in the streets of Calcutta.

To this modern conduct of Birmingham, in sending her sons to the foreign market, I ascribe the chief cause of her rapid increase.

By the poor's books it appears, there are not three thousand houses in Birmingham, that pay the parochial rates; whilst there are more then five thousand that do not, chiefly through inability. Hence we see what an amazing number of the laborious class of mankind is among us. This valuable part of the creation, is the prop of the remainder. They are the rise and support of our commerce. From this fountain we draw our luxuries and our pleasures. They spread our tables, and oil the wheels of our carriages. They are also the riches and the defence of the country.

How necessary then, is it to direct with prudence, the rough passions of this important race, and make them subservient to the great end of civil society. The deficiency of conduct in this useful part of our species ought to be supplied by the superior.

Let not the religious reader be surprised if I say, their follies, and even their vices, under certain restrictions, are beneficial. Corruption in the community, as well as in the natural body, accelerates vital existence.

Let us survey one of the men, who begin life at the lowest ebb; without property, or any other advantage but that of his own prudence.

He comes, by length of time and very minute degrees, from being directed himself, to have the direction of others. He quits the precincts of servitude, and enters the dominions of command: He laboured for others, but now others labour for him. Should the whole race, therefore, possess the same prudence, they would all become masters. Where then could be found the servant? Who is to perform the manual part? Who to execute the orders of the merchant? A world consisting only of masters, is like a monster consisting only of a head. We know that the head is no more than the leading power, the members are equally necessary. And, as one member is placed in a more elevated state than another, so are the ranks of men, that no void may be left. The hands and the feet, were designed to execute the drudgery of life; the head for direction, and all are suitable in their sphere.

If we turn the other side of the picture, we shall see a man born in affluence, take the reins of direction; but like Phæton, not being able to guide them, blunders on from mischief to mischief, till he involves himself in destruction, comes prone to the earth, and many are injured by his fall. From directing the bridle, he submits to the bit; seeks for bread in the shops, the line designed him by nature; where his hands become callous with the file, and where, for the first time in his life, he becomes useful to an injured society.

Thus, from imprudence, folly, and vice, is produced poverty;--poverty produces labour; from labour, arise the manufactures; and from these, the riches of a country, with all their train of benefits.

It would be difficult to enumerate the great variety of trades practised in Birmingham, neither would it give pleasure to the reader. Some of them, spring up with the expedition of a blade of grass, and, like that, wither in a summer. If some are lasting, like the sun, others seem to change with the moon. Invention is ever at work. Idleness; the manufactory of scandal, with the numerous occupations connected with the cotton; the linen, the silk, and the woollen trades, are little known among us.

Birmingham begun with the productions of the anvil, and probably will end with them. The sons of the hammer, were once her chief inhabitants; but that great croud of artists is now lost in a greater: Genius seems to increase with multitude.

Part of the riches, extension, and improvement of Birmingham, are owing to the late John Taylor, Esq; who possessed the singular powers of perceiving things as they really were. The spring, and consequence of action, were open to his view; whom we may justly deem the Shakespear or the Newton of his day. He rose from minute beginnings, to shine in the commercial hemisphere, as they in the poetical and philosophical--Imitation is part of the human character. An example of such eminence in himself, promoted exertion in others; which, when prudence guided the helm, led on to fortune: But the bold adventurer who crouded sail, without ballast and without rudder, has been known to overset the vessel, and sink insolvent.

To this uncommon genius we owe the gilt-button, the japanned and gilt snuff-boxes, with the numerous race of enamels-- From the same fountain also issued the paper snuff-box, at which one servant earned three pounds ten shillings per week, by painting them at a farthing each.

In his shop were weekly manufactured buttons to the amount of 800*l* exclusive of other valuable productions.

One of the present nobility, of distinguished taste, examining the works, with the master, purchased some of the articles, amongst others, a toy of eighty guineas value, and, while paying for them, observed with a smile, "he plainly saw he could not reside in Birmingham for less than two hundred pounds a day."

The toy trades first made their appearance in Birmingham, in the beginning of Charles the second, in an amazing variety, attended with all their beauties and their graces. The first in pre-eminence is

The BUTTON.

This beautiful ornament appears with infinite variation; and though the original date is rather uncertain, yet we well remember the long coats of our grandfathers covered with half a gross of high-tops, and the cloaks of our grandmothers, ornamented with a horn button nearly the size of a crown piece, a watch, or a John apple, curiously wrought, as having passed through the Birmingham press.

Though the common round button keeps on with the steady pace of the day, yet we sometimes see the oval, the square, the pea, and the pyramid, flash into existence. In some branches of traffic the wearer calls loudly for new fashions, but in this, the fashions tread upon each other, and crowd upon the wearer. The consumption of this article is astonishing. There seem to be hidden treasures couched within this magic circle, known only to a few, who extract prodigious fortunes out of this useful toy, whilst a far greater number, submit to a statute of bankruptcy.

Trade, like a restive horse, can rarely be managed; for, where one is carried to the end of a successful journey, many are thrown off by the way. The next that calls our attention is

The BUCKLE.

Perhaps the shoe, in one form or other, is nearly as ancient as the foot. It originally appeared under the name of, sandal; this was no other than a sole without an upper-leather. That fashion hath since been inverted, and we now, sometimes, see an upper-leather nearly without a sole. But, whatever was the cut of the shoe, it always demanded a fastening. Under the house of Plantagenet, it shot horizontally from the foot, like a Dutch scait, to an enormous length, so that the extremity was fattened to the knee, sometimes, with a silver chain, a silk lace, or even a pack-thread string, rather than avoid *genteel taste*.

This thriving beak, drew the attention of the legislature, who were determined to prune the exorbitant shoot. For in 1465 we find an order of council, prohibiting the growth of the shoe toe, to more than two inches, under the penalty of a dreadful curse from the priest, and, which was worse, the payment of twenty shillings to the king.

This fashion, like every other, gave way to time, and in its stead, the rose began to bud upon the foot. Which under the house of Tudor, opened in great perfection. No shoe was fashionable, without being fattened with a full-blown rose. Under the house of Stuart, the rose withered, which gave rise to the shoe-string.

The beaus of that age, ornamented their lower tier with double laces of silk, tagged with silver, and the extremities beautified with a small fringe of the same metal. The inferior class, wore laces of plain silk, linen, or even a thong of leather; which last is yet to be met with in the humble plains of rural life. But I am inclined to think, the artists of Birmingham had no great hand in fitting out the beau of the last century.

The revolution was remarkable, for the introduction of William, of liberty, and the minute buckle; not differing much in size and shape from the horse bean.

This offspring of fancy, like the clouds, is ever changing. The fashion of to-day, is thrown into the casting pot to-morrow.

The buckle seems to have undergone every figure, size and shape of geometrical invention: It has passed through every form in the whole zodiac of Euclid. The large square buckle is the *ton* of the present day. The ladies also, have adopted the reigning taste: It is difficult to discover their beautiful little feet, covered with an enormous shield of buckle; and we wonder to see the active motion under the massive load. Thus the British fair support the manufactures of Birmingham, and thus they kill by weight of metal.

GUNS.

Though the sword and the gun are equal companions in war, it does not appear they are of equal original. I have already observed, that the sword was the manufacture of Birmingham, in the time of the Britons.

But tradition tells us, King William was once lamenting "That guns were not manufactured in his dominions, but that he was obliged to procure them from Holland at a great expence, and greater difficulty."

One of the Members for Warwickshire being present, told the King, "He thought his constituents could answer his Majesty's wishes."--The King was pleased with the remark, and the Member posted to Birmingham. Upon application to a person in Digbeth, whose name I forget, the pattern was executed with precision, which, when presented to the royal board, gave entire satisfaction. Orders were immediately issued for large numbers, which have been so frequently repeated that they never lost their road; and the ingenious artists have been so amply rewarded, that they have rolled in their carriages to this day.--Thus the same instrument which is death to one man, is genteel life to another.

LEATHER.

It may seem singular to a modern eye, to view this place in the light of one vast tan-yard.--Though there is no appearance of that necessary article among us, yet Birmingham was once a famous market for leather. Digbeth not only abounded with tanners, but large numbers of hides arrived weekly for sale, where the whole country found a supply. When the weather would allow, they were ranged in columns in the High-street, and at other times deposited in the Leather-hall, at the East end of New-street, appropriated for their reception.

This market was of great antiquity, perhaps not less than seven hundred years, and continued till the beginning of the present century. We have two officers, annually chosen, by the name of *leather-sealers*, from a power given them by ancient charter, to mark the vendible hides; but now the leather-sealers have no duty, but that of taking an elegant dinner. Shops are erected upon tan-fats; the Leather-hall is gone to destruction, and we are reduced to one solitary tanner.

STEEL.

The progress of the arts, is equal to the progress of time; they began, and will end together. Though some of both are lost, yet they both accumulate.

The manufacture of iron, in Birmingham, is ancient beyond research; that of steel is of modern date.

Pride is inseparable from the human character, the man without it, is the man without breath: we trace it in various forms, through every degree of people; but like those objects about us, it is best discovered in our own sphere; those above, and those below us, rather escape our notice; envy attacks an equal.

Pride induced the Pope to look with contempt on the European Princes, and now induces them to return the compliment; it taught insolence to the Spaniard, selfishness to the Dutch; it teaches the rival nations of France and England to contend for power.

Pride preserves a man from mean actions, it throws him upon meaner; it whets the sword for destruction; it urges the laudable acts of humanity; it is the universal hinge on which we move; it glides the gentle stream of usefulness, it overflows the mounds of reason, and swells into a destructive flood; like the sun, in his milder rays, it animates and draws us towards perfection; but, like him, in his fiercer beams, it scorches and destroys.

Money is not the necessary attendant of pride, for it abounds no where more than in the lowest ranks. It adds a sprucer air to a sunday dress; casts a look of disdain from a bundle of rags; it boasts the *honor* of a family, while poverty unites a sole and upper-leather with a bandage of shop-thread. There are people who even *pride* themselves in humility.

This dangerous *good*, this necessary *evil*, supports the female character; without it, the brightest part of the creation would degenerate.

It will be asked, "What portion may be allowed?" Prudence will answer, "As much as you please, but *not* to disgust."

It is equally found in the senate-house, or the button-shop; the scene of action is the scene of pride; and I, unable to adorn this work with erudition, take a pride in cloathing a worn-out subject afresh, and that pride will increase, should the world smi ---- "But why, says my friend, do you forsake the title of your chapter, and lead us a dance through the mazes of pride? Can there be any connexion between that sovereign passion, and forging a bar of steel?" Yes, he who makes steel prides himself in carrying the art one step higher than he who makes iron.

This art appeared among us in the seventeenth century; was introduced by the family of Kettle. The name of Steelhouse-lane will convey to posterity the situation of the works, the commercial spirit of Birmingham, will convey the produce to the Antipodes.

From this warm, but dismal climate, issues the button, which shines on the breast, and the bayonet, intended to pierce it; the lancet, which bleeds the man, and the rowel, the horse; the lock, which preserves the beloved bottle, and the screw, to uncork it; the needle, equally obedient to the thimble and the pole.

NAILS.

In most occupations, the profit of the master and the journeyman bear a proportion: if the former is able to figure in genteel life, the latter is able to figure in silk stockings. If the matter can afford to allow upon his goods ten per cent. discount for money, the servant can afford to squander half his wages. In a worn-down trade, where the tides of profit are reduced to a low ebb, and where imprudence sets her foot upon the premises, the matter and the man starve together. Only *half* this is our present case.

The art of nail-making is one of the most ancient among us; we may safely charge its antiquity with four figures.

We cannot consider it a trade *in*, so much as *of* Birmingham; for we have but few nail-makers left in the town: our nailers are chiefly masters, and rather opulent. The manufacturers are so scattered round the country, that we cannot travel far, in any direction, out of the sound of the nail-hammer. But Birmingham, like a powerful magnet, draws the produce of the anvil to herself.

When I first approached her, from Walsall, in 1741, I was surprized at the prodigious number of blacksmiths shops upon the road; and could not conceive how a country, though populous, could support so many people of the same occupation. In some of these shops I observed one, or more females, stript of their upper garment, and not overcharged with their lower, wielding the hammer with all the grace of the sex. The beauties of their face were rather eclipsed by the smut of the anvil; or, in poetical phrase, the tincture of the forge had taken possession of those lips, which might have been taken by the kiss.

Struck with the novelty, I inquired, "Whether the ladies in this country shod horses?" but was answered, with a smile, "They are nailers."

A fire without heat, a nailer of a fair complexion, or one who despises the tankard, are equally rare among them. His whole system of faith may be comprised in one article--That the slender two-penny mug, used in a public house, *is deceitful above all things, and desperately wicked*.

While the master reaps the harvest of plenty, the workman submits to the scanty gleanings of penury, a thin habit, an early old age, and a figure bending towards the earth. Plenty comes not near his dwelling, except of rags, and of children. But few recruits arise from his nail-shop, except for the army. His hammer is worn into deep hollows, fitting the fingers of a dark and plump hand, hard as the timber it wears. His face, like the moon, is often seen through a cloud.

BELLOWS.

Man first catches the profession; the profession afterwards moulds the man.

In whatever profession we engage, we assume its character, become a part of it, vindicate its honor, its eminence, its antiquity; or feel a wound through its sides.

Though there may be no more pride in a minister of state, who opens a budget, than in a tinker who carries one, yet they equally contend for the honor of their trade.

Every man, from the attorney's clerk to the butcher's apprentice, feels his own honor, with that of his profession, wounded by travelling on foot. To be caught on his feet, is nearly the same as to be caught in a crime. The man who has gathered up his limbs, and hung them on a horse, looks *down* with dignity on him who has not; while the man on foot offers his humble bow, afraid to look up--If providence favours us with feet, is it a disgrace to use them?--I could instance a person who condescended to quit London, that center of trick, lace, and equipage; and in 1761, open a draper's shop in Birmingham: but his feet, or his *pride*, were so much hurt by walking, that he could scarcely travel ten doors from his own without a post-chaise--the result was, he became such an adept in riding, that in a few months, he rode triumphant into the Gazette. Being quickly scoured bright by the ill-judged laws of bankruptcy, he rode, for the last time, *out* of Birmingham, where he had so often rode *in*: but his injured creditors were obliged to *walk* after the slender dividend of eighteen pence in the pound. The man who *can* use his feet, is envied by him who *cannot*; and he, in turn, envies him who *will* not. Our health and our feet, in a double sense, go together. The human body has been justly compared to a musical instrument; I add, this instrument was never perfectly in tune, without a due portion of exercise.

The man of military character, puts on, with his scarlet, that martial air, which tells us, "he has formed a resolution to kill:" and we naturally ask, "Which sex?"

Some "*pert and affected author*" with anxiety on his brow, will be apt to step forward, and say, "Will you celebrate the man of the sword, who transfers the blush of his face to his back, and neglect the man of the quill, who, like the pelican, portions out his vitals to feed others? Which is preferable, he who lights up the mental powers, or he who puts them out? the man who stores the head with knowledge, or he who stores it with a bullet?"

The antiquarian supports his dignity with a solemn aspect; he treats a sin and a smile as synonymous; one half of which has been discarded from his childhood. If a smile in the house of religion, or of mourning, be absurd, is there any reason to expel it from those places where it is not? A tale will generally allow of two ingredients, *information* and *amusement*: but the historian and the antiquarian have, from time immemorial, used but *one*. Every smile, except that of contempt, is beneficial to the constitution; they tend to promote long life, and pleasure while that life lasts. Much may be said in favour of tears of joy, but more on joy without tears. I wonder the lively fancy of Hogarth never sketched the *dull* historian, in the figure of an ass, plodding to market under his panniers, laden with the fruits of antiquity, and old time driving up the *rear*, with his scythe converted into an hedge-stake.

The bellows-maker proclaims the *honor* of his art, by observing, he alone produces that instrument which commands the winds; his soft breeze, like that of the south, counter-acts the chill blasts of winter: by his efforts, like those of the sun, the world receives light: he creates when he pleases, and gives *breath* when he creates. In his caverns the winds deep at pleasure; and by his *orders* they set Europe in flames.

He pretends, that a gentle puff in the eyes of a *reviewer*, from a pair of his bellows, would tend to clear the sight, and enable him to distinguish between a smile and a serious face: that his circular board, like a ferula, applied by the handle to an inferior part, would induce him to peruse the *whole treatise*, and not partially pronounce from the preface.

He farther pretends, that the *antiquity* of his occupation will appear from the plenty of elm, once in the neighbourhood, but long cut up for his use: that the leather-market in Birmingham, for many ages, furnished him with sides; and though the manufacture of iron is allowed to be extremely ancient, yet the smith could not procure his heat without a blast, nor could that blast be raised without the bellows.

Two inferences arise from these remarks, that the antiquarian will frown on this little history; and that bellows-making is one of the oldest trades in Birmingham.

THREAD.

We, who reside in the interior parts of the kingdom, may observe the first traces of a river issue from its fountain; the current so extremely small, that if a bottle of liquor, distilled through the urinary vessels, was discharged into its course, it would manifestly augment the water, and quicken the stream: the reviving bottle, having added spirits to the man, seems to add spirits to the river.--If we pursue this river, winding through one hundred and thirty miles, we shall observe it collect strength as it runs, expand its borders, swell into consequence, employ multitudes of people, carry wealth in its bosom, and exactly resemble *thread-making* in Birmingham.

If we represent to our idea, a man able to employ three or four people, himself in an apron, one of the number; but being *unable* to write his name, shows his attachment to the christian religion, by signing the *cross* to receipts; whose method of book-keeping, like that of the publican, is *a door and a lump of chalk;* producing a book which none can peruse but himself: who, having manufactured 40lb. weight of thread, of divers colours, and rammed it into a pair of leather bags, something larger than a pair of boots, which we might deem the arms of his trade *empaled*; flung them on a horse, and placed himself on the top, by way of a *crest*; visits an adjacent market, to starve with his goods at a stall, or retail them to the mercer, nor return without the money--we shall see a thread-maker of 1652.

If we pursue this occupation, winding through the mazes of one hundred and thirty *years*, we shall see it enlarge its boundaries, multiply its people, increase its consequence and wealth, till 1782, when we behold the matter in possession of correct accounts, the apron thrown aside, the stall kicked over, the bags tossed into the garret, and the mercer overlooked in the grand prospect of exportation. We farther behold him take the lead in provincial concerns, step into his own carriage, and hold the king's commission as a magistrate.

PRINTING,

By JOHN BASKERVILLE.

The pen of an historian rejoices in the actions of the great; the fame of the deserving, like an oak tree, is of sluggish growth; and, like the man himself, they are not matured in a day. The present generation becomes debtor to him who excels, but the future will discharge that debt with more than simple interest. The still voice of fame may warble in his ears towards the close of life, but her trumpet seldom sounds in full clarion, till those ears are stopped with the finger of death.

This son of genius was born at Wolverley, in the county of Worcester, in 1706; heir to a paternal estate of 60*l*. per annum, which, fifty years after, while in his own possession, had increased to 90*l*. He was trained to no occupation; but, in 1726, became a writing-matter in Birmingham.--In 1737, he taught school in the Bull-ring, and is said to have written an excellent hand.

As painting suited his talents, he entered into the lucrative branch of japanning, and resided at No. 22, in Moor-street.

He took, in 1745, a building lease of eight acres, two furlongs north west of the town, to which he gave the name of *Easy-hill*, converted it into a little Eden, and built a house in the center: but the town, as if conscious of his merit, followed his retreat, and surrounded it with buildings.--Here he continued the business of a japanner for life: his carriage, each pannel of which was a distinct picture, might be considered *the pattern-card of his trade*, and was drawn by a beautiful pair of cream-coloured horses.

His inclination for letters induced him, in 1750, to turn his thoughts towards the press. He spent many years in the uncertain pursuit; sunk 600*l*. before he could produce one letter to please himself, and some thousands before the shallow stream of profit began to flow.

His first attempt, in 1756, was a quarto edition of Virgil, price one guinea, now worth several.--He afterwards printed Paradise Lost, the Bible, Common Prayer, Roman and English Classics, etc. in various sizes, with more satisfaction to the literary world than emolument to himself.

In 1765, he applied to his friend, Dr. Franklin, then at Paris, and now Ambassador from America, to sound the literati, respecting the purchase of his types; but received for answer, "That the French, reduced by the war of 1756, were so far from pursuing schemes of taste, that they were unable to repair their public buildings, but suffered the scaffolding to rot before them."

In private life he was a humorist; idle in the extreme; but his invention was of the true Birmingham model, active. He could well design, but procured others to execute; wherever he found merit he caressed it: he was remarkably polite to the stranger; fond of show: a figure rather of the smaller size, and delighted to adorn that figure with gold lace.--Although constructed with the light timbers of a frigate, his movement was solemn as a ship of the line.

During the twenty-five years I knew him, though in the decline of life, he retained the singular traces of a handsome man. If he exhibited a peevish temper, we may consider good-nature and intense thinking are not always found together.

Taste accompanied him through the different walks of agriculture, architecture, and the finer arts. Whatever passed through his fingers, bore the lively marks of John Baskerville.

His aversion to christianity would not suffer him to lie among christians; he therefore erected a mausoleum in his own grounds for his remains, and died without issue, in 1775, at the age of 69.--Many efforts were used after his death, to dispose of the types; but, to the lading discredit of the British nation, no purchaser could be found in the whole commonwealth of letters. The universities coldly rejected the offer. The London booksellers understood no science like that of profit. The valuable property, therefore, lay a dead weight, till purchased by a literary society at Paris, in 1779, for 3700*l*.

It is an old remark, that no country abounds with genius so much as this island; and it is a remark nearly as old, that genius is no where so little rewarded; how else came Dryden, Goldsmith, and Chatterton to want bread? Is merit, like a flower of the field, too common to attract notice? or is the use of money beneath the care of exalted talents?

Invention seldom pays the inventor. If you ask, what fortune Baskerville ought to have been rewarded with? "The *most* which can be comprised in five figures." If you farther ask, what he possessed? "The *least*;" but none of it squeezed from the press. What will the shade of this great man think, if capable of thinking, that he has spent a fortune of opulence, and a life of genius, in carrying to perfection the greatest of all human inventions; and his productions, slighted by his country, were hawked over Europe, in quest of a bidder?

We must *revere*, if we do not *imitate*, the taste and economy of the French nation, who, brought by the British arms, in 1762, to the verge of ruin, rising above distress, were able, in 17 years, to purchase Baskerville's elegant types, refused by his own country, and expend an hundred thousand pounds in printing the works of Voltaire!

BRASS FOUNDRY.

The curious art before us is perhaps less ancient than profitable, and less healthful than either. I shall not enquire whose grandfather was the first brass-founder here, but shall leave their grandsons to settle that important point with my successor who shall next write the History of Birmingham. Whoever was the first, I believe he figured in the reign of King William; but, though he sold his productions at an excessive price, he did not, like the moderns, possess the art of acquiring a fortune: but now the master knows the way to affluence, and the servant to liquor.

To enumerate the great variety of occupations amongst us, would be as useless, and as unentertaining to the reader, perhaps to the writer, as to count the pebbles in the street.

Having therefore visited a few, by way of specimen, I shall desist from farther pursuit, and wheel off in a

---

HACKNEY COACH.

Wherever the view of profit opens, the eyes of a Birmingham man are open to see it.

In 1775, a person was determined to try if a Hackney Coach would take with the inhabitants. He had not mounted the box many times before he inadvertently dropped the expression, "Thirty shillings a day!" The word was attended with all the powers of magic, for instantly a second rolled into the circus.

And these elevated sons of the lash are now augmented to fifteen, whom we may justly denominate a club of tippling deities, who preside over weddings, christenings, and pleasurable excursions.

It would give satisfaction to the curious calculator, could any mode be found of discovering the returns of trade, made by the united inhabitants. But the question is complicated. It only admits of surmise. From comparing many instances in various ranks of life among us, I have been led to suppose, that the weekly returns exceed the annual rent of the buildings. And as these rents are nearly ascertained, perhaps, we may conclude, that those returns are about 80,000. If we deduct for four weeks holidays, the annual returns will be--3,840,000*l*.

Now we have entered the visionary regions of fancy, let us pursue the thought a stage farther; and consider Birmingham as one great family, possessed of a capital of Eight Millions. Her annual returns in trade as above, from which we will deduct for the purchase of

Raw materials	1,920,000
House rent, repairs and taxes	100,000
Losses in trade	50,000
Maintenance, clothing, and pleasurable expences, for 50,000 people, at 10*s*. per week	1,300,000
	3,370,000

Annual addition to the capital	470,000

Should a future antagonist arise, and attack me in numbers, I promise beforehand to relinquish the field; for I profess only, to stand upon ideal ground.

BANK.

Perhaps a public bank is as necessary to the health of the commercial body, as exercise to the natural. The circulation of the blood and spirits are promoted by one, so are cash and bills by the other; and a stagnation is equally detrimental to both. Few places are without: Yet Birmingham, famous in the annals of traffic, could boast no such claim. To remedy this defect therefore, about every tenth trader was a banker, or, a retailer of cash. At the head of whom were marshalled the whole train of drapers and grocers, till the year 1765, when a regular bank was established by Messrs. Taylor and Lloyd, two opulent tradesmen, whose credit being equal to that of the bank of England, quickly collected the shining rays of sterling property into its focus.

GOVERNMENT.

Have you, my dear reader, seen a sword hilt, of curious, and of Birmingham manufactory, covered with spangles of various sizes, every one of which carries a separate lustre, but, when united, has a dazzling effect? Or, have you seen a ring, from the same origin, set with diamonds of many dimensions, the least of which, sparkles with amazing beauty, but, when beheld in cluster, surprize the beholder? Or, have you, in a frosty evening, seen the heavens bespangled with refulgent splendor, each stud shining with intrinsic excellence, but, viewed in the aggregate, reflect honour upon the maker, and enliven the hemisphere? Such is the British government. Such is that excellent system of polity, which shines, the envy of the stranger, and the protector of the native.

Every city, town and village in the English hemisphere, hath a separate jurisdiction of its own, and may justly be deemed *a stud in the grand lustre.*

Though the British Constitution is as far from perfection, as the glory of the ring and the hilt is from that of the sun which causes it, or the stars from the day; yet perhaps it stands higher in the scale of excellence, than that of its neighbours. We may, with propriety, allow that body to shine with splendor, which hath been polishing for seventeen hundred years. Much honour is due to the patriotic merit which advanced it to its present eminence.

Though Birmingham is but one sparkle of the brilliant clustre, yet she is a sparkle of the first *water*, and of the first *magnitude.*

The more perfect any system of government, the happier the people. A wise government will punish for the commission of crimes, but a wiser will endeavour to prevent them. Man is an active animal: If he is not employed in some useful pursuit, he will employ himself in mischief. Example is also prevalent: If one man falls into error, he often draws another. Though heaven, for wise purposes, suffers a people to fulfil the measure of their iniquities, a prudent state will nip them in the bud.

It is easy to point out some places, only one third the magnitude of Birmingham, whose frequent breaches of the law, and quarrels among themselves, find employment for half a dozen magistrates, and four times that number of constables; whilst the business of this, was for many years conducted by a single Justice, the late John Wyrley, Esq. If the reader should think I am mistaken and object, that parish affairs cannot be conducted without a second? Let me reply, He conducted that second also.

An History of Birmingham (1783)

As human nature is nearly the same, whether in or out of Birmingham; and as enormities seem more prevalent out than in, we may reasonably ascribe the cause to the extraordinary industry of the inhabitants, not allowing time to brood over, and bring forth mischief, equal to places of inferior diligence.

We have at present two acting magistrates to hold the beam of justice, the Rev. Benjamin Spencer, and Joseph Carles, Esq; who both reside at a distance.

Many of our corporate towns received their charters from that amiable, but unfortunate prince, Henry the Second. These were the first dawnings of British liberty, after fixing the Norman yoke. They were afterwards ratified and improved by the subsequent Kings of England; granting not only the manors, but many exclusive privileges. But at this day, those places which were so remarkably favoured with the smiles of royalty, are not quite so free as those that were not. The prosperity of this happy place proves the assertion, of which every man is free the moment he enters.

We often behold a pompous corporation, which sounds well in history, over something like a dirty village--This is a head without a body. The very reverse is our case--We are a body without a head. For though Birmingham has undergone an amazing alteration in extension, riches and population, yet the government is nearly the same as the Saxons left it. This part of my important history therefore must suffer an eclipse: This illustrious chapter, that rose in dazling brightness, must be veiled in the thick clouds of obscurity: I shall figure with my corporation in a despicable light. I am not able to bring upon the stage, a mayor and a group of aldermen, dressed in antique scarlet, bordered with fur, drawing a train of attendants; the meanest of which, even the pinder, is badged with silver: Nor treat my guest with a band of music, in scarlet cloaks with broad laces. I can grace the hand of my Birmingham fidler with only a rusty instrument, and his back with barely a whole coat; neither have I a mace for the inaugeration of the chief magistrate. The reader, therefore, must either quit the place, or be satisfied with such entertainment as the company affords.

The officers, who are annually chosen, to direct in this prosperous feat of fortune, are

An High Bailiff.	Two High Tasters.
Low Bailiff.	Two Low Tasters.
Two Constables.	Two Asseirers. And
Headborough.	Two Leather Sealers.

All which, the constables excepted, are no more than servants to the lord of the manor; and whose duty extends no farther, than to the preservation of the manorial rights.

The high bailiff is to inspect the market, and see that justice takes place between buyer and seller; to rectify the weights and dry measures used in the manor.

The low bailiff summons a jury, who choose all the other officers, and generally with prudence. But the most important part of his office is, to treat his friends at the expence of about Seventy Pounds.

The headborough is only an assistant to the constables, chiefly in time of absence.

High tasters examine the goodness of beer, and its measure.

Low tasters inspect the meat exposed to sale, and cause that to be destroyed which is unfit for use.

Asseirers ratify the chief rent and amercements, between the lord and the inhabitant. And the

Leather sealers, stamped a public seal upon the hides, when Birmingham was a market for leather.

These manorial servants, instituted by ancient charter, chiefly possess a name, without an office. Thus order seems assisted by industry, and thus a numerous body of inhabitants are governed without a governor.

Exclusive of the choice of officers, the jury impannelled by the low bailiff, have the presentation of all encroachments upon the lord's waste, which has long been neglected.

The duties of office are little known, except that of taking a generous dinner, which is punctually observed. It is too early to begin business till the table is well stored with bottles, and too late afterwards.

During the existence of the house of Birmingham, the court-leet was held at the Moat, in what we should now think a large and shabby room, conducted under the eye of the low bailiff, at the expence of the lord.

The jury, twice a year, were witnesses, that the famous dish of roast beef, ancient as the family who gave it, demanded the head of the table. The court was afterwards held at the Leather-hall, and the expence, which was trifling, borne by the bailiff. Time, prosperity, and emulation, are able to effect considerable changes. The jury, in the beginning of the present century, were impannelled in the Old Cross, then newly erected, from whence they adjourned to the house of the bailiff, and were feasted at the growing charge of *two or three pounds*.

This practice continued till about the year 1735, when the company, grown too bulky for a private house, assembled at a tavern, and the bailiff enjoyed the singular privilege of consuming ten pounds upon his guests.

It is easier to advance in expences than to retreat. In 1760, they had increased to forty pounds, and in the next edition of this work, we may expect to see the word *hundred*.

The lord was anciently founder of the feast, and treated his bailiff; but now that custom is inverted, and the bailiff treats his lord.

The proclamation of our two fairs, is performed by the high bailiff, in the name of the Lord of the Manor; this was done a century ago, without the least expence. The strength of his liquor, a silver tankard, and the pride of shewing it, perhaps induced him, in process of time, to treat his attendants.

His ale, without a miracle, was, in a few years, converted into wine, and that of various sorts; to which was added, a small collation; and now his friends are complimented with a card, to meet him at the Hotel, where he incurs an expence of twenty pounds.

While the spirit of the people refines by intercourse, industry, and the singular jurisdiction among us, this insignificant pimple, on our head of government, swells into a wen.

Habits approved are soon acquired: a third entertainment has, of late years, sprung up, termed *the constables feast*, with this difference, *it is charged to the public*. We may consider it a wart on the political body, which merits the caustic.

Deritend, being a hamlet of Birmingham, sends her inhabitants to the court-leet, where they perform suit and service, and where her constable is chosen by the same jury.

I shall here exhibit a defective list of our principal officers during the last century. If it should be objected, that a petty constable is too insignificant, being the lowest officer of the crown, for admission into history; I answer, by whatever appellation an officer is accepted, he cannot be insignificant who stands at the head of 50,000 people. Perhaps, therefore, the office of constable may be sought for in future, and the officer himself assume a superior consequence.

The dates are the years in which they were chosen, fixed by charter, within thirty days after Michaelmas.

CONSTABLES.

1680	John Simco	John Cottrill
1681	John Wallaxall	William Guest
1682	George Abel	Samuel White
1683	Thomas Russell	Abraham Spooner
1684	Roger Macham	William Wheely
1685	Thomas Cox	John Green
1686	Henry Porter	Samuel Carless
1687	Samuel Banner	John Jesson
1690	Joseph Robinson	John Birch
1691	John Rogers	Richard Leather
1692	Thomas Robins	Corbet Bushell
1693	Joseph Rann	William Sarjeant
1694	Rowland Hall	John Bryerly
1695	Richard Scott	George Wells
1696	Joseph Haddock	Robert Mansell
1697	James Greir	John Foster

1698	John Baker	Henry Camden
1699	William Kettle	Thomas Gisborn
1700	John Wilson	Joseph Allen
1701	Nicholas Bakewell	Richard Banner
1702	William Collins	Robert Groves
1703	Henry Parrot	Benjamin Carless
1704	William Brierly	John Hunt
1705	Jonathan Seeley	Thomas Holloway
1706	Robert Moore	John Savage
1707	Isaac Spooner	Samuel Hervey
1708	Richard Weston	Thomas Cope
1709	Samuel Walford	Thomas Green
1710	John Foxall	William Norton
1711	Stephen Newton	John Taylor
1712	William Russel	John Cotterell
1713	John Shaw	Thomas Hallford
1714	Randall Bradburn	Joseph May
1715	Stephen Newton	Samuel Russell
1716	Stephen Newton	Joseph Carless
1717	Abraham Foxall	William Spilsbury
1718	John Gisborn	Henry Carver
1719	Samuel Hays	Joseph Smith
1720	John Barnsley	John Humphrys
1721	William Bennett	Thomas Wilson
1722	John Harrison	Simon Harris

A LIST OF THE HIGH BAILIFFS, LOW BAILIFFS, AND CONSTABLES, Of the TOWN of BIRMINGHAM, from 1732, to 1782.

YEAR	HIGH BAILIFFS.	LOW BAILIFFS.	CONSTABLES.	
1732	Thomas Wilson	John Webster	Joseph Bradnock	John Wilson
1733	John Webster	Joseph Kettle	Thomas Nickin	James Baker
1734	John Wickins	Thomas Lakin	Joseph Scott, esq;[2]	James Taylor

1735	Joseph Marston	John Russell	John Webster	Thomas Ashfield
1736	Joseph Bradnock	Robert Moore	Thomas Wickins	Joseph Fullelove
1737	James Baker	Isaac Ingram	John Kettle	Richard Porter
1738	Joseph Smith	William Mason	William Hunt	Henry Hun
1739	Thomas Wickens	William Harvey	Edward Burton	John England
1740	Simon Harris	Thomas Russel	Joseph Richards	T. Honeyborn
1741	Daniel Gill	George Abney	Thomas Turner	John Bedford
1742				
1743	Josiah Jefferys	William Kettle	John Russel	Thomas
1744	George Davies	J. Humphrys, Jr.	William Mason	William Ward
1745	Edward Burton	Robert Moore	Joseph Wollaston	John Turner
1746				
1747	Thomas Ashwell	J. Taylor, esq;	Joseph Walker	Josiah Hunt
1748	Thomas Wickens	John Roe	Robert Moore	John Horton
1749	Joseph Fullelove	Richard Brett	Henry Hunt	Joseph Ruston
1750	Thomas Lakin	Joseph Smith	John Gill	Luke Bell
1751	Thomas Turner	Benj. Mansell	John Walters	W. Walsingham
1752	James Baker	John Taylor	Price Thomas	Joseph Thomas
1753	E. Jordan, esq;	Samuel Harvey	Samuel Birch	Samuel Richards
1754	Thomas Cottrell	Joseph Richards	John Bellears	John Camden
1755	Joseph Walker	John Wells[3]	Stephen Colmore	John Powell
1756	John Bellears	J. Kettle, esq;	Ambrose Foxall	John Gray
1757	William Patteson	Joseph Webster	J. Darbyshire	Richard Brett
1758	James Horton	T. Lawrence	Thomas Richards	Sam. Pemberton
1759	John Walker	Thomas Abney	G. Spilsbury	Edward Weston
1760	John Turner	Abel Humphrys	Richard Dingley	Web Marriott
1761	John Baskerville	Stephen Bedford	Michael Lakin	Nehemiah Bague
1762	Joseph Thomas	James Jackson	George Birch	John Green
1763	John Gold	John Lee	William Parks	John Daws
1764	Richard Hicks	J. Ryland	S. Bradburn, esq;	Geo. Anderton
1765	Thomas Vallant	Sam. Richards	Ed. H. Noble	Elias Wallin
1766	John Lane	Henry Venour	John Lane	Joseph Adams
1767	John Horn	Jo. Wilkinson	Richard Rabone	Thomas Care
1768	Gregory Hicks	W. Russell, esq;	Thomas Bingham	John Moody
1769	James Male	Samuel Ray	Thomas Gisborne	William Mansell
1770	Joshua Glover	Thomas Russell	T. Lutwyche	Thomas Barker
1771	John Harris	J. Hornblower	Thomas Cooper	Walter Salt
1772	William Holden	Jos. Tyndall	R. Anderton	T. Hunt

1773	Thomas Westley	John Richards	Ob. Bellamy	John Smart
1774	John Ward	John Francis	W. Hodgkins	Thomas Wight
1775	Thomas Hurd	John Taylor, esq;	John Startin	T. Everton
1776	E.W. Patteson	Josiah Rogers	Thomas Corden	Joseph Wright
1777	Ed. Thomason	S. Pemberton	Joseph Jukes	Joseph Sheldon
1778	Joseph Green	William Hunt	Thomas Wright	John Allen[4]
1779	T. Faulconbridge	W. Humphrys	John Guest	Jonathan Wigley
1780	Daniel Winwood	William Scott	William Thomas	John Bird
1781	William Hicks	W. Taylor, esq;	John Dallaway	Richard Porter
1782	Thomas Carless	G. Humphrys	John Holmes	Thomas Barrs

[2] Joseph Scott, Esq; not choosing the official part, procured a substitute to perform it, in the person of the late Constable James Baker.

[3] in office, Benjamin Mansell was chosen in his stead.

[4] was charged with a fine of 25*l.* by the lady of the manor, and John Miles chosen in his stead.

Three of the Inhabitants have, since I knew the place, served the Office of SHERIFF for the County, viz.

John Taylor, Esquire, in	1756.
Edward Jordan, Esquire, in	1757.
And Isaac Spooner, Esquire, in	1763.

COURT OF REQUESTS.

Law is the very basis of civil society, without it man would quickly return to his original rudeness; the result would be, robbery and blood:--and even laws themselves are of little moment, without a due execution of them--there is a necessity to annex punishment.

But there is no necessity to punish the living, who are innocent, by hanging the dead bodies of criminals in the air. This indecent and inhuman custom, which originated from the days of barbarism, reflects an indelible disgrace upon a civilized age. The intention, no doubt, was laudable; to prevent the commission of crimes, but does it answer that intention?

In 1759, two brothers, of the name of Darby, were hung in chains near Hales-Owen, since which time there has been only one murder committed in the whole neighbourhood, and that under the very gibbet upon which they hung[5].

[5] Joseph Skidmore, a carrier of Stourbridge, having Ann Mansfield, a young woman of Birmingham, under his care, ravished and murdered her in the evening of December 10, 1774.

Justice, however, points out a way wherein the dead body, by conveying chirurgical knowledge, may be serviceable to the living.

Laws generally tend, either directly, or remotely, to the protection of property.

All wise legislators have endeavoured to proportion the punishment to the crime, but never to exceed it: a well conducted state holds forth a scale of punishments for transgressions of every dimension, beginning with the simple reprimand, and proceeding downwards even to death itself.

It will be granted, that the line of equity ought to be drawn with critical exactness.

If by fair trade, persuasion, or finesse, I get the property of another into my hands, even to the trifling value of a shilling, my effects ought to be responsible for that sum.

If I possess no effects, he certainly retains a right of punishing to that amount: for if we do not lay this line in the boundaries of strict justice, it will not lie upon any other ground. And if I am allowed fraud in one shilling, I am allowed it in a greater sum. How far punishment may be softened by concurring circumstances, is another question.

It therefore follows of course, that if my creditor has a right to recover his unfortunate property, those laws are the nearest to perfection, that will enable him to recover it with the most expedition, and the least expence and trouble to us both.

If the charge of recovery is likely to exceed the debt, he will be apt to desist, I to laugh at him, and to try my skill at a second enterprize.

Trade and credit cannot be well separated; they are as closely connected as the wax and the paper. The laws of credit, therefore, ought to rest upon a permanent foundation: neither is law necessary to restrain credit; for if, in a commercial state, it becomes detrimental by its over growth, it finds itself a remedy.

Much has been said, and perhaps more than has been thought, concerning the court before us. The loser is expected to complain, and his friends to give him a partial hearing; and though he breathes *vengeance* against his antagonist, it ends in a *breath*.

The looker-on can easily spy an error in the actor. If a fault is committed, we are glad it was done by another; besides, it is no new thing for the *outs* to complain of the *ins*. It will plead strongly in excuse, to say, the intention was right, if the judgment was wrong. If perfection is required, she does not reside upon earth.

But if these pleadings are not found a balance against prejudice, and a man suffers his wrath to kindle against a valuable institution, because perfection does not preside over it, let him peruse an old author, who asks, "What shall we think of the folly of that man, who throws away the apple, because it contains a core? despises the nut, for the shell? or casts the diamond into the sea, because it has a flaw?"

Decision is usually established upon oath, both in criminal courts, and in those at Westminster, through which the oath is seen to pass with free currency.

A judge is sometimes fond of sheltering himself behind an oath; it may be had at an easy rate. Each of the contending parties wishes to win his cause by an oath: but though oaths would be willingly taken, they ought to be sparingly given.-- They may be considered what they generally are not, *of the last importance.*

We may observe, that two opponents are ready to swear directly contrary to each other; that if a man asserts a thing, he can do no less than swear it; and that, after all, an oath proves nothing.

The commissioners, therefore, wish rather to establish *fact* upon *proof*; but, if this is wanting, then upon circumstantial evidence; and if this support fails, they chuse to finish a quarrel by a moderate, though a random judgment.

Much honor is due to that judicial luminary, William Murray, Earl of Mansfield, who presides over the King's-Bench, for introducing equity into the courts of law, where she had long been a stranger.

The Court of Requests may justly be charged with weakness, and what court may not? It is inseparable from man.

A person cannot chuse his capacity, but he may chuse to be a rogue; one is an act of nature, the other of the will. The greater the temptation to go astray, the greater must be the resolution to conquer it.

One of the suitors presented a commissioner with a couple of chickens, as a powerful argument to strengthen a feeble case; but the commissioner returned his present, and the plaintiff lost his cause; and no wonder, he sent a chicken to plead it.

The defendant, by disobeying the orders of the court, falls under the power of the plaintiff, who can cause execution to issue against his goods, and reimburse himself; or, against his body, and confine him forty days, unless paid his demand.

There is no cause that can be brought before the Court of Requests, but may be brought before a higher court, and at a higher expence.

A cause passes through this court for seventeen-pence; and cannot well, by chicanery or neglect, amount to more than two shillings and nine-pence: So that ruin is not one of its imperfections.

Though law is said to produce quarrels among friends, yet the contending parties often go out of that court better friends than when they came in.

It has been objected, that the publicans give credit to the lower class, in expectation of relief from the court. But the debtor is equally apprized of the remedy, and often drinks deeper, in expectation of a mild sentence from the commissioners; besides, is not all credit founded on the laws of recovery?

It has also been urged, that while punishment pursues the debtor, for neglect of orders, his family falls upon the community.

But the community would not wish to put a bar between a man and his property--The precedent would be dangerous: Justice is no respector of persons. A culprit will soon procure a family, if they are able to plead his excuse: It would follow, that single men only would be obliged to be honest. She does not save the criminal, because he is an handsome man. If she did, beauty would increase in value; but honesty, seldom be its companion.

But can accusation lie against a fair tribunal of rectitude? The man does not exist that can quarrel with equity, and treat her as the offspring of fraud---The most amiable character in the creation, and the immediate representative of supreme excellence. She will be revered, even by the sons of plunder!

Many of the causes that pass this court, are of a disputable nature, and if not terminated there, would take a different turn.

From distant views of relief here, even sickness herself finds credit in the day of distress.

The use of the court is also favourable to trade, for, to oblige a man to pay his debts, is to oblige him to labour, which improves the manufactures.

Birmingham, in no period of her existence, has increased with such rapidity, in people, buildings and commerce, as since the erection of that court; so that depopulation is not one of its inconveniencies.

From a consideration of the prodigious intercourse subsisting in so vast a body of people, and the credit consequent thereon, it was wisely judged necessary to establish an easy, and expeditious method of ending dispute, and securing property.

The inhabitants of Birmingham, therefore, in 1752, procured an act for the recovery of debts under Forty Shillings; constituting seventy-two commissioners, three to be a quorum. They sit for the dispatch of business in the chamber over the Old Cross every Friday morning, and there usually appear before them between eighty and one hundred causes: Their determinations are final. Two clerks also, constituted by the act, attend the court to give judicial assistance; are always of the law, chosen alternately by the lord of the manor, and the commissioners, and to continue for life. Once in every two years, ten of the commissioners are ballotted out, and ten others of the inhabitants chosen in their stead.

LAMP ACT.

Order, is preserved by industry. In 1769 an act was obtained, and in 1773 an amendment of the act, for lighting and cleaning the streets of Birmingham, and for removing obstructions that were prejudicial to the health or convenience of the inhabitants.

These acts were committed to the care of about seventy-six irresolute commissioners, with farther powers of preventing encroachments upon public ground; for it was justly observed, that robbery was a work of darkness, therefore to introduce light would, in some measure, protect property. That in a town like Birmingham, full of commerce and inhabitants, where necessity leads to continual action, no part of the twenty four hours ought to be dark. That, to avoid darkness, is sometimes to avoid insult; and that by the light of 700 lamps, many unfortunate accidents would be prevented.

It was also observed, that in a course of time, the buildings in some of the ancient streets had encroached upon the path, four or five feet on each side; which caused an irregular line, and made those streets eight or ten feet narrower, that are now used by 50,000 people, than they were, when used only by a tenth part of that number; and, that their confined width rendered the passage dangerous to children, women, and feeble age, particularly on the market day and Saturday evening.

That if former encroachments could not be recovered, future ought to be prevented.

And farther, that necessity pleads for a wider street now, than heretofore, not only because the inhabitants, being more numerous, require more room, but the buildings being more elevated, obstruct the light, the sun, and the air, which obstructions tend to sickness and inconveniency.

Narrow streets with modern buildings are generally dirty, for want of these natural helps; as Digbeth, St. Martin's-lane, Swan-alley, Carr's-lane, &c. The narrower the street, the less it can be influenced by the sun and the wind, consequently, the more the dirt will abound; and by experimental observations upon stagnate water in the street, it is found extremely prejudicial to health. And also, the larger the number of people, the more necessity to watch over their interest with a guardian eye.

It may farther be remarked, that an act of parliament ought to distribute justice with an impartial hand, in which case, content and obedience may reasonably be expected. But the acts before us carry a manifest partiality, one man claims a right to an encroachment into the street, of three or four feet, whilst another is restricted to twelve inches.

This inactive body of seventy-six, who wisely argue against the annihilation of one evil, because another will remain; had also powers to borrow a thousand pounds, to purchase and remove some obstructive buildings; and to defray the expence by a rate on the inhabitants, which, after deducting about one hundred and twenty pounds per ann. for deficiencies, amounted in 1774, to 912*l*.

1775, -- 902*l.*
1776, -- 947*l.*
1777, -- 965*l.*
1778, -- 1,012*l.*
1779, -- 1,022*l.*
1780, -- 1,021*l.*

Though the town was averse to the measure, as an innovation, they quickly saw its utility, and seemed to wish a more vigorous exertion of the commissioners; but numbers sometimes procrastinate design. If it is difficult to find five men of one mind, it is more difficult to find a superior number. That business which would run currently through the hands of five, stagnates at fifteen, the number required.

It is curious to observe a body of commissioners, every one of whom conducts his own private affairs with propriety and success, attack a question by the hour, which is as plain as the simplest proposition in the mathematicks, when not being able to reduce it, and their ammunition spent, leave the matter undetermined, and retreat in silence.

In works of manual operation a large number may be necessary, but in works of direction a small one facilitates dispatch.

Birmingham, a capacious field, by long neglect is over-grown with encroaching weeds. The gentle commissioners, appointed to reduce them, behold it an arduous work, are divided in opinion, and some withdraw the hand from the plough; certainly, *the harvest is great, and the labourers are few*. The manorial powers, which alone could preserve order, have slept for ages. Regularity has been long extinct. The desire of trespass is so prevalent, that I have been tempted to question; if it were not for the powers of the lamp act, feeble as they are, whether the many-headed-public, ever watchful of prey, would not in another century, devour whole streets, and totally prevent the passenger. Thus a supine jurisdiction abounds with *street-robbers*.

There are cases where the line of the street should inviolably be preserved, as in a common range of houses; therefore all projections above a given dimension infringe this rule.

There are other cases where taste would direct this line to be broken, as in buildings of singular size and construction, which should be viewed in recess. Those of a public nature generally come under this description, as the free-school, and the hotel, which ought to have fallen two or three yards back. What pity, that so noble an edifice as the theatre in New-street, should lose any of its beauty, by the prominence of its situation!

As Birmingham abounds with new streets, that were once private property, it is a question often discussed, In what point of time the land appropriated for such streets, ceases to be private? But as this question was never determined, and as it naturally rises before me, and is of importance, suffer me to examine it.

When building leases are granted, if the road be narrow, as was lately the case at the West end of New-street, the proprietor engages to give a certain portion of land to widen it. From that moment, therefore, it falls to the lot of the public, and is under the controul of the commissioners, as guardians of public property. I allow, if within memory, the grantor and the lessees should agree to cancel the leases, which is just as likely to happen as the powers of attraction to cease, and the moon to descend from the heavens; in this case, the land reverts again to its original proprietor.

Though the streets of Birmingham have for many ages been exposed to the hand of the encroacher, yet, by a little care, and less expence, they might in about one century be reduced to a considerable degree of use and beauty. In what light then shall we be viewed by the future eye, if we neglect the interest of posterity?

RELIGION AND POLITICS.

Although these two threads, like the warp and the woof, are very distinct things; yet, like them, they are usually woven together. Each possesses a strength of its own, but when united, have often become extremely powerful, as in the case of Henry the Third and the clergy. This union, at times, subsisted from a very early date.

Power is the idol of man; we not only wish to acquire it, but also to increase and preserve it. If the magistrate has been too weak to execute his designs, he has backed his schemes with the aid of the church; this occurred with King Stephen and the Bishops.

Likewise, if a churchman finds his power ascendant in the human mind, he still wishes an addition to that power, by uniting another. Thus the Bishop of Rome, being master of the spiritual chair, stept also into the temporal.

Sometimes the ecclesiastical and civil governors appear in malign aspect, or in modern phrase, like a quarrel between the squire and the rector, which is seldom detrimental to the people. This was the case with Henry the Eighth and the church.

The curses of a priest hath sometimes brought a people into obedience to the King, when he was not able to bring them himself. One could not refrain from smiling, to hear a Bishop curse the people for obeying their Sovereign, and in a few months after, curse them again if they did not; which happened in the reign of King John. But, happy for the world, that these retail dealers in the wrath of heaven are become extinct, and the market is over.

Birmingham, in those remote periods of time, does not seem to have attended so much to religious and political dispute, as to the course music of her hammer. Peace seems to have been her characteristic--She paid obedience to that Prince had the good fortune to possess the throne, and regularly paid divine honours in St. Martin's, because there was no other church. Thus, through the long ages of Saxon, Danish, and Norman government, we hear of no noise but that of the anvil, till the reign of Henry the Third, when her Lord joined the Barons against the Crown, and drew after him some of his mechanics, to exercise the very arms they had been taught to make; and where, at the battle of Evesham, he staked his life and his fortune, and lost both.

Things quickly returning into their former channel, she stood a silent spectator during that dreadful contest between the two roses, pursuing the tenor of still life till the civil wars of Charles I. when she took part with the Parliament, some of whose troops were stationed here, particularly at the Garrison and Camp-hill; the names of both originating in that circumstance.

Prince Rupert, as hinted before, approaching Birmingham in 1643 with a superior power, forced the lines, and as a punishment set fire to the town. His vengeance burned fiercely in Bull-street, and the affrighted inhabitants quenched the flames with a heavy fine.

In 1660, she joined the wish of the kingdom, in the restoration of the Stuart family. About this time, many of the curious manufactures began to blossom in this prosperous garden of the arts.

In 1688, when the nation chose to expel a race of Kings, though replete with good nature, because they had forgot the limits of justice ; our peaceable sons of art, wisely considering, that oppression and commerce, like oil and water, could never unite, smiled with the rest of the kingdom at the landing of the Prince of Orange, and exerted their little assistance towards effecting the Revolution, notwithstanding the lessons of *divine right* had been taught near ninety years.

In the reign of Queen Anne, when that flaming luminary, Dr. Sacheverel, set half the kingdom in blaze, the inhabitants of this region of industry caught the spark of the day, and grew warm for the church--They had always been inured to *fire*, but now we behold them between *two*.

As the doctor rode in triumph through the streets of Birmingham, this flimsy idol of party snuffed up the incense of the populace, but the more sensible with held their homage; and when he preached at Sutton Coldfield, where he had family connections, the people of Birmingham crowded in multitudes round his pulpit. But it does not appear that he taught his hearers to *build up Zion*, but perhaps to pull her down; for they immediately went and gutted a meeting-house.

It is easy to point out a time when it was dangerous to have been of the established church, and I have here pointed out one, when it was dangerous to profess any other.

We are apt to think the zeal of our fathers died with them, for I have frequently beheld with pleasure, the churchman, the presbyterian, and the quaker uniting their efforts, like brethren, to carry on a work of utility. The bigot of the last age casts a malicious sneer upon the religion of another, but the man of this passes a joke upon his own.

A sameness in religious sentiment is no more to be expected, than a sameness of face. If the human judgment varies in almost every subject of plain knowledge, how can it be fixed in this, composed of mystery?

As the true religion is ever that which a man professes himself, it is necessary to enquire, What means, he that is right may use, to convert him that is wrong?

As the whole generations of faggot and torture, are extinct in this age of light, there seems only to remain fair arguments founded in reason, and these can only be brought as evidences upon the trial: The culprit himself, *by indefeasible right divine*, will preside as the judge. Upon a close enquiry it will be found, that his sentiments are as much his private property, as the coat that covers him, or the life which that coat incloses.

Is there not as much reason to punish my neighbour for differing in opinion from me, as to punish me, because I differ from him? Or, is there any to punish either?

If a man's sentiments and practice in religious matters, appear even absurd, provided society is not injured, what right hath the magistrate to interfere?

The task is as easy to make the stream run upwards, as to form a nation of one mind. We may pronounce with confidence, an age of bigotry is no age of philosophy.

The gentle hand of Brunswick, had swayed the British sceptre near half a century, ere all the sons of science in this meridian, were compleatly reconciled to this favourite line.

But unanimity, with benign aspect, seems now the predominant star of the zenith: A friendly intercourse succeeds suspicion. The difference of sentiment, that once created jealousy, now excites a smile; and the narrow views of our forefathers are prudently expanded.

St. John's Chapel, Deritend.

PLACES OF WORSHIP.

In a town like Birmingham, unfettered with charteral laws; which gives access to the stranger of every denomination, for he here finds a freedom by birthright; and where the principles of toleration are well understood, it is no wonder we find various modes of worship. The wonder consists in finding such *agreement*, in such variety.

We have fourteen places for religious exercise, six of the established church, three dissenting meeting houses, a quakers, baptist, methodist, roman catholic, and jewish. Two of these only are churches, of which elsewhere.

SAINT JOHN'S CHAPEL,

DERITEND.

This, tho' joining to the parish of Birmingham, is a chapel of ease belonging to Aston, two miles distant. Founded in the fifth of Richard the Second, 1382.

This chapel does not, like others in Birmingham, seem to have been erected first, and the houses brought round it: It appears, by its extreme circumscribed latitude, to have been founded upon the scite of other buildings, which were purchased, or rather given, by Sir John de Birmingham, Lord of Deritend, and situated upon the boundaries of the manor, perhaps to accommodate in some measure the people of Digbeth; because the church in Birmingham must, for many-ages, have been too small for the inhabitants.

Time seems to have worn out that building of 1382; in the windows of which were the arms of Lord Dudley, and Dudley empaling Barckley, both knights of the garter, descended from the Somery's, Barons of Dudley-castle: Also a whole figure of Walter Arden, Esq; of ancient family, often mentioned, Lord of Bordesley.

The present building was erected in 1735, and the steeple in 1762. In 1777 eight of the most musical bells, together with a clock, entered the steeple. The present chaplain, the Rev. Thomas Cox--Income 80*l*.

St. Bartholomew's Chapel.

SAINT BARTHOLOMEW'S.

Built in 1749, on the east side of the town, will accommodate about 800 hearers; is neat and elegant. The land was the gift of John Jennens, Esq; of Copsal, in the county of Leicester, possessor of a considerable estate in and near Birmingham.

By the solicitation of Mrs. Weaman, Mrs. Jennens gave 1000*l*. and the remainder was raised by contribution to accomplish the building.

Wherever a chapel is erected, the houses immediately, as if touched by the wand of magic, spring into existence. Here is a spacious area for interment, amply furnished by death. The infant steeple, if it will bear the name, is very small but beautiful.

The chancel hath this singular difference from others--that it veres towards the North. Whether the projector committed an error, I leave to the critics.

It was the general practice of the Pagan church to fix their altar, upon which they sacrificed, in the East, towards the rising sun, the object of worship.

The Christian church, in the time of the Romans, immediately succeeded the Pagan, and scrupulously adopted the same method; which has been strictly adhered to.

By what obligation the Christian is bound to follow the Pagan, or wherein a church would be injured by being directed to any of the thirty-two points in the compass, is doubtful. Certain it is, if the chancel of Bartholomew's had tended due East, the eye would have been exceedingly hurt, and the builder would have raised an object of ridicule for ages. The ground will admit of no situation but that in which the church now stands. But the inconsiderate architect of Deritend chapel, anxious to catch the Eastern point, lost the line of the street: we may therefore justly pronounce, *be sacrificed to the East*. Other enormities also, of little moment, have issued from the same fountain.

The altar piece was the gift of Basil Earl of Denbigh; and the communion plate, consisting of 182 ounces, that of Mary Carless. Income 100*l*.--Rev. William Jabbitt, chaplain.

St. Mary's Chapel.

SAINT MARY's.

Though the houses for divine worship were multiplied in Birmingham, yet the inhabitants increased in a greater proportion; so that in 1772 an act was obtained for two additional chapels.

St. Mary's, therefore, was erected in 1774, in the octagon form, not overcharged with light nor strength; in an airy situation and taste, but shews too little steeple, and too much roof. If a light balustrade was raised over the parapet, with an urn in the centre of the roof, the eye of the observer would be relieved.

The clock was seldom seen to go right, but the wonder ceases if there are NO WORKS within.

The land was the gift of Mary Weaman, in whom is the presentation, who inducted the Rev. John Riland. Annual income about 200*l*.

SAINT PAUL's.

The act was procured for this chapel at the same time as for that of St. Mary's; but it was not erected till 1779, upon a spot of ground given by Charles Colmore, Esq; upon the declivity of a hill, not altogether suitable for the elegant building it sustains, which is of stone--plain beauty unites with strength.

This roof, like that of St. Mary's, appears also too full. The steeple intended for this useful edifice, will do honour to the modern stile of architecture, whenever money can be procured to erect it; which at present is only delineated upon paper.

Chaplain, the Rev. William Toy Young.--Income nearly as St. Mary's.

OLD MEETING.

After the extinction of the Stuart race, who bore an invincible hatred to presbyterianism, the dissenters from the establishment procured a licence for a meeting at the bottom of Digbeth, which yet bears the name of Meeting-house-yard. Here the rigid sons of worship paid a weekly attendance. The place is now a work-shop: The sound of the pulpit is changed into that of the bellows: Instead of an impression upon the heart, it is now stamped upon the button. The visitants used to appear in a variety of colours, but now always in black.

St. Paul's Chapel.

New Meeting.

Old Meeting.

Another was erected in the reign of King William, now denominated The Old Meeting, and from whence the street in which it stands derives a name. This is large, and much attended.

Pastor, the Rev. Radcliff Scoldfield.

NEW MEETING.

Erected in the year 1730, at which time that in Digbeth went into disuse. This is in a stile of elegance, and has few equals. The Rev. Samuel Blyth, and the Rev. William Hawkes preside over it.

In December 1780, Mr. Hawkes declining the pastoral care, the congregation judiciously turned their thoughts towards the celebrated Doctor Priestley, F.R.S. one of the first philosophers of the age; whose merit seems obvious to every eye but his own.

CARR's LANE MEETING.

A scion of the Old Meeting, transplanted in 1748. The building cost about 700*l*. This society hath been favoured with two donations; one the interest of 800*l*. by the will of John England, in 1771: The other Scott's Trust, mentioned in another part.

This residence of divine light is totally eclipsed, by being surrounded with about forty families of paupers, crouded almost within the compass of a giant's span, which amply furnish the congregation with noise, smoak, dirt and dispute. If the place itself is the road to heaven, the stranger would imagine, that the road to the place led to something worse: The words, *Strait is the gate, and narrow is the way*, are here literally verified.--Pastor, the Rev. John Punfield.

BAPTIST MEETING.

Founded in Cannon-street, 1738. This hill of Zion is also hid from the public eye, but situated in a purer air.--The minister was the late Rev. James Turner.

Some trifling differences arising in the congregation, to which the human mind is everlastingly prone, caused discontent: Individuals began to sting each other, which in 1745, produced a swarm.

The destitute wanderers therefore, erected for themselves a small cell in Freeman-street, where they hived in expectation of harmony. Over this little society of separatists presided a journeyman woolcomber: What elevation he bore in the comb-shop, during six days of the week, history is silent; but having the good fortune to procure a black coat and a white wig, he figured on the seventh with parsonic elegance.

Whether *he* fed his people best, or *they* him, is uncertain; but whether they starved one another, is not. Disgust, which ever waits upon disappointment, appeared among them.

Though the preacher was certainly warmed in the shop, *with a live coal from the altar*; yet unfortunately, Sunday was the only day in which his *fire* was extinguished; *then* the priest and the people hit the taste of the day, and slumbered together; a priviledge never granted by a *reader* to an *author*. Thus the boasted *liberty of the press* submits to that of the pulpit.

This exalted shepherd dwelt upon the words of Paul, *He that preaches the gospel, ought to subsist by the gospel;* and *they* did not forget a portion in John, *Feed my sheep*. The word, he well knew, promised both wine and *oil*, but he was obliged to be satisfied with the latter.

Although the teacher might possess some *shining qualities* at the combe-pot, he did not possess that of protecting his flock, who in 1752, silently retreated to their original fold in Cannon-street; and the place was soon after converted into a dwelling, No. 16, when for the first time it produced *profit*.

The growing numbers of this prosperous society induced them, in 1780, to enlarge the place of worship, at the expence of about 800*l.* in which is observable some beauty, but more conveniency.

QUAKER's MEETING

In Bull-street. A large convenient place, and notwithstanding the plainness of the profession rather elegant. The congregation is very flourishing, rich, and peaceable. Chandler tells us, to the everlasting honour of the Quakers, that they are the only christian sect who have never exercised the cruel weapon of persecution.

METHODIST's MEETING.

We learn from ecclesiastical history, that the people in high life are always *followers* in religion. Though they are the best leaders in political and social concerns, yet all religions seem to originate from the lowest class. Every religion is first obstructed by violence, passes through the insults of an age, then rests in peace, and often takes up the rod against another.

The first preachers of the christian faith, the short-sighted apostles, were men of the meanest occupations, and their church, a wretched room in a miserable tenement. The superb buildings of St. Peter's in Rome, and St. Paul's in London, used by their followers, were not within the reach of their penetration. They were also totally ignorant of tripple crowns, red hats, mitres, crosiers, robes, and rochets, well known to their successors.

The religion of a private room, soon became the religion of a country: the church acquired affluence, for all churches hate poverty; and this humble church, disturbed for ages, became the church of Rome, the disturber of Europe.

John Wickliff, in 1377, began to renew her disturbance: this able theologist planted our present national church, which underwent severe persecutions, from its mother church at Rome; but, rising superior to the rod, and advancing to maturity, she became the mother of a numerous offspring, which she afterwards persecuted herself; and this offspring, like *their* mother, were much inclined to persecution.

Puritanism, her first born, groaned under the pressure of her hand. The Baptists, founded by a taylor, followed, and were buffeted by both.--Independency appeared, ponderous as an elephant, and trampled upon all three.

John Fox, a composition of the oddest matter, and of the meanest original, formed a numerous band of disciples, who suffered the insults of an age, but have carried the arts of prudence to the highest pitch.

The Muglitonians, the Prophets, the Superlapsarians, &c. like untimely births, just saw the light and disappeared.

The Moravians, under the influence of Zinzendorf, rose about 1740, but are not in a flourishing state; their circumscribed rules, like those of the cloister, being too much shackled to thrive in a land of freedom.

James Sandiman introduced a religion, about 1750, but, though eclipsed himself by poverty, he taught his preachers to shine; for he allowed them to grace the pulpit with ruffles, lace, and a cueque. Birmingham cannot produce one professor of the two last churches.

The christian religion has branched into more sectaries in the last two hundred years, than in the fifteen hundred before--the reason is obvious. During the tedious reign of the Romish priest, before the introduction of letters, knowledge was small, and he wished to confine that knowledge to himself: he substituted mystery for science, and led the people blindfold. But the printing-press, though dark in itself, and surrounded with yet *darker* materials, diffused a ray of light through the world, which enabled every man to read, think, and judge for himself; hence diversity of opinion, and the absurdity of reducing a nation to one faith, vainly attempted by Henry VIII.

In those distant ages, the priest had great influence, with little knowledge; but in these, great knowledge, with little influence. He was then revered according to his authority; but now, according to his merit: he shone in a borrowed, but now in a real lustre: then he was less deserving; but now less esteemed. The humble christian, in the strictest sense, worked out his salvation with fear and trembling, and with tools furnished by the priest: he built upon his opinions, but now he lays a foundation for his own.

Though we acknowledge the scriptures our guide, we take the liberty to guide them; we torture them to our own sentiments. Though we allow their *equal* weight, we suffer one portion to weigh down another. If we attend to twenty disputants, not one of them will quote a text which militates against his sentiments.

The artillery of vengeance was pointed at Methodism for thirty years; but, fixed as a rock, it could never be beaten down, and its professors now enjoy their sentiments in quiet.

After the institution of this sect by George Whitfield, in 1738, they were first covered by the heavens, equally exposed to the rain and the rabble, and afterwards they occupied, for many years, a place in Steelhouse-lane, where the wags of the age observed, "they were eat out by the bugs."--They therefore procured a cast off theatre in Moor-street, where they continued to exhibit till 1782; when, quitting the stage, they erected a superb meeting-house, in Cherry-street, at the expence of 1200*l*. This was opened, July 7, by John Wesley, the chief priest, whose extensive knowledge, and unblemished manners, give us a tolerable picture of apostolic purity; who *believes*, as if he were to be saved by faith; and who *labours*, as if he were to be saved by works.

Thus our composite order of religion, an assemblage of the Episcopalian, the Presbyterian, the Independent, and the Baptist; fled from the buffetings of the vulgar, and now take peaceable shelter from the dews of heaven.

ROMISH CHAPEL.

I have already remarked, there is nothing which continues in the same state: the code of manners, habits of thinking, and of expression, modes of living, articles of learning; the ways of acquiring wealth, or knowledge; our dress, diet, recreations, &c. change in every age.

But why is there a change in religion? eternal truth, once fixed, is everlastingly the same. Religion is purity, which, one would think, admits of no change; if it changes, we should doubt whether it is religion. But a little attention to facts will inform us, *there is nothing more changable:* nor need we wonder, because, man himself being changable, every thing committed to his care will change with him. We may plead his excuse, by observing, his sight is defective: he may be deceived by viewing an object in one light, or attitude, to-day, and another, to-morrow. This propensity to change might lead us to suspect the authenticity of our own sentiments.

The apostles certainly formed the church of Rome; but she, having undergone the variations of seventeen hundred years, St. Peter himself, should he return to the earth, could not discover one linament in her aspect; but would be apt to reject her as a changling.

The church of England has not only undergone a change since the reformation, but wishes a greater.

We should suppose the puritan of 1583, and the dissenter of 1783, were the same: but although substance and shadow exactly resemble each other, no two things differ more.

When pride sends a man in quest of a religion, if he does not discover something new, he might as well stay at home: nothing near the present standard can take. Two requisites are necessary to found a religion, capacity, and singularity: no fool ever succeeded. If his talents are not above mediocrity, he will not be able to draw the crowd; and if his doctrines are not singular, the crowd will not be drawn--novelty pleases.

Having collected, and brightened up a set of doctrines, wide of every other church, he fixes at a distance from all. But time, and unavoidable intercourse with the world, promote a nearer approximation; and, mixing with men, we act like men. Thus the Quaker under George III. shews but little of the Quaker under George Fox.

In two congregations of the same profession, as in two twins of the same family, though there is a striking likeness, the curious observer will trace a considerable difference.

In a religion, as well as a man, *there is a time to be born, and a time to die.* They both vary in aspect, according to the length of their existence, carry the marks of decline, and sink into obscurity.

We are well informed how much the Romish religion has declined in this country: three hundred years ago Birmingham did not produce one person of another persuasion; but now, out of 50,000 people, we have not 300 of this.

The Roman Catholics formerly enjoyed a place for religious worship near St. Bartholomew's-chapel, still called Masshouse-lane; but the rude hands of irreligion destroyed it. There is now none nearer than Edgbaston, two miles distant; yet the congregation is chiefly supplied from Birmingham.

If the Roman Catholics are not so powerful as in the sixteenth century, they seem as quiet, and as little addicted to knowledge; perhaps they have not yet learned to see through any eyes but those of the priest.--There appears, however, as much devotion in their public worship, as among any denomination of christians.

JEWISH SYNAGOGUE.

We have also among us a remnant of Israel. A people who, when masters of their own country, were scarcely ever known to travel, and who are now seldom employed in any thing else. But, though they are ever moving, they are ever at home: who once lived the favourites of heaven, and fed upon the cream of the earth; but now are little regarded by either: whose society is entirely confined to themselves, except in the commercial line.

Birmingham Theatre

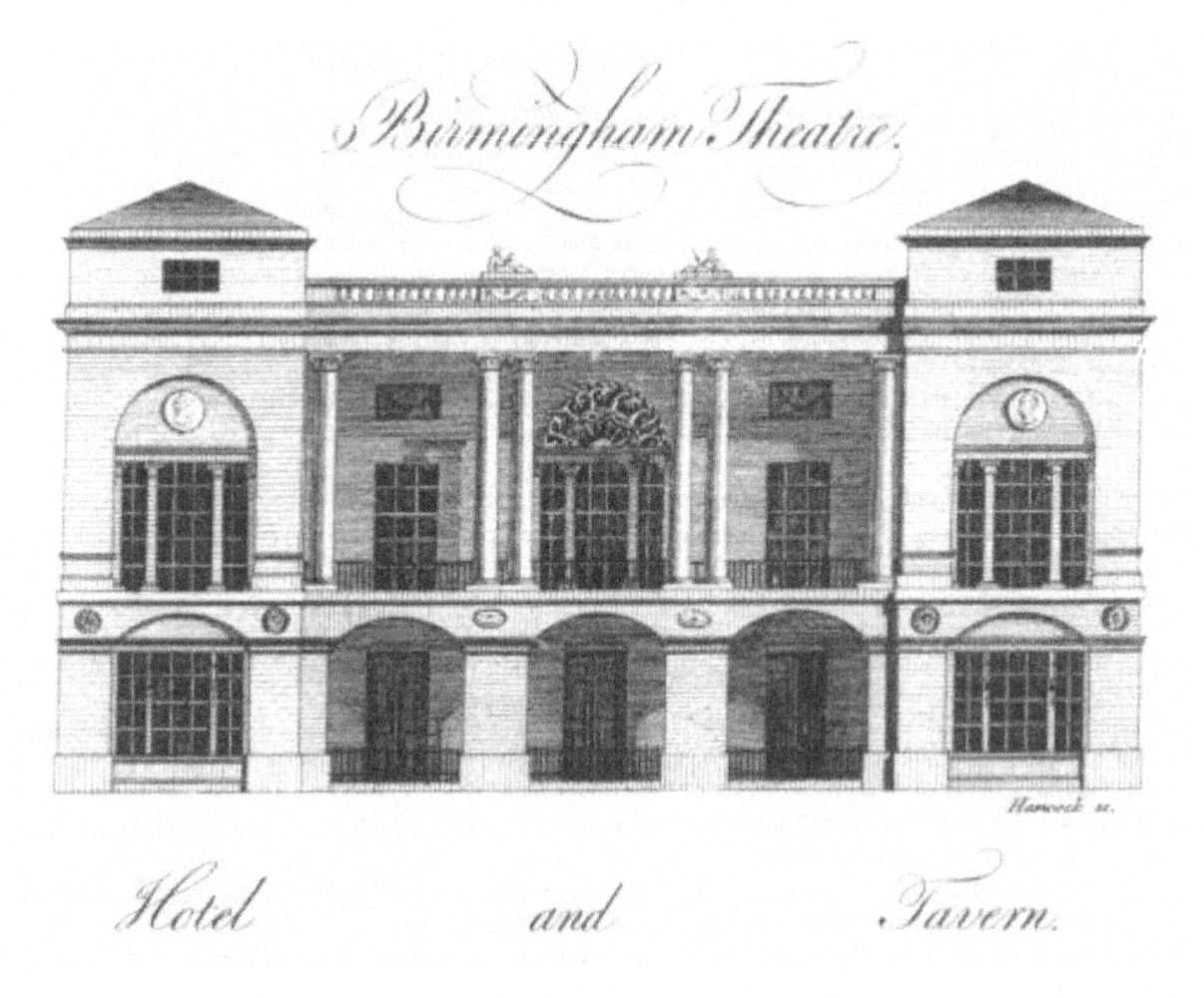

Hotel and Tavern.

In the Synagogue, situated in the Froggery, they still preserve the faint resemblence of the ancient worship. Their whole apparatus being no more than the drooping ensigns of poverty. The place is rather small, but tolerably filled; where there appears less decorum than in the christian churches. The proverbial expression "as rich as a jew," is not altogether verified in Birmingham, but perhaps, time is transfering it to the Quakers.

It is rather singular, that the honesty of a jew, is seldom pleaded but by the jew himself.

THEATRES.

The practice of the Theatre is of great antiquity. We find it in great repute among the Greeks; we also find, the more a nation is civilized, the more they have supported the stage. It seems designed for two purposes, improvement and entertainment.

There are certain exuberances that naturally grow in religion, government, and private life which may with propriety be attacked by the poet and the comedian, but which can scarcely be reduced by any other power. While the stage therefore keeps this great end in view, it answers a valuable purpose to the community. The poet should use his pen to reform, not to indulge a corrupt age, as was the case in the days of Charles the Second, when indecency was brought on to raise the laugh.

Perhaps there is no period of time in which the stage was less polluted, owing to the inimitable Garrick, than the present: notwithstanding there is yet room for improvement.

Tragedy is to melt the heart, by exhibiting the unfortunate; satiate revenge, by punishing the unjust tyrant: To discard vice, and to keep undue passions within bounds.

Comedy holds up folly in a ridiculous light: Whatever conduct or character is found in the regions of absurdity, furnishes proper materials for the stage; and out of these, the pen of a master will draw many useful lessons.

The pulpit and the stage have nearly the same use, but not in the same line--That of improving the man.

The English stage opened about the conquest, and was wholly confined to religion; in whose service it continued, with very little intermission, to the extinction of the Plantagenets. The play-houses were the churches, the principal actors the priests, and the performances taken from scripture; such as the Fall of Man, the Story of Joseph, Sampson, Histories of the Saints, the Sufferings of Christ, Resurrection, Day of Judgment, &c.

Theatrical exhibition in Birmingham, is rather of a modern date. As far as memory can penetrate, the stroller occupied, occasionally, a shed of boards in the fields, now Temple-street: Here he acted the part of Distress, in a double capacity. The situation was afterwards changed, but not the eminence, and the Hinkleys dignified the performers booth!

In about 1730, the amusements of the stage rose in a superior stile of elegance, and entered something like a stable in Castle-street. Here the comedian strutted in painted rags, ornamented with tinsel: The audience raised a noisy laugh, half real and half forced, at three-pence a head.

In about 1740, a theatre was erected in Moor-street, which rather gave a spring to the amusement; in the day time the comedian beat up for volunteers for the night, delivered his bills of fare, and roared out an encomium on the excellence of the entertainment, which had not always the desired effect.

In 1751, a company arrived, which anounced themselves, "His Majesty's servants, from the theatres-royal in London; and hoped the public would excuse the ceremony of the drum, as beneath the dignity of a London company." The novelty had a surprising effect; the performers had merit; the house was continually crouded; the general conversation turned upon theatrical exhibition, and the town was converted into one vast theatre.

In 1752 it was found necessary to erect a larger theatre, that in King Street, and we multiplied into two London companies.

The pulpits took the alarm, and in turn, roared after their customers: But the pious teachers forgot it was only the fervour of a day, which would cool of itself; that the fiercer the fire burns, the sooner it will burn out.

This declaration of war, fortunately happening at the latter end of summer, the campaign was over, and the company retreated into winter quarters, without hostilities.

It was afterwards found, that two theatres were more than the town chose to support; therefore that in Moor-street was set for a methodist meeting, where, it was said, though it changed its audience, it kept its primeval use, continuing the theatre of farce.

In 1774, the theatre in King-street was enlarged, beautified, and made more convenient; so that it hath very few equals.

About the same time that in New-street was erected upon a suitable spot, an extensive plan, and richly ornamented with paintings and scenery.--Expence seems the least object in consideration.

An additional and superb portico, was erected in 1780, which perhaps may cause it to be pronounced, "One of the first theatres in Europe."

Two busts, in relief, of excellent workmanship, are elevated over the attic windows; one is the father, and the other the refiner of the British, stage--Shakespear and Garrick.

Also two figures eight feet high, are said to be under the chissel, one of Thalia, and the other of Melpomene, the comic and the tragic muses; the value one hundred and sixty guineas. Places are reserved for their reception, to augment the beauty of the front, and shew the taste of the age.

AMUSEMENTS.

Man seems formed for variety, whether we view him in a rational or an animal light. A sameness of temper, habit, diet, pursuit, or pleasure, is no part of his character. The different ages of his life, also produce different sentiments; that which gives us the highest relish in one period, is totally flat in another. The rattle that pleases at three, would be cast into the fire at threescore: The same hand that empties the purse at twenty, would fill it at fifty: In age, he bends his knee to the same religion, which he laughed at in youth: The prayer book, that holds the attention of seventy, holds the lottery pictures of seven: And the amorous tale that awakes the ideas of twenty five, lulls old age to sleep.

Not only life is productive of change, but also every day in it. If a man would take a minute survey of his thoughts and employments, for only twenty-four hours, he would be astonished at their infinite variety.

Though industry be the ruling passion of this ingenious race, yet relaxation must follow, as one period to another. Society is therefore justly esteemed an everlasting fund of amusement, which is found at the tavern, in the winter evening: Intoxication is seldom met with, except in the inferior ranks, where it is visible in both sexes.

A regular concert is established, where the music is allowed to excel. This harmonious science, like other productions of taste, though it be not the general study of the inhabitants, hath made an amazing progress during the last thirty years.

In 1777, a coffee-house was opened at the East end of New-street, the first in this department; which, drawing into its vortex the transactions of Europe, finds employment for the politician.

Assemblies are held weekly, which give room for beauty to figure at cards, in conversation, and in the dance.

The pleasures of the field claim their votaries, but, in a populous country, like that of Birmingham, plenty of game is not to be expected; for want of wild fowl, therefore, the shooter has been sometimes known to attack the tame.

However, the farmer need not be under any great concern for his property; the sportsman seldom does any thing with his arms--but--*carry them*. We are more famous for *making*, than *using* the gun.

A pack of hounds have sometimes been kept by subscription, termed, The Birmingham Hunt; but, as the sound of the dogs and the anvil never harmonised together, they have been long in disuse: the jocund tribe, therefore, having no scent of their own, fall into that of the neighbouring gentry, many of whom support a pack.

The man of reflection finds amusement in domestic resources; and, in his own mind, if unoppressed. Here the treasures collected from men, books, and observation, *are laid up for many years*, from which he draws pleasure, without diminishing the flock. The universal riches of nature and of art; the part, the present, and a glympse of the future, lie open to his eye.

Two obstructions only bound his ideas, *time* and *space*. He steps from planet to planet, and if he cannot enter immensity, he can verge upon its borders.

I pity the man, who through poverty, cannot find warmth by his own fire-side; but I pity him more, who, through poverty of thought, cannot find happiness.

For the entertainment of summer, exclusive of the two theatres, there are five greens, where the gentlemen are amused with bowls, and the ladies with tea.

There are also great variety of public gardens, suited to every class of people, or which Duddeston, the ancient seat of the Holte family, claims the pre-eminence.

The fishing-rod, that instrument which *destroys in peace*, must find a place: other animals are followed with fire and tumult, but the fishes are entrapped with deceit. Of all the sportsmen, we charge the angler alone with *killing in cold blood*.

Just as a pursuit abounds with pleasure, so will it abound with votaries. The pleasure of angling depends on the success of the line: this art is but little practised here, and less known. Our rivers are small, and thinly stored; our pools are guarded as private property: the Birmingham spirit is rather too active for the sleepy amusement of fishing.

Patience seems the highest accomplishment of an angler. We behold him, fixed as a statue, on the bank; his head inclining towards the river, his attention upon the water, his eye upon the float; he often draws, and draws only his hook! But although he gets no bite, it may fairly be said *he is bit:* of the two, the fish display the most cunning.--He, surprized that he has *caught nothing*, and I, that he has kept his rod and his patience.

Party excursion is held in considerable esteem, in which are included Enville, the seat of Lord Stamford; Hagley, that of the late Lord Lyttelton; and the Leasowes, the property of the late Wm. Shenstone, Esq. We will omit the journey to London, a tour which some of us have made all our lives *without seeing it*.

Cards and the visit are linked together, nor is the billiard table totally forsaken. One man amuses himself in amassing a fortune, and another in dissolving one.

About thirty-six of the inhabitants keep carriages for their own private use; and near fifty have country houses. The relaxations of the humbler class, are fives, quoits, skittles, and ale.

Health and amusement are found in the prodigious number of private gardens scattered round Birmingham, from which we often behold the father returning with a cabbage, and the daughter with a nosegay.

HOTEL.

The spot where our great-grandmothers smiled in the lively dance, when they possessed the flower of beauty in the spring of life, is lost in forgetfulness. The floor that trembled under that foot which was covered with a leather shoe tied with a silken string, and which supported a stocking of dark blue worsted, not of the finest texture, is now buried in oblivion.

Hotel.

In 1750 we had two assembly rooms; one at No. 11. in the Square, the other No. 85. in Bull-street. This last was not much in use afterwards. That in the Square continued in repute till in the course of that evening which happened in October 1765, when Edward Duke of York had the honour of leading up the dance, and the ladies of Birmingham enjoyed that of the Duke's hand, He remarked, "That a town of such magnitude as Birmingham, and adorned with so much beauty, deserved a superior accomodation:--That the room itself was mean, but the entrance still meaner."

Truth is ever the same, whether it comes from a prince or a peasant; but its effects are not. Whether some secret charm attended the Duke's expression, that blasted the room, is uncertain, but it never after held its former eminence.

In 1772 a building was erected by subscription, upon the Tontine principle, at the head of Temple row, and was dignified with the French name of Hotel: From a handsome, entrance the ladies are now led through a spacious saloon, at the extremity of which the eye is struck with a grand flight of steps, opening into an assembly-room, which would not disgrace even the royal presence of the Duke's brother.

The pile itself is large, plain, and elegant, but standing in the same line with the other buildings, which before were really genteel, eclipses them by its superiority: Whereas, if the Hotel had fallen a few feet back, it would, by breaking the line, have preserved the beauty of the row, without losing its own.

WAKES.

This ancient custom was left us by the Saxons. Time, that makes alteration only in other customs, has totally inverted this.

When a church was erected, it was immediately called after a saint, put under his protection, and the day belonging to that saint kept in the church as an high festival. In the evening preceding the day, the inhabitants, with lights, approached the church, and kept a continual devotion during the whole night; hence the name *wake*: After which they entered into festivity.

But now the devotional part is forgot, the church is deserted, and the festivity turned into riot, drunkenness, and mischief.

Without searching into the mouldy records of time, for evidence to support our assertion, we may safely pronounce the wake the lowest of all low amusements, and compleatly suited to the lowest of tempers.

Wakes have been deemed a public concern, and legislature, more than once, been obliged to interpose for the sake of that order which private conduct could never boast.

In the reign of Henry the Sixth, every consideration, whether of a public or a private nature, gave way to the wake: The harvest in particular was neglected. An order therefore issued, confining the wakes to the first Sunday in October, consequently the whole nation run mad at once.

Wakes in Birmingham are not ancient: Why St. Martin's, then the only church, was neglected, is uncertain.

Although we have no wakes for the town, there are three kept in its borders, called Deritend, Chapel, and Bell wakes. The two first are in the spring of existence, the last in the falling leaf of autumn.

Deritend wake probably took its rise at the erection of her chapel, in 1382.

Chapel wake, in 1750, from St. Bartholomew's chapel, is held in the meridian of Coleshill-street; was hatched and fostered by the publicans, for the benefit of the spiggot.

Amongst other important amusements, was that of bull-baiting, till the year 1773, when the commissioners of lamps, in the amendment of their act, wisely broke the chain, and procured a reprieve for the unfortunate animal.

Another was the horse-race, 'till a few years ago a person being killed, rather slackened the entertainment. What singular genius introduced the horse-race into a crowded street, I am yet to learn.

In the evening the passenger cannot proceed without danger; in the morning, he may discover which houses are public, without other intelligence than the copious streams that have issued from the wall. The blind may also distinguish the same thing, by the strong scent of the tap.

Bell wake is the junior by one year, originating from the same cause, in 1751, in consequence of ten bells being hung up in St Philip's steeple.--'Till within these few years, we were at this wake struck with a singular exhibition, that of a number of boys running a race through the streets naked. Some of the inhabitants, seeing so fair a mark for chastisement, applied the rod with success, put a period to the sport, and obliged the young runners to run under cover.

CLUBS.

It may be expected, from the title of this chapter, that I shall introduce a set of ruffians armed with missive weapons; or, having named a trump, a set of gamblers shuffling and dealing out the cards: But whatever veneration I may entertain for these two fag ends of our species, I shall certainly introduce a class of people, which, though of the lower orders, are preferable to both.

Social compact is a distinguishing mark of civilization: The whole British empire may be justly considered as one grand alliance, united for public and private interest, and this vast body of people are subdivided into an infinity of smaller fraternities, for individual benefit.

Perhaps there are hundreds of these societies in Birmingham under the name of clubs; some of them boast the antiquity of a century, and by prudent direction have acquired a capital, at accumulating interest. Thousands of the inhabitants are thus connected, nay, to be otherwise is rather unfashionable, and some are people of sentiment and property.

A variety of purposes are intended by these laudable institutions, but the principal one is that of supporting the sick.

Each society is governed by a code of laws of its own making, which have at least the honour of *resembling* those of legislature, for words without sense are found in both, and we sometimes stumble upon contradiction.

The poor's-rates, enormous as they appear, are softened by these brotherly aids. They tend also to keep the mind at rest, for a man will enjoy the day of health, with double relish, when he considers he has a treasure laid up for that of sickness.

If a *member* only of a poor family be sick, the *head* still remains to procure necessaries; but if that head be disordered, the whole source of supply is dried up, which evinces the utility of such institutions.

The general custom is to meet at the public every fortnight, spend a trifle, and each contribute six-pence, or any stated sum, to the common stock. The landlord is always treasurer, or father, and is assisted by two stewards, annually or monthly chosen.

As honour and low life are not always found together, we sometimes see a man who is rather *idle*, wish the society may suppose him *sick*, that he may rob them with more security. Or, if a member hangs long upon the box, his brethren seek a pretence to expel him. On the other hand, we frequently observe a man silently retreat from the club, if another falls upon the box, and fondly suppose himself no longer a member; or if the box be loaded with sickness, the whole club has been known to dissolve, that they may rid themselves of the burthen; but the Court of Requests finds an easy remedy for these evils, and at a trifling expence.

The charity of the club, is also extended beyond the grave, and terminates with a present to the widow.

The philosophers tell us, "There is no good without its kindred evil." This amiable body of men, therefore, marshalled to expel disease, hath one small alloy, and perhaps but one. As liquor and labour are inseparable, the imprudent member is apt to forget to quit the club room when he has spent his necessary two-pence, but continues there to the injury of his family.

Another of these institutions is the *rent club*, where, from the weekly sums deposited by the members, a sop is regularly served up twice a year, to prevent the growlings of a landlord.

In the *breeches club* every member ballots for a pair, value a guinea, *promised* of more value by the maker. This club dissolves when all the members are served.

The intentions of the *book club* are well known, to catch the productions of the press as they rise.

The *watch club* has generally a watchmaker for its president, is composed of young men, and is always temporary.

If a taylor be short of employment, he has only to consult a landlord over a bottle, who, by their joint powers, can give birth to a *cloaths club*; where every member is supplied with a suit to his taste, of a stipulated price. These are chiefly composed of batchelors, who wish to shine in the eye of the fair.

Thus a bricklayer stands at the head of the *building club*, where every member perhaps subscribes two guineas per month, and each house, value about one hundred pounds, is balloted for, as soon as erected. As a house is a weighty concern, every member is obliged to produce two bondsmen for the performance of covenants.

I will venture to pronounce another the *capital club*, for when the contributions amount to 50*l.* the members ballot for this capital, to bring into business: Here also securities are necessary. It is easy to conceive the two last clubs are extremely beneficial to building and to commerce.

The last I shall enumerate is the *clock club*: When the weekly deposits of the members amount to about 4*l.* they call lots who shall be first served with a clock of that value, and continue the same method till the whole club is supplied; after which, the clockmaker and landlord cast about for another set, who are chiefly composed of young house-keepers. Hence the beginner ornaments his premises with furniture, the artist finds employment and profit, and the publican empties his barrel.

Thus we have taken a transient survey of this rising colony of arts, uniting observation with fact: We have seen her dark manufactures, in darker times: We have attended her through her commercial, religious, political, and pleasurable walks: Have viewed her in many points of light, but never in decline; 'till we have now set her in the fair sunshine of the present day.

Perhaps I shall not be charged with prolixity, that unpardonable sin against the reader, when it is considered, that three thousand years are deposited in the compass of one hundred and forty little pages.

Some other circumstances deserve attention, which could not be introduced without breaking the thread of history: But as that thread is now drawn to an end, I must, before I resume it, step back into the recesses of time, and slumber through the long ages of seventeen hundred years; if the active reader, therefore, has no inclination for a nod of that length, or, in simple phrase, no relish for antiquity, I advise him to pass over the five ensuing chapters.

IKENIELD STREET.

About five furlongs North of the Navigation Bridge, in Great Charles street, which is the boundary of the present buildings, runs the Ikenield-street; one of those famous pretorian roads which mark the Romans with conquest, and the Britons with slavery.

By that time a century had elapsed, from the first landing of Caesar in Britain the victorious Romans had carried their arms through the southern part of the isle. They therefore endeavoured to secure the conquered provinces by opening four roads, which should each rise in the shore, communicate with, and cross each other, form different angles, extend over the island several ways, and terminate in the opposite sea.

These are the Watling-street, which rises near Dover, and running North-west through London, Atherstone, and Shropshire, in the neighbourhood of Chester, ends in the Irish sea.

The Foss begins in Devonshlre, extends South-east through Leicestershire, continuing its course through Lincolnshire, to the verge of the German ocean.

These two roads, crossing each other at right angles, form a figure resembling the letter X, whose centre is the High Cross, which divides the counties of Warwick and Leicester.

The Ermine-street extends along the southern part of the island; near the British channel; and the Ikenield-street, which I cannot so soon quit, rises near Southampton, extends nearly North, through Winchester, Wallingford, and over the Isis, at New-bridge; thence to Burford, crossing the Foss at Stow in the Woulds, over Bitford-bridge, in the County of Warwick, to Alcester; by Studley, Ipsley, Beely, Wetherick-hill, Stutley-street; crosses the road from Birmingham to Bromsgrove, at Selley oak, leaving Harborne a mile to the left, also the Hales Owen road a mile West of Birmingham: Thence by the Observatory in Lady-wood-lane, where it enters the parish of Birmingham, crossing the Dudley road at the Sand-pits; along Worstone-lane; through the little pool, and Hockley-brook, where it quits the parish: Thence over Handsworth-heath, entering a little lane on the right of Bristle-lands-end, and over the river Tame, at Offord-mill, (Oldford-mill) directly to Sutton Coldfield. It passes the Ridgeway a few yards East of King's-standing, a little artificial mount, on which Charles the First is said to have stood when he harangued the troops he brought out of Shropshire, at the opening of the civil wars, in 1642. From thence the road proceeds through Sutton park, and the remainder of the Coldfield; over Radley-moor; from thence to Wall, a Roman station, where it meets the Watling-street: Leaving Lichfield a mile to the left, it leads through Street-hay; over Fradley-heath; thence through Alderwas hays, crossing the river Trent, at Wichnor-bridge, to Branson-turnpike: over Burton-moor, leaving the town half a mile to the right: thence to Monk's-bridge, upon the river Dove; along Egington-heath, Little-over, the Rue-dyches, Stepping-lane, Nun-green, and Darley-slade, to the river Derwent, one mile above Derby; upon the eastern banks of which stands Little Chester, built by the Romans.

If the traveller is tired with this tedious journey, and dull description, which admits of no variety, we will stop for a moment, and refresh in this Roman city.

In drawing the flewks of his oar along the bed of the river, as he boats over it, he may feel the foundations of a Roman bridge, nearly level with its bottom. Joining the water are the vestiges of a castle, now an orchard. Roman coins are frequently discovered--In 1765, I was presented with one of Vespasian's, found the year before in scowering a ditch; but I am sorry to observe, it has suffered more during the fifteen years in my possession, than during the fifteen hundred it lay in the earth.

The inhabitants being in want of materials to form a turnpike road, attempted to pull up this renowned military way, for the sake of those materials, but found them too strongly cemented to admit of an easy separation, and therefore desisted when they had taken up a few loads.

I saw the section of this road cut up from the bottom: the Romans seem to have formed it with infinite labour and expence. They took out the soil for about twenty yards wide, and one deep, perhaps, till they came to a firm bottom; and filled up the whole with stones of all sizes, brought from Duffield, four miles up the river; cemented with coarse mortar.

The road here is only discoverable by its barren track, along the cultivated meadows. It then proceeds over Morley-moor, through Scarsdale, by Chesterfield, Balsover, through Yorkshire, Northumberland, and terminates upon the banks of the Tine, near Tinmouth.

There are many roads in England formed by the Romans: they were of two kinds, the military, which crossed the island; and the smaller, which extended from one town to another. The four I have mentioned come under the first class: they rather avoided, than led through a town, that they might not be injured by traffic.

Two of these four, the Watling-street, and the Ikenield-street, are thought, by their names, to be British, and with some reason; neither of the words are derived from the Latin: but whatever were their origin, they are certainly of Roman construction.

These great roads were begun as soon as the island was subdued, to employ the military, and awe the natives, and were divided into stages, at the end of each was a fort, or station, to accommodate the guard, for the reception of stores, the conveniency of marching parties, and to prevent the soldiers from mixing with the Britons.

The stations upon the Ikenield-street, in our neighbourhood, are Little Chester (Derventione) a square fort, nearly half an acre; joining the road to the south, and the Derwent to the west.

The next is Burton upon Trent (Ad Trivonam) thirteen miles south. Here I find no remains of a station.

Then Wall (Etocetum) near Lichfield, which I have examined with great labour, or rather with great pleasure: Here the two famous consular roads cross each other. We should expect a fort in the angle, commanding both, which is not the case. The Watling-street is lost for about half a mile, leading over a morass, only the line is faintly preserved, by a blind path over the inclosures: the Ikenield-street crosses it in this morass, not the least traces of which remain. But, by a strict attention, I could point out their junction to a few yards.

Six furlongs west of this junction, and one hundred yards north of the Watling-street, in a close, now about three acres, are the remains of the Roman fortress. This building, of strength and terror, is reduced to one piece of thick wall, visibly of Roman workmanship, from whence the place derives its modern name.

Can you, says I to a senior peasant, for I love to appeal to old age, tell the origin of that building?

"No; but we suppose it has been a church. The ruins were much larger in my memory; but they were lately destroyed, to bring the land into that improved state of cultivation in which you see it."--And so you reduced a fortress in four years, which the Britons never could in four hundred. For a trifling profit, you eraze the work of the ancients, and prevent the wonder of the moderns.--Are you apprised of any old walls under the surface?

"Yes; the close is full of them: I have broke three ploughs in one day; no tool will stand against them. It has been more expensive to bring the land into its present condition, than the freehold is worth." Why, you seem more willing to destroy than your tools; and more able than time. The works which were the admiration of ages, you bury under ground. What the traveller comes many miles to see, you assiduously hide.

What could be the meaning that the Romans erected their station on the declivity of this hill, when the summit, two hundred yards distant, is much more eligible; are there no foundations upon it? "None."

The commandry is preferable: the Watling-street runs by it, and it is nearer the Ikenield-street. Pray, are you acquainted with another Roman road which crosses it? "No."

Do you know any close about the village, where a narrow bed of gravel, which runs a considerable length, has impeded the plough?

"Yes; there is a place, half a mile distant, where, when a child, I drove the plough; we penetrated a land of gravel, and my companion's grandfather told us, it had been an old road."--That is the place I want, lead me to it. Being already master of both ends of the road, like a broken line, with the center worn out, the gravel bed enabled me to recover it.

The next station upon the Ikenield-street is Birmingham (Bremenium) I have examined this country with care; but find no vestiges of a station: nor shall we wonder; dissolution is the preserver of antiquity, nothing of which reigns here; the most likely place is Wor-ston (Wall-stone) which a younger brother of Birmingham might afterwards convert into the fashionable moat of the times, and erect a castle. The next station is Alcester (Alauna) all which are nearly at equal distances.

In forming these grand roads, a strait direction seems to have been their leading maxim. Though curiosity has lead me to travel many hundred miles upon their roads, with the eye of an enquirer, I cannot recollect one instance, where they ever broke the line to avoid a hill, a swamp, a rock, or a river.

They were well acquainted with the propriety of an old English adage, *Once well done is twice done*; an idea new cloathed by Lord Chesterfield, *If a a thing be worth doing at all, it is worth doing well*.

An History of Birmingham (1783)

For their roads were so durably constructed, that, had they been appropriated only to the use intended, they might have withstood the efforts of time, and bid fair for eternity.--Why is this useful art so lost among the moderns?

When time and intercourse had so far united the Romans and the Britons, that they approached nearly to one people, the Romans formed, or rather *improved*, many of the smaller roads; placed stones of intelligence upon them; hence, London Stone, Stony Stratford (the stone at the Street-ford) Atherstone, stone (hither, near, or first stone from Witherly-bridge, a Roman camp) and fixed their stations in the places to which these roads tended.

The great roads, as observed before, were chiefly appropriated for military purposes, and instituted in the beginning of their government; but the smaller were of later date, and designed for common use. As these came more in practice, there was less occasion for the military; which, not leading to their towns, were, in process of time, nearly laid aside.

Antonine, and his numerous train of commentators, have not bestowed that attention on the roads they deserve: a curious acquaintance with the roads of a country, brings us acquainted with the manners of the people: in one, like a mirror, is exactly represented the other. Their state, like a master key, unlocks many apartments.

The authors I have seen are *all in the wrong*; and as my researches are confined, it is a mortification, I am not able to set them right. They have confounded the two classes together, which were very distinct in chronology, the manner of making, and their use. If an author treats of one old road, he supposes himself bound to treat of all in the kingdom, a task no man can execute: by undertaking much, we do nothing well; the journey of an antiquarian mould never be rapid. If fortune offers a small discovery, let him think, and compare. Neither will they ever be set right, but continue to build a mouldering fabric, with untempered mortar, till a number of intelligent residents, by local enquiries can produce solid materials for a lasting monument.

The Romans properly termed their ways streets, a name retained by many of them to this day; one of the smaller roads, issuing from London, penetrates through Stratford upon Avon (Street-ford) Monks-path-street, and Shirley-street, to Birmingham, which proves it of great antiquity, and the Ikenield-street running by it, proves it of greater. We may from hence safely conclude, Birmingham was a place of note in the time of Caesar, because she merited legislative regard in forming their roads; which will send us far back among the Britons, to find her first existence.

Though we are certain the Ikenield-street passes about a mile in length through this parish, as described above; yet, as there are no Roman traces to be seen, I must take the curious traveller to that vast waste, called Sutton-Coldfield, about four miles distant, where he will, in the same road, find the footsteps of those great mailers of the world, marked in lasting characters.

He will plainly see its straight line pass over the Ridgeway, through Sutton Park, leaving the West hedge about 200 yards to the left; through the remainder of the Coldfield, till lost in cultivation.

This track is more than three miles in length, and is no where else visible in these parts. I must apprize him that its highest beauty is only discovered by an horizontal sun in the winter months.

I first saw it in 1762, relieved by the transverse rays, in a clear evening in November; I had a perfect view upon the Ridgeway, near King's-standing of this delightful scene: Had I been attacked by the chill blasts of winter, upon this bleak mountain, the sensation would have been lost in the transport. The eye, at one view, takes in more than two miles. Struck with astonishment, I thought it the grandest sight I had ever beheld; and was amazed, so noble a monument of antiquity should be so little regarded.

The poets have long contended for the line of beauty--they may find it here. I was fixed as by enchantment till the sun dropt, my prospect with it, and I left the place with regret.

If the industrious traveller chooses to wade up to the middle in gorse, as I did, he may find a roughish journey along this famous military way.

Perhaps this is the only road in which money is of no use to the traveller; for upon this barren wild he can neither spend it, nor give it away.

He will perceive the Coldfield to be one vast bed of gravel, covered with a moderate depth of soil of eight or ten inches: During this journey of three miles, he will observe all the way, on each side, a number of pits, perhaps more than a thousand, out of which the Romans procured the gravel to form the road; none of them many yards from it. This great number of pits, tends to prove two points--That the country was full of timber, which they not choosing to fall, procured the gravel in the interstices; for the road is composed of nothing else--And, that a great number of people were employed in its formation: They would also, with the trees properly disposed, which the Romans must inevitably cut to procure a passage, form a barrier to the road.

This noble production was designed by a master, is every where straight, and executed with labour and judgement.

Here he perceives the date of his own conquest, and of his civilization. Thus the Romans humbled a ferocious people.

If he chooses to measure it he will find it exactly sixty feet wide, divided into three lands, resembling those in a ploughed field. The centre land thirty-six feet, and raised from one to three, according to the nature of the ground. The side lands, twelve each, and rising seldom more than one foot.

This centre land no doubt was appropriated for the march of the troops, and the small one, on each side, for the out-guards, who preserved their ranks, for fear of a surprize from the vigilant and angry Britons.

The Romans held these roads in great esteem, and were severe in their laws for their preservation.

This famous road is visible all the way, but in some parts greatly hurt, and in others, compleat as in the first day the Romans made it. Perhaps the inquisitive traveller may find here, the only monument in the whole island left us by the Romans, that *time* hath not injured.

The philosophical traveller may make some curious observations in the line of agriculture, yet in its infancy.

The only growth upon this wild, is gorse and ling: The vegetation upon the road and the adjacent lands, seem equal: The pits are all covered with a tolerable turf.

As this road has been made about 1720 years, and, as at the time of making, both that and the pits must have been surfaces of neat gravel; he will be led to examine, what degree of soil they have acquired in that long course of years, and by what means?

He well knows, that the surface of the earth is very far from being a fixed body: That there is a continual motion in every part, stone excepted: That the operations of the sun, the air, the frost, the dews, the winds, and the rain, produce a constant agitation, which changes the particles and the pores, tends to promote vegetation, and to increase the soil to a certain depth.

This progress is too minute for the human eye, but the effects are visible. The powers above mentioned operate nearly as yeast in a lump of dough, that enlivens the whole. Nature seems to wish that the foot would leave the path, that she may cover it with grass. He will find this vegetative power so strong, that it even attends the small detached parts of the soil where-ever they go, provided they are within reach of air and moisture: He will not only observe it in the small pots, appropriated for garden use, but on the tops of houses, remote from any road, where the wind has carried any small dust. He will also observe it in cracks of the rocks; but in an amazing degree in the thick walls of ruined castles, where, by a long course of time, the decayed materials are converted into a kind of soil, and so well covered with grass, that if one of our old castle builders could return to his possessions, he might mow his house as well as his field, and procure a tolerable crop from both.

In those pits, upon an eminence, the soil will be found deep enough for any mode of husbandry. In those of the vallies, which take in the small drain of the adjacent parts, it is much deeper. That upon the road, which rather gives than receives any addition from drain, the average depth is about four inches.

The soil is not only increased by the causes above, but also by the constant decays of the growth upon it. The present vegetable generation falling to decay, adds to the soil, and also, assists the next generation, which in a short time follows the same course.

The author of the History of Sutton says, "The poor inhabitants are supplied with fuel from a magazine of peat, near the Roman road, composed of thousands of fir trees cut down by the Romans, to enable them to pass over a morass. The bodies of the trees are sometimes dug up found, with the marks of the axe upon them."

Are we then to suppose, by this curious historical anecdote, that the inhabitants of Sutton have run away with this celebrated piece of antiquity? That the cart, instead of rolling *over* the military way, has rolled *under* it, and that they have boiled the pot with the Roman road?

Upon inquiry, they seemed more inclined to credit the fact, than able to prove it; but I can find no such morass, neither is the road any where broken up. Perhaps it would be as difficult to find the trees, as the axe that cut them: Besides, the fir is not a native of Britain, but of Russia; and I believe our forefathers, the Britons, were not complete masters of the art of transplanting. The park of Sutton was probably a bed of oaks, the natural weed of the country, long before Moses figured in history.

Whilst the political traveller is contemplating this extraordinary production of antiquity, of art, and of labour, his thoughts will naturally recur to the authors of it.

He will find them proficients in science, in ambition, in taste: They added dominion to conquest, 'till their original territory became too narrow a basis to support the vast fabric acquired by the success of their arms: The monstrous bulk fell to destruction by its own weight.--Man was not made for universality; if he grasps at little, he may retain it; if at much, he may lose all.

The confusion, natural on such occasions, produced anarchy: At that moment, the military stept into the government, and the people became slaves.

Upon the ruins of this brave race, the Bishop of Rome founded an ecclesiastical jurisdiction. His power increasing with his votaries, he found means to link all christendom to the triple crown, and acquired an unaccountable ascendency over the human mind: The princes of Europe were harnessed, like so many coach horses. The pontiff directed the bridle. He sometimes used the whip, and sometimes the curse. The thunder of his throne rattled through the world with astonishing effect, 'till that most useful discovery, the art of printing, in the fifteenth century, dissolved the charm, and set the oppressed cattle at liberty; who began to kick their driver. Henry the Eighth of England, was the first unruly animal in the papal team, and the sagacious Cranmer assisted in breaking the shackles.

We have, in our day, seen an order of priesthood in the church of Rome, annihilated by the consent of the European princes, which the Pope beheld in silence.

"There is an ultimate point of exaltation, and reduction, beyond which human affairs cannot proceed." Rome, seems to have experienced both, for she is at this day one of the most contemptible states in the scale of empire.

This will of course lead the traveller's thoughts towards Britain, where he will find her sons by nature inclined to a love of arms, of liberty, and of commerce. These are the strong outlines of national character, the interior parts of which are finished with the softer touches of humanity, of science, and of luxury. He will also find, that there is a natural boundary to every country, beyond which it is dangerous to add dominion. That the boundary of Britain is the sea: That her external strength is her navy, which protects her frontiers, and her commerce: That her internal is unanimity: That when her strength is united within herself, she is invincible, and the balance of Europe will be fixed in her hand, which she ought never to let go.

But if she accumulates territory, though she may profit at first, she weakens her power by dividing it; for the more she fends abroad, the less will remain at home; and, instead of giving law to the tyrant, she may be obliged to receive law from him.

That, by a multiplicity of additions, her little isles will be lost in the great map of dominion.

That, if she attempts to draw that vast and growing empire, America, she may herself be drawn to destruction; for, by every law of attraction, the greater draws the less--The mouse was never meant to direct the ox. That the military and the ecclesiastical powers are necessary in their places, that is, subordinate to the civil.

But my companion will remember that Birmingham is our historical mark, therefore we must retreat to that happy abode of the smiling arts. If he has no taste for antiquity, I have detained him too long upon this hungry, though delightful spot. If he has, he will leave the enchanted ground with reluctance; will often turn his head to repeat the view, 'till the prospect is totally lost.

LORDS OF THE MANOR.

By the united voice of our historians, it appears, that as the Saxons conquered province after province, which was effected in about one hundred and thirty years, the unfortunate Britons retreated into Wales: But we are not to suppose that all the inhabitants ran away, and left a desolate region to the victor; this would have been of little more value to the conqueror, than the possession of Sutton Coldfield or Bromsgrove Lickey. The mechanic and the peasant were left, which are by far the greatest number; they are also the riches of a country; stamp a value upon property, and it becomes current. As they have nothing to lose, so they have nothing to fear; for let who will be master, they must be drudges: Their safety consists in their servitude; the victor is ever conscious of their utility, therefore their protection is certain.

But the danger lies with the man of substance, and the greater that substance, the greater his anxiety to preserve it, and the more danger to himself if conquered: These were the people who retreated into Wales. Neither must we consider the wealth of that day to consist of bags of cash, bills of exchange, India bonds, bank stock, etc. no such thing existed. Property lay in the land, and the herds that fed upon it. And here I must congratulate our Welch neighbours, who are most certainly descended from gentlemen; and I make no doubt but the Cambrian reader will readily unite in the same sentiment.

The Saxons, as conquerors, were too proud to follow the modes of the conquered, therefore they introduced government, laws, language, customs and habits of their own. Hence we date the division of the kingdom into manors.

Human nature is nearly the same in all ages. Where value is marked upon property or power, it will find its votaries: Whoever was the most deserving, or rather could make the most interest, procured land sufficient for an Elderman, now Earl; the next class, a Manor; and the inferior, who had borne the heat and burthen of the day--nothing.

I must now introduce an expression which I promised not to forget.--In the course of a trial between William de Birmingham, and the inhabitants of Bromsgrove and King's-norton, in 1309, concerning the right of tollage; it appeared, That the ANCESTORS of the said William had a market here before the Norman conquest. This proves, that the family of Birmingham were of Saxon race, and Lords of the Manor prior to that period.

Mercia was not only the largest, but also the last of the seven conquered kingdoms--It was bounded on the North by the Humber, on the West by the Severn, on the South by the Thames, and on the East by the German ocean. Birmingham lies nearly in the centre. Cridda, a Saxon, came over with a body of troops, and reduced it in 582; therefore, as no after revolution happened that could cause Birmingham to change its owner, and as land was not in a very saleable state at that time, there is the greatest reason to suppose the founder of the house of Birmingham Came over with Cridda, as an officer in his army, and procured this little flourishing dominion as a reward for his service.

The succeeding generations of this illustrious family are too remote for historical penetration, 'till the reign of Edward the Confessor, the last of the Saxon Kings, when we find, in 1050,

---

ULUUINE, (since ALWYNE, now ALLEN,)

master of this improving spot.

RICHARD,

1066,

seems to have succeeded him, and to have lived in that unfortunate period for property, the conquest.

The time was now arrived when this ancient family, with the rest of the English gentry, who had lived under the benign climate of Saxon government, and in the affluence of fortune, must quit the happy regions of hospitality, and enter the gloomy precincts of penury--From givers, they were to become beggars.

The whole conduct of William seems to have carried the strongest marks of conquest. Many of the English lost their lives, some their liberty, and nearly all their estates. The whole land in the kingdom was insufficient to satisfy the hungry Normans.

Perhaps William took the wisest method to secure the conquered country that could be devised by human wisdom; he parcelled out the kingdom among his greater Barons; the whole county of Chester is said to have fallen to the share of Hugh Lupus: and these were subdivided into 62,000 Knight's-sees, which were held under the great Barons by military service. Thus the Sovereign by only signifying his pleasure to the Barons, could instantly raise an army for any purpose. We cannot produce a stronger indication of arbitrary government: But, it is happy for the world, that perfection is not found even in human wisdom; for this well laid scheme destroyed itself. Instead of making the crown absolute, as was intended, it threw the balance into the hands of the Barons, who became so many petty Sovereigns, and a scourge to the King in after ages, 'till Henry the Seventh sapped their power, and raised the third estate, the Commons, which quickly eclipsed the other two.

The English gentry suffered great distress: Their complaints rung loud in the royal ear, some of them therefore, who had been peaceable and never opposed the Normans, were suffered to enjoy their estates in dependance upon the great Barons.

This was the case with Richard, Lord of Birmingham, who held this manor by knight's-service of William Fitz-Auscoulf, Lord of Dudley castle, and perhaps all the land between the two places.

Thus Birmingham, now rising towards the meridian of opulence, was a dependant upon Dudley castle, now in ruins; and thus an honourable family, who had enjoyed a valuable freehold, perhaps near 500 years, were obliged to pay rent, homage, suit and service, attend the Lord's court at Dudley every three weeks, be called into the field at pleasure, and after all, possess a precarious tenure in villainage.

The blood of the ancient English was not only tainted with the breath of that destructive age, but their lands also. The powerful blast destroyed their ancient freehold tenures, reducing them into wretched copyholds: and to the disgrace of succeeding ages, many of them retain this mark of Norman slavery to the present day. How defective are those laws, which give one man power over another in neutral cases? That tend to promote quarrels, prevent cultivation, and which cannot draw the line between property and property?

Though a spirit of bravery is certainly a part of the British character, yet there are two or three periods in English history, when this noble flame was totally extinguished. Every degree of resolution seems to have been cut off at the battle of Hastings. The English acted contrary to their usual manner:--Danger had often made them desperate, but now it made them humble. This conquest is one of the most extraordinary held forth in history; the flower of nobility was wholly nipped off; the spirit of the English depressed, and having no head to direct, or hand to cultivate the courage of the people and lead it into action, it dwindled at the root, was trampled under the foot of tyranny, and, according to *Smollet*, several generations elapsed before any one of the old English stock blossomed into peerage.

It is curious to contemplate the revolution of things--Though the conquering Romans flood first in the annals of same at the beginning of the Christian era, yet they were a whole century in carrying their illustrious arms over the island, occupied only by a despicable race of Britons. Though the Saxons were invited, by one false step in politics, to assist the Britons in expelling an enemy, which gave them an opportunity of becoming enemies themselves; yet it was 130 years before they could complete their conquest. And though the industrious Dane poured incessant numbers of people into Britain, yet it cost them 200 years, and 150,000 men before they reduced it. But William, at one blow, finished the dreadful work, shackled her sons to his throne, and governed them with a sceptre of iron. Normandy, a petty dukedom, very little larger than Yorkshire, conquered a mighty nation in one day. England seems to have been taken by storm, and her liberties put to the sword: Nor did the miseries of this ill-fated kingdom end here, for the continental dominions, which William annexed to the crown, proved a whirlpool for 400 years, which drew the blood and treasure of the nation into its vortex, 'till those dominions were fortunately lost in the reign of Mary the First.

Thus the Romans spent one century in acquiring a kingdom, which they governed for four. The Saxons spent 130 years, and ruled for 459. The Danes spent 200 and reigned for 25--But the Norman spent one day only, for a reign of 700 years: They continue to reign still.

It is easy to point out some families of Norman race, who yet enjoy the estates won by their ancestors at the battle of Hastings.

WILLIAM,

1130,

Like his unfortunate father, was in a state of vassalage. The male line of the Fitz-Ausculfs soon became extinct, and Gervase Paganell marrying the heiress, became Baron of Dudley-castle.

PETER DE BIRMINGHAM,

1154.

It is common in every class of life, for the inferior to imitate the superior: If the real lady claims a head-dress sixteen inches high, that of the imaginary lady will immediately begin to thrive. The family, or surname, entered with William the First, and was soon the reigning taste of the day: A person was thought of no consequence without a surname, and even the depressed English, crept into the fashion, in imitation of their masters. I have already mentioned the Earl of Warwick, father of a numerous race now in Birmingham; whose name before the conquest was simply Turchill, but after, Turchill de Arden, (Matter of the Woods) from his own estate.

Thus the family of whom I speak, chose to dignify themselves with the name of *de Birmingham*.

Peter wisely consulted his own interest, kept fair with Paganall his Lord, and obtained from him, in 1166, nine Knight's-fees, which he held by military service.

A Knight's-fee, though uncommon now, was a word well understood 600 years ago. It did not mean, as some have imagined, fifteen pounds per annum, nor any determinate sum; but as much land as would support a gentleman. This Peter was fewer to Paganall, (waited at his table) though a man of great property.

The splendor in which the great Barons of that age lived, was little inferior to royalty.

The party distinctions also of Saxon and Norman, in the twelfth century, began to die away, as the people became united by interest or marriage, like that of Whig and Tory, in the eighteenth. And perhaps there is not at present a native that does not carry in his veins the blood of the four nations that were grafted upon the Britons.

Peter himself lived in affluence at his castle, then near Birmingham, now the Moat, of which in the next section. He also obtained from Henry the Second, as well as from Paganall the Lord paramount, several valuable privileges for his favourite inheritance of Birmingham. He bore for his arms, *azure, a bend lozenge*, of five points, *or*; the coat of his ancestors.

WILLIAM DE BIRMINGHAM,

1216.

At the reduction of Ireland, in the reign of Henry the Second, a branch of this family, and perhaps uncle to William, was very instrumental under Richard Strongbow, Earl of Pembroke, in accomplishing that great end; for which he was rewarded with a large estate, and the title of Earl of Lowth, both which continue in his family. Perhaps they are the only remains of this honorable house.

WILLIAM DE BIRMINGHAM,

1246.

By this time, the male line of the Paganalls was worn out, and Roger de Someri marrying the heiress, became Baron of Dudley, with all its dependencies; but Someri and Birmingham did not keep peace, as their fathers had done. William, being very rich, forgot to ride to Dudley every three weeks, to perform suit and service at Someri's court.

Whereupon a contest commenced to enforce the performance. But, in 1262, it was agreed between the contending parties-- That William should attend the Lord's court only twice a year, Easter and Michaelmas, and at such other times, as the Lord chose to command by special summons. This William, having married the daughter of Thomas de Astley, a man of great eminence, and both joining with the Barons under Simon Mountfort, Earl of Leicester, against Henry the Third, William fell, in 1265, at the battle of Evesham; and as the loser is ever the rebel, the Barons were prescribed, and their estates confiscated.

The manor of Birmingham, therefore, valued at forty pounds per annum, was seized by the King, and given to his favorite, Roger de Clifford.

WILLIAM DE BIRMINGHAM,

1265.

By a law called the statute of Kenilworth, every man who had forfeited his estate to the crown, by having taken up arms, had liberty to redeem his lands, by a certain fine: William therefore paid that fine, and recovered the inheritance of his family. He also, in 1283 strengthened his title by a charter from Edward the First, and likewise to the other manors he possessed, such as Stockton, in the County of Worcester; Shetford, in Oxfordshire; Maidencoat, in Berkshire; Hoggeston, in the county of Bucks; and Christleton, in Cheshire.

In 1285, Edward brought his writ of quo warranto, whereby every holder of land was obliged to show by what title he held it. The consequence would have been dreadful to a Prince of less prudence than Edward. Some showed great unwillingness; for a dormant title will not always bear examination--But William producing divers charters, clearly proved his right to every manorial privilege, such as market, toll, tem, sack, sok, insangenthief, weyfs, gallows, court-leet, and pillory, with a right to fix the standard for bread and beer; all which were allowed.

William, Lord of Birmingham, being a military tenant, was obliged to attend the King into Gascoigne, 1297, where he lost his liberty at the siege of Bellgard, and was carried prisoner in triumph to Paris.

WILLIAM DE BIRMINGHAM,

1306.

This is the man who tried the right of tollage with the people of Bromsgrove and King's norton.

WILLIAM DE BIRMINGHAM,

LORD BIRMINGHAM.
1316.

Was knighted in 1325; well affected to Edward the Second, for whose service he raised four hundred foot. Time seems to have put a period to the family of Someri, Lords of Dudley, as well as to those of their predecessors, the Paganalls, and the Fitz-Ausculfs.

In 1327, the first of Edward the Third, Sir William was summoned to Parliament, by the title of William Lord Birmingham, but not after.

It was not the fashion of that day to fill the House of Peers by patent. The greater Barons held a local title from their Baronies; the possessor of one of these, claimed a seat among the Lords.

I think, they are now all extinct, except Arundel, the property of the Norfolk family, and whoever is proprietor of Arundel castle, is Earl thereof by ancient prescription.

The lesser Barons were called up to the House by writ, which did not confer an hereditary title. Of this class was the Lord of Birmingham.

Hugh Spencer, the favourite of the weak Edward the Second, had procured the custody of Dudley-castle, with all its appendages, for his friend William, Lord Birmingham.

Thus the family who had travelled from Birmingham to Dudley every three weeks, to perform humble suit at the Lord's court, held that very court by royal appointment, to receive the fealty of others.

By the patent which constituted William keeper of Dudley-castle, he was obliged to account for the annual profits arising from that vast estate into the King's exchequer. When, therefore, in 1334, he delivered in his accounts, the Barons refused to admit them, because the money was defective. But he had interest enough with the crown to cause a mandamus to be issued, commanding the Barons to admit them.

SIR FOUK DE BIRMINGHAM,

1340.

This man advanced to Sir Baldwin Freville, Lord of Tamworth, forty eight marks, upon mortgage of five mills. The ancient coat of the *bend lozenge*, was now changed for the *partie per pale, indented, or, and gules*.

In 1352, and 1362 he was returned a member for the county of Warwick; also, in three or four succeeding Parliaments.

SIR JOHN DE BIRMINGHAM,

1376.

Served the office of Sheriff for the county of Warwick, in 1379, and was successively returned to serve in Parliament for the counties of Warwick, Bedford, and Buckingham. He married the daughter of William de la Planch, by whom he had no issue. She afterwards married the Lord Clinton, retained the manor of Birmingham as her dower, and lived to the year 1424.

It does not appear in this illustrious family, that the regular line of descent, from father to son, was ever broken, from the time of the Saxons, 'till 1390. This Sir John left a brother, Sir Thomas de Birmingham, heir at law, who enjoyed the bulk of his brother's fortune; but was not to possess the manor of Birmingham 'till the widow's death, which not happening 'till after his own, he never enjoyed it.

The Lord Clinton and his Lady seem to have occupied the Manor-house; and Sir Thomas, unwilling to quit the place of his affections and of his nativity, erected a castle for himself at Worstone, near the Sand-pits, joining the Ikenield-street; street; where, though the building is totally gone, the vestiges of its liquid security are yet complete. This Sir Thomas enjoyed several public offices, and figured in the style of his ancestors. He left a daughter, who married Thomas de la Roche, and from this marriage sprang two daughters; the eldest of which married Edmund, Lord Ferrers of Chartley, who, at the decease of Sir John's widow, inherited the manor, and occupied the Manor house. There yet stands a building on the North-east side of the Moat, erected by this Lord Ferrers, with his arms in the timbers of the ceiling, and the crest, a horse-shoe.

I take this house to be the oldest in Birmingham, though it hath not that appearance; having stood about 350 years.

By an entail of the manor upon the male line, the Lady Ferrers seems to have quitted her title in favor of a second cousin, a descendant of William de Birmingham, brother to Sir Fouk.

WILLIAM DE BIRMINGHAM,

1430.

In the 19th of Henry the Sixth, 1441, is said to have held his manor of Birmingham, of Sir John Sutton, Lord of Dudley, by military service; but instead of paying homage, fealty, escuage, &c. as his ancestors had done, which was very troublesome to the tenant, and brought only empty honour to the Lord: and, as sometimes the Lord's necessities taught him to think that money was more *Solid* than suit and service; an agreement was entered into, for money instead of homage, between the Lord and the tenant--Such agreements now became common. Thus land became a kind of bastard freehold:--The tenant held a certainty, while he conformed to the agreement; or, in other words, the custom of the manor--And the Lord still possessed a material control. He died in 1479, leaving a son,

SIR WILLIAM BIRMINGHAM,

1479,

Aged thirty at the decease of his father. He married Isabella, heiress of William Hilton, by whom he had a son, William, who died before his father, June 7, 1500, leaving a son,

---

EDWARD BIRMINGHAM,

1500,

Born in 1497, and succeeded his grandfather at the age of three. During his minority, Henry the Seventh, 1502, granted the wardship to Edward, Lord Dudley.

The family estate then consisted of the manors of Birmingham, Over Warton, Nether Warton, Mock Tew, Little Tew, and Shutford in the county of Oxford, Hoggeston in Bucks, and Billesley in the county of Worcester. Edward afterwards married Elizabeth, widow of William Ludford, of Annesley, by whom he had one daughter, who married a person of the name of Atkinson.

But after the peaceable possession of a valuable estate, for thirty seven years; the time was now arrived, when the mounds of justice must be broken down by the weight of power, a whole deluge of destruction enter, and overwhelm an ancient and illustrious family, in the person of an innocent man. The world would view the diabolical transaction with amazement, none daring to lend assistance to the unfortunate; not considering, that property should ever be under the protection of law; and, what was Edward's case to-day, might be that of any other man to-morrow. But the oppressor kept fair with the crown, and the crown held a rod of iron over the people.--Suffer me to tell the mournful tale from Dugdale's Antiquities of Warwickshire.

1537,

John Dudley, Duke of Northumberland, a man of great wealth, unbounded ambition, and one of the basest characters of the age, was possessor of Dudley-castle, and the fine estate belonging to it:--He wished to add Birmingham to his vast domain. Edward Birmingham therefore was privately founded, respecting the disposal of his manor; but as money was not wanted, and as the place had been the honor and the residence of his family for many centuries, it was out of the reach of purchase.

Northumberland was so charmed with its beauty, he was determined to possess it; and perhaps the manner in which he accomplished his design, cannot be paralleled in the annals of infamy.

He procured two or three rascals of his own temper, and rather of mean appearance, to avoid suspicion, to take up their quarters for a night or two in Birmingham, and gain secret intelligence when Edward Birmingham should ride out, and what road: This done, one of the rascals was to keep before the others, but all took care that Edward should easily overtake them. Upon his arrival at the first class, the villains joined him, entered into chat, and all moved soberly together 'till they reached the first man; when, on a sudden, the strangers with Edward drew their pistols and robbed their brother villain, who no doubt lost a considerable sum after a decent resistance. Edward was easily known, apprehended, and committed as one of the robbers; the others were not to be found.

Edward immediately saw himself on the verge of destruction. He could only *alledge*, but not *prove* his innocence: All the proof the case could admit of, was against him.

Northumberland (then only Lord L'Isle) hitherto had succeeded to his wish; nor was Edward long in suspence--Private hints were given him, that the only way to save his life, was to make Northumberland his friend; and this probably might be done, by resigning to him his manor of Birmingham; with which the unfortunate Edward reluctantly complied.

Northumberland thinking a common conveyance insufficient, caused Edward to yield his estate into the hands of the King, and had interest enough in that age of injustice to procure a ratification from a weak Parliament, by which means he endeavoured to throw the odium off his own character, and fix it upon theirs, and also, procure to himself a safer title.

An extract from that base act is as follows:--

"Whereas Edward Byrmingham, late of Byrmingham in the countie of Warwick, Esquire, otherwise callid Edward Byrmingham, Esquire, ys and standyth lawfully indettid to our soverene Lord the Kinge, in diverse grete summes of money; and also standyth at the mercy of his Highness, for that the same Edward ys at this present convected of felony: Our seide soverene Lord the Kinge ys contentid and pleasid, that for and in recompence and satisfaction to his Grace of the seyde summes of money, to accept and take of the seyde Edward the mannour and lordship of Byrmingham, otherwise callid Byrmincham, with the appurtinances, lying and being in the countie of Warwick, and all and singuler other lands and tenements, reversions, rents, services, and hereditaments of the same Edward Byrmingham, set, lying and beying in the countie of Warwick aforesaid. Be yt therefore ordeyned and enacted, by the authoritie of this present Parliament, that our seyde soverene Lord the Kinge shall have, hold, and enjoy, to him and his heires and assignes for ever, the seyde mannour and lordship of Byrmingham, &c."

In the act there is a reservation of 40*l.* per annum, during the lives only of the said Edward and his wife.

It appears also, by an expression in the act, that Edward was brought to trial, and found guilty. Thus innocence is depressed for want of support; property is wrested for want of the protection of the law; and a vile minister, in a corrupt age, can carry an infamous point through a court of justice, the two Houses of Parliament, and complete his horrid design by the sanction of a tyrant.

The place where tradition tells us this diabolical transaction happened, is the middle of Sandy-lane, in the Sutton road; the upper part of which begins at the North east corner of Aston park wall; at the bottom, you bear to the left, for Sawford-bridge, or to the right, for Nachell's-green; about two miles from the Moat, the place of Edward's abode.

Except that branch which proceeded from this original stem, about 600 years ago, of which the Earl of Lowth is head, I know of no male descendant from this honourable stock; who, if we allow the founder to have come over with Cridda, the Saxon, in 582, must have commanded this little Sovereignty 955 years.

I met with a person sometime ago of the name of Birmingham, and was pleased with the hope of finding a member of that ancient and honorable house; but he proved so amasingly ignorant, he could not tell whether he was from the clouds, the sea, or the dunghill: instead of traceing the existence of his ancestors, even so high as his father, he was scarcely conscious of his own.

As this house did not much abound with daughters, I cannot at present recollect any families among us, except that of Bracebridge, who are descended from this illustrious origin, by a female line; and Sir John Talbot Dillon, who is descended from the ancient Earls of Lowth, as he is from the De Veres, the more ancient Earls of Oxford.

Here, then, I unwillingly extinguish that long range of lights, which for many ages illuminated the house of Birmingham.

But I cannot extinguish the rascallity of the line of Northumberland. This unworthy race, proved a scourge to the world, at least during three generations. Each, in his turn, presided in the British cabinet; and each seems to have possessed the villainy of his predecessor, united with his own. The first, only *served* a throne; but the second and the third intended to *fill* one. A small degree of ambition warms the mind in pursuit of fame, through the paths of honor; while too large a portion tends to unfavorable directions, kindles to a flame, consumes the finer sensations of rectitude, and leaves a stench behind.

Edmund, the father of this John, was the voracious leech, with Empson, who sucked the vitals of the people, to feed the avarice of Henry the Seventh.

It is singular that Henry, the most sagacious prince since the conquest, loaded him with honours for filling the royal coffers with wealth, which the penurious monarch durst never enjoy: but his successor, Henry the Eighth, enjoyed the pleasure of consuming that wealth, and *executed* the father for collecting it! How much are our best laid schemes defective? How little does expectation and event coincide? It is no disgrace to a man that he died on the scaffold; the question is--What brought him there? Some of the most inoffensive, and others the most exalted characters of the age in which they lived, have been cut off by the axe, as Edward Plantagenet, Earl of Warwick, for being the last male heir of the Anjouvin Kings; John Fisher, Bishop of Rochester, Sir Thomas Moore, Sir Walter Raleigh, Algernon Sidney, William Lord Russell, &c. whose blood ornamented the scaffold on which they fell.

The son of this man, Robert Dudley, Earl of Leicester, favorite of Queen Elizabeth, is held up by our historians as a masterpiece of dissimulation, pride, and cruelty. He married three wives, all which he is charged with sending to the grave by untimely deaths; one of them, to open a passage to the Queen's bed, to which he aspired. It is surprising, that he should deceive the penetrating eye of Elizabeth: but I am much inclined to think she *knew him* better than the world; and they knew him rather to well. He ruined many of the English gentry, particularly the ancient family of Arden, of Park-hall, in this neighbourhood: he afterwards ruined his own family by disinheriting a son, more worthy than himself.--If he did not fall by the executioner, it is no proof that he did not deserve it.--We now behold

JOHN, DUKE OF NORTHUMBERLAND,

1537,

Lord of the manor of Birmingham; a man, who of all others the least deserved that honor; or rather, deserved the axe for being so.

Some have asserted, "That property acquired by dishonesty cannot prosper." But I shall leave the philosopher and the enthusiast to settle that important point, while I go on to observe, That that the lordship of Birmingham did not prosper with the Duke. Though he had, in some degree, the powers of government in his hands, he had also the clamours of the people in his ears. What were his inward feelings, is uncertain at this distance--Fear seems to have prevented him from acknowledging Birmingham for his property. Though he exercised every act of ownership, yet he suffered the fee-simple to rest in the crown, 'till nine years had elapsed, and those clamours subsided, before he ventured to accept the grant, in 1546.

As the execution of this grant was one of the last acts of Henry's life, we should be apt to suspect the Duke carried it in his pocket ready for signing, but deferred the matter as long as he could with safety, that distance of time might annihilate reflection; and that the King's death, which happened a few weeks after, might draw the attention of the world too much, by the importance of the event, to regard the Duke's conduct.

The next six years, which carries us through the reign of Edward the Sixth, is replete with the intrigues of this illustrious knave. He sought connections with the principal families: He sought honours for his own: He procured a match between his son, the Lord Guildford Dudley, and the Lady Jane Gray, daughter of the Duke of Suffolk, and a descendant from Henry the Seventh, with intent of fixing the crown in his family, but failing in the attempt, he brought ruin upon the Suffolk family, and himself to the block, in the first of Queen Mary, 1553.

Though a man be guilty of many atrocious acts that deserve death, yet in the hour of distress humanity demands the tear of compassion; but the case was otherwise at the execution of John, Duke of Northumberland, for a woman near the scaffold held forth a bloody handkerchief and exclaimed, "Behold the blood of the Duke of Somerset, shed by your means, and which cries for vengeance against you."

Thus Northumberland kept a short and rough possession of glory; thus he fell unlamented; and thus the manor of Birmingham reverted to the crown a second time, the Duke himself having first taught it the way.

Birmingham continued two years in the crown, 'till the third of Queen Mary, when she granted it to

THOMAS MARROW,

1555,

Whose family, for many descents, resided at Berkeswell, in this county.

In the possession of the High Bailiff is a bushel measure, cast in brass, of some value; round which in relief is, SAMUEL MARROW, LORD OF THE MANOR OF BIRMINGHAM, 1664.

The Lordship continued in this family about 191 years, 'till the male line failing, it became the joint property of four coheirs--Ann, married to Sir Arthur Kaye; Mary, the wife of John Knightley, Esq; Ursulla, the wife of Sir Robert Wilmot; and Arabella, unmarried; who, in about 1730, disposed of the private estate in the manor, amounting to about 400*l.* per annum, to Thomas Sherlock, Bishop of London, as before observed, and the manor itself to

THOMAS ARCHER, ESQ.

for 1,700*l.* in 1746,

Of an ancient family, who have resided at Umberslade in this county more than 600 years--from him it descended to

---

ANDREW, LORD ARCHER,

And is now enjoyed by his relict,

SARAH, LADY ARCHER,

1781,

Possessing no more in the parish than the royalty; as it does not appear that the subsequent Lords, after the extinction of the house of Birmingham, were resident upon the manor, I omit particulars.

Let me remark, this place yet gives title to the present Lord Viscount Dudley and Ward, as descended, by the female line, from the great Norman Barons, the Fitz-Ausculfs, the Paganalls, the Somerys, the Suttons, and the Dudleys, successively Lords paramount, whose original power is reduced to a name.

MANOR HOUSE.

(The Moat.)

The natural temper of the human mind, like that of the brute, is given to plunder: This temper is very apt to break forth into action. In all societies of men, therefore, restraints have been discovered, under the name of laws, attended with punishment, to deter people from infringing each others property. Every thing that a man can possess, falls under the denomination of property; whether it be life, liberty, wealth or character.

The less perfect these laws are, the less a people are removed from the rude state of nature, and the more necessity there is for a man to be constantly in a state of defence, that he may be able to repel any force that shall rise up against him.

It is easy to discover, by the laws of a country, how far the people are advanced in civilization. If the laws are defective, or the magistrate too weak to execute them, it is dangerous for a man to possess property.

But when a nation is pretty far advanced in social existence; when the laws agree with reason, and are executed with firmness, a man need not trouble himself concerning the protection of his property--his country will protect it for him.

The laws of England have, for many ages, been gradually refining; and are capable of that protection which violence never was.

But if we penetrate back into the recesses of time, we shall find the laws inadequate, the manners savage, force occupy the place of justice, and property unprotected. In those barbarous ages, therefore, men sought security by intrenching themselves from a world they could not trust. This was done by opening a large ditch round their habitation, which they filled with water, and which was only approachable by a draw-bridge. This, in some degree, supplied the defect of the law, and the want of power in the magistrate. It also, during the iron reign of priesthood, furnished that table in lent, which it guarded all the year.

The Britons had a very slender knowledge of fortification. The camps they left us, are chiefly upon eminences, girt by a shallow ditch, bordered with stone, earth, or timber, but never with water. The moat, therefore, was introduced by the Romans; their camps are often in marshes; some wholly, and some in part surrounded by water.

These liquid barriers were begun in England early in the christian æra, they were in the zenith of their glory at the barons wars, in the reign of king John, and continued to be the mode of fortification till the introduction of guns, in the reign of Edward the fourth, which shook their foundation; and the civil wars of Charles the first totally annihilated their use, after an existence of twelve hundred years.

Perhaps few parishes, that have been the ancient habitation of a gentleman, are void of some traces of these fluid bulwarks. That of Birmingham has three; one of these, of a square form, at Warstone, erected by a younger brother of the house of Birmingham, hath already been mentioned; it is fed by a small rivulet from Rotton Park, which crosses the Dudley Road, near the Sand pits.

Another is the Parsonage house, belonging to St. Martin's, formerly situated in the road to Bromsgrove, now Smallbrook street, of a circular figure, and supplied by a neighbouring spring. If we allow this watery circle to be a proof of the great antiquity of the house, it is a much greater with regard to the antiquity of the church.

The third is what we simply denominate the Moat, and was the residence of the ancient lords of Birmingham, situated about sixty yards south of the church, and twenty west of Digbeth; this is also circular, and supplied by a small stream that crosses the road to Bromsgrove, near the first mile stone; it originally ran into the river Rea, near Vaughton's hole, dividing the parishes of Birmingham and Edgbaston all the way, but at the formation of the Moat, was diverted from its course, into which it never returned.

No certain evidence remains to inform us when this liquid work was accomplished: perhaps in the Saxon heptarchy, when there were few or no buildings south of the church. Digbeth seems to have been one of the first streets added to this important school of arts; the upper part of that street must of course have been formed first: but, that the Moat was completed prior to the erection of any buildings between that and Digbeth, is evident, because those buildings stand upon the very soil thrown out in forming the Moat.

The first certain account that we meet with of this guardian circle, is in the reign of Henry the Second, 1154, when Peter de Birmingham, then lord of the see, had a cattle here, and lived in splendor. All the succeeding Lords resided upon the same island, till their cruel expulsion by John Duke of Northumberland in 1537.

The old castle followed its lords, and is buried in the ruins of time. Upon the spot, about forty years ago, rose a house in the modern style, occupied by a manufacturer (John Francis;) in one of the out-buildings is shewn, the apartment where the ancient lords kept their court leet; another out-building which stands to the east, I have already observed, was the work of Edmund Lord Ferrers.

The ditch being filled with water, has nearly the same appearance now as perhaps a thousand years ago, but not altogether the same use. It then served to protect its master, but now, to turn a thread-mill.

PUDDING BROOK.

Near the place where the small rivulet discharges itself into the Moat, another of the same size is carried over it, called Pudding Brook, and proceeds from the town as this advances towards it, producing a curiosity seldom met with; one river running South, and the other North, for half a mile, yet only a path-road of three feet asunder; which surprised Brindley the famous engineer.

THE PRIORY.

The site of this ancient edifice is now the Square; some small remains of the old foundations are yet visible in the cellars, chiefly on the South-east. The out-buildings and pleasure-grounds perhaps occupied the whole North east side of Bull-street, then uninhabited, and only the highway to Wolverhampton; bounded on the North-west by Steelhouse-lane; on the North-east by Newton and John's-street; and on the South-east by Dale-end, which also was no other than the highway to Lichfield--The whole, about fourteen acres.

The building upon this delightful eminence, which at that time commanded the small but beautiful prospect of Bristland-fields, Rowley-hills, Oldbury, Smethewick, Handsworth, Sutton-Coldfield, Erdington, Saltley, the Garrison, and Camp-hill, and which then stood at a distance from the town, though now near its centre; was founded by the house of Birmingham, in the early reigns of the Norman Kings, and called the Hospital of Saint Thomas,--The priest being bound to pray for the souls of the founders every day, to the end of the world.

In 1285, Thomas de Madenhache, Lord of the manor of Aston, gave ten acres of land in his manor. William de Birmingham ten, which I take to be the land where the Priory stood; and Ranulph de Rakeby three acres, in Saltley: About the same time, sundry others gave houses and land in smaller quantities: William de Birmingham gave afterwards twenty-two acres more. The same active spirit seems to have operated in our ancestors, 500 years ago, that does in their descendants at this day: If a new scheme strikes the fancy, it is pursued with vigor.

The religious fervor of that day ran high: It was unfashionable to leave the world, and not remember the Priory. Donations crowded in so fast, that the prohibiting act was forgot; so that in 1311, the brotherhood were prosecuted by the crown, for appropriating lands contrary to the act of mortmain; But these interested priests, like their sagacious brethren, knew as well how to preserve as to gain property; for upon their humble petition to the throne, Edward the Second put a stop to the judicial proceedings, and granted a special pardon.

In 1351, Fouk de Birmingham, and Richard Spencer, jointly gave to the priory one hundred acres of land, part lying in Aston, and part in Birmingham, to maintain another priest, who should celebrate divine service daily at the altar of the Virgin Mary, in the church of the hospital, for the souls of William la Mercer, and his wife. The church is supposed to have stood upon the spot now No. 27, in Bull-street.

In the premises belonging to the Red Bull, No. 83, nearly opposite, have been discovered human bones, which has caused some to suppose it the place of interment for the religious, belonging to the priory, which I rather doubt.

At the dissolution of the abbies, in 1536, the King's visitors valued the annual income at the trifling sum of 8*l.* 8s. 9d.

The patronage continued chiefly in the head of the Birmingham family. Dugdale gives us a list of some of the Priors, who held dominion in this little common wealth, from 1326, 'till the total annihilation, being 210 years.

Robert Marmion,
Robert Cappe,
Thomas Edmunds,
John Frothward,
Robert Browne,
John Port,
William Priestwood,
Henry Drayton,
John Cheyne,
Henry Bradley,
Thomas Salpin,
Sir Edward Toste,
    AND
Henry Hody.

Thomas Cromwell, Earl of Essex, a man of much honour, more capacity, and yet more spirit, was the instrument with which Henry the Eighth destroyed the abbies; but Henry, like a true politician of the house of Tudor, wisely threw the blame upon the instrument, held it forth to the public in an odious light, and then sacrificed it to appease an angry people.

This destructive measure against the religious houses, originated from royal letchery, and was replete with consequence.

It opened the fountains of learning, at that day confined to the monastry, and the streams diffused themselves through various ranks of men. The revival of letters and of science made a rapid progress: It soon appeared, that the stagnate knowledge of the priest, was abundantly mixed with error; but now, running through the laity, who had no private interest to serve, it became more pure.

It removed great numbers of men, who lay as a dead weight upon the community, and they became useful members of society: When younger sons could no longer find an asylum within the gloomy walls of a convent, they sought a livelihood in trade. Commerce, therefore, was taught to crowd her sails, cross the western ocean, fill the country with riches, and change an idle spirit into that of industry.

By the destruction of religious houses, architecture sustained a temporary wound: They were by far the most magnificent and expensive buildings in the kingdoms, far surpassing those of the nobility; some of these structures are yet habitable, though the major part are gone to decay. But modern architecture hath since out-done the former splendor of the abbey, in use and elegance and sometimes with the profits arising from the abbey lands.

It also shut the door of charity against the impostor, the helpless, and the idle, who had found here their chief supply; and gave rise to one of the best laws ever invented by human wisdom that of each parish supporting its own poor.

By the annihilation of abbots, the church lost its weight in Parliament, and the vote was thrown into the hands of the temporal Lords.

It prevented, in some degree, the extinction of families; for, instead of younger branches becoming the votaries of a monastic life, they became the votaries of hymen: Hence the kingdom was enriched by population. It eased the people of a set of masters, who had for ages ruled them with a rod of iron.

The hands of superstition were also weakened, for the important sciences of astrology, miracle, and divination, supported by the cell, have been losing ground ever since.

It likewise recovered vast tracts of land out of dead hands, and gave an additional vigor to agriculture, unknown to former ages. The monk, who had only a temporary tenancy, could not give a permanant one; therefore, the lands were neglected, and the produce was small: But these lands falling into the hands of the gentry, acquired an hereditary title. It was their interest; to grant leases, for a superior rent; and it was the tenant's interest to give that rent, for the sake of security: Hence the produce of land is become one of the most advantageous branches of British commerce.

Henry, by this seisure, had more property to give away, than any King of England since William the Conqueror, and he generously gave away that which was never his own. It is curious to survey the foundation of some of the principal religions that have taken the lead among men.

Moses founded a religion upon morals and ceremonies, one half of which continues with his people to this day.

Christ founded one upon *love* and *purity*; words of the simplest import, yet we sometimes mistake their meaning.

The Bishop of Rome erected his, upon deceit and oppression; hence the treasures of knowledge were locked up, an inundation of riches and power flowed into the church, with destructive tendency.

And Henry the Eighth, built his reformation upon revenge and plunder: He deprived the *head* of the Romish see, of an unjust power, for pronouncing a just decision; and robbed the *members*, for being annexed to that head. Henry wished the world to believe, what he believed himself, that he acted from a religious principle; but his motive seems to have been *savage love*.

Had equity directed when Henry divided this vast property, he would have restored it to the descendants of those persons, whose mistaken zeal had injured their families; but his disposal of it was ludicrous--sometimes he made a free gift, at others he exchanged a better estate for a a worse, and then gave that worse to another.

I have met with a little anecdote which says, "That Henry being upon a tour in Devonshire, two men waited on him to beg certain lands in that county; while they attended in the anti-room for the royal presence, a stranger approached, and asked them a trifling question; they answered, they wished to be alone--at that moment the King entered: They fell at his feet: The stranger seeing them kneel, kneelt with them. They asked the favor intended; the King readily granted it: They bowed: The stranger bowed also. By this time, the stranger perceiving there was a valuable prize in the question, claimed his thirds; they denied his having anything to do with the matter: He answered, he had done as much as they, for they only asked and bowed, and he did the same. The dispute grew warm, and both parties agreed to appeal to the King, who answered, He took them for joint beggars, therefore had made them a joint present. They were then obliged to divide the land with the stranger, whose share amounted to 240*l*. per annum."

The land formerly used for the priory of Birmingham, is now the property of many persons. Upon that spot, whereon stood one solitary house, now stand about four hundred. Upon that ground, where about thirty persons lived upon the industry of others, about three thousand live upon their own: The place, which lay as a heavy burden upon the community, now tends to enrich it, by adding its mite to the national commerce, and the national treasury.

In 1775, I took down an old house of wood and plaister, which had stood 208 years, having been erected in 1567, thirty-one years after the dissolution of abbies. The foundation of this old house seemed to have been built chiefly with stones from the priory; perhaps more than twenty wagon loads: These appeared in a variety of forms and sizes, highly finished in the gothic taste, parts of porticos, arches, windows, ceilings, etc. some fluted, some cyphered, and otherwise ornamented, yet complete as in the first day they were left by the chizel. The greatest, part of them were destroyed by the workmen: Some others I used again in the fireplace of an under kitchen. Perhaps they are the only perfect fragments that remain of that venerable edifice, which once stood the monument of ancient piety, the ornament of the town, and the envy of the priest out of place.

JOHN A DEAN'S HOLE.

At the bottom of Digbeth, about thirty yards North of the bridge, on the left, is a water-course that takes in a small drain from Digbeth, but more from the adjacent meadows, and which divides the parishes of Aston and Birmingham, called John a Dean's Hole; from a person of that name who is said to have lost his life there, and which, I think, is the only name of antiquity among us.

The particle *de*, between the christian and surname, is of French extraction, and came over with William the First: It continued tolerably pure for about three centuries, when it in some degree assumed an English garb, in the particle *of*: The *a*, therefore is only a corruption of the latter. Hence the time of this unhappy man's misfortune may be fixed about the reign of Edward the Third.

LENCH'S TRUST.

In the reign of Henry the Eighth, William Lench, a native of this place, bequeathed his estate for the purpose of erecting alms houses, which are those at the bottom of Steelhouse-lane, for the benefit of poor widows, but chiefly for repairing the streets of Birmingham. Afterwards others granted smaller donations for the same use, but all were included under the name of Lench; and I believe did not unitedly amount, at that time, to fifteen pounds per annum.

Over this scattered inheritance was erected a trust, consisting of gentlemen in the neighborhood of Birmingham.

All human affairs tend to confusion: The hand of care is ever necessary to keep order. The gentlemen, therefore at the head of this charity, having too many modes of pleasure of their own, to pay attention to this little jurisdiction, disorder crept in apace; some of the lands were lost for want of inspection; the rents ran in arrear, and were never recovered; the streets were neglected, and the people complained.

Misconduct, particularly of a public nature, silently grows for years, and sometimes for ages, 'till it becomes too bulky for support, falls in pieces by its own weight, and out of its very destruction rises a remedy. An order, therefore, from the Court of Chancery was obtained, for vesting the property in other hands, consisting of twenty persons, all of Birmingham, who have directed this valuable estate, now 227*l*. 5s. per annum, to useful purposes. The man who can guide his own private concerns with success, stands the fairest chance of guiding those of the public.

If the former trust went widely astray, perhaps their successors have not exactly kept the line, by advancing the leases to a rack rent: It is worth considering, whether the tenant of an expiring lease, hath not in equity, a kind of reversionary right, which ought to favour him with the refusal of another term, at one third under the value, in houses, and one fourth in land; this would give stability to the title, secure the rents, and cause the lessee more chearfully to improve the premises, which in time would enhance their value, both with regard to property and esteem.

But where business is well conducted, complaint should cease; for perfection is not to be expected on this side the grave.

Exclusive of a pittance to the poor widows above, the trust have a power of distributing money to the necessitous at Christmas and Easter, which is punctually performed.

I think there is an excellent clause in the devisor's will, ordering his bailiff to pay half a crown to any two persons, who, having quarreled and entered into law, shall stop judicial proceedings, and make peace by agreement--He might have added, "And half a crown to the lawyer that will suffer them." I know the sum has been demanded, but am sorry I do *not* know that it was ever paid.

If money be reduced to one fourth its value, since the days of Lench, it follows, that four times the sum ought to be paid in ours; and perhaps ten shillings cannot be better laid out, than in the purchase of that peace, which tends to harmonise the community, and weed a brotherhood not the most amicable among us.

The members choose annually, out of their own body a steward, by the name of bailiff Lench: The present fraternity, who direct this useful charity, are

Thomas Colmore, *bailiff*.
George Davis,
Win. Walsingham, *dead*,
Michael Lakin,
Benjamin May,
Michael Lakin, *jun.*
James Bedford,
Samuel Ray,
John Ryland,
James Jackson,
Stephen Bedford, *dead*,
Joseph Tyndall,
Joseph Smith,
Robert Mason,
Joseph Webster, *dead*,
Abel Humphreys,
Thomas Lawrence,
Samuel Pemberton,
Joseph Webster, *jun.*
John Richards.

FENTHAM'S TRUST.

In 1712, George Fentham, of Birmingham, devised his estate by will, consisting of about one hundred acres, in Erdington and Handsworth, of the value then, of 20*l*. per annum, vesting the same in a trust, of which no person could be chosen who resided more than one hundred yards from the Old Cross. We should be inclined to think the devisor entertained a singular predilection for the Old Cross, then in the pride of youth. But if we unfold this whimsical clause, we shall find it contains a shrewd intention. The choice was limited within one hundred yards, because the town itself, in his day, did not in some directions extend farther. Fentham had spent a life in Birmingham, knew well her inhabitants, and like some others, had found honour as well as riches among them: He knew also, he could with safety deposit his property in their hands, and was determined it should never go out,--The scheme will answer his purpose.

The uses of this estate, now about 100*l*. per annum, are for teaching children to read, and for clothing ten poor widows of Birmingham: Those children belonging to the charity school, in green, are upon this foundation.

The present trust are
Francis Coales, and Edmund Wace Pattison.

CROWLEY'S TRUST.

Ann Crowley bequeathed, by her last will, in 1733, six houses in Steelhouse-lane, amounting to eighteen pounds per annum, for the purpose of supporting a school, consisting of ten children. From an attachment to her own sex, she constituted over this infant colony of letters a female teacher: Perhaps we should have seen a female trust, had they been equally capable of defending the property. The income of the estate increasing, the children are now augmented to twelve.

By a subsequent clause in the devisor's will, twenty shillings a year, forever, issues out of two houses in the Lower Priory, to be disposed of at discretion of the trust.

The governors of this female charity are

Thomas Colmore, *bailiff*,
Joseph Cartwright,
Thomas Lee,
John Francis,
Samuel Colmore,
William Russell, *esq*.
Josiah Rogers,
Joseph Hornblower,
John Rogers.

SCOTT'S TRUST.

Joseph Scott, Esq; yet living, assigned, July 7, 1779, certain messuages and lands in and near Walmer-lane, in Birmingham, of the present rent of 40*l*. 18s. part of the said premises to be appropriated for the interment of protestant dissenters; part of the profits to be applied to the use of a religious society in Carr's lane, at the discretion of the trust; and the remainder, for the institution of a school to teach the mother tongue.

Free School.

That part of the demise, designed for the reception of the dead, is about three acres, upon, which stands one messuage, now the Golden Fleece, joining Summer-lane on the west, and Walmer-lane on the east; the other, which hath Aston-street on the south, and Walmer-lane on the west, contains about four acres, upon which now stand ninety-one houses. A building lease, in 1778, was granted of these last premises, for 120 years, at 30*l.* per annum; at the expiration of which, the rents will probably amount to twenty times the present income. The trust, to whose direction this charity is committed, are

Abel Humphrys, *bailiff,*
John Allen,
John Parteridge,
William Aitkins,
Joseph Rogers,
Thomas Cock,
John Berry,
William Hutton,
Thomas Cheek Lea,
Durant Hidson,
Samuel Tutin.

FREE SCHOOL.

It is entertaining to contemplate the generations of fashion, which not only influences our dress and manner of living, but most of the common actions of life, and even the modes of thinking. Some of these fashions, not meeting with the taste of the day, are of short duration, and retreat out of life as soon as they are well brought in; others take a longer space; but whatever fashions predominate, though ever so absurd, they carry an imaginary beauty, which pleases the fancy, 'till they become ridiculous with age, are succeeded by others, when their very memory becomes disgusting.

Custom gives a sanction to fashion, and reconciles us even to its inconveniency. The fashion of this year is laughed at the next.

There are fashions of every date, from five hundred years, even to one day; of the first, was that of erecting religious houses; of the last, was that of destroying them.

Our ancestors, the Saxons, after their conversion to christianity, displayed their zeal in building churches: though the kingdom in a few centuries was amply supplied, yet that zeal was no way abated; it therefore exerted itself in the abbey.-- When a man of fortune had nearly done with time, he began to peep into eternity through the windows of an abbey; or, if a villian had committed a piece of butchery, or had cheated the world for sixty years, there was no doubt but he could burrow his way to glory through the foundations of an abbey.

In 1383, the sixth of Richard the Second, before the religious fervor subsided that had erected Deritend-chapel, Thomas de Sheldon, John Coleshill, John Goldsmith, and William att Slowe, all of Birmingham, obtained a patent from the crown to erect a building upon the spot where the Free School now stands in New-street, to be called *The Gild of the Holy Cross*; to endow it with lands in Birmingham and Edgbaston, of the annual value of twenty marks, for the maintenance of two priests, who were to perform divine service to the honor of God, our blessed Lady his Mother, the Holy Cross, St. Thomas, and St. Catharine.

The fashion seemed to take with the inhabitants, many of whom wished to join the four happy men, who had obtained the patent for so pious a work; so that, in 1393, a second patent was procured by the bailiff and inhabitants of Birmingham, for confirming the gild, and making the addition of a brotherhood in honor of the Holy Cross, consisting of both sexes, with power to constitute a master and wardens, and also to erect a chantry of priests to celebrate divine service in the chapel of the gild, for the souls of the founders, and all the fraternity; for whose support there were given, by divers persons, eighteen messuages, three tofts, (pieces of ground) six acres of land, and forty shillings rent, lying in Birmingham and Edgbaston aforesaid.

But, in the 27th of Henry the Eighth, 1536, when it was the fashion of that day, to multiply destruction against the religious, and their habitations, the annual income of the gild was valued, by the King's random visitors, at the sum of 31*l*. 2s. 10d. out of which, three priests who sung mass, had 5*l*. 6s. 8d. each; an organist, 3*l*. 13s. 4d. the common midwife, 4s. the bell-man, 6s. 8d. with other salaries of inferior note.

These lands continued in the crown 'till 1552, the fifth of Edward the Sixth, when, at the humble suit of the inhabitants, they were assigned to

William Symmons, *gent.*
Richard Smallbrook, *bailiff of the town,*
John Shilton,
William Colmore,
Henry Foxall,
William Bogee,
Thomas Cooper,
Richard Swifte,
Thomas Marshall,
John Veysy,
John King,
John Wylles,
William Paynton,
William Aschrig,
Robert Rastall,
Thomas Snowden,

John Eyliat,
William Colmore, *jun.*
    AND
William Mychell,

all inhabitants of Birmingham, and their successors, to be chosen upon death or removal, by the appellation of the Bailiff and Governors of the Free Grammar School of King Edward the Sixth, for the instruction of children in grammar; to be held of the crown in common soccage, paying for ever twenty shillings per annum. Over this seminary of learning were to preside a master and usher, whose united income seems to have been only twenty pounds per annum. Both are of the clergy. The hall of the gild was used for a school-room. In the glass of the windows was painted the figure of Edmund Lord Ferrers; who, marrying, about 350 years ago, the heiress of the house of Birmingham, resided upon the manor, and seems to have been a benefactor to the gild, with his arms, empaling Belknap; and also, those of Stafford, of Grafton, of Birmingham, and Bryon.

The gild stood at that time at a distance from the town, surrounded with inclosures; the highway to Hales Owen, now New-street, running by the north. No house could be nearer than those in the High-street.

The first erection, wood and plaister, which had stood about 320 years, was taken down in 1707, to make way for the present flat building. In 1756, a set of urns were placed upon the parapet, which give relief to that stiff air, so hurtful to the view: at the same time, the front was *intended* to have been decorated, by erecting half a dozen dreadful pillars, like so many over-grown giants marshalled in battalia, to guard the entrance, which the boys wish to shun; and, being sufficiently tarnished with Birmingham smoak, may become dangerous to pregnancy. Had the wings of this building fallen two or three yards back, and the line of the street been preserved by a light palisade, it would have risen in the scale of beauty, and removed the gloomy aspect of the area.

The tower is in a good taste, except being rather too narrow in the base, and is ornamented with a sleepy figure of the donor, Edward the Sixth, dressed in a royal mantle, with the ensigns of the Garter; holding a bible and sceptre.

The lands that support this foundation, and were in the reign of Henry the Eighth, valued at thirty-one pounds per annum, are now, by the advance of landed property, the reduction of money, and the increase of commerce, about 600*l.*

The present governors of this royal donation are

John Whateley, *bailiff*,
Rev. Charles Newling,
Abraham Spooner, *esq*;
Thomas Russell,
John Ash, *M.D.*
Richard Rabone,
Francis Goodall,
Francis Parrott, *esq*;
William Russell, *esq*;
John Cope, *dead*,
Thomas Hurd,
Thomas Westley,
Wm. John Banner,
Thomas Salt,
William Holden,
Thomas Carless,
John Ward,
Edward Palmer, *esq*;
Francis Coales,
    AND
;Robert Coales.

Charity School.

Over this nursery of science presides a chief master, with an annual salary of one hundred and twenty pounds; a second master sixty; two ushers; a master in the art of writing, and another in that of drawing, at forty pounds each: a librarian, ten: seven exhibitioners at the University of Oxford, twenty-five pounds each. Also, eight inferior schools in various parts of the town, are constituted and fed by this grand reservoir, at fifteen pounds each, which begin the first rudiments of learning.

CHIEF MASTERS.

John Brooksby, 1685.

---- Tonkinson.
John Husted.
Edward Mainwaring, 1730.
John Wilkinson, 1746
Thomas Green, 1759.
William Brailsford, 1766.
Rev. Thomas Price, 1776.

CHARITY SCHOOL:

COMMONLY,
The BLUE SCHOOL.

There seems to be three clases of people, who demand the care of society; infancy, old age, and casual infirmity. When a man cannot assist himself, it is necessary he should be assisted. The first of these only is before us. The direction of youth seems one of the greatest concerns in moral life, and one that is the least understood: to form the generation to come, is of the last importance. If an ingenious master hath flogged the a b c into an innocent child, he thinks himself worthy of praise. A lad is too much terrified to march that path, which is marked out by the rod. If the way to learning abounds with punishment, he will quickly detest it; if we make his duty a task, we lay a stumbling-block before him that he cannot surmount.

We rarely know a tutor succeed in training up youth, who is a friend to harsh treatment.

Whence is it, that we so seldom find affection subsisting between master and scholar? From the moment they unite, to the end of their lives, disgust, like a cloud, rises in the mind, which reason herself can never dispel.

The boy may pass the precincts of childhood, and tread the stage of life upon an equality with every man in it, except his old school-master; the dread of him seldom wears off; the name of Busby founded with horror for half a century after he had laid down the rod. I have often been delighted when I have seen a school of boys break up; the joy that diffuses itself over every face and action, shews infant nature in her gayest form--the only care remaining is, to forget on one side of the walls what was taught on the other.

One would think, if *coming out* gives so much satisfaction, there must be something very detestable *within*.

If the master thinks he has performed his task when he has taught the boy a few words, he as much mistakes his duty, as he does the road to learning: this is only the first stage of his journey. He has the man to form for society with ten thousand sentiments.

It is curious to enter one of these prisons of science, and observe the children not under the least government: the master without authority, the children without order; the master scolding, the children riotous. We never *harden* the wax to receive the impression. They act in a natural sphere, but he in opposition: he seems the only person in the school who merits correction; he, unfit to teach, is making them unfit to be taught.

A man does not consider whether his talents are adapted for teaching, so much, as whether he can *profit* by teaching: thus, when a man hath taught for twenty years, he may be only fit to go to school.

To that vast group of instructors, therefore, whether in, or out of petticoats, who teach, without having been taught; who mistake the tail for the feat of learning, instead of the head; who can neither direct the passions of others nor their own; it may be said, "Quit the trade, if bread can be procured out of it. It is useless to pursue a work of error: the ingenious architect must take up your rotten foundation, before he can lay one that is solid."

But, to the discerning few, who can penetrate the secret windings of the heart; who know that nature may be directed, but can never be inverted; that instruction should ever coincide with the temper of the instructed, or we sall against the wind; that it is necessary the pupil should relish both the teacher and the lesson; which, if accepted like a bitter draught, may easily be sweetened to his taste: to these valuable few, who, like the prudent florist, possessed of a choice root, which he cultivates with care, adding improvement to every generation; it may be said, "Banish tyranny out of the little dominions over which you are absolute sovereigns; introduce in its stead two of the highest ornaments of humanity, love and reason." Through the medium of the first, the master and the lesson may be viewed without horror; when the teacher and the learner are upon friendly terms, the scholar will rather invite than repel the assistance of the master. By the second, reason, the teacher will support his full authority. Every period of life in which a man is capable of attending to instruction, he is capable of attending to reason: this will answer every end of punishment, and something more.

Thus, an irksome task will be changed into a friendly intercourse.

This School, by a date in the front, was erected in 1724, in St. Philip's church-yard; is a plain, airy, and useful building, ornamented over the door with the figures of a boy and a girl in the uniform of the school, and executed with a degree of elegance, that a Roman statuary would not have blushed to own.

This artificial family consists of about ninety scholars, of both sexes; over which preside a governor and governess, both single. Behind the apartments, is a large area appropriated for the amusement of the infant race, necessary as their food. Great decorum is preserved in this little society; who are supported by annual contribution, and by a collection made after sermon twice a year.

At twelve, or fourteen, the children are removed into the commercial world, and often acquire an affluence that enables them to support that foundation, which formerly supported them.

It is worthy of remark, that those institutions which are immediately upheld by the temporary hand of the giver, flourish in continual spring, and become real benefits to society; while those which enjoy a perpetual income, are often tinctured with supineness, and dwindle into obscurity.--The first, usually answer the purpose of the living; the last, seldom that of the dead.

DISSENTING CHARITY-SCHOOL.

About twenty years ago, the Dissenters established a school, upon nearly the same plan as the former, consisting of about eighteen boys and eight girls; with this improvement, that the boys are innured to moderate labour, and the girls to house-work.

The annual subscriptions seem to be willingly paid, thankfully received, and judiciously expended.

Work House.

WORKHOUSE.

During the long reign of the Plantagenets in England, there do not seem many laws in the code then existing for the regulation of the poor: distress was obliged to wander for a temporary and uncertain relief:--idleness usually mixed with it.

The nobility then kept plain and hospitable houses, where want frequently procured a supply; but, as these were thinly scattered, they were inadequate to the purpose.

As the abbey was much more frequent, and as a great part of the riches of the kingdom passed through the hands of the monk, and charity being consonant to the profession of that order, the weight of the poor chiefly lay upon the religious houses; this was the general mark for the indigent, the idle, and the impostor, who carried meanness in their aspect, and the words *Christ Jesus* in their mouth. Hence arise the epithets of stroller, vagrant, and sturdy beggar, with which modern law is intimately acquainted.

It was too frequently observed, that there was but a slender barrier between begging and stealing, that necessity seldom marks the limits of honesty, and that a country abounding with beggars, abounds also with plunderers. A remnant of this urgent race, so justly complained of, which disgrace society, and lay the country under contribution, are still suffered, by the supineness of the magistrate.

When the religious houses, and all their property, in 1536, fell a sacrifice to the vindictive wrath of Henry the Eighth, the poor lost their dependence, and as want knows no law, robbery became frequent; justice called loudly for punishment, and the hungry for bread; which gave rise, in the reign of Queen Elizabeth, to that most excellent institution, of erecting every parish into a distinct fraternity, and obliging them to support their own members; therefore, it is difficult to assign a reason, why the blind should go abroad to *see* fresh countries, or the man *without feet to travel*.

Though the poor were nursed by parochial law, yet workhouses did not become general 'till 1730: that of Birmingham was erected in 1733, at the expence of 1173*l*. 3s. 5d. and which, the stranger would rather suppose, was the residence of a gentleman, than that of four hundred paupers. The left wing, called the infirmary, was added in 1766, at the charge of 400*l*. and the right, a place for labour, in 1779, at the expence of 700*l*. more.

Let us a second time, consider the 50,000 people who occupy this *grand toy shop of Europe*[6] as one great family, where, though the property of individuals is ascertained and secured, yet a close and beneficial compact subsists. We behold the members of this vast family marked with every style of character. Forlorn infancy, accidental calamity, casual sickness, old age, and even inadvertent distress, all find support from that charitable fund erected by industry. No part of the family is neglected: he that cannot find bread for himself, finds a ready supply; he that can, ought to do so. By cultivating the young suckers of infancy, we prudently establish the ensuing generation, which will, in the commercial walk, abundantly repay the expence: temporary affliction of every kind also merits pity; even those distresses which arise from folly ought not to be neglected: the parish hath done well to many a man, who would not do well to himself; if imprudence cannot be banished out of the world, companion ought not: he that cannot direct himself, must be under the direction of another.--If the parish supported none but the prudent, she would have but few to support. The last stage of human life demands, as well as the first, the help of the family. The care of infancy arises from an expectation of a return; that of old age from benefits already received. Though a man may have passed through life without growing rich, he may, by his labour, have contributed to make others so; though he could not pursue the road to affluence himself, he may have been the means of directing others to find it.

[6] Burke.

The number of persons depending upon this weekly charity in Birmingham were, April 14, 1781, about 5240.

Whether the mode of distributing the bounty of the community, is agreeable to the intentions of legislature, or the ideas of humanity, is a doubt. For in some parishes the unfortunate paupers have the additional misery of being sold to a mercenary wretch to starve upon twelve pence a head. It is matter of surprise that the magistrate should wink at this cruelty; but it is matter of pleasure, that no accusation comes within the verge of my historical remarks, for the wretched of Birmingham are not made more so by ill treatment, but meet with a kindness acceptable to distress. One would think *that* situation could not be despicable, which is often *wished for*, and often *sought*, that of becoming one of the poor of Birmingham.

We cannot be conversant in parochial business, without observing a littleness predominant in most parishes, by using every finesse to relieve themselves of paupers, and throwing them upon others. Thus the oppressed, like the child between two fathers, is supported by neither.

There is also an enormity, which, though agreeable to law, can never be justified by the rules of equity That a man should spend the principal part of his life in a parish, add wealth to it by his labour, form connexions in it, bring up a family which shall all belong to it, but having never gained a settlement himself, shall, in old age be removed by an order, to perish among strangers. In 1768, a small property fell into my hands, situated in a neighbouring village; I found the tenant had entered upon the premises at the age of twenty-two; that he had resided upon them, with poverty and a fair character, during the long space of forty six years--I told him he was welcome to spend the residue of his life upon the spot gratis. He continued there ten years after, when finding an inability to procure support from labour, and meeting with no assistance from the parish in which he had been resident for an age, he resigned the place with tears, in 1778, after an occupation of fifty six years, and was obliged to recoil upon his own parish, about twelve miles distant; to be farmed with the rest of the poor; and where, he afterwards assured me, "They were murdering him by inches." -- But no complaint of this ungrateful kind lies against that people whose character I draw.

Perhaps it may be a wise measure, in a place like Birmingham, where the manufactures flourish in continual sunshine, not to be over strict with regard to removals. Though it may be burdensome to support the poor of another parish, yet perhaps it is the least of two evils: to remove old age which hath spent a life among us, is ungenerous; to remove temporary sickness, is injurious to trade; and to remove infancy is impolitic, being upon the verge of accommodating the town with a life of labour. It may be more prudent to remove a rascal than a pauper. Forty pounds hath been spent in removing a family, which would not otherwise have cost forty shillings, and whose future industry might have added many times that sum to the common capital. The highest pitch of charity, is that of directing inability to support itself. Idleness suits no part of a people, neither does it find a place here; every individual ought to contribute to the general benefit, by his head or his hands: if he is arrived at the western verge of life, when the powers of usefulness decline, let him repose upon his fortune; if no such thing exists, let him rest upon his friends, and if this prop fail, let the public nurse him, with a tenderness becoming humanity.

We may observe, that the manufactures, the laborious part of mankind, the poor's rates, and the number of paupers, will everlastingly go hand in hand; they will increase and decrease together; we cannot annihilate one, but the others will follow, and odd as the expression may sound, we become rich by payment and poverty. If we discharge the poor, who shall act the laborious part? Stop the going out of one shilling, and it will prevent the coming in of two.

At the introduction of the poor's laws, under Elizabeth, two pence halfpenny in the pound rent was collected every fortnight, for future support: time has made an alteration in the system, which is now six-pence in the pound, and collected as often as found necessary. The present levy amounts to above 10,000*l.* per ann. but is not wholly collected.

As the overseers are generally people of property, payment in advance is not scrupulously observed.

It was customary, at the beginning of this admirable system of jurisprudence, to constitute two overseers in each parish; but the magnitude of Birmingham pleaded for four, which continued 'till the year 1720, when a fifth was established: in 1729 they were augmented to half a dozen; the wishes of some, who are frighted at office, rise to the word *dozen*, a number very familiar in the Birmingham art of reckoning: but let it be remembered, that a vestry filled with overseers is not calculated for the meridian of business; that the larger the body, the slower the motion; and that the time and the necessities of the poor demand dispatch.

From the annual disbursements in assisting the poor, which I shall here exhibit from undoubted evidence, the curious will draw some useful lessons respecting the increase of manufactures, of population, and of property.

No memoirs are found prior to 1676.

Year.	Disbursed.			Year.	Disbursed.		
	l.	s.	d.		l.	s.	d.
1676	328	17	7	1684	451	0	5-1/2
1677	347	9	10-1/2	1685	324	2	8
1678	398	8	0-1/2	1686	338	12	11
1679	omitted			1687	343	15	6
1680	342	11	2-1/2	1688	308	17	9-1/2
1681	363	15	7	1689	395	14	11
1682	337	2	8-1/2	1690	396	15	2-1/2
1683	410	12	1	1691	354	1	5-1/2
1691	360	0	4-1/2	1720	950	14	0
1693	376	12	3-1/2	1721	1024	6	6-1/2
1694	423	12	1-1/2	1722	939	18	0-1/2
1695	454	2	1-1/2	1739	678	8	5

An History of Birmingham (1783)

1696	385	8	11-1/2	1740	938	0	6
1697	446	11	5	1742	888	1	1-1/2
1698	505	0	2-1/2	1743	799	6	1
1699	592	11	2	1744	851	12	5-1/2
1700	661	7	4-1/2	1745	746	2	7
1701	487	13	0	1746	1003	14	9-1/2
1702	413	14	0-1/2	1747	1071	7	3
1703	476	13	10	1748	1175	8	7-1/2
1704	555	11	11-1/2	1749	1132	11	7-1/2
1705	510	0	10	1750	1167	16	6
1706	519	3	6	1751	1352	0	8-1/2
1707	609	0	4-1/2	1752	1355	6	4
1708	649	15	9	1756	3255	18	3-1/4
1709	744	17	0-1/2	1757	3402	7	2-1/2
1710	960	8	8-1/2	1758	3306	12	5
1711	1055	2	10	1759	2708	9	5-3/4
1712	734	0	11	1760	3221	18	7
1713	674	7	6	1761	2935	4	1-1/2
1714	722	15	6-1/2	1762	3078	18	2-1/2
1715	718	2	1	1763	3330	13	11-1/2
1716	788	3	2-1/2	1764	3963	11	0-1/2
1717	764	0	6-1/2	1765	3884	18	9
1718	751	2	4	1766	4716	2	10-1/2
1719	1094	10	7	1767	4940	2	2
1768	4798	2	5	1775	6509	10	10
1769	5082	0	9	1776	5203	4	9-1/2
1770	5125	13	2-1/4	1777	6012	5	5
1771	6132	5	10	1778	6866	10	8-1/2
1772	6139	6	5-1/2	1779	8081	19	7-1/2
1773	5584	18	8-1/2	1780	9910	4	11-3/4
1774	6115	17	11				

We cannot pass through this spacious edifice without being pleased with its internal oeconomy; order influences the whole, nor can the cleanliness be exceeded: but I am extremely concerned, that I cannot pass through without complaint.

There are evils in common life which admit of no remedy; but there are very few which may not be lessened by prudence.

The modes of nursing infancy in this little dominion of poverty, are truly defective. It is to be feared the method intended to train up inhabitants for the earth, annually furnishes the regions of the grave.

Why is so little attention paid to the generation who are to tread the stage after us? as if we suffered them to be cut off that we might keep possession for ever. The unfortunate orphan that none will own, none will regard: distress, in whatever form it appears, excites compassion, but particularly in the helpless. Whoever puts an infant into the arms of decrepit old age, passes upon it a sentence of death, and happy is that infant who finds a reprieve. The tender sprig is not likely to prosper under the influence of the tree which attracts its nurture; applies that nurture to itself, where the calls occasioned by decay are the most powerful--An old woman and a sprightly nurse, are characters as opposite as the antipodes.

If we could but exercise a proper care during the first two years, the child would afterwards nurse itself; there is not a more active animal in the creation, no part of its time, while awake, is unemployed: why then do we invert nature, and confine an animal to still life, in what is called a school, who is designed for action?

We cannot with indifference behold infants crouded into a room by the hundred, commanded perhaps by some disbanded soldier, termed a school-master, who having changed the sword for the rod, continues much inclined to draw blood with his arms; where every individual not only re breathes his own air, but that of another: the whole assembly is composed of the feeble, the afflicted, the maimed, and the orphan; the result of whose confinement, is a fallow aspect, and a sickly frame: but the paltry grains of knowledge gleaned up by the child in this barren field of learning, will never profit him two-pence in future; whereas, if we could introduce a robust habit, he would one day be a treasure to the community, and a greater to himself. Till he is initiated into labour, a good foundation for health may be laid in air and exercise.

Whenever I see half a dozen of these forlorn innocents quartered upon a farm house, a group of them taking the air under the conduct of a senior, or marshalled in rank and file to attend public worship, I consider the overseer who directed it, as possessed of tender feelings: their orderly attire, and simplicity of manners, convey a degree of pleasure to the mind; and I behold in them, the future support of that commercial interest; upon which they now lie as a burden.

If I have dwelt long upon the little part of our species, let it plead my excuse to say, I cannot view a human being, however diminutive in stature, or depressed in fortune, without considering, *I view an equal*.

OLD CROSS,

So called, because prior to the Welch Cross; before the erection of this last, it was simply called, The Cross.

The use of the market cross is very ancient, though not equal to the market, for this began with civilization.

Christianity first appeared in Britain under the Romans; but in the sixth century, under the Saxon government, it had made such an amazing progress, that every man seemed to be not only *almost a Christian*, but it was unfashionable not to have been a zealous one. The cross of Christ was frequently mentioned in conversation, and afterwards became an oath. It was hacknied about the streets, sometimes in the pocket, or about the neck; sometimes it was fixed upon the church, which we see at this day, and always hoisted to the top of the steeple. The rudiments of learning began with the cross; hence it stands to this moment as a frontispiece to the battledore, which likewise bears its name.

This important article of religion was thought to answer two valuable purposes, that of collecting the people; and containing a charm against ghosts, evil spirits, etc. with the idea of which, that age was much infested.

To accomplish these singular ends, it was blended into the common actions of life, and at that period it entered the market-place. A few circular steps from the centre of which issued an elevated pillar, terminating in a cross, was the general fashion throughout the kingdom; and perhaps our Vulcanian ancestors knew no other for twelve hundred years, this being renewed about once every century, 'till the year 1702, when the present cross was erected, at the expence of 80*l*. 9s. 1d. This was the first upon that spot, ever honoured with a roof: the under part was found a useful shelter for the market-people. The room over it was designed for the court leet, and other public business, which during the residence of the lords upon the manor, had been transacted in one of their detached apartments, yet in being: but after the removal of the lords, in 1537, the business was done in the Leather-hall, which occupied the whole east end of New-street, a covered gateway of twelve feet excepted, and afterwards in the Old Cross.

Welch Cross.

Old Cross.

WELCH CROSS.

If a reader, fond of antiquity, should object, that I have comprized the *Ancient state of Birmingham* in too small a compass, and that I ought to have extended it beyond the 39th page; I answer, when a man has not much to say, he ought to be hissed out of authorship, if he picks the pocket of his friend, by saying much; neither does antiquity end with that page, for in some of the chapters, I have led him through the mazes of time, to present him with a modern prospect.

In erecting a new building, we generally use the few materials of the old, as far as they will extend. Birmingham may be considered as one vast and modern edifice, of which the ancient materials make but a very small part: the extensive *new*, seems to surround the minute *old*, as if to protect it.

Upon the spot where the Welch Cross now stands, probably stood a finger-post, to direct the stranger that could read, for there were not many, the roads to Wolverhampton and Lichfield.

Though the ancient post, and the modern cross, might succeed each other, yet this difference was between them, one stood at a distance from the town, the other stands near its centre.

By some antique writings it appears, that 200 years ago this spot bore the name of the Welch End, perhaps from the number of Welch in its neighbourhood; or rather, from its being the great road to that principality, and was at that time the extremity of the town, odd houses excepted. This is corroborated by a circumstance I have twice mentioned already, that when Birmingham unfortunately fell under the frowns of Prince Rupert, 137 years ago, and he determined to reduce it to ashes for succouring an enemy, it is reasonable to suppose he began at the exterior, which was then in Bull-street, about twelve houses above the cross.

If we were ignorant of the date of this cross, the style of the building itself would inform us, that it rose in the beginning of the present century, and was designed, as population encreased, for a Saturday market; yet, although it is used in some degree for that purpose, the people never heartily adopted the measure.

In a town like Birmingham, a commodious market-place, for we have nothing that bears the name, would be extremely useful. Efforts have been used to make one, of a large area, now a bowling-green, in Corbet's-alley; but I am persuaded the market-people would suffer the grass to grow in it, as peaceably as in their own fields. We are not easily drawn from ancient custom, except by interest.

For want of a convenient place where the sellers may be collected into one point, they are scattered into various parts of the town. Corn is sold by sample, in the Bull-ring; the eatable productions of the garden, in the same place: butchers stalls occupy Spiceal-street; one would think a narrow street was preferred, that no customer should be suffered to pass by. Flowers, shrubs, etc. at the ends of Philip-street and Moor-street: beds of earthen-ware lie in the middle of the foot ways; and a double range of insignificant stalls, in the front of the shambles, choak up the passage: the beast market is kept in Dale-end: that for pigs, sheep and horses in New-street: cheese issues from one of our principal inns: fruit, fowls and butter are sold at the Old Cross: nay, it is difficult to mention a place where they are not. We may observe, if a man hath an article to sell which another wants to buy, they will quickly find each other out.

Though the market-inconveniencies are great, a man seldom brings a commodity for the support of life, or of luxury, and returns without a customer. Yet even this crowded state of the market, dangerous to the feeble, hath its advantages: much business is transacted in a little time; the first customer is obliged to use dispatch, before he is justled out by a second: to *stand all the day idle in the market place*, is not known among us.

The upper room of this cross is appropriated for a military guard-house. We find, December 16, 1723, an order made at a public meeting, that "A guard house should be erected in a convenient part of the town, because neither of the crosses were eligible." But this old order, like some of the new, was never carried into execution. As no complaint lies against the cross, in our time, we may suppose it suitable for the purpose; and I know none but its prisoners that pronounce against it.

SAINT MARTIN's.

It has been remarked, that the antiquity of this church is too remote for historical light.

The curious records of those dark ages, not being multiplied, and preserved by the art of printing, have fallen a prey to time, and the revolution of things.

Saint Martin's Church.

   There is reason for fixing the foundation in the eighth century, perhaps rather sooner, and it then was at a small distance from the buildings. The town stood upon the hill, whose centre was the Old Cross; consequently, the ring of houses that now surrounds the church, from the bottom of Edgbaston-street, part of Spiceal-street, the Bull-ring, Corn-cheaping, and St. Martin's-lane, could not exist.

   I am inclined to think that the precincts of St. Martin's have undergone a mutilation, and that the place which has obtained the modern name of Bull-ring, and which is used as a market for corn and herbs, was once an appropriation of the church, though not used for internment; because the church is evidently calculated for a town of some size, to which the present church-yard no way agrees, being so extremely small that the ancient dead must have been continually disturbed, to make way for the modern, that little spot being their only receptacle for 900 years.

A son not only succeeds his father in the possession of his property and habitation, but also in the grave, where he can scarcely enter without expelling half a dozen of his ancestors.

The antiquity of St. Martin's will appear by surveying the adjacent ground. From the eminence upon which the High-street stands, proceeds a steep, and regular descent into Moor-street, Digbeth, down Spiceal-street, Lee's-lane, and Worcester-street. This descent is broken only by the church-yard; which, through a long course of internment, for ages, is augmented into a considerable hill, chiefly composed of the refuse of life. We may, therefore, safely remark, in this place, *the dead are raised up*. Nor shall we be surprised at the rapid growth of the hill, when we consider this little point of land was alone that hungry grave which devoured the whole inhabitants, during the long ages of existence, till the year 1715, when St. Philip's was opened. The curious observer will easily discover, the fabric has lost that symmetry which should ever attend architecture, by the growth of the soil about it, causing a low appearance in the building, so that instead of the church burying the dead, the dead would, in time, have buried the church.

It is reasonable to allow, the original approach into this place was by a flight of steps, not by descent, as is the present case; and that the church-yard was surrounded by a low wall. As the ground swelled by the accumulation of the dead, wall after wall was added to support the growing soil; thus the fence and the hill sprang up together; but this was demonstrated, August 27, 1781, when, in removing two or three old houses, to widen St. Martin's Lane, they took down the church-yard wall, which was fifteen feet high without, and three within. This proved to be only an outward case, that covered another wall twelve feet high; in the front of which was a stone, elevated eight feet, and inscribed, "Robert Dallaway, Francis Burton." Church-wardens, anno dom. (supposed) "1310." As there is certain evidence, that the church is, much older then the above date, we should suspect there had been another fence many ages prior to this. But it was put beyond a doubt, when the workmen came to a third wall, four feet high, covered with antique coping, probably erected with the fabric itself, which would lead us far back into the Saxon times.

The removal of the buildings to accommodate the street, the construction of the wall, beautified with pallisades, is *half* an elegant plan, well executed. If we can persuade ourselves to perform the other half, by removing the remainder of the buildings, and continuing the line to the steps, at the bottom of Spiceal-street, the work will stand in the front of modern improvement.

In the south-east part of the wall, covered by the engine-house, upon another stone, nearly obliterated, is, John Enser, Richard Higginson, Church-wardens, 1709.

Other church-yards are ornamented with the front of the buildings, but that of St. Martin submits to the rear.

The present church is of stone; the first upon the premises; and perhaps the oldest building in these parts.

As the country does not produce stone of a lasting texture, and as the rough blasts of 900 years, had made inroads upon the fabric, it was thought necessary, in 1690, to case both church and steeple with brick, except the spire, which is an elegant one. The bricks and the workmanship are excellent.

Though the fabric is not void of beauty, yet being closely surrounded with houses, which destroy the medium of view, that beauty is totally hid.

The steeple has, within memory, been three times injured by lightning. Forty feet of the spire, in a decayed state, was taken down and rebuilt in 1781, with stone from Attleborough, near Nuneaton; and strengthened by a spindle of iron, running up its centre 105 feet long, secured to the side walls every ten feet, by braces--the expence, 165*l*. 16s.

Inclosed is a ring of twelve musical bells, and though I am not master of the bob major and tripple-grandfire, yet am well informed, the ringers are masters of the bell-rope: but to excel in Birmingham is not new.

The seats in the church would disgrace a meaner parish than that of Birmingham; one should be tempted to think, they are the first ever erected upon the spot, without taste or order: the timber is become hard with age, and to the honour of the inhabitants, bright with use. Each sitting is a private freehold, and is farther disgraced, like the coffin of a pauper, with the paltry initials of the owner's name. These divine abodes are secured with the coarse padlocks of a field gate.

By an attentive survey of the seats, we plainly discover the increasing population of Birmingham. When the church was erected, there was doubtless sufficient room for the inhabitants, and it was probably the only place for public worship during 800 years: as the town increased, gallery after gallery was erected, 'till no conveniency was found for more. Invention was afterwards exerted to augment the number of sittings; every recess capable only of admitting the body of an infant, was converted into a seat, which indicates, the continual increase of people, and, that a spirit of devotion was prevalent among them.

The floor of the church is greatly injured by internment, as is also the light, by the near approach of the buildings, notwithstanding, in 1733, the middle roof of the chancel was taken off, and the side walls raised about nine feet, to admit a double range of windows.

An History of Birmingham (1783)

Dugdale, who wrote in 1640, gives us twenty-two drawings of the arms, in the windows, of those gentry who had connection with Birmingham.

1. Astley.
2. Sumeri.
3. Ancient Birmingham.
4. Ancient Birmingham, the 2nd house.
5. Seagreve.
6. Modern Birmingham.
7. Ancient and modern Birmingham, quartered.
8. Peshale quartering Bottetort.
9. Birmingham quartering Wyrley.
10. Freville.
11. Ancient Birmingham.
12. Knell.
13. Fitz-Warrer.
14. Montalt.
15. Modern Birmingham.
16. Hampden.
17. Burdet.
18. Montalt.
19. Modern Birmingham.
20. Beauchamp.
21. Ferrers.
22. Latimere.

These twenty-two coats are now reduced to three, which are,

Number two, in the east window of the chancel, which is *or, two lions passant azure*, the arms of the family of Someri, Lords of Dudley-castle, and superior Lords of Birmingham; which having been extinct about 450 years, the coat of arms must have been there at least during that period.

Number three, in the south window of the chancel, *azure, a bend lozenge of five points, or*, the ancient arms of the family of Birmingham, which perhaps is upwards of 400 years old, as that coat was not used after the days of Edward the First, except in quarterings.

And number ten, in the north window, *or, a cross, indented gules*; also, *five fleurs de lis*, the ancient arms of Freville, Lords of Tamworth, whose ancestor, Marmion, received a grant of that castle from William the Conqueror, and whose descendant, Lord Viscount Townshend, is the present proprietor. Perhaps this coat hath been there 400 years, for the male line of the Freville family, was extinct in the reign of Henry the Fourth.

Under the south window of the chancel, by the door, are two monuments a-breast, of white marble, much injured by the hand of rude time, and more by that of the ruder boys. The left figure, which is very ancient, I take to be William de Birmingham, who was made prisoner by the French, at the siege of Bellegard, in the 25th of Edward the First, 1297. He wears a short mantle, which was the dress of that time, a sword, expressive of the military order, and he also bears a shield with the bend lozenge, which seems never to have been borne after the above date.

The right hand figure, next the wall, is visibly marked with a much older date, perhaps about the conquest. The effigy does not appear in a military character, neither did the Lords of that period. The value of these ancient relicts have long claimed the care of the wardens, to preserve them from the injurious hand of the boys, and the foot of the window cleaner, by securing them with a pallisade. Even Westminster abbey, famous for departed glory, cannot produce a monument of equal antiquity.

At the foot of these, is another of the same materials, belonging to one of the Marrows, Lords of Birmingham.

Under the north east window, is a monument of white marble, belonging to one of the Lords of the house of Birmingham: but this is of modern date compared with the others, perhaps not more than 300 years; he bearing the *parte per pale, indented or, and gules*.

In the church is an excellent organ, and in the steeple a set of chimes, where the ingenious artist treats us with a fresh tune every day of the week.

Upon one of the CENTRE PILLARS.

Here lieth the bodies of William Colmore, Gent. who died in 1607, and Ann his wife, in 1591: also the body of Henry Willoughby, Esq; father to Frances, wife of William Colmore, now living; he died 1609.

NORTH GALLERY.

John Crowley, in 1709, gave twenty shillings per annum, payable out of the lowermost house in the Priory, to be distributed in bread, in the church on St. John's day, to house-keepers in Birmingham, who receive no pay.

Joseph Hopkins died in 1683, who gave 200*l.* with which an estate was purchased in Sutton Coldfield; the rents to be laid out in coats, gowns, and other relief for the poor of Birmingham: he also gave 200*l.* for the poor of Wednesbury: 200*l.* to distresed quakers: 5*l.* 10s. to the poor of Birmingham, and the same sum to those of Wednesbury, at his death.

SAME GALLERY.

Whereas the church of St. Martin's, in Birmingham, had only 52 ounces of plate, in 1708, for the use of the communion table; it was, by a voluntary subscription of the inhabitants, increased to 275--Two flaggons, two cups, two covers and pattens, with cases: the whole, 80*l.* 16s. 6d.

Richard Banner ordered one hundred pounds to be laid out in lands within ten miles of Birmingham; which sum, lying at interest, and other small donations being added, amounted to 170*l.* with which an estate at Erdington, value 8*l.* 10s. per annum, was purchased for the poor of Birmingham.

Richard Kilcup gave a house and garden at Spark-brook, for the church and poor.

John Cooper gave a croft for making of love-days (merriments) among Birmingham men.

William Rixam gave a house in Spiceal-street, No. 26, for the use of the poor, in 1568.

John Ward, in 1591, gave a house and lands in Marston Culey.

William Colmore gave ten shillings per ann. payable out of the house, No. 1, High-street.

John Shelton gave ten shillings per annum, issuing out of a house occupied by Martin Day.

Several of the above donations are included in Lench's trust.

John Peak gave a chest bound with iron for the use of the church; seemingly about 200 years old, and of 200 lb. weight.

Edward Smith gave 20*l.* per ann. to the poor, in 1612, and also erected the pulpit.

John Billingsley, in 1629, gave 26 shillings yearly, chargeable upon a house in Dale-end, to be given in bread, by six-pence every Sunday.

One croft to find bell-ropes.

Richard Dukesayle, in 1630, gave the utensils belonging to the communion table.

Barnaby Smith, 1633, gave 20*l.* to be lent to ten poor tradesmen, at the discretion of the church-wardens for two or three years.

Catharine Roberts, wife of Barnaby Smith, in 1642, gave 20*l.* the interest of which was to be given to the poor, the first Friday in Lent.

John Jennens, 1651, gave 2*l.* 10s. for the use of the poor, born and living in Birmingham; and also 20s. on St. Thomas's day.

John Milward gave 26*l* per annum, lying in Bordesley: one third to the school-master of Birmingham, (Free-school); one third to the Principal of Brazen nose College, Oxford, for the maintenance of one scholar from Birmingham or Haverfordwest, and the remainder to the poor.

Joseph Pemberton gave 40s. per annum, payable out of an estate at Tamworth, and 20s. out of an estate in Harbourne.

Richard Smallbrook gave to the poor of Birmingham 10s. per annum, arising out of a salt vat in Droitwich.

Robert Whittall gave the pall, or beere cloth.

Widow Cooper, of the Talbot, No. 20, in High-street, gave one towel and one sheet, to wrap the poor in the grave.

Mrs. Jennens gave 10*l*. per annum to support a lecture, the second and third Thursday in every month.

The following offspring of charity seems to have expired at its birth, but rose from the dead a few months ago, after an internment of fifty-four years.

The numerous family of Piddock flourished in great opulence for many ages, and though they were not lords of a manor, they were as rich as those who were: they yet boast, that their ancestors could walk seven miles upon their own land. It sometimes may be prudent, however, to believe only *half* what a man says; besides, a person with tolerable vigour of limb, might contrive to walk seven miles upon his own land, if he has but one acre--a lawyer is not the only man who can double.

Perhaps they were possessed of the northern part of this parish, from Birmingham-heath to Shirland-brook, exclusive of many estates in the manors of Smethwick and Oldbury.

Their decline continued many years, till one of them, in 1771, extinguished their greatness by a single dash of his pen, in selling the last foot of land.--I know some of them now in distress.

William Piddock, in 1728, devised his farm at Winson-green, about nine acres, to his wife Sarah, during life, and at her death, to his nephews and executors William and John Riddall, their heirs and assigns for ever, in trust, for educating and putting out poor boys of Birmingham; or other discretional charities in the same parish.

But William and John wisely considered, that they could not put the money into any pocket sooner than their own; that as the estate was in the family it was needless to disturb it; that as the will was not known to the world, there was no necessity to publish it; and, as it gave them a discretional power of disposal, they might as well consider themselves *the poor*, for they were both in the parish.

There is nothing easier than to coin excuses for a fault;--there is nothing harder than to make them pass.

What must be his state of mind, who is in continual apprehensions of a disgraceful discovery? No profits can compensate his feelings.

Had the deviser been less charitable, William and John had been less guilty: the gift of one man becomes a temptation to another. These nine acres, from which the donor was to spring upwards, lay like a mountain on the breasts of William and John, tending to press them downwards. Although poverty makes many a rogue, yet had William and John been more poor, they would have been more innocent. The children themselves would have been the least gainers by the bequest, for, without this legacy, they could just as well have procured trades; the profit would have centered in the inhabitants, by softening their levies.--Thus a donation runs through many a private channel, unseen by the giver.

Matters continued in this torpid state till 1782, when a quarrel between the brothers and a tenant, broke the enchantment, and shewed the actors in real view.

The officers, in behalf of the town, filed a bill in Chancery, and recovered the dormant property, which was committed in trust to

John Dymock Griffith,
John Harwood,
Thomas Archer,   > Overseers, 1781.
William Hunt,
Joseph Robinson,
James Rollason,

John Holmes,   > Constables, 1782.
Thomas Barrs,
Joseph Sheldon,
Charles Primer,   > Church-wardens,
William Dickenson,
Edmund Tompkins,

Claud Johnson,
Nathaniel Lawrence,

Edward Homer,   > Overseers, 1782.
Thomas Cock,
Samuel Stretch,
Joseph Townsend,
John Startin.

The presentation of St. Martin's was vested in the family of Birmingham, until the year 1537, since which it has passed through the Dudleys, the Crown, the Marrows, the Smiths, and now rests in the family of Tennant.

RECTORS.

1300	Thomas de Hinckleigh.
1304	Stephen de Segrave.
1304	John de Ayleston.
1336	Robert de Shuteford.
1349	William de Seggeley.
1354	Thomas de Dumbleton.
1369	Hugh de Wolvesey.
1396	Thomas Darnall.
1412	William Thomas.
1414	Richard Slowther.
1428	John Waryn.
1432	William Hyde.
1433	John Armstrong.
1433	John Wardale.
1436	Henry Symon.
1444	Humphrey Jurdan.
1504	Richard Button.
1536	Richard Myddlemore.
1544	William Wrixam.
1578	Lucus Smith.

Thus far Dugdale.

----	------ Smith.
1641	Samuel Wills.
1654	------ Slater.
1660	John Riland.
1672	Henry Grove.
----	William Daggett.
----	Thomas Tyrer.

1732   Richard Dovey.

1771   ------ Chase.

1772   John Parsons.

1779   William Hinton, D.D.

1781   Charles Curtis.

During Cromwell's government, ---- Slater, a broken apothecary of this place, having been unsuccessful in curing the body, resolved to attempt curing the soul. He therefore, to repair his misfortunes, assumed the clerical character, and cast an eye on the rectory of St. Martin's; but he had many powerful opponents: among others were Jennens, an iron-master, possessor of Aston-furnace; Smallbroke, another wealthy inhabitant, and Sir Thomas Holt.

However, he with difficulty, triumphed over his enemies, stept into the pulpit, and held the rectory till the restoration.

Being determined, in his first sermon, to lash his enemies with the whip of those times, he told his people, "The Lord had carried him through many troubles; for he had passed, like Shadrach, Meshach, and Abednego, through the *fiery furnace*. And as the Lord had enabled the children of Israel to pass over the Red Sea, so he had assisted him in passing over the *Small-brooks*, and to overcome the strong *Holts* of sin and satan."

At the restoration, suspecting the approach of the proper officers to expel him from the Parsonage-house, he crept into a hiding-place under the stairs; but, being discovered, was drawn out by force, and the place ever after, bore the name of *Slater's Hole*.

John Riland succeeded him, who is celebrated for piety, learning, and a steady adherence to the interest of Charles the First; in whose cause he seems to have lost every thing he possessed, but his life. He was remarkable for compromising quarrels among his neighbours, often at an expence to himself; also for constantly carrying a charity box, to relieve the distress of others; and, though robbed of all himself, never thought he was poor, except when his box was empty.--He died in 1672, aged 53.

A succeeding rector, William Daggett, is said to have understood the art of boxing, better than that of preaching: his clerk often felt the weightier argument of his hand. Meeting a quaker, whose profession, then in infancy, did not stand high in esteem, he offered some insults, which the other resenting, told him, "If he was not protected by his cloth, he would make him repent the indignity." Dagget immediately stripped, "There, now I have thrown off my protection."

They fought--but the spiritual bruiser proved too hard for the injured quaker.

Among the rectors we sometimes behold a magistrate; at others, those who for misconduct ought to have been taken before one.

The rectory, in the King's books, was valued, in 1291, at 5*l*. per annum; and, in 1536, at 19*l*. 3s. 6d.

A terrier of the rectory, written by the rector, about 1680.

A house wherein the present rector, Mr. Dagget, resides. [Parsonage-house.]

Two other houses in Birmingham, [now three, at No. 15, Spiceal-street.]

Three pieces of glebe land, nineteen acres, between the school land and Sheepcoat-lane.

Three pieces, called the Five-way-closes twenty-one acres, bounded by the lands of Samuel Smallbroke, Esq; and Josiah Porter.

One close, two acres, bounded by Lady-wood-lane.

Parsons-meadow, two acres, bounded by the lands of Thomas Smith, Sir Richard Gough, and Sir Arthur Kaye.

Horse pool-croft, half an acre, bounded by Bell's-barn-lane, [Brickiln-lane] the lands of Robert Phillips and Samuel Smallbrook, Esqrs.

Tythe of all kinds of grain: but instead of hay, wool and lamb, a due of 12d. in the pound rent, called herbage, in all the parish, except foreign, wherein the custom is 4d. per acre for meadow land; 3d. per acre for leas; 3d. for each lamb; 1d. 1/2 for a cow and calf: and except part of the estate of William Colmore, Esq; with the Hall-ring, Tanter-butts, Bell's-barns, [No. 1, Exeter-row] and Rings; for the herbage of which is paid annually 13s. 4d. and also, except part of the estate of Samuel Smallbrook, Esq; for which he pays 8s. per annum; and, except the estate of Thomas Weaman, called Whittall's-farm, [Catharine-street] for which he pays 2s. 8d.

All the above estates pay the customary modus, whether in or out of tillage.

SURPLICE FEES.

	Rector. s.	Rector. d.	Clerk. s.	Clerk. d.
For burying in the church,	1	0	1	0
Ditto church-yard,	0	6	0	6
Churching a woman,	0	4	0	4
Marrying by licence,	5	0	2	6
Ditto without,	2	6	1	0
Tythe pig, if seven or upwards,	0	4	0	0
Easter dues, man and wife,	0	4	0	0
---- each person above sixteen,	0	4	0	0

Clerk's salary 20s. paid by the wardens; also 2d. from each house keeper at Easter.

From the above terrier, I am inclined to value the income at about 90*l.* per annum.

The benefice, in 1771, was about 350*l.* per annum: the late Rector, John Parsons, procured an act, in 1773, to enable the incumbent to grant building leases; the grant of a single lease, in 1777, brought the annual addition of about 170*l.* The income is now about 700*l.* and is expected, at the expiration of the leases, to exceed 2000*l.*

The repairs of the chancel belong to the rector, and the remainder of the building to the parish.

St. Philip's Church.

SAINT PHILLIP's.

We have touched upon various objects in our peregrinations through Birmingham, which meet with approbation, though viewed through the medium of smoke; some of these, being covered with the rust of time, command our veneration; but the prospect before us is wholly modern.

We have mounted, by imperceptable gradations, from beauty to beauty, 'till we are now arrived at the summit.

If an historian had written in the last century, he would have recorded but two places of worship; I am now recording the fourteenth: but my successor, if not prevented by our own imprudence, in driving away the spirit of commerce, may record the four-and-twentieth. The artist, who carries the manufactures among foreigners, or the overseer, who wantonly loads the people with burdens, draws the wrath of the place upon his own head.

This curious piece of architecture, the steeple of which is erected after the model of St. Paul's, in London, but without its weight, does honour to the age that raised it, and to the place that contains it. Perhaps the eye of the critic cannot point out a fault, which the hand of the artist can mend: perhaps too, the attentive eye cannot survey this pile of building, without communicating to the mind a small degree of pleasure. If the materials are not proof against time, it is rather a misfortune to be lamented, than an error to be complained of, the country producing no better.

Yet, amidst all the excellencies we boast, I am sorry to charge this chief ornament with an evil which admits no cure, that of not ranging with its own coemetery, or the adjacent buildings: out of seven streets, with which it is connected, it lines with none.--Like Deritend chapel, of which I have already complained, from a strong attachment to a point of religion, or of the compass, it appears twisted out of its place. We may be delighted with a human figure, complete in stature, exactly moulded with symmetry, and set off with the graces of dress; but we should be disgusted, if his right side seemed to attempt to out-walk his left.

This defect, in religious architecture, arises from a strict adherence to the custom of the ancients, who fixed their altars towards the east. It is amasing, that even weakness itself, by long practice, becomes canonical; it gains credit by its age and its company. Hence, Sternhold and Hopkins, by being long bound up with scripture, acquired a kind of scripture authority.

The ground, originally, was part of a farm, and bore the name of the Horse-close; afterwards *Barley-close*.--Thus a benign spot of earth, gave additional spirits to a man when living, and kindly covered him in its bosom when dead.

This well chosen spot, is the summit of the highest eminence in Birmingham, with a descent every way; and, when the church was erected, there were not any buildings nearer than those in Bull-street.

The land was the gift of Robert Phillips, Esq; whence the name, ancestor to William Theodore Inge, Esquire.

In all degrees of people, from the bishop to the beadle, there seems a propensity in the mind to arrive at the honours of Sainthood: by joining our names in partnership with a faint, we share with him a red letter in the almanack.

Out of six churches in Birmingham, three bear the names of the donors. St. Bartholomew's would, probably, have taken that of its founder, John Jennens, Esq; but that name happened to be anticipated by Sir John de Birmingham, who conferred it upon Deritend chapel. St. Mary's could readily perpetuate the name of its benefactress, because we had no place of worship that bore it. But as neither the popish, nor the protestant kalendar produced a St. Charles, the founder of St. Paul's was unfortunately excluded.

The gifts, which the benefactor himself believes are charitable, and expects the world to believe the same, if scrutinized, will be found to originate from various causes--counterfeits are apt to be offered in currency for sterling.

Perhaps *ostentation* has brought forth more acts of beneficence than charity herself; but, like an unkind parent, she disowns her offspring, and charges them upon charity.

Ostentation is the root of charity; why else are we told, in capitals, by a large stone in the front of a building--"This hospital was erected by William Bilby, in the sixty-third year of his age, 1709." Or, "That John Moore, yeoman, of Worley Wigorn, built this school, in 1730."--Nay, pride even tempts us to strut in a second-hand robe of charity, left by another; or why do we read--"These alms-houses were erected by Lench's trust, in 1764. W. WALSINGHAM, BAILIFF."

Another utters the word *charity*, and we rejoice in the echo. If we miss the substance, we grasp at the shadow.

Sometimes we assign our property for religious uses, late in the evening of life, when *enjoyment* is over, and almost *possession*. Thus we bequeath to piety, what we can keep no longer. We convey our name to posterity at the expence of our successor, and scaffold our way towards heaven up the walls of a steeple.

Will charity chalk up one additional score in our favour, because we grant a small portion of our land to found a church, which enables us to augment the remainder treble its value, by granting building leases? a man seldom makes a bargain for heaven, and forgets himself. Charity and self-interest, like the apple and the rind, are closely connected, and, like them, we cannot separate one without trespassing on the other.

In contributions of the lesser kind, the giver examines the quantum given by those of his own station; *pride* will not suffer him to appear less than his neighbour.

Sometimes he surrenders merely through importunity, which indicates as much *charity*, as the garrison does *merit*, which surrenders when closely besieged. Neither do we fear *our left hand knowing what our right hand doth*, our only fear is, left the world should *not* know it.

This superb edifice was begun by act of Parliament, in 1711, under a commission consisting of twenty of the neighbouring gentry, appointed by the bishop of the diocese, under his episcopal seal. Their commission was to end twelve months after the erection of the church.

Though Birmingham ever was, and perhaps ever will be considered as one parish, yet a portion of land, about one hundred acres, nearly triangular, and about three fourths built up, was taken out of the centre of St. Martin's, like a shred of cloth out of a great coat, to make a less, and constituted a separate parish, by the appellation of St Philip's.

We shall describe this new boundary by an imaginary journey, for a real one perhaps was never taken since the land was first laid out, nor ever will to the end of time.

We include the warehouse, then of John Jenens, Esq; now No. 26, in High-street, penetrate through the buildings, till we come within twenty yards, of Moor-street, turn sharp to the left, cross the lower part of Castle-street, Carr's-lane, and New Meeting-street; pass close by the front of the Meeting-house, through Bank-alley, into Hen's-walk, having kept Moor-street about twenty yards to the right, all the way; we now enter that street, at the bottom of Hen's-walk, pass through the east part of Dale-end, through Stafford-street, Steelhouse-lane (then called Whittal-lane) Bull-lane (then New-hall-lane) and Mount-pleasant.

Our journey now leads us on the west of Pinfold-street, keeping it about twenty yards on our left; up Peck-lane, till we come near the top, when we turn to the right, keeping the buildings, with the Free-school in New street, on our left, into Swan-alley. We now turn up the Alley into New-street, then to the right, which leads us to the Party-wall, between No. 25 and 26, in High-street, late Jennens's, where we began.

In the new parish I have described, and during the journey, kept on the left, there seems to have been, at passing the act, twelve closes, all which are filled with buildings, except the land between New-street and Mount-pleasant, which only waits a word from the owner, to speak the houses into being.

The church was consecrated in 1715, and finished in 1719, the work of eight years; at which time the commissioners resigned their powers into the hands of the diocesan, in whom is the presentation, after having paid, it is said, the trifling sum of 5012*l*.--but perhaps such a work could not be completed for 20,000*l*.

Three reasons may be assigned, why so small a sum was expended; many of the materials were given; more of the carriage, and some heavy debts were contracted.

The urns upon the parapet of the church, which are highly ornamental, were fixed at the same time with those of the school, in about 1756.

When I first saw St. Philip's, in the year 1741, at a proper distance, uncrowded with houses, for there were none to the north, New-hall excepted, untarnished with smoke, and illuminated by a western sun, I was delighted with its appearance, and thought it then, what I do now, and what others will in future, *the pride of the place*.

If we assemble the beauties of the edifice, which cover a rood of ground; the spacious area of the church-yard, occupying four acres; ornamented with walks in great perfection; shaded with trees in double and treble ranks; and surrounded with buildings in elegant taste: perhaps its equal cannot be found in the British dominions.

The steeple, 'till the year 1751, contained a peal of six bells, which were then augmented to ten; at which time St. Martin's, the mother church, having only eight, could not bear to be out-numbered by a junior, though of superior elegance, therefore ordered twelve into her own steeple: but as room was insufficient for the admission of bells by the dozen, means were found to hoist them tier over tier. Though the round dozen is a complete number in the counting-house, it is not altogether so in the belfry: the octave is the most perfect concord in music, but diminishes by rising to an octave and a half; neither can that dozen well be crowded into the peal.

But perhaps the artist had another grand scheme in view, that of accommodating the town with the additional harmony of the chimes; for only a few tunes can be played on the octave, whilst the dozen will compass nearly all.

Whether we are entertained even by this *exalted* style of music, admits a doubt; for instead of the curious ear being charmed with distinct notes, we only hear a bustle of confused sounds, which baffle the attention too much to keep pace with the tune.

These two steeples, are our *public* band of music: they are the only *standing* Waits of the place. Two thousand people may be accommodated in the church, but, at times, it has contained near three thousand.

In the vestry is a theological library, bequeathed by the first rector, William Higgs, for the use of the clergy in Birmingham and its neighbourhood; who left 200*l*. for future purchase.

Under the centre isle runs a vault, the whole length of the church, for the reception of those who chuse to pay an additional guinea.

The organ excels; the paintings, mouldings and gildings are superb: whether the stranger takes an external or an internal survey, the eye is struck with delight, and he pronounces the whole the work of a matter. Its conveniency also, can only be equalled by its elegance.

In the FRONT GALLERY.

Upon application of Sir Richard Gough, to Sir Robert Walpole, then in power, George the First gave 600*l*. in 1725, towards finishing this church.

Three remarks naturally arise from this declaration; That the prodigious sums expended upon this pious undertaking, were beyond the ability of the inhabitants; that the debts contracted, were many years in discharging; and that one of the best of Kings, the head of the Brunswick line, bestowed a liberal benefaction upon a people not compleatly reconciled to his house.

Whether monumental decoration adds beauty to a place already beautiful, is a question. There are three very small and very elegant monuments in this church. Upon one of the south pillars, is that of the above William Higgs, who died in 1733. Upon another is that of William Vyse, the second rector, who died in 1770, at the age of 61. And, upon a north pillar, that of Girton Peak, Esq; an humane magistrate, who died in 1770, aged 48.

Internment in the church is wisely prohibited; an indecency incompatible with a civilized people. The foreigner will be apt to hold forth the barbarity of the English nation, by observing, "They introduce corruption in their very churches, and pay divine adoration upon the graves of their ancestors."

Places of worship were designed for the living, the dead give up their title with their life: besides, even small degrees of putrefaction, confined in a room where the air cannot circulate, may become prejudicial to health: it also ruins the pavement, as is done at St. Martin's. Our first inhabitants, therefore, lie contented in the church yard, by their unfortunate equals; having private sepulchres appropriated for family use--Perhaps at the last day, no inquiry will be made whether they lay on the in, or the outside of the walls.

It is difficult to traverse the elegant walks that surround this gulf of death, without contemplating, that time is drawing us towards the same focus, and that we shall shortly fall into the centre: that this irregular circle contains what was once generous and beautiful, opulent and humane. The arts took their rise in this fruitful soil: this is the grave of invention and of industry; here those who figured upon the stage are fallen, to make way for others, who must follow: though multitudes unite with the dead, the numbers of the living increase; the inhabitants change, while the genius improves. We cannot pass on without reading upon the stones, the short existence of our departed friends, perusing the end of a life with which we were well acquainted. The active motion that veered with the rude blasts of seventy years, slops in this point for ever.

The present rector, who is the third, is the Rev. Charles Newling, and the benefice something like the following:

	l.	s.	d.
A prebendal stall in the cathedral church of Lichfield,	6	0	0
Eight acres and a half of glebe land, at Long bridge, near Birmingham,	32	0	0
Emoluments arising from the seats of the church,	140	0	0
Surplice fees,	50	0	0
Easter offerings,	10	0	0
An estate at Sawley, in the county of Derby, under lease for three lives,			

renewable by fine, at the annual rent of	66	13	4
	304	13	4
Out of which is paid to the rector of St. Martin's, in consideration fees and offerings once appropriated to that church,	15	0	0
	289	13	4

BIRTHS AND BURIALS.

There are many inducements for an author to take up the pen, but the leading motives, however disguised, seem to be pride and poverty; hence, two of the most despicable things among men, furnish the world with knowledge.

One would think, however, there can be no great inducement for a man to write what he is conscious will never be read. Under this class may be comprehended alphabetical collections, chronological tables, books of figures, occasional devotions, etc. here also I range the lists of officers in Birmingham, the annual sums expended upon the poor, and the present chapter of numbers. These are intended for occasional inspection, rather than for regular perusal: we may consider them as deserts served up for a taste only, not a dinner; yet even this rule may be broken by a resolute reader, for the late Joseph Scott, Esq; founder of the trust before-mentioned, assured me, in 1751, that he had perused Bailey's Dictionary as methodically as he had done Tom Jones; and, though a dissenter, he continued to read the Common Prayer Book from end to end, about twice a year; which is more than, perhaps, the greatest lover of that excellent composition can boast.

I shall, to avoid prolixity in a barren chapter of the two extremes of life, select about every tenth year from the register. Those years at the time of the plague, make no addition to the burials, because the unhappy victims were conveyed to Lady-wood for internment.

These lists inform us, that the number of streets, houses, inhabitants, births, burials, poor's rates, and commercial productions, increase with equal rapidity. It appears also from the register, that there were more christenings lately at St. Martin's, in one day, than the whole town produced in a year, in the 16th century--The same may be found in that of St. Phillip's.

The deaths in Deritend are omitted, being involved with those of Aston.

Year.	Births.	Burials.	Year.	Births.	Burials.
1555	37	27	1667	146	140
1560	--	37	1668	113	102
1571	48	26	1681	251	139
1580	37	25	1690	127	150
1590	52	47	1700	172	171
1600	62	32	1719	334	270
1610	70	45	1720	423	355
1623	81	66	1730	449	415

1628	100	96	1740	520	573
1653	--	47	1750	860	1020
1660	--	75	1760	984	1143
1665	--	109	1770	1329	899
1666	144	121	1780	1636	1340

GENERAL HOSPITAL.

Though charity is one of the most amiable qualities of humanity, yet, like Cupid, she ought to be represented blind; or, like Justice, hood-winked. None of the virtues have been so much misapplied; giving to the *hungry*, is sometimes only another word for giving to the *idle*. We know of but two ways in which this excellence can exert itself; improving the *mind*, and nourishing the *body*. To help him who *will not* help himself; or, indiscriminately to relieve those that want, is totally to mistake the end; for want is often met with: but to supply those who *cannot* supply themselves, becomes real charity. Some worthy Christians have taken it into their heads to relieve *all*, for fear of omitting the right. What should we think of the constable who seizes every person he meets with, for fear of missing the thief? Between the simple words, therefore, of WILL NOT and CANNOT, runs the fine barrier between real and mistaken charity.

This virtue, so strongly inculcated by the christian system, hath, during the last seventeen centuries, appeared in a variety of forms, and some of them have been detrimental to the interest they were meant to serve: *Such was the cloister*. Man is not born altogether to serve himself, but the community; if he cannot exist without the assistance of others, it follows, that others ought to be assisted by him: but if condemned to obscurity in the cell, he is then fed by the aid of the public, while that public derives none from him.

General Hospital.

Estates have sometimes been devised in trust for particular uses, meant as charities by the giver, but have, in a few years, been diverted out of their original channel to other purposes.

The trust themselves, like so many contending princes, ardently druggie for sovereignty; hence, *legacy* and *discord* are intimate companions.

The plantation of many of our English schools sprang up from the will of the dead; but it is observable, that sterility quickly takes place; the establishment of the master being properly secured, supineness enters, and the young scions of learning are retarded in their growth.

It therefore admits a doubt, whether charitable donation is beneficial to the world; nay, the estate itself becomes blasted when bequeathed to public use, for, being the freehold of none, none will improve it: besides, the more dead land, the less scope for industry.

At the reformation, under Queen Elizabeth, charity seemed to take a different appearance: employment was found for the idle; he that was able, was obliged to labour, and the parish was obliged to assist him who could not. Hence the kingdom became replete with workhouses: these are the laudable repositories of distress.

It has already been observed, that three classes of people merit the care of society: forlorn infancy, which is too weak for its own support; old age, which has served the community, without serving itself; and accidental calamity: the two first, fall under the eye of the parish, the last, under the modern institution of the General Hospital.

The shell of this plain, but noble edifice, was erected in 1766, upon a situation very unsuitable for its elegant front, in a narrow dirty lane, with an aspect directing up the hill, which should ever be avoided.

The amiable desire of doing good in the inhabitants, seemed to have exceeded their ability; and, to the grief of many, it lay dormant for twelve years. In 1778, the matter was revived with vigor; subscriptions filled apace, and by the next year the hospital was finished, at the expence of 7137*l*. 10s. Though the benefactions might not amount to this enormous sum, yet they were noble, and truly characteristic of a generous people. The annual subscriptions, as they stood at Michaelmas, 1779, were 901*l*. 19s. and, at Midsummer, 1780, 932*l*. 8s. During these nine months, 529 patients were admitted, of which, 303 were cured, 93 relieved, 112 remained on the books, only 5 died, and but *one* was discharged as incurable; an incontestible proof of the *skill* of the faculty, which is at least equalled by their *humanity*, in giving their attendance gratis.

The rules by which this excellent charity is conducted, are worthy of its authors: success hath fully answered expectation, and the building will probably stand for ages, to tell posterity a favourable tale of the present generation.

PUBLIC ROADS.

Man is evidently formed for society; the intercourse of one with another, like two blocks of marble in friction, reduces the rough prominences of behaviour, and gives a polish to the manners.

Whatever tends to promote social connection, improve commerce, or stamp an additional value upon property, is worthy of attention.

Perhaps, there is not a circumstance that points more favourably towards these great designs, than commodious roads.

According as a country is improved in her roads, so will she stand in the scale of civilization. It is a characteristic by which we may pronounce with safety. The manners and the roads of the English, have been refining together for about 1700 years. If any period of time is distinguished with a more rapid improvement in one, it is also in the other.

Our Saxons ancestors, of dusky memory, seldom stepped from under the smoke of Birmingham. We have a common observation among us, that even so late as William the Third, the roads were in so dangerous a state, that a man usually made his will, and took a formal fare-well of his friends, before he durst venture upon a journey to London; which, perhaps, was thought then, of as much consequence as a voyage to America now.

A dangerous road is unfavourable both to commerce and to friendship; a man is unwilling to venture his neck to sell his productions, or even visit his friend: if a dreadful road lies between them, it will be apt to annihilate friendship.

Landed property in particular, improves with the road. If a farmer cannot bring his produce to market, he cannot give much for his land, neither can that land well be improved, or the market properly supplied. Upon a well formed road, therefore, might, with propriety, be placed the figures of commerce, of friendship, and of agriculture, as presiding over it.

There are but very few observations necessary in forming a road, and those few are very simple; to expel whatever is hurtful, and invite whatever is beneficial.

The breaking up of a long frost, by loosening the foundations, is injurious, and very heavy carriages ought to be prevented, 'till the weather unites the disjointed particles, which will soon happen.

But the grand enemy is water; and as this will inevitably fall, every means should be used to discharge it: drains ought to be frequent, that the water may not lie upon the road.

The great benefits are *the sun* and the *wind:* the surveyor should use every method for the admission of these friendly aids, that they may dispel the moisture which cannot run off.

For this purpose, all public roads ought to be sixty feet wide; all trees and hedges within thirty feet of the centre, be under the controul of the commissioners, with full liberty of drawing off the water in what manner they judge necessary.

The Romans were the most accomplished masters we know of in this useful art; yet even they seem to have forgot the under drain, for it is evident at this day, where their road runs along the declivity of a hill, the water dams up, flows over, and injures the road.

Care should be taken, in properly forming a road at first, otherwise you may botch it for a whole century, and at the end of that long period, it will be only a botch itself.

A wide road will put the innocent traveller out of fear of the waggoners; not the most civilized of the human race.

From Birmingham, as from a grand centre, issues twelve roads, that point to as many towns; some of these, within memory, have scarcely been passable; all are mended, but though much is done, more is wanted. In an upland country, like that about Birmingham, where there is no river of size, and where the heads only of the streams show themselves: the stranger would be surprised to hear, that through most of these twelve roads he cannot travel in a flood with safety. For want of causeways and bridges, the water is suffered to flow over the road, higher than the stirrup: every stream, though only the size of a tobacco-pipe, ought to be carried through an under drain, never to run over the road.

At Saltley, in the way to Coleshill, which is ten miles, for want of a causeway, with an arch or two, every flood annoys the passenger and the road: at Coleshill-hall, 'till the year 1779, he had to pass a dangerous river.

One mile from Birmingham, upon the Lichfield road, sixteen miles, to the disgrace of the community, is yet a river without a bridge. In 1777, the country was inclined to solicit Parliament for a turnpike-act, but the matter fell to the ground through private views: one would think, that the penny can never be ill laid out, which carries a man ten miles with pleasure and safety. The hand of nature hath been more beneficent, both to this, and to the Stafford road, which is twenty-eight miles, than that of art.

The road to Walfall, ten miles, is rather *below indifferent.*

That to Wolverhampton, thirteen miles, is much improved since the coal-teams left it.

The road to Dudley, ten miles, is despicable beyond description. The unwilling traveller is obliged to go two miles about, through a bad road, to avoid a worse.

That to Hales-Owen, eight miles, like the life of man, is checkered with good and evil; chiefly the latter.

To Bromsgrove, thirteen miles, made extremely commodious for the first four, under the patronage of John Kettle, Esq; in 1772, at the expence of near 5000*l.* but afterwards is so confined, that two horses cannot pass without danger; the sun and the winds are excluded, the rivers lie open to the stranger, and he travels through dirt 'till Midsummer.

To Alcester, about twenty, formed in 1767, upon a tolerable plan, but is rather too narrow, through a desolate country, which at present scarcely defrays the expence; but that country seems to improve with the road.

Those to Stratford and Warwick, about twenty miles each, are much used and much neglected.

That to Coventry, about the same distance, can only be equalled by the Dudley road. The genius of the age has forgot, in some of these roads to accommodate the foot passenger with a causeway.

The surveyor will be inclined to ask, How can a capital be raised to defray this enormous expence? Suffer me to reply with an expression in the life of Oliver Cromwell, "He that lays out money when necessary, and only then, will accomplish matters beyond the reach of imagination."

Government long practised the impolitic mode of transporting vast numbers of her people to America, under the character of felons; these, who are generally in the prime of life, might be made extremely useful to that country which they formerly robbed, and against which, they are at this moment carrying arms. It would be easy to reduce this ferocious race under a kind of martial discipline; to badge them with a mark only removeable by the governors, for hope should ever be left for repentance, and to employ them in the rougher arts of life, according to the nature of the crime, and the ability of body; such as working the coal mines in Northumberland, the lead mines in Derbyshire, the tin mines in Cornwall, cultivating waste lands, banking after inundations, forming canals, cleansing the beds of rivers, assisting in harvest, and in FORMING and MENDING the ROADS: *these hewers of wood and drawers of water* would be a corps of reserve against any emergency. From this magazine of villiany, the British navy might be equipped with, considerable advantage.

CANAL.

An act was obtained, in 1767, to open a cut between Birmingham and the coal delphs about Wednesbury.

The necessary article of coal, before this act, was brought by land, at about thirteen shillings per ton, but now at seven.

It was common to see a train of carriages for miles, to the great destruction of the road, and the annoyance of travellers.

This dust is extended in the whole to about twenty-two miles in length, 'till it unites with what we may justly term the grand artery, or Staffordshire Canal; which, eroding the island, communicates with Hull, Bristol and Liverpool. The expence was about 70,000*l.* divided into shares 140*l.* each, of which no man can purchase more than ten, and which now sell for about 370*l.*

The proprietors took a perpetual lease of six acres of land, of Sir Thomas Gooch, at 47*l.* per annum, which is converted into a wharf, upon the front of which is erected an handsome office for the dispatch of business.

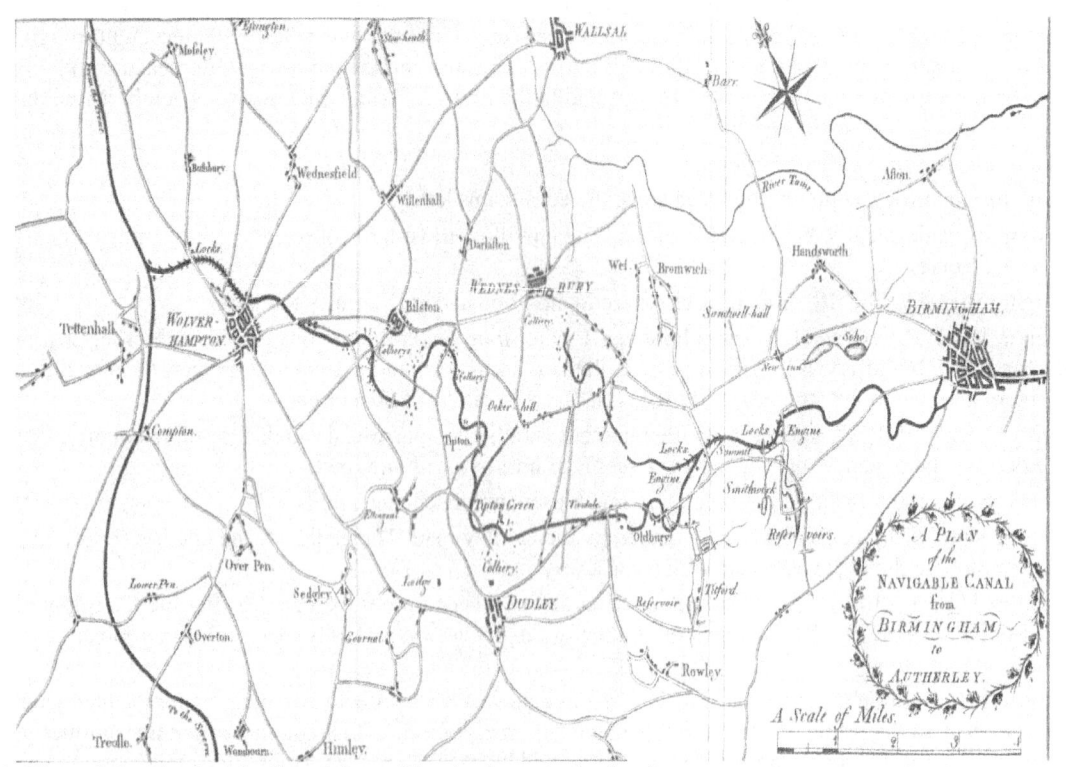

A Plan of the Navigable Canal from Birmingham to Autherley.

Navigation Office.

This watery passage, exclusive of loading the proprietors with wealth, tends greatly to the improvement of some branches of trade, by introducing heavy materials at a small expence, such as pig iron for the founderies, lime-stone, articles for the manufacture of brass and steel, also stone, brick, slate, timber, &c.

It is happy for the world, that public interest is grafted upon private, and that both flourish together.

This grand work, like other productions of Birmingham birth, was rather hasty; the managers, not being able to find patience to worm round the hill at Smethwick, or cut through, have wisely travelled over it by the help of twelve locks, with six they mount the summit, and with six more descend to the former level; forgetting the great waste of water, and the small supply from the rivulets, and also, the amazing loss of of time in climbing this curious ladder, consisting of twelve liquid steps. It is worthy of remark, that the level of the earth, is nearly the same at Birmingham as at the pits: what benefit then would accrue to commerce, could the boats travel a dead flat of fourteen miles without interruption? The use of the canal would increase, great variety of goods be brought which are now excluded, and these delivered with more expedition, with less expence, and the waste of water never felt; but, by the introduction of twelve unnecessary locks, the company may experience five plagues more than fell on Egypt.

The boats are nearly alike, constructed to fit the locks, carry about twenty-five tons, and are each drawn by something like the skeleton of a horse, covered with skin: whether he subsists upon the scent of the water, is a doubt; but whether his life is a scene of affliction, is not; for the unfeeling driver has no employment but to whip him from one end of the canal to the other. While the teams practised the turnpike road, the lash was divided among five unfortunate animals, but now the whole wrath of the driver falls upon one.

We can scarcely view a boat travelling this liquid road, without raising opposite sensations--pleased to think of its great benefit to the community, and grieved to behold wanton punishment.

I see a large field of cruelty expanding before me, which I could easily prevail with myself to enter; in which we behold the child plucking a wing and a leg off a fly, to try how the poor insect can perform with half his limbs; or running a pin through the posteriors of a locust, to observe it spinning through the air, like a comet, drawing a tail of thread. If we allow, man has a right to destroy noxious animals, we cannot allow he has a right to protract their pain by a lingering death. By fine gradations the modes of cruelty improve with years, in pinching the tail of a cat for the music of her voice, kicking a dog because we have trod upon his foot, or hanging him for *fun*, 'till we arrive at the priests in the church of Rome, who burnt people for opinion; or to the painter, who begged the life of a criminal, that he might torture him to death with the severest pangs, to catch the agonizing feature, and transfer it into his favourite piece, of a dying Saviour. But did that Saviour teach such doctrine? Humanity would wish rather to have lost the piece, than have heard of the cruelty. What, if the injured ghost of the criminal is at this moment torturing that of the painter?--

But as this capacious field is beyond the line I profess, and, as I have no direct accusation against the people of my regard, I shall not enter.

DERITEND BRIDGE.

Cooper's-mill, situated upon the verge of the parishes of Afton and Birmingham, 400 yards below this bridge, was probably first erected in the the peaceable ages of Saxon influence, and continued a part of the manorial estate 'till the disposal of it in 1730.

Before the water was pounded up to supply the mill, it must have been so shallow, as to admit a passage between Digbeth and Deritend, over a few stepping stones; and a gate seems to have been placed upon the verge of the river, to prevent encroachments of the cattle.

This accounts for the original name, which Dugdale tells us was *Derry-yate-end:* derry, low; yate, gate; end, extremity of the parish; with which it perfectly agrees.

The mill afterwards causing the water to be dammed up, gave rise to a succession of paltry bridges, chiefly of timber, to preserve a communication between the two streets.

But in later ages, the passage was dignified with those of stone. In 1750, a wretched one was taken down, and the present bridge erected by Henry Bradford and John Collins, overseers of the highway, consisting of five arches; but the homely style, the deep ascent, and the circumscribed width prevents encomium.

ADJACENT REMARKS.

SOHO.

If we travel two miles from the centre of Birmingham, upon the Wolverhampton road, which may be called, the road to taste, and is daily travelled by the nobility and gentry, we shall arrive at the epitome of the arts.

Though this little spot lies in the county of Stafford, we must accept it as part of Birmingham; neither is it many yards distant from the parish.

The proprietor, invited by a genius, a fortune of 30,000*l.* and a little stream, which promised to facilitate business, has erected the most elegant works in these parts, said to accommodate seven hundred persons. Upon that hungry ground, where, in 1758 stood one paltry cottage, we now behold, a city in miniature.

From this nursery of ingenuity, originated the Soho button, the single wheel clock, the improvement of the steam engine, the platina button, the method of taking exact copies of painting, writing, &c. also, the productions of fancy, in great variety; with which some of the European princes are well acquainted.

To the genius of the place is owing the assay-office, for marking standard wrought plate, which, prior to the year 1773, was conveyed to London to receive the sanction of that office; but by an act then obtained, the business is done here by an assay master, superintended by four wardens: these are annually chosen out of thirty-six guardians, whose chief duty consists in dining together, at least once a year; for it appears from the chapter upon government, that feasting makes a principal part of a Birmingham office; and, however unwilling a man may seem to *enter in* we generally find him pleased when he *is in*.

DANES CAMP:

DANES BANK, OR BURY FIELDS.

About five miles south of Birmingham, and five furlongs off Solihull Lodge, is a place called *The Danes Camp*. But although neither history nor tradition speak of this particular event, it probably was raised in the ninth century.

The situation is well chosen, upon an eminence, about nine acres, nearly triangular, is yet in tolerable perfection; the ditch is about twenty feet wide; the base of the bank about the same; admits but of one entrance, and is capable of being secured by water. From the bottom of the ditch, to the top of the mound, was, when made, about twenty feet; and is a production of great labour.

GENTLEMEN'S SEATS.

This neighbourhood may justly be deemed the seat of the arts, but not the seat of the gentry.

None of the nobility are near us, except William Legge, Earl of Dartmouth, at Sandwell, four miles from Birmingham. The principal houses in our environs, are those of Sir Charles Holte, late member for the county, at Aston; Sir Henry Gough, member for Bamber, at Edgbaston; George Birch, Esq; at Handsworth; John Gough, Esq; at Perry; and John Taylor, Esq; at Bordesley and at Moseley; all joining to the manor of Birmingham. Exclusive of these, are many elegant retreats of our first inhabitants, acquired by commercial success.

Full fed with vanity is an author, when two readers strive to catch up his work, for the pleasure of perusing it:--but, perchance, if two readers dip into this chapter, they may strive to lay it down.

I have hitherto written to the *world*, but now to a small part, *the antiquarians*; nay, a small part of the sensible part; for a fool and an antiquary is a contradiction: they are, to a man, people of letters and penetration. If their judgment is sometimes erroneous, we may consider, man was never designed for perfection; there is also less light to guide them in this, than in other researches. If the traveller slips upon common ground, how will he fare if he treads upon ice?--Besides, in dark questions, as in intricate journies, there are many erroneous ways for one right.

If, like the mathematician, he can establish one point, it ascertains another. We may deem his pursuit one of the most arduous, and attended with the least profit: his emoluments consist in the returns of pleasure to his own mind.

The historian only collects the matter of the day, and hands it to posterity; but the antiquarian brings his treasures from remote ages, and presents them to this: he examines forgotten repositories, calls things back into existence, which are past; counter-acts the efforts of time, and of death; possesses something like a re-creative power; collects the dust of departed matter, moulds it into its prestine state, exhibits the figure to view, and stamps it with a kind of immortality.

Every thing has its day, whether it be a nation, a city, a castle, a man, or an insect; the difference is, one is a winter's day, the other may be extended to the length of a summer's--an *end* waits upon all. But we cannot contemplate the end of grandeur, without gloomy ideas.

Birmingham is surrounded with the melancholy remains of extinguished greatness; the decayed habitations of decayed gentry, fill the mind with sorrowful reflections. Here the feet of those marked the ground, whose actions marked the page of history. Their arms glistened in the field; their eloquence moved the senate. Born to command, their influence was extensive; but who now rest in peace among the paupers, fed with the crumbs of their table. The very land which, for ages, was witness to the hospitality of its master, is itself doomed to stirility. The spot which drew the adjacent country, is neglected by all; is often in a wretched state of cultivation, sets for a trifle; the glory is departed; it demands a tear from the traveller, and the winds teem, to sigh over it.

THE MOATS.

In the parish of King's-norton, four miles south west of Birmingham, is *The Moats*, upon which long resided the ancient family of Field. The numerous buildings, which almost formed a village, are totally erased, and barley grows where the beer was drank.

BLACK GREVES.

Eight miles south west of Birmingham, in the same parish, near Withod Chapel, is *Black Greves* (Black Groves) another seat of the Fields; which, though a family of opulence, were so far from being lords of the manor, that they were in vassalage to them.

The whole of that extensive parish is in the crown, which holds the detestable badge of ancient slavery over every tenant, of demanding under the name of harriot, the best moveable he dies possessed of--Thus death and the bailiff make their inroads together; they rob the family in a double capacity, each taking the best moveable.

As the human body descends into the regions of sickness, much sooner than it can return into health; so a family can decline into poverty by hastier steps, than rise into affluence. One generation of extravagance puts a period to many of greatness.

A branch of the Fields, in 1777, finished their ancient grandeur, by signing away the last estate of his family.--Thus he blotted out the name of his ancestors by writing his own.

ULVERLEY, OR CULVERLEY.

Four miles from Birmingham, upon the Warwick road, entering the parish of Solihull, in Castle-lane, is Ulverle, in doom's-day Ulverlei. Trifling as this place now seems, it must have been the manor-house of Solihull, under the Saxon heptarchy; but went to decay so long ago as the conquest.

The manor was the property of the Earls of Mercia, but whether their residence is uncertain.--The traces of a moat yet remain, which are triangular, and encircle a wretched farm-house of no note: one of the angles of this moat is filled up, and become part of Castle-lane; which proves that Ulverley went into disuse when Hogg's-moat was erected: it also proves that the lane terminated here, which is about two hundred yards from the turnpike road. The great width of the lane, from the road to Ulverley, and the singular narrowness from thence to Hogg's-moat, is another proof of its prior antiquity.

If we pursue our journey half a mile Farther along this lane, which by the way is scarcely passable, it will bring us to

HOGG'S-MOAT.

At Oltenend (Old Town) originally Odingsell's-moat, now Hobb's-moat, the ancient manor-house of Solihull, after it had changed its lords at the conquest. The property, as before observed, of Edwin Earl of Mercia, in the reign of Edward the the Confessor.

William the First granted the manor to a favourite lady, named Cristina, probably a handsome lass, of the same complexion as his mother; thus we err when we say William gave all the land in the kingdom to his followers--some little was given to those *he* followed.

This lady, like many of her successors, having tired the arms of royalty, was conveyed into those of an humble favourite; Ralph de Limesie married her, who became lord of the place, but despising Ulverley, erected this castle.

The line of Limesie continued proprietors four descents; when, in the reign of King John, it became the property of Hugh de Odingsells, by marrying a co-heiress.

The last of the Odingsells, in 1294, left four daughters, one of whom, with the lordship, fell into the hands of John de Clinton; but it is probable the castle was not inhabited after the above date, therefore would quickly fall to decay.

The moat is upon a much larger plan than Ulverley, takes in a compass of five acres, had two trenches; the outer is nearly obliterated, but the inner is marked with the strongest lines we meet with. This trench is about twenty feet deep, and about thirty yards from the crown of one bank to the other.

When Dugdale saw it, about a hundred and fifty years ago, the center, which is about two acres, where the castle stood, was covered with old oaks; round this center are now some thousands, the oldest of which is not more than a century; so that the timber is changed since the days of Dugdale, but not the appearance of the land.

The center is bare of timber, and exhibits the marks of the plough. The late Benjamin Palmer, Esq; a few years ago, planted it with trees, which are in that dwindling state, that they are not likely to grow so tall as their master[7].

[7] He measured about six feet five inches, but was singularly short in the lower parts: his step was not larger than a child's of ten years old. His carriage, by its extraordinary height, looked at a distance like a moving steeple; he sat as high in a common chair, as a man of the middle-size stands: he was as immoderately heavy as he was tall, and as remarkable for good-nature as either. As a man, he shone by his bulk; as a magistrate, in a dull but honest light--his decisions were *intended* to be just. He seemingly dozed as he walked; but if his own eyes were half shut, those of every other person were open to see him.

It lies in a pleasant situation, upon a descent, so that the trench in one part is dry, and in another three or four yards deep in water.

A place of such desolation, one would think, was a place of silence--just the reverse. When I saw it, Feb. 23, 1783, the trees were tall, the winds high, and the roar tremendous.

Exclusive of Ulverley and Hogg's-moat, there are many old foundations in Solihull, once the residence of gentry now extinct; as Solihull-hall, the Moat-house, and Kynton, the property of the Botolers; Bury-hall, that of the Warings; who both came over with William: Henwood, belonging to the Hugfords; Hillfield-hall, the ancient seat of the Greswolds, as Malvern was their modern.

YARDLEY.

At Yardley church, four miles east of Birmingham, is *The Moat*, now a pasture; the trench still retains its water, as a remembrance of its former use.

This was anciently the property of the Allestrees, lords of Witton; but about thirty years ago, the building and the family expired together.

KENT'S-MOAT.

One mile farther east is Kent's-moat, in which no noise is heard but the singing of birds, as if for joy that their enemy is fled, and they have regained their former habitation.

This is situate on an eminence, like that of Park-hall, is capacious, has but one trench, supplied by its own springs; and, like that, as complete as earth and water can make it.

This was part of Coleshill, and vested in the crown before the conquest, but soon after granted with that to Clinton, who gave it with a daughter to Verdon; and he, with another, to Anselm de Scheldon, who kept it till the reign of Edward the

Third: it afterwards passed through several families, till the reign of Henry the Seventh, when it came into that of De Gray, Earl of Kent, whence the name; though, perhaps, the works were erected by Scheldon.

It is now, with Coleshill, the property of Lord Digby; but the building has been so long gone, that tradition herself has lost it.

SHELDON.

One mile east is Sheldon-hall, which anciently bore the name of East-hall, in contradistinction from Kent's-moat, which was West-hall. This, in 1379, was the property of Sir Hugh le Despenser, afterwards of the family of Devereux, ancestor of the present Viscount Hereford, who resided here till about 1710. In 1751, it was purchased by John Taylor, Esq; and is now possessed by his tenant.

The moat, like others on an eminence, has but one trench, fed by the land springs; is filled up in the front of the hall, as there is not much need of water protection. The house, which gives an idea of former gentility, seems the first erected on the spot; is irregular, agreeable to the taste of the times, and must have been built many centuries. All the ancient furniture fled with its owners, except an hatchment in the hall, with sixteen coats of arms, specifying the families into which they married.

KING'S-HURST.

Two furlongs east of Sheldon-hall, and one mile south of Castle Bromwich, is *Kings-hurst*; which, though now a dwelling in tenancy, was once the capital of a large track of land, consisting of its own manor, Coleshill, and Sheldon; the demesne of the crown, under the Saxon kings, from whom we trace the name.

The Conqueror, or his son William, granted it; but whether for money, service, caprice, or favour, is uncertain; for he who wears a crown acts as whimsically as he who does not.

Mountfort came over with William, as a knight, and an officer of rank; but, perhaps, did not immediately receive the grant, for the king would act again much like other people, *give away their property, before he would give away his own*.

If this unfortunate family were not the first grantees, they were lords, and probably residents of King's-hurst, long before their possession of Coleshill, in 1332, and by a younger branch, long after the unhappy attainder of Sir Simon, in 1497.

Sir William Mountfort, in 1390, augmented the buildings, erected a chapel, and inclosed the manor. His grandson, Sir Edmund, in 1447, paled in some of the land, and dignified it with the fashionable name of *park*.

This prevailing humour of imparking was unknown to the Saxons, it crept in with the Norman: some of the first we meet with are those of Nottingham, Wedgnock, and Woodstock--Nottingham, by William Peveral, illegitimate son of the Conqueror; Wedgnock, by Newburg, the first Norman Earl of Warwick; and Woodstock, by Henry the First. So that the Duke of Marlborough perhaps may congratulate himself with possessing the oldest park in use.

The modern park is worth attention; some are delightful in the extreme: they are the beauties of creation, terrestrial paradises; they are just what they ought to be, nature cautiously assisted by invisible art. We envy the little being who presides over one--but why mould we envy him? the pleasure consists in *seeing*, and one man may *see* as well as another: nay, the stranger holds a privilege beyond him; for the proprietor, by often seeing, sees away the beauties, while he who looks but seldom, sees with full effect. Besides, one is liable to be fretted by the mischievous hand of injury, which the stranger seldom sees; he looks for excellence, the owner for defect, and they both find.

These proud inclosures, guarded by the growth within, first appeared under the dimension of one or two hundred acres; but fashion, emulation, and the park, grew up together, till the last swelled into one or two thousand.

If religions rise from the lowest ranks, the fashions generally descend from the higher, who are at once blamed, and imitated by their inferiors.

The highest orders of men lead up a fashion, the next class tread upon their heels, the third quickly follow, then the fourth, fifth, &c. immediately figure after them. But as a man who had an inclination for a park, could not always spare a thousand acres, he must submit to less, for a park must be had: thus Bond, of Ward-end, set up with thirty; some with one half, till the very word became a burlesque upon the idea. The design was a display of lawns, hills, water, clumps, &c. as if ordered by the voice of nature; and furnished with herds of deer. But some of our modern parks contain none of these beauties, nor scarcely land enough to support a rabbit.

I am possessed of one of these jokes of a park, something less than an acre:--he that has none, might think it a *good* joke, and wish it his own; he that has more would despise it: that it never was larger, appears from its being surrounded by Sutton Coldfield; and that it has retained the name for ages, appears from the old timber upon it.

The manor of King's-hurst was disposed of by the Mountforts, about two hundred years ago, to the Digbys, where it remains.

COLESHILL.

One mile farther east is *Coleshill-hall*, vested in the crown before, and after the conquest; purchased, perhaps, of William Rufus, by Geoffrey de Clinton, ancestor to the present Duke of Newcastle. In 1352, an heiress of the house of Clinton, gave it, with herself, to Sir John de Mountfort, of the same family with Simon, the great Earl of Leicester, who fell, in 1265, at Evesham, in that remarkable contest with Henry the Third.

With them it continued till 1497, when Sir Simon Mountfort, charged, but perhaps unjustly, with assisting Perkin Warbeck with 30*l*. was brought to trial at Guildhall, condemned as a traitor, executed at Tyburn, his large fortune confiscated, and his family ruined. Some of his descendants I well know in Birmingham; and *they* are well known to poverty, and the vice.

In the reign of Henry the Seventh, it was almost dangerous, particularly for a rich man, even to *think* against a crafty and avaricious monarch.--What is singular, the man who accused Sir Simon at the bar, succeeded him in his estate.

Simon Digby procured a grant of the place, in whose line it still continues. The hall is inhabited, but has been left about thirty years by the family; was probably erected by the Mountforts, is extensive, and its antique aspect without, gives a venerable pleasure to the beholder, like the half admitted light diffused within. Every spot of the park is delightful, except that in which the hall stands: our ancestors built in the vallies, for the sake of water; their successors on the hills, for the sake of air.

From this uncouth swamp sprung the philosopher, the statesman, and tradition says, the gunpowder-plot.

DUDDESTON.

Four furlongs north-east of Birmingham, is *Duddeston* (Dud's-town) from Dud, the Saxon proprietor, Lord of Dudley, who probably had a seat here; once a considerable village, but long reduced to the manor-house, till Birmingham, swelling beyond its bounds, in 1764, verged upon this lordship; and we now, in 1783, behold about eighty houses, under the names of Duke-street, Prospect-row, and Woodcock-lane.

It afterwards descended to the Paganalls, the Sumeris, then to the Bottetourts, and was, in 1323, enjoyed by Joan Bottetourt, lady of Weoley castle, a daughter of the house of Sumeri.

Sir Thomas de Erdington held it of this lady, by a chief-rent, which was a pair of gilt spurs, or six-pence, at the option of the tenant.

Erdington sold it, in 1327, to Thomas de Maidenhache, by whose daughter, Sibell, it came in marriage to Adam de Grymforwe; whose posterity, in 1363, conveyed it for 26*l*. 13s. 4d. now worth 20,000*l*. to John atte Holt; and his successors made it their residence, till the erection of Aston-hall, in the reign of James I.

It is now converted into beautiful gardens, as a public resort of pleasure, and dignified with the London name of Vauxhall. The demolished fish-ponds, and the old foundations, which repel the spade, declare its former grandeur.

In 1782 it quitted, by one of the most unaccountable alignments that ever resulted from human weakness, the ancient name of Holte, familiar during four hundred and nineteen years, for that of Legge.

Could the ghost of Sir Lister re-visit his departed property, one might ask, What reception might you meet with, Sir Lister, in 1770, among your venerable ancestors in the shades, for barring, unprovoked, an infant heiress of 7000*l.* a year, and giving it, unsolicited, to a stranger? Perhaps you experience repeated buffetings; a sturdy figure, with iron aspect, would be apt to accost you--"I with nervous arm, and many a bended back, drew 40*l.* from the Birmingham forge, with which, in 1330, I purchased the park and manor of Nechels, now worth four hundred times that sum. I planted that family which you have plucked up by the roots: in the sweat of my brow, I laid a foundation for greatness; many of my successors built on that foundation--but you, by starving your brother, Sir Charles, into compliance, wantonly cut off the entail, and gave away the estate, after passing through seventeen descents, merely to shew you had a power to give it. We concluded here, that a son of his daughter, the last hope of the family, would change his own name to preserve ours, and not the estate change its possessor."--"I," another would be apt to say, "with frugal hand, and lucrative employments under the crown, added, in 1363, the manor of Duddeston; and, in 1367, that of Alton. But for what purpose did I add them? To display the folly of a successor."--A dejected spectre would seem to step forward, whose face carried the wrinkles of eighty-four, and the shadow of tear; "I, in 1611, brought the title of baronet among us, first tarnished by you; which, if your own imbecility could not procure issue to support, you ought to have supported it by purchase. I also, in 1620, erected the mansion at Afton, then, and even now, the most superb in that neighbourhood, fit to grace the leading title of nobility; but you forbad my successors to enter. I joined, in 1647, to our vast fortune, the manor of Erdington.--Thus the fabric we have been rearing for ages, you overthrew in one fatal moment."--The last angry spectre would appear in the bloom of life. "I left you an estate which you did not deserve: you had no more right to leave it from your successor, than I to leave it from you: one man may ruin the family of another, but he seldom ruins his own. We blame him who wrongs his neighbour, but what does he deserve who wrongs himself?--You have done both, for by cutting off the succession, your name will be lost. The ungenerous attorney, instead of making your absurd will, ought to have apprized you of our sentiments, which exactly coincide with those of the world, or how could the tale affect a stranger? Why did not some generous friend guide your crazy vessel, and save a sinking family? Degenerate son, he who destroys the peace of another, should forfeit his own--we leave you to remorse, may she quickly *find, and weep over you.*"

SALTLEY.

A mile east of Duddeston is *Saltley-hall*, which, with an extensive track of ground, was, in the Saxon times, the freehold of a person whom we should now call Allen; the same who was Lord of Birmingham. But at the conquest, when justice was laid asleep, and property possessed by him who could seize it, this manor, with many others, fell into the hands of William Fitz-Ausculf, Baron of Dudley-castle, who granted it in knight's-service to Henry de Rokeby.

A daughter of Rokeby carried it by marriage to Sir John Goband, whose descendants, in 1332, sold it to Walter de Clodshale; an heiress of Clodshale, in 1426, brought it into the ancient family of Arden, and a daughter of this house, to that of Adderley, where it now rests.

The castle, I have reason to think, was erected by Rokeby, in which all the lords resided till the extinction of the Clodshales.--It has been gone to ruin about three hundred years, and the solitary platform seems to mourn its loss.

WARD-END.

Three miles from Birmingham, in the same direction, is *Wart-end*, anciently *Little Bromwich*; a name derived from the plenty of broom, and is retained to this day by part of the precincts, *Broomford* (Bromford).

This manor was claimed by that favourite of the conqueror, Fitz-Ausculf, and granted by him to a second-hand favourite, who took its name.

The old castle has been gone about a century; the works are nearly complete, cover about nine acres, the most capacious in this neighbourhood, those of Weoley-castle excepted. The central area is now an orchard, and the water, which guarded the castle, guards the fruit. This is surrounded with three mounds, and three trenches, one of them fifty yards over, which, having lost its master, guards the fish.

The place afterwards passed through several families, till the reign of Henry the Seventh. One of them bearing the name of *Ward*, changed the name to *Ward-end*.

In 1512, it was the property of John Bond, who, fond of his little hamlet, inclosed a park of thirty acres, stocked it with deer; and, in 1517, erected a chapel for the conveniency of his tenants, being two miles from the parish church of Afton. The skeleton of this chapel, in the form of a cross, the fashion of the times, is yet standing on the outward mound: its floor is the only religious one I have seen laid with horse-dung; the pulpit is converted into a manger--it formerly furnished husks for the man, but now corn for the horse. Like the first christian church, it has experienced a double use, a church and a stable; but with this difference, *that* in Bethlehem, was a stable advanced into a church; this, on the contrary, is reduced into a stable.

The manor, by a female, passed through the Kinardsleys, and is now possessed by the Brand-woods; but the hall, erected in 1710, and its environs, are the property of Abraham Spooner, Esq.

CASTLE BROMWICH.

Simply *Bromwich*, because the soil is productive of broom.

My subject often leads me back to the conquest, an enterprize, wild without parallel: we are astonished at the undertaking, because William was certainly a man of sense, and a politician. Harold, his competitor, was a prince much superior in power, a consummate general, and beloved by his people. The odds were so much against the invader, that out of one hundred such imprudent attempts, ninety-nine would miscarry: all the excuse in his favour is, *it succeeded*. Many causes concurred in this success, such as his own ambition, aided by his valour; the desperate fortune of his followers, very few of whom were men of property, for to the appearance of gentlemen, they added the realities of want; a situation to which any change is thought preferable; but, above all, *chance*. A man may dispute for religion, he may contend for liberty, he may run for his life, but he will *fight* for property.

By the contest between William and Harold, the unhappy English lost all they had to lose; and though this all centered in the Normans, they did not acquire sufficient to content them.

History does not inform us who was then the proprietor of Castle Bromwich, but that it belonged to the Mercian Earls scarcely admits a doubt; as Edwin owned some adjoining manors, he probably owned this. Fitz-Ausculf was his fortunate successor, who procured many lordships in the neighhood of Birmingham; Castle Bromwich was one. He granted it to an inferior Norman, in military tenure; who, agreeable to the fashion of those times, took the surname of Bromwich.

Henry de Castel was a subsequent proprietor. Dugdale supposes the village took its name from a castle, once on the premises; and that the castle-hill yet remains: but this hill is too small, even to admit a shelter for a Lilliputian, and is evidently an artificial trifle, designed for a monument. It might hold, for its ancient furniture, a turret, termed a castle-- perhaps it held nothing in Dugdale's time: the modern is a gladiator, in the attitude of fighting, supported by a pedestal, containing the Bridgeman arms.

Castle, probably, was added by the family of that name, lords of the place, to distinguish it from *woody* and *little* Bromwich. They bore for their arms, three castles and a chevron.

Lord Ferrers of Chartley, who was proprietor of Birmingham in the reign of Henry the Sixth, enjoyed it by marriage; and his grand daughter brought it, by the same channel, into the family of Devereux, Lords of Sheldon. Edward, about the latter end of Queen Elizabeth's reign, erected the present building, which is capacious, is in a stile between ancient and modern, and has a pleasing appearance.

The Bridgeman family acceded to possession about eighty years ago, by purchase, and made it their residence till about 1768. We should naturally enquire, Why Sir Harry quitted a place so delightfully situated? Perhaps it is not excelled in this country, in the junction of three great roads, a a desirable neighbourhood, the river Tame at its back, and within five miles of the plentiful market of Bimingham--but, alas, *it has no park*.

The gentry seem to have resided in our vicinity, when there was the greatest inducement to leave it, *impassable roads*: they seem also to have quitted the country, now there is the greatest inducement to reside there; roads, which improve their estates, and may be travelled with pleasure. It may be objected, that "the buildings become ancient." But there is no more disgrace in an old house, than in an old man; they may both be dressed in character, and look well. A gentleman, by residing in the family seat, pays a compliment to his ancestors.

PARK-HALL.

Six miles north-east of Birmingham, and one from Castle Bromwich chapel, is a spacious moat, with one trench, which, for many centuries guarded *Park-hall*. This is another of those desolate islands, from which every creature is fled, and every sound, except that of the winds; nay, even the very clouds seem to lament the desolation with tears.

This was possessed by none but the Ardens, being part of their vast estate long before the conquest, and five hundred years after. A delightful situation on the banks of the Tame; to which we are led through a dirty road.

We may consider this island, the treasury into which forty-six lordships paid their tribute. The riches of the country were drawn to this center, and commands were issued from it. The growth of these manors supplied that spot, which now grows for another. The lordships are in forty-six hands; the country is in silence; the island ploughed up, and the family distressed-- At the remembrance of their name, the smile quits the face of history; she records their sad tale with a sigh; while their arms are yet displayed in some of the old halls in the neighbourhood.

BERWOOD.

Crossing the river, one mile farther east, is *Berwood-hall*, where the forsaken moat, at this day, guards--nothing. This, with the manor to which it belongs, was also the property of the Ardens; one of which in the reign of Henry the Second, granted it to the canons of Leicester; who added a chapel, which went to decay four hundred years ago. After the grant, the Ardens seem to have become tenants to the canons for the land, once their own: we frequently observe a man pay rent for what he *sells*, but seldom for what he *gives*.

At the dissolution of abbies, in 1537, Thomas Arden, the head of the family, purchased it of Henry the Eighth, for 272*l*. 10s. uniting it again to his estate, after a separation of three hundred and fifty years, in whose posterity it continued till their fall.

Thus, the father first purchased what the son gave away, and his offspring re-purchased again. The father lays a tax on his successor; or, climbs to heaven at the expence of the son. In one age it is meritorious to *give* to the church, in another, to *take* from her.

ERDINGTON.

Three miles north-east of Birmingham, is *Erdington-hall*, which boasts a long antiquity. The manor was the property of the old Earls of Mercia: Edwin possessed it at the conquest, but lost it in favour of William Fitz-Ausculf, who no doubt granted it in knight's service to his friend and relation, of Norman race, who erected the hall; the moat, took his residence in, and his name Erdington, from the place. His descendants seem to have resided here with great opulence near 400 years.

Dugdale mentions a circumstance of Sir Thomas de Erdington, little noticed by our historians. He was a faithful adherent to King John, who conferred on him many valuable favours: harrassed by the Pope on one side, and his angry Barons on the other, he privately sent Sir Thomas to Murmeli, the powerful King of Africa, Morocco, and Spain; with offers to forsake the christian faith, turn mahometan, deliver up his kingdom, and hold it of him in tribute, for his assistance against his enemies. But it does not appear the ambassador succeeded: the Moorish Monarch did not chuse to unite his prosperous fortune with that of a random prince; he might also consider, the man who could destroy his nephew and his sovereign, could not be an honour to any profession.

The manor left the Erdington family in 1472, and, during a course of 175 years, acknowledged for its owners, George Plantagenet, Duke of Clarence, Sir William Harcourt, Robert Wright, Sir Reginald Bray, Francis Englefield, Humphry Dimock, Walter Earl, Sir Walter Devereux, and was, in 1647, purchased by Sir Thomas Holte, in whose family it continued till 1782, when Henage Legge, Esq; became seised of the manor.

As none of the Lords seem to have resided upon the premises since the departure of the Erdingtons, it must be expected they have gradually tended to decay.

We may with some reason conclude, that as Erdington was the freehold of the Earls of Mercia, it was not the residence of its owners, therefore could not derive its name from them. That as the word *Arden* signifies a wood, the etymology of that populous village is, *a town in the wood*. That one of the first proprietors, after the conquest, struck with the security offered by the river, erected the present fortifications, which cover three parts of the hall, and the river itself the fourth. Hence it follows, that the neighbouring work, which we now call Bromford-forge, was a mill prior to the conquest; because the stream is evidently turned out of its bed to feed it. That the present hall is the second on the premises, and was erected by the Erdingtons, with some later additions.

PIPE.

One mile north-east of Erdington, is *Pipe-hall*; which, with its manor, like the neighbouring land, became at the conquest the property of Fitz-Ausculf; and afterwards of his defendants, Paganall, Sumeri, Bottetort, and St. Leger.

It was common at that fatal period, for one of these great barons, or rather great robbers, to procure a large quantity of land for himself; some of them two or three hundred thousand acres--too much for one man to grasp. He therefore kept what he pleased for his private use, and granted the other in knight's-service, reserving annually a rent. These rents were generally small, so as never to hurt the tenant: however, the lord could order him to arms whenever he pleased.

A few of the grants were procured by the disinherited English, but chiefly by the officers of William's army, being more respected, and more proper to be trusted: they were often relations, or favourites of the great barons. The lord could not conveniently sell, without the consent of the crown, but he could set at what price he pleased. Time made this chief-rent permanent, and gave the tenant stability of title.

The manor of Pipe, with some others, was granted to William Mansell, who resided in the hall, and executed some of the chief offices of the county.

The last of the name, in the reign of Henry the Third, left a daughter, who married Henry de Harcourt; and his daughter married John de Pipe, who seems to have taken its name.

Henry, his descendant, had many children, all of whom, with his lady, died of the plague, except a daughter, Margery. He afterwards married, in 1363, Matilda, the daughter of George de Castell, of Castle Bromwich; but soon after the happy wedding, he perceived his bride was pregnant, which proved, on enquiry, the effect of an intrigue with her father's menial servant; a striking instance of female treachery, which can only be equalled by--male.

The shock proving too great for his constitution, brought on a decline, and himself to the grave, before the birth of the child.

John was the fruit of this unlawful amour, whose guardian, to prevent his inheriting the estate, made him a canon of Ouston, in Leicestershire; and afterwards persuaded the unhappy Margery to grant the manor to the abbot of Stonely.

Thomas de Beauchamp, Earl of Warwick, afterwards purchased it for 133*l*. 6s. 8d. It came to the crown by attainder, in the reign of Henry the Seventh; then to Sir William Staunford, one of his judges, John Buttler; Edward Holte, in 1568; Francis Dimock, whose daughter married Walter Earl; then to Walter Devereux, by marrying Earl's daughter; afterwards to Sir Thomas Holte, by purchase; and is now in the family of Bagot.

Though the hall is antique, its front is covered in the modern barbarous stile, by a clump of venerable trees; which would become any situation but that in which they stand. It is now inhabited by a gentleman of Birmingham, who has experienced the smiles of commerce.

ASTON.

Two miles north of Birmingham, is Aston (East-town) being east of Westbury (Wednesbury) it lies on a steep descent towards the river Tame.

This place, like that of Erdington, belonged to the Earls of Mercia in the Saxon times; and, at the conquest, was the property of the unfortunate Edwin. Fitz-Ausculf became his successor in this, and in other lands: the survey calls it eight hides, valued at 5*l*. per annum; a mill, 3s. and a wood, three miles long, and half a mile broad. The mill, I make no doubt, stood where a mill now stands, near Sawford-bridge; but neither the hides, nor the wood, could be confined within the boundary of Afton; the manor is too little for either. The lordship extends about a square mile, and that part which is now the park, I have reason to think, was then a common, and for ages after.

A Saxon, of the name of Godmund, held it under the Mercian Earls, and found means, at the conquest, to hold it under the Norman.

One hundred yards north of the church, in a perfect swamp, stood the hall; probably erected by Godmund, or his family: the situation shews the extreme of bad taste--one would think, he endeavoured to lay his house under the water. The trenches are obliterated by the floods, so as to render the place unobserved by the stranger: it is difficult to chuse a worse, except he had put his house under the earth. I believe there never was more than one house erected on the spot, and that was one too much.

Whether this Saxon family of Godmund became extinct, or had lost their right, is uncertain; but Sumeri, Fitz-Ausculf's successor, about 1203, granted the manor to Sir Thomas de Erdington, Ambassador to King John, mentioned before, who had married his sister; paying annually a pair of spurs, or six-pence, as a nominal rent, but meant, in reality, as a portion for the lady.

The family of Erdington, about 1275, sold it to Thomas de Maidenhache, who did not seem to live upon friendly terms with his neighbour, William de Birmingham; for, in 1290, he brought an action against him for fishing in his water, called Moysich (Dead-branch) leading into Tame, towards Scarford-bridge (Shareford, dividing the shares, or parts of the parish, Aston manor from Erdington, now Sawford-bridge) which implies a degree of unkindness; because William could not amuse himself in his own manor of Birmingham, for he might as well have angled in one of his streets, as in the river Rea. The two lords had, probably, four years before been on friendly terms, when they jointly lent their assistance to the hospital of St. Thomas, in Birmingham.

Maidenhache left four daughters; Sibel, married Adam de Grymsorwe, who took with her the manor of Aston; a daughter of this house, in 1367, sold it to John atte Holte, of Birmingham, in whose family it continued 415 years, till 1782, when Henage Legge, Esq; acceded to possession.

This wretched bog was the habitation of all the lords, from Godmund to the Holtes, the Erdington's excepted; for Maud Grymsorwe executing the conveyance at Aston, indicates that she resided there; and Thomas Holte, being possessed of Duddeston, proves that he did not: therefore I conclude, that the building, as it ought, went to decay soon after; so that desolation has claimed the place for her own near four hundred years. This is corroborated by some old timber trees, long since upon the spot where the building stood.

The extensive parish of Aston takes in the two extremes of Birmingham, which supplies her with more christenings, weddings, and burials, than were, a few years ago, supplied by the whole parish of Birmingham.

WITTON.

Three miles north of Birmingham, and one from Aston, is *Witton*, (Wicton) from the bend of the river, according to Dugdale: the property of a person at the conquest whose name was Staunchel. Fitz-Ausculf seized it, and Staunchel, more fortunate than the chief of his country men, became his tenant; valued in the conqueror's survey at 20s. per ann.

It was afterwards vested in the crown: in 1240, Henry the third granted it to Andrew de Wicton, who took his name from the place, for in Dooms-day it is Witone; therefore the name being prior, proves the remark.

Andrew, anxious after the boundary of his new purchase, brought an action against his neighbour, William de Pyrie (Perry) for infringing his property. Great disputes arise from small beginnings; perhaps a lawyer blew the flame.

The king issued his precept to the Sheriff of Staffordshire, in which Perry lies, to bring with him twelve lawful and discreet knights; and the same to the Sheriff of Warwickshire, of which Witton is part, to ascertain the bounds between them.

Which was the aggressor, is hard to determine, but I should rather suppose Squire Perry, because *man* is ever apt to trespass; he resided on the premises, and the crown is but a sleepy landlord; not so likely to rob, as be robbed.

There is a road, where foot seldom treads, mounded on each side, leading over the Coldfield, from Perry-bridge towards the Newlands, undoubtedly the work of this venerable band of discreet knights.

The stranger, of course, would deem the property between the contending parties, of great value, which, twenty-four of the principal characters of the age, the flower of two counties, marshalled by two chief officers, were to determine. But what will he think of the quarrelsome spirit of the times, when, I tell him, it was only a few acres, which is, even at this day, waste land, and scarcely worth owning by either.

In 1290, Witton was the property of William Dixley; in 1340, that of Richard de Pyrie, descendant of him, who, a hundred years before, held the contest. In 1426, Thomas East, of Hay-hall, in Yardley, was owner; who sold it to John Bond, of Ward-end, of whose descendants William Booth purchased it, in 1620: an heiress of Booth brought it by marriage to Allestree, of Yardley, who enjoyed it in our days; it was sold to John Wyrley, and is now possessed by George Birch, Esq; of Handsworth.

The house, left by its owners, is in that low, or rather boggy situation, suitable to the fashion of those times. I can discover no traces of a moat, though there is every conveniency for one: We are doubly hurt by seeing a house in a miserable hole, when joining an elegible spot.

BLAKELEY.

Five miles north-west of Birmingham, is *Blakely-hall*, the manor house of Oldbury. If we see a venerable edifice without a moat, we cannot from thence conclude, it was never the residence of a gentleman, but wherever we find one, we may conclude it was.

Anciently, this manor, with those of Smethwick and Harborn, belonged to the family of Cornwallis, whose habitation was Blakeley-hall: the present building seems about 300 years old.

The extinction of the male line, threw the property into the hands of two coheirs; one of whom married into the family of Grimshaw, the other into that of Wright, who jointly held it. The family of Grimshaw failing, Wright became then, and is now, possessed of the whole.

I am unacquainted with the principal characters who acted the farce of life on this island, but it has long been in the tenancy of a poor farmer, who, the proprietor allured me, was *best* able to stock the place with children. In 1769, the Birmingham canal passing over the premises, robbed the trench of its water. Whether it endangers the safety is a doubt, for *poverty* is the best security against violence.

WEOLEY

Four miles west of Birmingham, in the parish of Northfield, are the small, but extensive ruins of *Weoley-castle*, whose appendages command a track of seventeen acres, situate in a park of eighteen hundred.

These moats usually extend from half an acre to two acres, are generally square, and the trenches from eight yards over to twenty.

This is large, the walls massy; they form the allies of a garden, and the rooms, the beds; the whole display the remains of excellent workmanship. One may nearly guess at a man's consequence, even after a lapse of 500 years, by the ruins of his house.

The steward told me, "they pulled down the walls as they wanted the stone." Unfeeling projectors: there is not so much to pull down. Does not time bring destruction fast enough without assistance? The head which cannot contemplate, offers its hand to destroy. The insensible taste, unable itself to relish the dry fruits of antiquity, throws them away to prevent another. May the fingers *smart* which injure the venerable walls of Dudley, or of Kenilworth. Noble remains of ancient grandeur! copious indexes, that point to former usage! We survey them with awful pleasure. The mouldering walls, as if ashamed of their humble state, hide themselves under the ivies; the generous ivies, as if conscious of the precious relics, cover them from the injuries of time.

When land frequently undergoes a conveyance, necessity, we suppose, is the lot of the owner, but the lawyer fattens: *To have and to hold* are words of singular import; they charm beyond music; are the quintessence of language; the leading figure in rhetoric. But how would he fare if land was never conveyed? He must starve upon quarrels.

Instances may be given of land which knows no title, except those of conquest and descent: Weoley Castle comes nearly under this description. *To sign, seal, and deliver*, were wholly unknown to our ancestors. Could a Saxon freeholder rise from the dead, and visit the land, once his own, now held by as many writings as would half spread over it, he might exclaim, "Evil increases with time, and parchment with both. You deprive the poor of their breeches; I covered the ground with sheep, you with their skins; I thought, as you were at variance with France, Spain, Holland, and America, those numerous deeds were a heap of drum heads, and the internal writing, the *articles of war*. In one instance, however, there is a similarity between us; we unjustly took this land from the Britons, you as unjustly took it from us; and a time may come, when another will take it from you. Thus, the Spaniards founded the Peruvian empire in butchery, now tottering towards a fall; you, following their example, seized the northern coast of America; you neither bought it nor begged it, you took it from the natives; and thus your children, the Americans, with equal violence, have taken it from you: No law binds like that of arms. The question has been, whether they shall pay taxes? which, after a dispute of eight years, was lost in another, *to whom* they shall pay taxes? The result, in a future day will be, domestic struggles for sovereignty will stain the ground with blood."

When the proud Norman cut his way to the throne, his imperious followers seized the lands, kicked out the rightful possessors, and treated them with a dignity rather beneath that practiced to a dog.--This is the most summary title yet discovered.

Northfield was the fee-simple of Alwold (Allwood) but, at the conquest, Fitz-Ausculf seized it, with a multitude of other manors: it does not appear that he granted it in knight's-service to the injured Allwood, but kept it for his private use, Paganall married his heiress, and Sumeri married Paganall's, who, in the beginning of the 13th century, erected the castle. In 1322, the line of Sumeri expired.

Bottetourt, one of the needy squires, who, like Sancho Panza, attended William his master, in his mad, but *fortunate* enterprize, procured lands which enabled him to *live* in England, which was preferable to starving in Normandy. His descendant became, in right of his wife, coheir of the house of Sumeri, vested in Weoley-castle. He had, in 1307, sprung into peerage, and was one of our powerful barons, till 1385, when the male line dropt. The vast estate of Bottetourt, was then divided among females; Thomas Barkley, married the eldest, and this ancient barony was, in 1761, revived in his descendant, Norborne Barkley, the present Lord Bottetourt; Sir Hugh Burnel married another, and Sir John St. Leger a third.

Weoley-castle was, for many years, the undivided estate of the three families; but Edward Sutton, Lord Dudley, having married a daughter of Barkley, became possessed of that castle, which was erected by Sumeri, their common ancestor, about nine generations before.

In 1551, he sold it to William Jervoise, of London, mercer, whose descendant, Jervoise Clark Jervoise, Esq; now enjoys it.

Fond of ranging, I have travelled a circuit round Birmingham, without being many miles from it. I wish to penetrate farther from the center, but my subject forbids. *Having therefore finished my discourse, I shall*, like my friends, the pulpitarians, many of whom, and of several denominations, are characters I revere, *apply what has been said*.

We learn, that the land I have gone over, with the land I have not, changed its owners at the conquest: this shuts the door of inquiry into pedigree, the old families chiefly became extinct, and few of the present can be traced higher.--Destruction then overspread the kingdom.

The seniors of every age exclaim against the growing corruption of the times: my father, and perhaps every father, dwelt on the propriety of his conduct in younger life, and placed it in counter-view with that of the following generation. However, while I knew him, it was much like other people's--But I could tell him, that he gave us the bright side of his character; that he was, probably, a piece of human nature, as well as his son; that nature varies but little, and that the age of William the Conqueror was the most rascally in the British annals. One age may be marked for the golden, another for the iron, but this for plunder.

We farther learn, there is not one instance in this neighbourhood, where an estate has continued till now in the male line, very few in the female. I am acquainted with only one family near Birmingham, whose ancestor entered with William, and who yet enjoy the land granted at that period: the male line has been once broken--perhaps this land was never conveyed. They shone with splendour near six hundred years. In the sixteenth century, their estate was about 1400*l.* a year; great for that time, but is now, exclusive of a few *pepper-corns* and *red roses*, long since withered, reduced to one little farm, tilled for bread by the owner. This setting glympse of a shining family, is as indifferent about the matter, and almost as ignorant, as the team he drives.

Lastly, we learn that none of the lords, as formerly, reside on the above premises: that in four instances out of twenty-one, the buildings are now as left by the lords, Sheldon, Coleshill, Pipe, and Blakeley: two have undergone some alteration, as Duddeston and Erdington: five others are re-erected, as Black Greves, Ulverley, King's-hurst, Castle Bromwich, and Witton; which, with all the above, are held in tenancy: in eight others all the buildings are swept away, and their moats left naked, as Hogg's-moat, Yardley, Kent's-moat, Saltley, Ward-end, Park-hall, Berwood, and Weoley; and in two instances the moats themselves are vanished, that of King's-norton is filled up to make way for the plough, and that of Aston demolished by the floods. Thus the scenes of hospitality and grandeur, become the scenes of antiquity, and then disappear.

SUTTON COLDFIELD.

Though the topographical historian, who resides upon the premises, is most likely to be correct; yet if *he*, with all his care, is apt to be mistaken, what can be expected from him who trots his horse over the scenes of antiquity?

I have visited, for twenty years, some singular places in this neighbourhood, yet, without being master of their history; thus a man may spend an age in conning his lesson, and never learn it.

When the farmer observes me on his territories, he eyes me *ascance*; suspecting a design to purchase his farm, or take it out of his hands.--I endeavour to remove his apprehensions, by approaching him; and introduce a conversation tending to my pursuit, which he understands as well as if, like the sons of Jacob, I addressed him in Hebrew; yet, notwithstanding his total ignorance of the matter, he has sometimes dropt an accidental word, which has thrown more light on the subject, than all my researches for a twelvemonth. If an honest farmer, in future, should see upon his premises a plumpish figure, five feet six, with one third of his hair on, a cane in his left hand, a glove upon each, and a Pomeranian dog at his heels, let him fear no evil; his farm will not be additionally tythed, his sheep worried, nor his hedges broken--it is only a solitary animal, in quest of a Roman phantom.

Upon the north west extremity of Sutton Coldfield, joining the Chester road, is *The Bowen Pool*; at the tail of which, one hundred yards west of the road, on a small eminence, or swell of the earth, are the remains of a fortification, called *Loaches Banks*; but of what use or original is uncertain, no author having mentioned it.

Four hundred yards farther west, in the same flat, is a hill of some magnitude, deemed, by the curious, a tumolus--it is a common thing for an historian to be lost, but not quite so common to acknowledge it. In attempting to visit this tumolus, I soon found myself in the center of a morass; and here, my dear reader might have seen the historian set fast in a double sense. I was obliged, for that evening, February 16, 1783, to retreat, as the sun had just done before me. I made my approaches from another quarter, April 13, when the hill appeared the work of nature, upon too broad a base for a tumolus; covering about three acres, perfectly round, rising gradually to the center, which is about sixteen feet above the level, surrounded by a ditch, perhaps made for some private purpose by the owner.

The Roman tumoli were of two sorts, the small for the reception of a general, or great man, as that at Cloudsley-bush, near the High Cross, the tomb of Claudius; and the large, as at Seckington, near Tamworth, for the reception of the dead, after a battle: they are both of the same shape, rather high than broad. That before us comes under the description of neither; nor could the dead well be conveyed over the morass.

The ground-plot, in the center of the fort, at Loaches Banks, is about two acres, surrounded by three mounds, which are large, and three trenches, which are small; the whole forming a square of four acres. Each corner directs to a cardinal point, but perhaps not with design; for the situation of the ground would invite the operator to chuse the present form. The northwest joins to, and is secured by the pool.

As the works are much in the Roman taste, I might, at first view, deem it the residence of an opulent lord of the manor; but, the adjacent lands carrying no marks of cultivation, destroys the argument; it is also too large for the fashion; besides, all these manorial foundations have been in use since the conquest, therefore tradition assists the historian; but here, tradition being lost, proves the place of greater antiquity.

One might judge it of Danish extraction, but here again, tradition will generally lend her assistance; neither are the trenches large enough for that people: of themselves they are no security, whether full or empty; for an active young fellow might easily skip from one bank to another. Nor can we view it as the work of some whimsical lord, to excite the wonder of the moderns; it could never pay for the trouble. We must, therefore, travel back among the ancient Britons, for a solution, and here we shall travel over solid ground.

It is, probably, the remains of a British camp, for near these premises are Drude-heath (Druid's-heath) and Drude-fields, which we may reasonably suppose was the residence of a British priest: the military would naturally shelter themselves under the wing of the church, and the priest with the protection of the military. The narrowness of the trenches is another proof of its being British; they exactly correspond with the stile of that people. The name of the pool, *Bowen*, is of British derivation, which is a farther proof that the work originated from the Britons. They did not place their security so much in the trenches, as in the mounds, which they barracaded with timber. This camp is secured on three sides by a morass, and is only approachable on the fourth, that from the Coldfield. The first mound on this weak side, is twenty-four yards over, twice the size of any other; which, allowing an ample security, is a farther evidence of its being British, and tradition being silent is another.

PETITION FOR A CORPORATION.

Every man upon earth seems fond of two things, riches and power: this fondness necessarily springs from the heart, otherwise order would cease. Without the desire of riches, a man would not preserve what he has, nor provide for the future. "My thoughts," says a worthy christian, "are not of this world; I desire but one guinea to carry me through it." Supply him with that guinea, and he wishes another, lest the first should be defective.

If it is necessary a man mould possess property, it is just as necessary he should possess a power to protect it, or the world would quickly bully him out of it: this power is founded on the laws of his country, to which he adds, by way of supplement, bye-laws, founded upon his own prudence. Those who possess riches, well know they are furnished with wings, and can scarcely be kept from flying.

The man who has power to secure his wealth, seldom stops there; he, in turn, is apt to triumph over him who has less. Riches and power are often seen to go hand in hand.

Industry produces property; which, when a little matured, looks out for command; thus the inhabitants of Birmingham, who have generally something upon the anvil besides iron, near seventy years ago having derived wealth from diligence, wished to derive power from charter; therefore, petitioned the crown that Birmingham might be erected into a corporation. Tickled with the title of alderman, dazzled with the splendour of a silver mace, a furred gown, and a magisterial chair, they could not see the interest of the place: had they succeeded, that amazing growth would have been crippled, which has since astonished the world, and those trades have been fettered which have proved the greatest benefit.

When a man loudly pleads for public good, we shrewdly suspect a private emolument lurking beneath. There is nothing more detrimental to good neighbourhood, than men in power, where power is unnecessary; free as the air we breathe, we subsist by our freedom; no command is exercised among us, but that of the laws, to which every discreet citizen pays attention--the magistrate who distributes justice, tinctured with mercy, merits the thanks of society. A train of attendants, a white wand, and a few fiddles, are only the fringe, lace, and trappings of charteral office.

Birmingham, exclusive of her market, ranks among the very lowest order of townships; every petty village claims the honour of being a constable-wick--we are no more. Our immunities are only the trifling privileges anciently granted to the lords; and two thirds of these are lost. But, notwithstanding this seemingly forlorn state, perhaps there is not a place in the British dominions, where so many people are governed by so few officers; nor a place better governed: pride, therefore, must have dictated the humble petition before us.

I have seen a copy of this petition, signed by eighty-four of the inhabitants; and though without a date, seems to have been addressed to King George the First, about 1716: it alledges, "That Birmingham is, of late years, become very populous, from its great increase of trade; is much superior to any town in the county, and but little inferior to any inland town in the kingdom: that it is governed only by a constable, and enjoys no more privileges than a village: that there is no justice of peace in the town; nor any in the neighbourhood, who dares act with vigour: that the country abounds with rioters, who, knowing the place to be void of magistrates, assemble in it, pull down the meeting-houses, defy the king, openly avow the pretender, threaten the inhabitants, and oblige them to keep watch in their own houses: that the trade decays, and will stagnate, if not relieved. To remedy these evils, they beseech his majesty to incorporate the town, and grant such privileges as will enable them to support their trade, the king's interest, and destroy the villainous attempts of the jacobites. In consideration of the requested charter, they make the usual offering of *lives* and *fortunes*".

A petition and the petitioner, like Janus with his two faces, looks different ways; it is often treated as if it said one thing, and meant another; or as if it said any thing but truth. Its use, in some places, is to *lie on the table*. Our humble petition, by some means, met with the fate it deserved.

We may remark, a town without a charter, is a town without a shackle. If there was then a necessity to erect a corporation, because the town was large, there is none now, though larger: the place was not better governed a thousand years ago, when only a tenth of its present magnitude; it may also be governed as well a thousand years hence, if it should swell to ten times its size.

The *pride* of our ancestors was hurt by a petty constable; the *interest* of us, their successors, would be hurt by a mayor: a more simple government cannot be instituted, or one more efficacious: that of some places is designed for parade, ours for use; and both answers their end. A town governed by a multitude of governors, is the most likely to be ill-governed.

The New Brass Works.

BRASS WORKS.

The manufacture of brass was introduced by the family of Turner, about 1740, who erected those works at the south end of Coleshill-street; then, near two hundred yards beyond the buildings, but now the buildings extend about five hundred beyond them.

Under the black clouds which arose from this corpulent tunnel, some of the trades collected their daily supply of brass; but the major part was drawn from the Macclesfield, Cheadle, and Bristol companies.

'Causes are known by their effects;' the fine feelings of the heart are easily read in the features of the face: the still operations of the mind, are discovered by the rougher operations of the hand.

Every creature is fond of power, from that noble head of the creation, man, who devours man, down to that insignificant mite, who devours his cheese: every man strives to be free himself, and to shackle another.

Where there is power of any kind, whether in the hands of a prince, a people, a body of men, or a private person, there is a propensity to abuse it: abuse of power will everlastingly seek itself a remedy, and frequently find it; nay, even this remedy may in time degenerate to abuse, and call loudly for another.

Brass is an object of some magnitude, in the trades of Birmingham; the consumption is said to be a thousand tons per annum. The manufacture of this useful article had long been in few, and opulent hands; who, instead of making the humble bow, for favours received, acted with despotic sovereignty, established their own laws, chose their customers, directed the price, and governed the market.

In 1780, the article rose, either through caprice, or necessity, perhaps the *former*, from 72*l.* a ton to 84*l.* the result was, an advance upon the goods manufactured, followed by a number of counter-orders, and a stagnation of business.

In 1781, a person, from affection to the user, or resentment to the maker, perhaps, the *latter*, harangued the public in the weekly papers; censured the arbitrary measures of the brazen sovereigns, shewed their dangerous influence over the trades of the town, and the easy manner in which works of our own might be constructed--good often arises out of evil; this fiery match, dipt in brimstone, quickly kindled another furnace in Birmingham. Public meetings were advertised, a committee appointed, and subscriptions opened to fill two hundred shares, of 100*l.* each, deemed a sufficient capital: each proprietor of a share, to purchase one ton of brass, annually. Works were immediately erected upon the banks of the canal, for the advantage of water carriage, and the whole was conducted with the true spirit of Birmingham freedom.

If a man can worm himself *into* a lucrative branch, he will use every method to keep another *out*. All his powers may prove ineffectual; for if that other smells the sweet profits of the first, *he* will endeavour to worm himself *in*: both may suffer by the contest, and the public be gainers.

The old companies, which we may justly consider the directors of a south sea bubble in miniature, sunk the price from 84*l.* to 56*l.* Two inferences arise from this measure; that their profits were once very high, or are now very low; and, like some former monarchs, in the abuse of power, they repented one day too late.

Schemes are generally proclaimed, *for public good!* but as often meant, *for private interest*.--This, however, varied from that rule, and seemed less calculated to benefit those immediately, than those remotely concerned: they chose to sustain a smaller injury from making brass, than a greater from the makers.

PRISON.

If the subject is little, but little can be said upon it; I shall shine as dimly in this chapter on confinement, as in that on government. The traveller who sets out lame, will probably limp through the journey.

Many of my friends have assured me, "That I must have experienced much trouble in writing the history of Birmingham." But I assure them in return, that I range those hours among the happiest of my life; and part of that happiness may consist in delineating the bright side of human nature. Pictures of deformity, whether of body or of mind, disgust--the more they approach towards beauty, the more they charm.

All the chapters which compose this work, were formed with pleasure, except the latter part of that upon *births and burials*; there, being forced to apply to the parish books, I *figured* with some obstruction. Poor *Allsop*, full of good-nature and affliction, fearful lest I should sap the church, could not receive me with kindness. When a man's resources lie within himself, he draws at pleasure; but when necessity throws him upon the parish, he draws in small sums, and with difficulty.

I either *have*, or *shall* remark, for I know not in what nich I shall exhibit this posthumous chapter, drawn like one of our sluggish bills, *three months after date*, "That Birmingham does not abound in villainy, equal to some other places: that the hand employed in business, has less time, and less temptation, to be employed in mischief; and that one magistrate alone, corrected the enormities of this numerous people, many years before I knew them, and twenty-five after." I add, that the ancient lords of Birmingham, among their manorial privileges, had the grant of a gallows, for capital punishment; but as there are no traces even of the name, in the whole manor, I am persuaded no such thing was ever erected, and perhaps the *anvil* prevented it.

Many of the rogues among us are not of our own growth, but are drawn hither, as in London, to shelter in a crowd, and the easier in that crowd to pursue their game. Some of them fortunately catch, from example, the arts of industry, and become useful: others continue to cheat for one or two years, till frightened by the grim aspect of justice, they decamp.

Our vile and obscure prison, termed *The Dungeon*, is a farther proof how little that prison has been an object of notice, consequently of use.

Anciently the lord of a manor exercised a sovereign power in his little dominion; held a tribunal on his premises, to which was annexed a prison, furnished with implements for punishment; these were claimed by the lords of Birmingham. This crippled species of jurisprudence, which sometimes made a man judge in his own cause, from which there was no appeal, prevailed in the highlands of Scotland, so late as the rebellion in 1745, when the peasantry, by act of parliament, were restored to freedom.

Early perhaps in the sixteenth century, when the house of Birmingham, who had been chief gaolers, were fallen, a building was erected, which covered the east end of New-street, called the Leather-hall: the upper part consisted of a room about fifty feet long, where the public business of the manor was transacted. The under part was divided into several: one of these small rooms was used for a prison: but about the year 1728, *while men slept an enemy came*, a private agent to the lord of the manor, and erazed the Leather-hall and the Dungeon, erected three houses on the spot, and received their rents till 1776, when the town purchased them for 500*l.* to open the way. A narrow passage on the south will be remembered for half a century to come, by the name of the *dungeon-entry*.

A dry cellar, opposite the demolished hall, was then appropriated for a prison, till the town of all bad places chose the worst, the bottom of Peck-lane; dark, narrow, and unwholesome within; crowded with dwellings, filth and distress without, the circulation of air is prevented.

As a growing taste for public buildings has for some time appeared among us, we might, in the construction of a prison, unite elegance and use; and the west angle of that land between New-street and Mount-pleasant, might be suitable for the purpose; an airy spot in the junction of six streets. The proprietor of the land, from his known attachment to Birmingham, would, I doubt not, be much inclined to grant a favour.--Thus, I have expended ten *score* words, to tell the world what another would have told them in *ten*--"That our prison is wretched, and we want a better."

CLODSHALES CHANTRY.

It is an ancient remark, "The world is a farce." Every generation, and perhaps every individual, acts a part in disguise; but when the curtain falls, the hand of the historian pulls off the mask, and displays the character in its native light. Every generation differs from the other, *yet all are right*. Time, fashion, and sentiment change together. We laugh at the oddity of our fore-fathers--our successors will laugh at us.

The prosperous anvil of Walter de Clodshale, a native of this place, had enabled him to acquire several estates in Birmingham, to purchase the lordship of Saltley, commence gentleman, and reside in the manor-house, now gone to decay, though its traces remain, and are termed by common people, *the Giant's Castle*. This man, having well provided for the *present*, thought it prudent, at the close of life, to provide for the *future*: he therefore procured a licence, in 1331, from William de Birmingham, lord of the see, and another from the crown, to found a chantry at the altar in St. Martin's church, for one priest, to pray for his soul, and that of his wife.

He gave, that he might be safely wafted into the arms of felicity, by the breath of a priest, four houses, twenty acres of land, and eighteen-pence rent, issuing out of his estates in Birmingham.

The same righteous motive induced his son Richard, in 1348, to grant five houses, ten acres of land, and ten shillings rent, from the Birmingham estates, to maintain a second priest, who was to secure the souls of himself and his wife. The declaration of Christ, in that pious age, seems to have been inverted; for instead of its being difficult for a rich man to enter the kingdom of heaven, it was difficult for him to miss it. We are not told what became of him who had nothing to give! If the profits of the estate tended the right way, perhaps there was no great concern which way either *Walter* or *Richard* tended.

The chantorial music continued two hundred and four years, till 1535, when Henry the Eighth closed the book, turned out the priests, who were Sir Thomas Allen and Sir John Green, and seized the property, valued at 5*l*. 1s. per annum. Permit me again to moralize upon this fashionable practice of ruining the family, for the health of the soul: except some lawful creditor puts in a claim, which justice ought to allow, a son has the same right to an estate, after the death of his father, as that father had before him.

Had Walter and Richard taken *equal* care of their souls, and their estate, the first might have been as safe as in the hands of a priest, and the last, at this day, have been the property of that ancient, and once noble race of Arden, long since in distress; who, in 1426, married the heiress of their house.--Thus, a family, benefited by the hammer, was injured by the church.

Had the hands of these two priests ministered to their wants, in the construction of tents and fishing-nets, like those of their predecessors, St. Paul and St. Peter, though their pride would have been eclipsed, their usefulness would have shone, and the world have been gainers by their labour. Two other lessons may be learnt from this little ecclesiastical history--

The astonishing advance of landed property in Birmingham: nine houses, and thirty acres of land, two hundred and fifty years ago, were valued at the trifling rent of 4*l*. 9s. 6d. per annum; one of the acres, or one of the houses, would at this day bring more. We may reasonably suppose they were under-rated; yet, even then, the difference is amasing. An acre, within a mile of Birmingham, now sells for about one hundred pounds, and lets from three pounds to five, some as high as seven.

And, the nation so overswarmed with ecclesiastics, that the spiritual honours were quickly devoured, and the race left hungry; they therefore fastened upon the temporal--hence we boast of two knighted priests.

OCCURRENCES.

EARTHQUAKE, &c.

It is a doctrine singular and barbarous, but it is nevertheless true, that *destruction is necessary*. Every species of animals would multiply beyond their bounds in the creation, were not means devised to thin their race.

I perused an author in 1738, who asserts, "The world might maintain sixty times the number of its present inhabitants." Two able disputants, like those in religion, might maintain sixty arguments on the subject, and like them, leave the matter where they found it. But if restraint was removed, the present number would be multiplied into sixty, in much less than one century.

Those animals appropriated for use, are suffered, or rather invited, to multiply without limitation. But *luxury* cuts off the beast, the pig, the sheep, and the fowl, and ill treatment the horse: vermin of every kind, from the lion to the louse, are hunted to death; a perpetual contest seems to exist between them and us; they for their preservation, and we for their extinction. The kitten and the puppy are cast *into* the water, to end their lives; *out* of which the fishes are drawn to end theirs--animals are every were devoured by animals.

Their grand governor, man himself, is under controul; some by religious, others by interested motives. Even the fond parent, seldom wishes to increase the number of those objects, which of all others he values most!

In civilized nations the superior class are restrained by the laws of honour, the inferior by those of bastardy; but, notwithstanding these restraints, the human race would increase beyond measure, were they not taken off by casualties. It is in our species alone, that we often behold the infant flame extinguished by the wretched nurse.

Three dreadful calamities attending existence, are inundations, fires, and earthquakes; devestation follows their footsteps, But *one* calamity, more destructive than them all, rises from man himself, *war*.

Birmingham, from its elevation, is nearly exempt from the flood; our inundations, instead of sweeping away life and fortune, sweep away the filth from the kennel.

It is amasing, in a place crowded with people, that so *much* business, and so *little* mischief is done by fire: we abound more with party walls, than with timber buildings. Utensils are ever ready to extinguish the flames, and a generous spirit to use them. I am not certain that a conflagration of 50*l*. damage, has happened within memory.

I have only one earthquake to record, felt Nov. 15, 1772, at four in the morning; it extended about eight miles in length, from Hall-green to Erdington, and four in breadth, of which Birmingham was part. The shaking of the earth continued about five seconds, with unequal vibration, sufficient to awake a gentle sleeper, throw down a knife carelessly reared up, or rattle the brass drops of a chest of drawers. A flock of sheep, in a field near Yardley, frightened at the trembling, ran away.--No damage was sustained.

PITMORE AND HAMMOND.

Thomas Pitmore, a native of Cheshire, after consuming a fortune of 700*l.* was corporal in the second regiment of foot; and John Hammond, an American by birth, was drummer in the thirty-sixth; both of recruiting parties in Birmingham.

Having procured a brace of pistols, they committed several robberies in the dark, on the highways.

At eight in the evening of November 22, 1780, about five hundred yards short of the four mile-stone, in the Coleshill road, they met three butchers of Birmingham, who closely followed each other in their return from Rugby fair. One of the robbers attempted the bridle of the first man, but his horse, being young, started out of the road, and ran away. The drummer then attacked the second, Wilfred Barwick, with "Stop your horse," and that moment, through the agitation of a timorous mind, discharged a pistol, and lodged a brace of slugs in the bowels of the unfortunate Barwick, who exclaimed, "I am a dead man!" and fell.

The corporal instantly disappeared, and was afterwards, by the light of the show upon the ground, seen retreating to Birmingham. The drummer ran forwards about forty yards, and over a stile into Ward-end field. A fourth butcher of their company, and a lad, by this time came up, who, having heard the report of a pistol, seen the flash, and the drummer enter the field, leaped over the hedge in pursuit of the murderer. A frey ensued, in which the drummer was seized, who desired them not to take his life, but leave him to the laws of his country.

Within half an hour, the deceased and the captive appeared together in the same room, at the Horse-shoe. What must then be the feelings of a mind, susceptible of impression by nature, but weakly calloused over by art? This is one instance, among many, which shews us, a life of innocence, is alone a life of happiness.

The drummer impeached his companion, who was perhaps the most guilty of the two, and they were both that night lodged in the dungeon.

Upon the trial, March 31, 1781, the matter was too plain to be controverted. The criminals were executed, and hung in chains at Washwood-heath, April 2; the corporal at the age of 25, and the drummer 22.

RIOTS.

Three principal causes of riot are, the low state of wages, the difference in political sentiment, and the rise of provisions: these causes, like inundations, produce dreadful effects, and like them, return at uncertain periods.

The journeyman in Birmingham is under no temptation to demand an additional price for his labour, which is already higher than the usual mark.

There is no nation fonder of their king than the English; which is a proof that monarchy suits the genius of the people: there is no nation more jealous of his power, which proves that liberty is a favourite maxim. Though the laws have complimented him with *much*, yet he well knows, a prerogative upon the stretch, is a prerogative in a dangerous state.

The more a people value their prince, the more willing are they to contend in his favour.

The people of England revered the memory of their beloved Saxon kings, and doubly lamented their fall, with that of their liberties.

They taxed themselves into beggary, to raise the amasing sum of 100,000*l*. to release Richard the First, unjustly taken captive by Leopold.

They protected Henry the Fifth from death, at Agincourt, and received that death themselves.

They covered the extreme weakness of Henry the Sixth, who *never said a good thing, or did a bad one*, with the mantle of royalty; when a character like his, without a crown, would have been hunted through life: they gave him the title of *good king Henry*, which would well have suited, had the word *king* been omitted; they sought him a place in the kalendar of saints, and made *him* perform the miracles of an angel when dead, who could never perform the works of a man, when living.

The people shewed their attachment to Henry the Eighth, by submitting to the faggot and the block, at his command; and with their last breath, praying for their butcher.

Affection for Charles the First, induced four of his friends to offer their own heads, to save his.--The wrath, and the tears of the people, succeeded his melancholy exit.

When James the Second eloped from the throne, and was casually picked up at Feversham, by his injured subjects, *they remembered he was their king*.

The church and Queen Anne, like a joyous co-partnership, were toasted together. The barrel was willingly emptied to honour the queen, and the toaster lamented he could honour her no more.

The nation displayed their love to Charles the Second, by latticing the forests. His climbing the oak at Boscobel, has been the destruction of more timber than would have filled the harbour of Portsmouth; the tree which flourished in the field, was brought to die in the street. Birmingham, for ninety years, honoured him with her vengeance against the woods; and she is, at this day, surrounded with mutilated oaks, which stand as martyrs to royalty.

It is singular, that the oak, which assisted the devotion of the Britons, composed habitations for the people, and furniture for those habitations; that, while standing, was an ornament to the country that bore it; and afterwards guarded the land which nursed it, should be the cause of continual riots, in the reign of George the First. We could not readily accede to a line of strangers, in preference to our ancient race of kings, though loudly charged with oppression.

Clubs and tumults supported the spirit of contention till 1745, when, as our last act of animosity, we crowned an ass with turnips, in derision of one of the worthiest families that ever eat them.

Power, in the hand of ignorance, is an edge-tool of the most dangerous kind. The scarcity of provisions, in 1766, excited the murmurs of the poor. They began to breathe vengeance against the farmer, miller, and baker, for doing what they do themselves, procure the greatest price for their property.

On the market day, a common labourer, like Massenello of Naples, formed the resolution to lead a mob.

He therefore erected his standard, which was a mop inverted, assembled the crowd, and roared out the old note, "Redress of Grievances." The colliers, with all their dark retinue, were to bring destruction from Wednesbury. Amazement seised the town! the people of fortune trembled: John Wyrley, an able magistrate, for the first time frightened in office, with quivering lips, and a pale aspect, swore in about eighty constables, to oppose the rising storm, armed each of them with a staff of authority, warm from the turning-lathe, and applied to the War-office for a military force.

The lime-powdered monarch began to fabricate his own laws, direct the price of every article, which was punctually obeyed.

Port, or power, soon overcome a weak head; the more copious the draught, the more quick intoxication: he entered many of the shops, and was every where treated with the utmost reverence; took whatever goods he pleased, and distributed them among his followers; till one of the inhabitants, provoked beyond measure at his insolence, gave him a hearty kick on the posteriors, when the hero and his consequence, like that of Wat Tyler, fell together.--Thus ended a reign of seven hours; the sovereign was committed to prison, as sovereigns ought, in the abuse of power, and harmony was restored without blood.

THE CONJURERS.

No *head* is a vacuum. Some, like a paltry cottage, are ill accommodated, dark, and circumscribed; others are capacious as Westminster-Hall. Though none are immense, yet they are capable of immense furniture. The more room is taken up by knowledge, the less remains for credulity. The more a man is acquainted with things, the more willing to *give up the ghost*. Every town and village, within my knowledge, has been pestered with spirits; which appear in horrid forms to the imagination in the winter night--but the spirits which haunt Birmingham, are those of industry and luxury.

If we examine the whole parish, we cannot produce one *old* witch; but we have plenty of young, who exercise a powerful influence over us. Should the ladies accuse the harsh epithet, they will please to consider, I allow them, what of all things they most wish for, *power*, therefore the balance is in my favor.

If we pass through the planitary worlds, we shall be able to muster up two conjurers, who endeavoured to *shine with the stars*. The first, John Walton, who was so busy in calling the nativity of others, he forgot his own.

Conscious of an application to himself, for the discovery of stolen goods, he employed his people to steal them. And though, for many years confined to his bed by infirmity, he could conjure away the property of others, and, for a reward, reconjure it again.

The prevalence of this evil, induced the legislature, in 1725, to make the *reception* of stolen goods capital. The first sacrifice to this law was the noted Jonathan Wild.

The officers of justice, in 1732, pulled Walton out of his bed, in an obscure cottage, one furlong from the town, now Brickhill-Lane, carried him to prison, and from thence to the gallows--they had better have carried him to the workhouse, and his followers to the anvil.

To him succeeded Francis Kimberley, the only reasoning animal, who resided at No. 60, in Dale-End, from his early youth to extreme age.--An hermit in a crowd! The windows of his house were strangers to light! The shutters forgot to open; the chimney to smoak. His cellar, though amply furnished, never knew moisture.

He spent threescore years in filling six rooms with such trumpery as is just too good to be thrown away, and too bad to be kept. His life was as inoffensive as long. Instead of *stealing* the goods which other people use, he *purchased* what he could not use himself. He was not anxious what kind of property entered his house; if there was *bulk* he was satisfied.

His dark house, and his dark figure corresponded with each other. The apartments, choaked up with lumber, scarcely admitted his body, though of the skeleton order. Perhaps leanness is an appendage to the science, for I never knew a corpulent conjurer.

His diet, regular, plain, and slender, shewed at how little expence life may be sustained.

His library consisted of several thousand volumes, not one of which, I believe, he ever read: having written, in characters unknown to all but himself, his name, price, and date, in the title-page, he laid them by for ever. The highest pitch of his erudition was the annual almanack.

He never wished to approach a woman, or be approached by one. Should the rest of men, for half a century, pay no more attention to the fair, some angelic hand might stick up a note, like the artic circle over one of our continents, *this world to be let*.

If he did not cultivate the human species, the spiders, more numerous than his books, enjoyed an uninterrupted reign of quiet. The silence of the place was not broken: the broom, the book, the dust, or the web, was not disturbed. Mercury and his shirt, changed their revolutions together; and Saturn changed *his*, with his coat.

He died, in 1756, as conjurers usually die, unlamented.

MILITARY ASSOCIATION.

The use of arms is necessary to every man who has something to lose, or something to gain. No property will protect itself. The English have liberty and property to lose, but nothing to win. As every man is born free, the West-Indian slaves have liberty to gain, but nothing to lose. If a rascally African prince attempts to sell his people, he ought to be first sold himself; and the buyer, who acts so daringly opposite to the Christian precept, is yet more blameable. He ought to have the first whip, often mended, worn out upon his own back.

It may seem unnecessary to tell the world, what they already know; recent transactions come under this description; but they are not known to the stranger, nor to posterity.

Upon a change of the Northean ministry, in 1782, the new premier, in a circular letter, advised the nation to arm, as the dangers of invasion threatened us with dreadful aspect. Intelligence from a quarter so authentic, locked up the door of private judgment, or we might have considered, that even without alliance, and with four principal powers upon our hands, we were rather gaining ground; that the Americans were so far from attacking us, that they wished us to run ourselves out of breath to attack them; that Spain had slumbered over a seven years war; that the Dutch, provoked at their governors, for the loss of their commerce, were more inclinable to invade themselves than us; and that as France bore the weight of the contest, we found employment for her arms, without invasion; but, perhaps, the letter was only an artifice of the new state doctor, to represent his patient in a most deplorable state, as a complement to his own merit in recovering her.

Whatever was the cause, nothing could be more agreeable than this letter to the active spirit of Birmingham. Public meetings were held. The rockets of war were squibbed off in the news-papers. The plodding tradesman and the lively hero assembled together in arms, and many a trophy was won in thought.

Each man purchased a genteel blue uniform, decorated with epaulets of gold, which, together with his accoutrements, cost about 17*l*. The gentleman, the apprentice, &c. to the number of seventy, united in a body, termed by themselves, *The Birmingham Association*; by the wag, *the brazen walls of the town*. Each was to be officer and private by ballet, which gives an idea of equality, and was called to exercise once a week.

The high price of provisions, and the 17th of October, brought a dangerous mob into Birmingham. They wanted bread: so did we. But little conference passed between them and the inhabitants. They were quiet; we were pleased; and, after an hour or two's stay, they retreated in peace.

In the evening, after the enemy were fled, our champions beat to arms, breathing vengeance against the hungry crew; and, had they returned, some people verily thought our valiant heroes would have *discharged* at them.

However laudable a system, if built upon a false basis, it will not stand. Equality and command, in the same person, are incompatible; therefore, cannot exist together. Subordination is necessary in every class of life, but particularly in the military. Nothing but severe discipline can regulate the boisterous spirit of an army.

A man may be bound to another, but if he commands the bandage, he will quickly set himself free. This was the case with the military association. As their uniform resembled that of a commander, so did their temper. There were none to submit. The result was, the farce ended, and the curtain dropt in December, by a quarrel with each other; and, like *John* and *Lilborn*, almost with themselves.

BILSTON CANAL ACT.

Envy, like a dark shadow, follows closely the footsteps of prosperity; success in any undertaking, out of the circle of genius, produces a rival.--This I have instanced in our hackney coaches.

Profits, like a round-bellied bottle, may seem bulky, which, like that, will not bear dividing: Thus Orator Jones, in 1774, opened a debating society at the Red Lion; he quickly filled a large room with customers, and his pockets with money, but he had not prudence to keep either. His success opened a rival society at the King's-head, which, in a few weeks, annihilated both.

The growing profits of our canal company, already mentioned, had increased the shares from 140*l*. in 1768, to 400 guineas, in 1782. These emoluments being thought enormous, a rival company sprung up, which, in 1783, petitioned Parliament to partake of those emoluments, by opening a parallel cut from some of the neighbouring coal-pits; to proceed along the lower level, and terminate in Digbeth.

A stranger might ask, "How the water in our upland country, which had never supplied one canal, could supply two? Whether the second canal was not likely to rob the first? Whether one able canal is not preferable to two lame ones? If a man sells me an article cheaper than I can purchase it elsewhere, whether it is of consequence to me what are his profits? And whether two companies in rivalship would destroy that harmony which has long subsisted in Birmingham."

The new company urged, "The necessity of another canal, lest the old should not perform the business of the town; that twenty per cent. are unreasonable returns; that they could afford coals under the present price; that the south country teams would procure a readier supply from Digbeth, than from the present wharf, and not passing through the streets, would be prevented from injuring the pavement; and that the goods from the Trent would come to their wharf by a run of eighteen miles nearer than to the other."

The old company alledged, "That they ventured their property in an uncertain pursuit, which, had it not succeeded, would have ruined many individuals; therefore the present gains were only a recompense for former hazard: that this property was expended upon the faith of Parliament, who were obliged in honour to protect it, otherwise no man would risk his fortune upon a public undertaking; for should they allow a second canal, why not a third; which would become a wanton destruction of right, without benefit; that although the profit of the original subscribers might seem large, those subscribers are but few; many have bought at a subsequent price, which barely pays common interest, and this is all their support; therefore a reduction would be barbarous on one side, and sensibly felt on the other: and, as the present canal amply supplies the town and country, it would be ridiculous to cut away good land to make another, which would ruin both."

I shall not examine the reasons of either, but leave the disinterested reader to weigh both in his own balance.

When two opponents have said all that is true, they generally say something more; rancour holds the place of argument.

Both parties beat up for volunteers in the town, to strengthen their forces; from words of acrimony, they came to those of virulence; then the powerful batteries of hand-bills, and news-papers were opened: every town within fifty miles, interested, on either side, was moved to petition, and both prepared for a grand attack, confident of victory.

Perhaps a contest among friends, in matters of property, will remove that peace of mind, which twenty per cent. will not replace.

Each party possessed that activity of spirit, for which Birmingham is famous, and seemed to divide between them the legislative strength of the nation: every corner of the two houses was ransacked for a vote; the throne was the only power unsolicited. Perhaps at the reading, when both parties had marshalled their forces, there was the fullest House of Commons ever remembered on a private bill.

The new company promised much, for besides the cut from Wednesbury to Digbeth, they would open another to join the two canals of Stafford and Coventry, in which a large track of country was interested.

As the old company were the first adventurers, the house gave them the option to perform this Herculean labour, which they accepted.

As parliament have not yet given their determination, and as the printer this moment raps at my door, "Sir, the press waits, more copy if you please," I cannot stay to tell the world the result of the bill; but perhaps, the new proprietors, by losing, will save 50,000*l.* and the old, by winning, become sufferers.

WORKHOUSE BILL.

I have often mentioned an active spirit, as the characteristic of the inhabitants of Birmingham. This spirit never forsakes them. It displays itself in industry, commerce, invention, humanity, and internal government. A singular vivacity attends every pursuit till compleated, or discarded for a second.

The bubble of the day, like that at the end of a tobacco-pipe, dances in air, exhibits divers beauties, pleases the eye, bursts in a moment, and is followed up by another.

There is no place in the British dominions easier to be governed than Birmingham; and yet we are fond of forging acts of parliament to govern her.

There is seldom a point of time in which an act is not in agitation; we fabricate them with such expedition, that we could employ a parliament of our own to pass them. But, to the honor of our ladies, not one of these acts is directed against them. Neither is there an instance upon record, that the torch of Hymen was ever extinguished by the breath of Marriot in Doctors-Commons.

In the present spring of 1783, we have four acts upon the anvil: every man, of the least consequence, becomes a legislator, and wishes to lend his assistance in framing an act; so that instead of one lord, as formerly, we now, like the Philistines, have three thousand.

An act of parliament, abstractedly considered, is a dead matter: it cannot operate of itself: like a plaister, it must be applied to the evil, or that evil will remain. We vainly expect a law to perform the intended work; if it does not, we procure another to make it. Thus the canal, by one act in 1767, hobbled on, like a man with one leg; but a second, in 1770, furnished a pair. The lamp act, procured in 1769, was worn to rags, and mended with another in 1773; and this second has been long out of repair, and waits for a third.

We carry the same spirit into our bye-laws, and with the same success. Schemes have been devised, to oblige every man to pay levies; but it was found difficult to extract money from him who had none.

In 1754, we brought the manufacture of pack-thread into the workhouse, to reduce the levies; the levies increased. A spirited overseer afterwards, for the same reason, as if poverty was not a sufficient stigma, badged the poor; the levies still increased.

The advance of bread in 1756, induced the officers to step out of the common track, perhaps, out of their knowledge; and, at the expence of half a levy, fit up an apparatus for grinding corn in the house: thus, by sacrificing half *one levy, many would be saved*. However, in the pursuit, many happened to be lost. In 1761, the apparatus was sold at a farther loss; and the overseers sheltered themselves under the charge of idleness against the paupers.

In 1766, the spinning of mop-yarn was introduced, which might, with attention, have turned to account; but unfortunately, the yarn proved of less value than the wool.

Others, with equal wisdom, were to ease the levies, by feeding a drove of pigs, which, agreeable to their own nature--ran backwards.--Renting a piece of ground, by way of garden, which supplied the house with a pennyworth of vegetables, for two-pence, adding a few cows, and a pasture; but as the end of all was *loss*, the levies increased.

In 1780, two collectors were appointed, at fifty guineas each, which would save the town *many a hundred*; still the levies increased.

A petition is this sessions presented, for an Act to overturn the whole pauper system (for our heads are as fond of new fashions, in parochial government, as in the hats which cover them) to erect a superb workhouse, at the expence of 10,000*l*. with powers to borrow 15,000*l*. which grand design is to reduce the levies *one third*.--The levies will increase.

The reasons *openly* alledged are, "The Out-pensioners, which cost 7000*l*. a year, are the chief foundation of our public grievances: that the poor ought to be employed *in* the house, lest their morals become injured by the shops; which prevents them from being taken into family service; and, the crowded state of the workhouse."--But whether the pride of an overseer, in perpetuating his name, is not the pendulum which set the machine in motion? Or, whether a man, as well as a spider, may not create a *place*, and, like that--*fill it with himself*?

The bill directs, That the inhabitants mall chuse a number of guardians by ballot, who shall erect a workhouse, on Birmingham-heath--a spot as airy as the scheme; conduct a manufacture, and the poor; dispose of the present workhouse; seize and confine idle or disorderly persons, and keep them to labour, till they have reimbursed the parish all expences.

But it may be asked, Whether spending 15,000*l*. is likely to reduce the levies?

Whether we shall be laughed at, for throwing by a building, the last wing of which cost a thousand pounds, after using it only three years?

Our commerce is carried on by reciprocal obligation. Every overseer has his friends, whom he cannot refuse to serve; nay, whom he may even wish to serve, if that service costs him nothing: hence, that over-grown monster so justly complains of, *The Weekly Tickets*; it follows, whether *sixty* guardians are not likely to have more friends to serve, than six overseers?

Whether the trades of the town, by a considerable manufacture established at the workhouse, will not be deprived of their most useful hands?

Whether it is not a maxim of the wisest men who have filled the office, "to endeavour to keep the poor *out* of the house, for if they are admitted, they become more chargeable; nor will they leave it without clothing?"

A workhouse is a kind of prison, and a dreadful one to those of tender feelings--Whether the health of an individual, the ideas of rectitude, or the natural right of our species, would not be infringed by a cruel imprisonment.

If a man has followed an occupation forty years, and necessity sends him to the parish, whether is it preferable to teach him a new trade, or suffer him to earn what he can at his old? If we decide for the latter, whether he had better walk four hundred yards to business, or four miles? His own infirmity will determine this question.

If a young widow be left with two children, shall she pay a girl six-pence a week to tend them, while she earns five shillings at the mops, and is allowed two by the parish, or shall all three reside in the house, at the weekly expence of six, and she be employed in nursing them? If we again declare for the latter, it follows, that the parish will not only have four shillings a week, but the community may gain half a crown by her labour.

Whether the morals of the children are more likely to be injured by the shops, than the morals of half the children in town; many of whom labour to procure levies for the workhouse?

Whether the morals of a child will be more corrupted in a small shop, consisting of a few persons, or in a large one at the workhouse, consisting of hundreds?

Whether the grand shop at Birmingham-heath, or at any heath, will train girls for service, preferable to others?

Shall we, because the house has been crowded a few weeks, throw away 15000*l*. followed by a train of evils? A few months ago, I saw in it a large number of vacant beds. Besides, at a small expence, and without impeding the circulation of air, conveniency may be made for one hundred more.

Did a manufacture ever prosper under a multitude of inspectors, not one of which is to taste the least benefit?

As public business, which admits no profit, such as vestry assemblies, commissions of lamps, turnpike meetings, &c. are thinly attended, even in town; what reason is there to expect a board two miles in the country?

The workhouse may be deemed *The Nursery of Birmingham*, in which she deposits her infants, for future service: the unfortunate and the idle, till they can be set upon their own basis; and the decrepid, during the few remaining sands in their glass. If we therefore carry the workhouse to a distance, whether we shall not interrupt that necessary intercourse which ought to subsist between a mother and her offspring? As sudden sickness, indications of child-birth, &c. require immediate assistance, a life in extreme danger may chance to be lost by the length of the road.

If we keep the disorderly till they have reimbursed the parish, whether we do not acquire an inheritance for life?

We censure the officer who pursues a phantom at the expence of others; we praise him who *teaches the poor to live.*

All the evils complained of, may be removed by *attention in the man*; the remedy is not in an act. He therefore accuses his own want of application, in soliciting government to *do* what he might do himself--Expences are saved by private acts of oeconomy, not by public Acts of Parliament.

It has long been said, *think* and *act*; but as our internal legislators chuse to reverse the maxim by fitting up an expensive shop; then seeking a trade to bring in, perhaps they may place over the grand entrance, *act* and *think*.

One remark should never be lost sight of, *The more we tax the inhabitants, the sooner they leave us, and carry off the trades.*

THE CAMP.

I have already remarked, *a spirit of bravery is part of the British character*. The perpetual contests for power, among the Britons, the many roads formed by the Romans, to convey their military force, the prodigious number of camps, moats, and broken castles, left us by the Saxons, Danes, and Normans, our common ancestors, indicate *a martial temper*. The names of those heroic sovereigns, Edward the Third, and Henry the Fifth, who brought their people to the fields of conquest, descend to posterity with the highest applause, though they brought their kingdom to the brink of ruin; while those quiet princes, Henry the Seventh, and James the First, who cultivated the arts of peace, are but little esteemed, though under their sceptre, England experienced the greatest improvement.--The man who dare face an enemy, is the most likely to gain a friend. A nation versed in arms, stands the fairest chance to protect its property, and secure its peace: war itself may be hurtful, the knowledge of it useful.

In Mitchly-park, three miles west of Birmingham, in the parish of Edgbaston, is *The Camp*; which might be ascribed to the Romans, lying within two or three stones cast of their Ikenield-street, where it divides the counties of Warwick and Worcester, but is too extensive for that people, being about thirty acres: I know none of their camps more than four, some much less; it must, therefore, have been the work of those pilfering vermin the Danes, better acquainted with other peoples property than their own; who first swarmed on the shores, then over-ran the interior parts of the kingdom, and, in two hundred years, devoured the whole.

No part of this fortification is wholly obliterated, though, in many places, it is nearly levelled by modern cultivation, that dreadful enemy to the antiquary. Pieces of armour are frequently ploughed up, particularly parts of the sword and the battle-axe, instruments much used by those destructive sons of the raven.

The platform is quadrangular, every side nearly four hundred yards; the center is about six acres, surrounded by three ditches, each about eight yards over, at unequal distances; though upon a descent, it is amply furnished with water. An undertaking of such immense labour, could not have been designed for temporary use.

The propriety of the spot, and the rage of the day for fortification, seem to have induced the Middlemores, lords of the place for many centuries, and celebrated for riches, but in the beginning of this work, for poverty, to erect a park, and a lodge; nothing of either exist, but the names.

MORTIMER's BANK.

The traveller who undertakes an extensive journey, cannot chuse his road, or his weather: sometimes the prospect brightens, with a serene sky, a smooth path, and a smiling sun; all within and without him is chearful.

Anon he is assailed by the tempests, stumbles over the ridges, is bemired in the hollows, the sun hides his face, and his own is sorrowful--this is the lot of the historian; he has no choice of subject, merry or mournful, he must submit to the changes which offer; delighted with the prosperous tale, depressed with the gloomy.

I am told, this work has often drawn a smile from the reader; it has often drawn a sigh from me. A celebrated painter fell in love with the picture he drew; I have wept at mine--Such is the chapter of the Lords, and the Workhouse. We are not always proof against a melancholy or a tender sentiment.

Having pursued our several stages, with various fortune, through fifty chapters, at the close of this last tragic scene, emotion and the journey cease together.

Upon King's-wood, five miles from Birmingham, and two hundred yards east of the Alcester-road, runs a bank for near a mile in length, unless obliterated by the new inclosure; for I saw it complete in 1775. This was raised by the famous Roger Mortimer, Earl of March, about 1324, to inclose a wood, from whence the place derives its name.

Then that feeble monarch, Edward the Second, governed the kingdom; the amorous Isabella, his wife, governed the king, and the gallant Mortimer governed the queen.

The parishes of King's-norton, Solihull, Yardley, uniting in this wood, and enjoying a right of commons, the inhabitants conceived themselves injured by the inclosure, assembled in a body, threw down the fence, and murdered the Earl's bailiff.

Mortimer, in revenge, procured a special writ from the Court of Common Pleas, and caused the matter to be tried at Bromsgrove, where the affrighted inhabitants, over-awed with power, durst not appear in their own vindication. The Earl, therefore, recovered a verdict, and the enormous sum of 300*l*. damage. A sum nearly equal, at that time, to the fee-simple of the three parishes.

The confusion of the times, and the poverty of the people, protracted payment, till the unhappy Mortimer, overpowered by his enemies, was seized as a criminal in Nottingham-castle; and, without being heard, executed at Tyburn, in 1328.

The distressed inhabitants of our three parishes humbly petitioned the crown, for a reduction of the fine; when Edward the Third was pleased to remit about 260*l*.

We can assign no reason for this imprudent step of inclosing the wood, unless the Earl intended to procure a grant of the manor, then in the crown, for his family. But what he could not accomplish by family, was accomplished by fortune; for George the Third, King of Great Britain, is lord of the manor of King's-norton, and a descendant from the house of Mortimer.

FINIS.

CPSIA information can be obtained
at www.ICGtesting.com
Printed in the USA
LVOW03s1530070816
499409LV00028B/246/P